Independent, strong ...and pregnant!

These women intend to carve a future for their children on their own.

Then they meet two confirmed bachelors—but these men may not be as committed to their single lives as they seem.

Could it be that there is a family in the making?

*Harlequin, Harlequin Duets and Colophon are
trademarks used under licence.*

*First published in Great Britain 2001
by Harlequin Mills & Boon Limited,
Eton House, 18-24 Paradise Road,
Richmond, Surrey TW9 1SR*

MUM'S THE WORD © Rosaline Fox 2000
(formerly titled Mom's the Word)

THREE FOR THE ROAD © Kathleen Shannon 1995

ISBN 0 373 04812 2

20-1101

*Printed and bound in Spain
by Litografía Rosés S.A., Barcelona*

MUM'S THE WORD

Roz Denny Fox

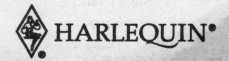

TORONTO • NEW YORK • LONDON
AMSTERDAM • PARIS • SYDNEY • HAMBURG
STOCKHOLM • ATHENS • TOKYO • MILAN • MADRID
PRAGUE • WARSAW • BUDAPEST • AUCKLAND

For Denny. I couldn't have written any of the previous books without your love and support. But with this one I *really* owe you—for driving to ghost towns where there weren't any roads. For finding a spring that, according to the map, was supposed to exist but turned out not to be so easily located. And especially for not complaining when the water was too deep to cross and we needed to reach the highway we could see in the distance. You probably felt like leaving me there, but you still had a smile after bouncing twenty long, dusty miles over terrain that was really only accessible on horseback. Thanks, with all my heart.

CHAPTER ONE

"YOU'RE PREGNANT, Hayley." Kindly old Dr. Gerrard looked over the top of his half glasses at the young woman seated on the examining table. "Given your circumstances, my dear, I hate to be the bearer of bad tidings."

Hayley Ryan stopped pleating folds in the loose-fitting paper gown and gasped as she spread both hands protectively across her stomach. "But I...I've been losing weight. Not gaining. Are you sure your diagnosis is correct?"

The doctor patted Hayley's suntanned hand. "My practice here in Tombstone may be winding down, child, but I haven't been wrong in predicting blessed events in thirty years. Why, twenty-six years ago your mama sat in this very room, asking the same question." He chuckled. "Nine months later out you popped."

"I didn't mean to imply that...that you don't know what you're doing." Hayley swallowed hard to keep from crying. "It's just that this isn't the best time in my life to be learning I'll soon have another mouth to feed. I'm not sure how I'll take care of myself let alone a baby."

Dr. Gerrard sobered at once. "I know. Gossip's running rampant about how your husband left town with that sassy-faced Cindy Trent from the nail-painting place." The doctor removed his glasses and gazed with unfocused sympathy into Hayley's turbulent eyes. "What kind of man, I'd like to know, leaves his wife while she's still grieving from burying her grandpa? I said it before, girl, and I'll say it again—Joe Ryan's worse than a snake-oil salesman."

Hayley glanced away. She could do without having that fact driven home. A little more than a year ago, Grandpa O'Dell and many of his friends had cautioned her against marrying Joe. If she had a dime for every person in Tombstone who'd warned her Joe Ryan was the kind of guy who blew into town on his own wind and would likely blow out the same way, she wouldn't be sitting here now, alone and worrying about how to feed herself and the baby Joe had planted before he pulled his vanishing act. "It's easier for me to see now that Joe only married me so he could get his hands on the Silver Cloud mine," Hayley murmured.

"Big Ben O'Dell would turn over in his grave if he knew that four-flushing louse stole his mine and left you in this fix."

"What's done is done. There's no use crying over it, Dr. Gerrard." Even as the words left Hayley's lips, tears slid down her cheeks.

"This isn't something I'd normally suggest—" Dr. Gerrard hesitated "—but you might think about terminating the pregnancy. I don't perform the procedure, but I'll recommend a reputable clinic in Phoenix. I calculate the child is due around Christmas." He turned and picked up a calendar. "Let's see, it's June. You're eight to ten weeks along. You'll have to decide soon. The surgery does carry some risk, but you're still within the limits set by the state."

Hayley looked horrified and linked her fingers across her stomach. "I appreciate your concern, really I do. But the good Lord entrusted me with a new life. I expect He'll eventually put my feet on a path that'll allow me to take care of myself and this baby.''

"I wish I had your faith, Hayley. If the Man upstairs takes care of His own, He shouldn't have let Joe and that floozy forge your name on the Silver Cloud's deed. Wasn't more'n six months ago that Ben told me he felt so poorly he'd decided to sign it to you. Joe was sittin' right here. If you ask me, that's when the lowlife hatched his plan.''

"Probably so. Then I suppose you could say I brought this mess on myself," she said glumly. "Gramps didn't like Joe to drive him to his breathing treatments. That day, Dee Dee Johnson phoned and asked me to go to the gem show in Tucson with her. I'd never been to a gem show, even though I've lived in Arizona all my life. I practically begged Joe to take Gramps for me.''

"Don't be taking the blame, girl. Joe's the bad apple. He and that deputy-sheriff pal of his would steal a cross from the church if they thought they could melt it down and sell it for a dollar.''

"You don't mean Shad Tilford?" Hayley frowned.

"The very same.''

"He…he's in charge of my complaint. Sheriff Bonner assigned Shad to my case when I asked the law to go after Joe for half the money from the mine sale. Shad hasn't been very helpful. He insinuated it was Joe's right, as my husband, to sell the Silver Cloud. He finally said he'd issue a warrant to bring Joe in for questioning.''

"Humph! I'll wager Tilford got a cut of the money Joe received from the deal. I've suspected for some time that our deputy's a little shady. How he ever wound up wearing a badge is beyond me.''

"Francesca said he was an L.A. city cop before he came to Tombstone."

"Just 'cause a chicken's got wings don't mean it can fly. I know Francesca has her fingers in a lot of pies in town, but how does she know Tilford didn't dummy up those fancy recommendations he flashed at the city council meeting?"

Francesca Portolo was one of the former lady friends of Big Ben O'Dell, and as such, she'd had a hand in raising Hayley. Hayley's dad had died in a mining accident when she was only a few weeks old. When she was three, her mother succumbed to breast cancer. Hayley's maternal grandfather, Ben O'Dell, a local prospector who'd—more than once—lost his shirt mining for silver, gold and copper, became guardian and caretaker of his grandchild. He, in turn, relied on the women who fostered dreams of becoming the second Mrs. Ben O'Dell to raise Hayley.

She had a soft spot in her heart for all of them, but Francesca, owner of the local fabric store, had taught Hayley how to sew and cook. In addition, she'd shown a lonely little girl tricks she needed to know about becoming a woman. So Hayley tended to believe Francesca.

"Like I said, Dr. Gerrard, I'm in a fix and it's not likely to change. Gramps had more downs than ups, but he was never a quitter. Nor am I. To tell you the truth, I'm relieved to hear it's a baby making me sick and not cancer, like killed Mama. If my health's otherwise okay, I'll get by without Joe."

"You're fit as a fiddle, Hayley, though a mite on the skinny side. Ask Esther at the front desk for the booklet I give all my prospective mothers. Tells you pretty much everything you need to know about prenatal care. Follow the book's advice and eat right. You'll have a healthy baby."

"Thanks, Dr. Gerrard. I guess my biggest worry, then, is how to earn the money to keep the rent paid, eat right and pay for my delivery."

"Your grandpa and I went back a long way. I'll arrange terms to make it easy on you, Hayley. Tell Esther that, too."

Hayley smiled, the first real smile since her grandfather's chronic asthma facilitated a persistent bacterial pneumonia from which he never recovered. Thank God, she thought, the world still held a few good men like Dr. Gerrard.

As Hayley left the clinic with the booklet and a supply of prenatal vitamins clutched in her hand, she set her sights on doing whatever was necessary to make a life for herself and the new life growing inside her.

Which seemed easier said than done when she returned home and found the mail had brought overdue notices on her utilities. Not only that, rent on the house was due in three days. She phoned Sheriff Bonner and voiced her concerns about Shad. Bonner said she had to be patient. They'd issued a warrant for Joe. It seemed he'd disappeared.

On hanging up, Hayley reviewed her options. She had the thousand dollars' guilt money Joe had left on the kitchen table. In the note he'd clipped to it, he'd said the money should tide her over until she found work. Of course, Joe ignored the fact that in a community-property state, he owed her half of the two hundred and fifty thousand he'd received from a mining consortium. Even so, it wasn't his taking the money that hurt so much. It was his betrayal. Never very outgoing, Hayley hadn't made a lot of friends her own age before Joe had come to town selling mining explosives. She'd been flattered by his interest. He was good-looking and charismatic. And he'd centered his attention on her.

Gramps had said disparaging things about Joe. So had several of the old-timers in town. Now Hayley wished she'd listened. But no one, especially not Gramps, understood how lonely she'd been for most of her life. Ben O'Dell had been a tough old codger who liked his solitude. He often took off for weeks on end, prospecting. When he was home, he was preoccupied with the Silver Cloud mine.

Mining was virtually all Hayley knew, too. And mining was tough. There hadn't been money for college at the time she graduated from high school. While her contemporaries moved on, Hayley had been stuck in Tombstone. Was it any wonder that at twenty-five, she'd latched on to Joe like a drowning woman with a life preserver? It was painful now to admit she'd been hoodwinked—that she'd been stupidly trusting despite all the warnings.

Not a chance she'd make *that* mistake again. No, siree! Hayley Ryan was through with men. Anyway, she had bigger worries now. A thousand dollars wouldn't pay two months' rent, let alone keep up with utilities and buy food.

She needed a long-term plan. She needed a job. But…doing what? Hayley drew stars on the back of her electric bill. Shoot, she didn't have a lot of skills, and Tombstone wasn't exactly a job mecca. Sometimes months went by without an opening being listed in the paper. If she knew anyone in Tucson or Phoenix, she could go there, where unskilled jobs were more plentiful. Thing was, she didn't even have transportation. Joe had traded in his car and Ben's sedan on a flashy convertible—or so she'd heard. The pencil lead broke as she bore down on the last star.

"Lord," she muttered, propping her chin in one palm, "if you're going to show me a path, now would be as good a time as any to do it." Idly she sorted a stack of bills while gazing blankly around at the meager accumulation of a lifetime. Dinnertime came, but she had no appetite. Although now she had to think about someone besides herself. The first item in Dr. Gerrard's prenatal care booklet said to eat nutritious meals.

Hayley finally settled on a salad with some grated cheese for protein. She was in the middle of halfheartedly tearing apart limp lettuce when someone knocked timidly on her door.

For a moment her stomach pitched. *Had Joe repented?* As quickly, Hayley knew she'd never take him back even if he crawled in on hands and knees.

It wasn't him she saw, anyway, as she peeped through the window beside the door. It was Virgil Coleman, one of her grandfather's retired mining buddies.

"Virgil, hi," she greeted the crusty gentleman who stood on the porch, crumpling a battered hat between his gnarled hands.

"Hate to bother you, little lady, you being in mourning and all." The old fellow carefully picked his way through condolences, as men his age were prone to do. Clearing his throat, he added, "My oldest boy, Hank, is coming tomorrow to move me up to his place in Flagstaff. We're putting my property up for sale. I wondered if you'd mind moving Ben's old pickup and camp trailer out of my shed? The Realtor said I gotta clean the place up."

"Pickup and camp trailer? I thought all of Gramps's

equipment went to the consortium that bought the mine.''

"Ben never used this stuff at the Silver Cloud. It's his prospecting outfit. In fact, the whole kit and caboodle was once your dad's. So I guess you know it's old. Truck still runs okay, though.''

"I'd forgotten those things.'' Hayley could barely contain her excitement. "The unit is self-contained, right?''

When Virgil scratched the fringe of hair that ringed his bald pate, Hayley elaborated. "I mean, the trailer has a kitchen, bedroom and bathroom, doesn't it?''

"About the size of a postage stamp, but yep. Once Big Ben stepped inside, he filled the place. I reckon it served his purpose, though. A man huntin' ore travels light. He made do with it when he worked his claim down Ruby way.''

"Wait—are you saying Gramps had a mine other than the Silver Cloud?''

"Not a mine, but a claim site.''

Hayley was floored by the news. And thrilled. And suddenly hopeful. "A duly registered claim?'' she asked, her heart beginning to flutter excitedly.

Virgil stammered a bit. "'Spect so. Don't rightly know. If Ben worked it, I knowed he'd have filed right and proper.''

"A name, Virgil.'' She grabbed the old man's scrawny wrist. "If you know what he called his claim, I can find the location in the recorder's office.''

Shaking his head, the old man backed out the door. "Wish I could help you more, missy. Ben was real secretive about that claim. So can I tell Hank you'll pick up the truck and trailer tomorrow or the next day?''

"Yes. You bet. Virgil, you just made my day.'' Hay-

ley flung her arms around his wasted shoulders and gave
him a resounding kiss on his leathery cheek. Typical of
an old miner, Virgil blushed and hurriedly stammered
out a goodbye.

Hayley spent only a moment hugging herself in glee
and dancing around the room. Then she went to the one
place she thought her grandfather might have kept a record of the claim. The same antique strongbox where he'd
stored the deed that Joe had stolen. But even if Joe had
found placer or lode claims for the Ruby site, she'd still
have the pickup and trailer.

As she took down the box with hands that shook,
Hayley recalled reading a magazine in Dr. Gerrard's office about campers who parked their RVs for free out
on the desert near Quartzsite. If nothing else, it'd be a
place she could live rent free until the baby arrived. A
place where she could stretch the money Joe had left
her.

It'd be too much to hope for—to think she might actually have claim rights to a parcel of land.

After a deep breath, Hayley began unloading the
strongbox. She found her birth certificate and her parents' certificate of marriage, along with old family pho-
tos. She paused to look at one of her mom before reverently laying it aside. Taped to the back of her
grandmother's photo was her worn gold wedding band.
Old-timers in town said that Hayley, except for her
lighter hair color, resembled her grandmother, a full-
blooded Apache.

Hayley lightly traced the woman's high cheekbones
and straight black hair. She saw a resemblance both to
herself and her mother. It was easy to see why Grandpa
had never given his heart to another woman, even
though he'd taken numerous females to his bed. There

was a strength and beauty about her grandmother that made her very different from softer ladies Ben squired around town.

Hayley neared the bottom of the box and her hopes of finding a claim dimmed. Suddenly, stuck to the lining, there it was. A claim form, yellowed with age, stapled to a hand-drawn map. Hayley could tell by the dates stamped on the form that Ben had refiled on the same site for ten years. To retain rights to any claim, a miner had to do a minimum of a hundred dollars' worth of work on it every calendar year. The recording calendar ran from July 1 to June 30.

Yikes! She had a week left to ready an outfit and refile on the property.

A week! Yet it felt like a beautiful, wonderful, stupendous reprieve. Hayley hugged the papers to her breast and skipped across the threadbare living-room carpet. She had no idea what Gramps thought he'd find near the old ghost town of Ruby. But certainly something worth going there for year after year.

Gold? Arizona had a rich history of gold deposits. Ben had fascinating stories to tell about placer-gold and flour-gold strikes. He'd taken Hayley prospecting in her younger days. Those trips had been idyllic. Out of her memories, Hayley suddenly formed a vision of cottonwoods shading a lazy stream. It was a vision she couldn't shake throughout a sleepless night or as she walked over to Virgil's the next day to claim her truck and camp trailer. Once again life held purpose. Purpose and dreams.

By the end of the following week, she'd paid her bills and said her goodbyes to the people who mattered. Only a very few people knew she'd bought stores for a lengthy outing. Cradling her still-flat stomach, she smiled.

"Hang in there, wee one. Your mama's going to find gold. You'll never have to worry about where your next meal's coming from—and you'll never have to rely on a man to take care of you."

Monday morning she left Tombstone behind and aimed the old pickup toward the county seat to renew Ben's claim.

When she got to the courthouse in Nogales, she filed for a divorce from Joe Ryan and posted her filing fee on the claim. Her dreams didn't stretch so far that she dared believe she'd ever become a millionaire, though she did allow herself to hope that Ben's secret claim would produce enough ore to provide her child with the kind of life she'd always wanted herself. Including a house. A permanent home in some friendly city that no one could ever take away.

After leaving the courthouse, she began the trek to Ruby. Twice she had doubts—although she never considered turning back. Once when she lost sight of the jutting red rock known as Montana Peak, which she'd been using as her compass since leaving the highway, and a second time when she passed the ghost town of Ruby. One-hundred-degree heat sizzled off the dented hood of the pickup. The remnants of dilapidated buildings depressed her. They stood as grim reminders that this scorched earth had beaten stronger men and women than Hayley Andrews Ryan ever thought of being.

She touched her stomach, where the flutter she felt was fear, not the movement of her child. What insanity had possessed her to come to this desolate land alone? *Pregnant* and alone.

Then, when the vegetation became greener and Hayley spotted a frolicking white-faced cow and calf, she reminded herself how alone she'd been in Tombstone.

"There's just you and me, kid," she murmured, patting her stomach again.

The trailer bumped when she hit a rocky dip. Hayley bounced on the seat and settled back with a giggle. "I hope you like roller coasters, kiddo. The track from here on is a real washboard."

According to the map, she was near the claim. While she'd hoped for an oasis of deer grass and cottonwoods, what lay ahead was an occasional mesquite, ironwood and rock. Sheer cliffs of reddish rock. Turning left around a promontory, Hayley saw a cascade of water falling between the two sentinel rocks drawn on the map. The falling water formed a natural spring. But it didn't feed the Santa Cruz River as she'd hoped.

A crushing disappointment descended as Hayley stopped her rig in the clearing also indicated on the crude map. So her grandfather hadn't been panning for gold. What riches had enticed him to come to this desolate place year after year—and to keep it such a secret?

She pulled the trailer beneath the shade of a huge mesquite. Maybe this *wasn't* the place, she thought as she climbed down from the cab.

But a hand-carved wooden sign carefully wedged in a stack of rocks said Blue Cameo Mine. Tears sprang to her eyes and it suddenly seemed absolutely right that she be here. A cameo carved in blue was the only memento she had of her mother. Another legacy stolen by Joe Ryan. Losing the cameo had hurt worse than his selling the Silver Cloud.

Ben O'Dell had carved his name in the sign. That was how prospectors staked a claim. Hayley could expect to find a similar mound at each of the claim's four corners. Twenty acres in all was the limit one person could work.

Night was sneaking up on her. The sun had slipped

behind the Sierrita Mountains. Tomorrow would be plenty of time to take stock of the land Hayley planned to call home for at least the next six months. What she needed to do in the remaining daylight was unhitch the pickup and level the trailer. With luck, she'd have time to gather a bit of wood and build a campfire. The trailer's utilities ran on butane, but she wanted to save that for when inclement weather drove her inside. She hadn't passed a convenience store or gas station, in the past thirty miles. Twenty of those miles had been unpaved road. Yes, she'd do well to save her store-bought re-sources and live off the land for as long as possible.

One indulgence she'd bought—a portable radio. And she'd laid in a good supply of batteries. It had seemed a frivolous purchase at the time, but as she snapped it on and twirled the dial until she found the faint strains of Tejano music coming from across the border, Hayley thanked whatever had prompted her to make the impul-sive buy. With music, she didn't feel half so alone.

As she built a fire, hammered pegs to hold the trailer's awning and dragged out the two lawn chairs that had belonged to Gramps, Hayley paused a moment to ap-preciate a truly glorious sunset. Life wasn't so bad, she decided on a rush of emotion. In fact, things had turned out pretty darned good. The thought ended abruptly. Over a lull in the twangy music, Hayley heard the steady clip-clop, clip-clop of a horse's hooves.

Holding her breath, she lowered the music. Yes, a horse and rider were definitely coming closer. The squeak of leather told her the horse was saddled. Gramps had taught her well to listen for and delineate sounds in the wild. And he obviously didn't consider this site to-tally safe; in the pickup's window rack, Ben had left a twelve-gauge, double-barreled shotgun and a well-oiled rifle.

Hayley dashed to the truck and grabbed the shotgun. She'd never shoot a person, but scaring someone, now, that was a different story. No stranger to guns, Hayley counted on being able to run a good bluff. She carefully put the crackling fire between her and the approaching rider.

Unfortunately he came at her out of the west, forcing her to look directly into the brilliant red glow of the sinking sun. Horse and rider rounded an outcrop of granite, appearing as a huge dark shadow. The horse snorted and blew as if he'd been ridden hard. The man sat tall and menacing in the saddle. These few facts registered with Hayley as she raised the gun to her shoulder and said in the toughest voice she could muster, "Stop right there." Squinting, she saw that the stranger wore a battered Stetson. His shoulders were wide, his legs long, and he looked like he hadn't shaved in a while. Even in modern times, Tombstone attracted its share of saddle tramps; Hayley had heard that the farther south one went, the more likelihood there was of encountering men who made their living rustling cattle or running contraband across the border. Just another show of her bad luck that she'd meet one of the unsavory types her first night out.

"Who the hell are you?" a rough voice asked. "This is private property. I'll give you two seconds to pack up and scram off Triple C land."

Hayley had to hand it to the stranger. He ran a fair bluff, too. "Scram yourself, cowboy. I have a piece of paper that says this twenty acres belongs to me as long as I work my claim. And I've got a loaded gun backing up my right to be here. I suggest you hightail it back wherever you came from.''

''You've staked a claim? For mining?''

''Not your business, cowboy.'' Hayley drew back one shotgun hammer. Instead of withdrawing as she expected, her visitor touched his boot heels to the big gelding and crow-hopped toward her.

Hayley didn't want to shoot, but the closer he got, the bigger he seemed. His sweating horse might as well have been breathing fire. Hayley panicked. She envisioned her life and that of her unborn child ending here in no-man's-land, where the buzzards would pick her bones clean and no living soul would care. Aiming above his head, hoping to make him think she meant business, she fired.

The force of the explosion slammed the stock of the gun against her shoulder and spun her sideways. But not before she saw a limb on the mesquite splinter. A thick limb, about to drop on the stranger's head. If she didn't do something, it could strike him dead. Hayley dropped the shotgun and lunged at the bay gelding.

''Are you plumb crazy, woman?'' The rider jerked back on his reins, which was the wrong thing to do. The limb hit him hard and scared his mount, who reared high on his hind legs and bolted, sending his rider flying.

The man landed hard enough to shake the ground.

''Oh, no. Oh, no!'' This was not at all what Hayley had intended. Muttering a prayer, she hurried to the stranger's side, fell to her knees and peered anxiously at his face. A great bloody gash spread above his left ear. Hesitantly she slipped her fingers beneath the red bandanna he had tied around his neck, checking for a pulse.

''Thank God.'' Hayley heaved a sigh and pillowed

his head on her knees. His pulse beat slow and steady. At least she hadn't killed him.

JACOB COOPER opened his eyes. He felt the world spin, so he shut them again. There was a hollow ringing in his ears. It took Jake several moments to realize he was no longer seated in his saddle but lay horizontally on the ground—with his head resting on something soft. Good, since his head hurt like hell.

What the devil had happened? It'd been years since he'd tumbled from a horse. Not since his rodeo days.

All at once Jake remembered the woman with the big eyes and the even bigger gun. Had she shot him? He struggled to sit up and, though woozy, nearly smacked his nose into a face peering at him from close range. Had he met his maker? Was this the angel of death? Somehow he'd never expected the angel of death to be so pretty.

So pretty, or so solidly real. It dawned on Jake that his head lay on the lap of a flesh-and-blood woman. He was so deliriously happy to discover he was alive he started to laugh.

His angel of death's beautiful eyes narrowed warily. Jake noticed they weren't blue as he'd thought at first but almost lavender—unless it was a trick of the light created by a fading sun.

"What's so funny?" the woman demanded, beginning to edge out from beneath his shoulders.

"You are," Jake said, planting a hand near her hip so he could lever himself into a sitting position. "If I'd been the kind of guy you thought I was—the kind who needed killing— you'd be in a heap of trouble about now, lady."

She scrambled backward, still on her knees. "I wasn't

trying to kill you. I'll have you know I generally hit what I aim for.''

Jake touched his bloody head. "I'll vouch for that." He climbed shakily to his feet and whistled for his horse, who now stood quietly lapping water from the spring.

"I aimed over your head. The sun was in my eyes. I didn't know the shot would sever a dead limb on that big old mesquite.''

Jacob now understood why he couldn't hear so well. It'd been the nearness of the shotgun blast. He glanced at the ground, saw the size of the limb and thought it was a miracle he and Mojave hadn't both been killed. The base of the limb was as big around as his thigh, and the front portion looked like a spike. "Loggers call limbs like this widow makers," he muttered. "Only I don't have a wife.''

The woman obviously wasn't anywhere near ready to trust him. While he patted down his horse, checking him for injuries, she stretched out a hand to retrieve her gun.

It was then that Jake noticed how dark it had become. The only light now came from the woman's campfire. Yet he could clearly see what she had in mind. In two long strides he beat her to the weapon. "Oh, no, you don't. I'm not letting you finish the job." As easily as taking a lollipop from a toddler, Jake divested her of her weapon.

"How about we start with introductions," he said when she shied away. "I'm Jacob—Jake—Cooper from the Triple C ranch. I admit this spring is on Bureau of Land Management property, but it's got water crucial to our cattle. In fact, there are some ten ranchers in the area who need that water. July to October our range land is almost dry. The vaqueros we hire to help with roundup start that pump over there at intervals to feed water through the ditches. Well, it's not really a pump, but a set of four flow valves that work off the water pressure when someone turns the wheels and opens the valves.'' He pointed.

''I don't think so, Mr. Cooper.'' She crossed her arms. ''I've recorded a legal claim to prospect here. My claim starts at that pile of rocks—at the sign declaring it the Blue Cameo Mine. This plot of ground is mine from now until next July.''

''Sorry. I didn't catch your name.''

''Hayley. Hayley Ryan. Feel free to check with the county recorder and the state BLM office. You'll find my paperwork in order and my fees paid.''

Jake bent at the waist and scooped up his hat from where it had fallen. He jammed it on his head and then grimaced because it scraped the bloody reminder of his encounter with this woman. ''I hate to burst your bubble, Hayley Ryan. You're claim-jumping. A man by the name of Ben O'Dell filed on this site—and the Triple C has an agreement with Ben. He promised to notify us when he's finished prospecting, and we're going to the recording office with him when he releases the mineral rights. Then we'll buy this twenty acres, plus the hundred that adjoins it.''

''Did my grandfath…uh…Ben…did he put that in writing?''

Jake removed his hat again and slapped it against his thigh. ''I shot the breeze with Ben a lot. We swapped stories and drank coffee or an occasional beer. I suppose you could call what we had a gentlemen's agreement. Are you and he related? He never mentioned having a family.''

''Everyone has a family. Ben passed on recently. That

nullifies his claim. If you two had an agreement, he didn't tell anyone. My claim is good, Mr. Cooper.''

Jake's eyes narrowed suspiciously. ''Well, I hope you'll pardon me if I ride into Tombstone to see if you're telling the truth.''

''Be my guest.'' Hayley waved him off. ''Don't let me keep you. It's been a long day. I'd like to eat my evening meal in peace, if you don't mind, Mr. Cooper.''

''It's Jake, or Jacob, please.''

''Jacob, then,'' she said sweetly, extending a hand. ''And, if you don't mind, I'll take my shotgun before you go.''

Jake let his disgruntled gaze circle the isolated campsite before he silently handed back her gun. ''Ben never said what he was digging for. It must be something valuable for a pretty lady like you to bury herself in such a desolate place. Are you aware of how far it is to the nearest ranch house?''

When she said nothing, only clamped her pointed little jaw tighter, Jake went ahead and filled her in before he swung into the saddle. ''Your closest neighbor would be the Triple C. Eight miles from here as the crow flies. Closer to twelve if you follow the trail. Our ranch sits practically on the Mexican border.''

Again Hayley said nothing. She simply cocked her head.

''Dang! It goes against my grain to leave a lady alone among coyotes and wolves. To say nothing of any two-legged varmints who drift past here, or any illegals jumping the border. Say the word and I'll help you hitch up that trailer so you can park closer to civilization.''

''I just unhitched, Mr. Cooper, er, Jake.'' Hayley enunciated clearly, as if to a child.

"I'm offering you the Triple C's hospitality, woman."

"My name is Hayley," she said pointedly as he'd done with his earlier. "Nice try, but nothing you say is going to frighten me off my claim. You may as well give up. If you have eight miles to travel before sitting down to supper, hadn't you better take off?" Hayley delivered the advice through a dazzling smile.

Jake pinched the bridge of his nose. Stubborn didn't begin to describe Hayley Ryan. He could just imagine what his dad and his brother, Dillon, who lived with his wife in a separate house on Triple C land, were going to say when he delivered the news about this squatter. He'd catch hell from his mom and his sister-in-law, Eden, too, for leaving a defenseless woman to fend for herself. Jake was torn between going home to impart the news or sticking close to look after the damn little fool.

A sharp pain sliced through his skull. He changed his mind about calling the woman defenseless. She was one tough cookie.

Touching two fingers curtly to the brim of his hat, he wheeled Mojave and rode off the way he'd come. If she didn't run out of lead for that scattergun, she ought to be safe enough by herself—for one night.

CHAPTER TWO

WADE COOPER met his son in the barn where Jake had stopped to rub down and feed Mojave. A Border collie Jake had raised from a pup yapped excitedly.

"Sit, Charcoal," ordered Wade, a lean handsome man in his midsixties. Without being asked, he pitched in to help Jake take care of his horse. "Expected you back by suppertime. Why don't you let me finish here? Go wash up. Your mother saved you a plate in the oven. You know Nell won't admit to worrying, but she still frets and peeks down the road when she thinks I'm not looking."

"Yeah, well, I'd have been here sooner, but I ran into a snag." Jake removed his Stetson and gingerly touched his swollen temple. It still hurt like hell.

"Literally a snag?" Wade stepped closer and frowned at the blood matted in his son's close-cropped sideburns.

"In more ways than one, I'm afraid." Jake left nothing out as he replayed his encounter with Hayley Ryan at Ben O'Dell's claim.

"Well, hell!" Wade exclaimed. His chin sagged to his chest by the time Jake finished his story. "I feel bad about Ben. Would've attended his funeral if I'd known about it. Your brother subscribes to all those damned papers—Tombstone, Nogales, Tubac. Wonder how he missed O'Dell's obituary?"

"You'll have to ask him. Perhaps Eden lined the bird

cage with it.'' Jake grinned. His brother was sappy in
love with his wife. He'd do anything for her. But Dillon
really had a hard time liking Eden's beloved parrot. Coronado talked a blue streak to everyone who walked into
the couple's house—but reserved special treatment for
Dillon, screeching at him and biting him every chance
he got.

"Quit needling Dillon over that bird. Tell me more
about the Ryan woman."

Jake scowled. "What's to tell? She's no bigger than
a flea. One of our stiff Baja winds will blow her and
that tomfool toy trailer of hers right off the map.''

"That's not what I meant. Ben led me to believe he'd
kept this claim a secret.''

"Hayley Ryan alleges she's Ben's granddaughter. But
he never mentioned any kin to me. I wonder if she's
trying to pull a fast one. She told me Ben never said a
word about our water deal. And asked me if I had something in writing. I thought I'd drive to Tombstone tomorrow and snoop a little.''

"Let Mom and me go," Wade said. "We'll drive on
to Tucson. Nell's been badgering me to go before
roundup starts. She heard about a new pottery-supply
store.''

"Fine by me. I'd just as soon not drive the pickup
over that graveled track between here and Arivaca.''
Jake hunkered down to pat Charcoal, then let the dog
lick his face.

"Probably wouldn't hurt if you were to ride back out
and check on the woman tomorrow. Someone should
warn her about the rattlers nesting back in those rocks.
Ben tangled with a couple of big ones.''

"It's a waste of breath trying to scare her off. I

brought up wolves, coyotes and mentioned illegals coming through. Didn't faze her.''

"Hmm. Then turn on the Cooper charm and see if you can work the same deal with her as we set up with Ben.''

Jake snorted and wrinkled his nose.

"Wha-at? You think I haven't heard Eden and Nell talk about how all the ranchers' daughters around here make cow eyes at you? I hear Dillon teasing you about all those single artists in Tubac who'd like to become Mrs. Jacob Cooper.''

"You're forgetting Hayley Ryan took a potshot at me, Dad.'' Jake didn't tell his father, however, that she'd also cushioned his injured head in her lap. Falling off his horse had been humiliating. But her hands had felt cool against his skin, and she'd smelled good. Very, very good. Jake recalled enjoying the faint scent of apple blossoms when he'd come to. Thinking about it again made him go a little breathless. He took a step back, threw the brush into a box of supplies and led Mojave into a stall.

"What do you suppose Ben hoped to find?'' Jake asked Wade, to take his mind off the way Hayley Ryan felt and looked and smelled.

"Can't recall the old guy saying. I don't know if he just needed to escape town life for a month or so every summer, or if he actually found ore.''

"You'd think it'd have to be more than just an escape to drag a guy out to live in primitive conditions every year for some ten years.''

"I figured he was halfheartedly hunting silver. A couple of times he talked like the ore was slowly playing out of his mine near Tombstone. But then, I'm a cattleman through and through. I don't pretend to know what makes a prospector tick."

"*There* you two are." Nell Cooper poked her head inside the barn. Still slender at fifty-five, she had smooth skin and warm gray eyes, which contributed to the fact that she didn't look much older than her sons, Dillon, thirty-five and Jacob, thirty-two. "Goodness, Jacob, what happened to your head?" Very much in command of the Triple C in her role as family caretaker, Nell silenced Charcoal and bustled the men toward the house.

She clucked sympathetically as Jake and Wade alternately explained Jake's clash with Hayley Ryan. "Well," Nell declared as she gently sponged her son's wound, "that woman sounds crazy. I say leave her alone, Jacob. We used to haul water from the ranch out to some troughs your father and his dad constructed from fifty-gallon barrels. I guess we can do that again."

Wade and Jake exchanged a very male rolling of the eyes. "After we successfully dickered to use Ben's spring, it cut our work by half," Wade reminded his wife. "Not only that, we're running twice the summer herd now. Jake, Dillon and I can certainly handle one contrary female."

As Nell got out first-aid supplies, she wore a look that said they should heed her advice and that the matter wasn't closed by a long shot.

Jake knew that look. "Mom, don't you be doing anything dumb. You and Dad are going to Tombstone tomorrow to check out the Ryan woman's story. I'm counting strays that may have drifted up around Pena Blanca Lake. I'll keep tabs on her when I head out in the morning."

"You'd better spy on her from a distance," his mother said as she rubbed antibacterial cream across

Jake's nasty-looking wound. "Her aim might be truer next time."

Jake sighed. "I told you she was shooting over my head. She stared square into the sun and didn't see the limb. I peg her as a stubborn female, not a criminal."

"Jacob Cooper." Nell wagged a finger. "Now, mind you, I'm not condoning what she did. But I hope you're not one to be calling her stubborn simply because she's a woman. If it were a man protecting his claim, you'd give him his due."

"Now, Mama, I give women their due. What I was trying to say is that Hayley Ryan isn't all that dangerous."

"Doesn't hurt to take it easy until we know more, son," Wade said, clapping Jake on the shoulder. "I mean, we don't know anything about her, and we don't know how old Ben died, now do we?"

"Oh, for crying out loud." Jake threw up his hands and stalked into the kitchen, away from his parents. As they entered the room behind him, he faced them again and ran a hand across his jaw with its three-day growth of beard. He directed his question at Nell. "Look at me. If I rode in and surprised you, and you were camped alone, wouldn't you pull a gun if you had one?"

Nell studied her second-born son. The love she felt for him shone from her eyes.

"Okay, so it's not a fair question," Jake allowed. "All I'm saying is I'm willing to cut her some slack."

Nell removed a warming plate from the oven and set it on the table, then motioned Jake to have a seat. "You can be respectful without being too trusting, Jacob. Oh, I know, females young and old fall naturally under your spell. At times it's music to a mother's ears, even if some of them insult me with their flattery when they're angling to become my daughter-in-law. But remember, this Hayley Ryan is a total stranger. Just because she appears helpless and vulnerable doesn't mean she is. Don't forget the women's prisons are full of baby-faced stinkers.''

A peal of laughter burst from Jake. His eyes, a shade lighter gray than his mother's, reflected his mirth. ''That must be lecture number ten million nine hundred and ninety-nine thousand. Dillon said you quit lecturing him altogether when he married Eden. Is that what I have to do to get you to ease up, Mom? Find me a wife?''

She looked sheepish for a moment, then playfully slapped one of his broad shoulders. ''Go ahead, laugh. You'll understand when you have kids of your own. A mother wants her children's lives to be perfect. They never get so old that you stop worrying.''

''You worry too much,'' Jake told her.

Wade looped his arms around his wife. He pinioned her arms and nuzzled her neck. ''Our boys are men, Nell. Time they worried about themselves. In fact, Jake and I were talking yesterday. After the next roundup we thought we'd start clearing that mesa he's had his eye on. You know, the one overlooking Hell's Gate.''

The news brought a happy cry from Nell. ''Jake. Does this mean you've made up your mind to put a ring on some lucky girl's finger? No, don't tell me. Let me guess. Cayla Burke.'' She glanced from her husband to her son and back again. ''Granted, Cayla can be a little chatty, but she knows ranching. No?'' She pursed her lips. ''Who, then? Oh, Jake, not Sierra Mackey. I know Eden said you danced with her three times at the grange dance last month. But she's…she's…''

''Well, don't stop there,'' Jake teased. ''Sierra's what?''

Nell gulped. ''If she's your choice, Jake, I don't want

to be critical of her. I'll support your decision and make her welcome here, of course.''

"I'm not marrying Sierra. Just because I'm ready to have a place of my own doesn't mean I've found a partner. Not that I'm not looking. I am. But I'm holding out for what you and Dad have. And I'll finish the sentence for you. Sierra is exactly like her mother. Myra drinks too much and she can't keep her hands off other women's husbands. I've got eyes, Mom.''

"And brains," Wade said, drawing his wife around for a more complete kiss. "Enough said, Nell," he muttered. "Let's retire and let Jacob eat."

Jake watched them leave arm in arm. An emptiness washed over him. He despaired of ever finding a mate who compared to his mother or to Dillon's wife, Eden. Both were one-man women. Yet they were strong and independent. His mom was a talented potter. Eden, a silversmith. Her jewelry sold in fine stores all over the world. Underneath, at a very basic level, each loved the land. Jake wouldn't settle for less.

The ranch was important to him. Many of the women he'd dated over the past five years couldn't wait to shake the dust of the country off their feet. Jake had known from the time he was five that he never wanted to do anything but raise beeves like his dad. Maybe it wasn't meant for him to get married, he mused as he polished off the last of the casserole and carried his plate to the dishwasher.

Maybe, unlike his father and brother, he couldn't have both.

HAYLEY SAT BESIDE her campfire and toyed with the hasty meal of biscuits and stew she'd fixed after the cowboy had gone. She couldn't remember a night so dark. There must have been some, she thought. Those times she'd gone prospecting with her grandfather. But back then, his larger-than-life presence had dispelled all the fears a young girl might associate with the darkness.

Hayley wished Jake Cooper hadn't ridden into her camp. In doing so, he'd reminded her how isolated she was. As melancholy overtook her, Hayley recognized that she'd fallen into the grip of a terrible homesickness.

Not only that, her uninvited visitor's unsubtle warning had turned the surrounding blackness into a potential place of terror. No stranger to the yip of coyotes, Hayley now gave a start and shivered whenever she heard distant calls.

She'd intended to stoke the fire after doing her dishes and then read one of the Luke Short westerns she'd brought to spice up lonely evenings. When an owl hooted nearby and she practically jumped out of her skin, Hayley changed her mind about staying up. She scraped her uneaten food into an airtight container to be disposed of later, and banked the fire, instead of feeding it.

She made one last check of the food sacks she'd hung in a tree. Jacob Cooper hadn't mentioned bears in his list of things she needed to fear, but Hayley would rather be safe than sorry.

Collecting her shotgun and rifle, she retreated into the tiny trailer, where she tossed and turned for hours. One thought she couldn't shut out: What if Jacob Cooper didn't belong to any Triple C ranch? What if, even now, he was rounding up pals to jump her claim? Things like that happened with regularity in the books she read. Perhaps she should have stocked some contemporary novels. People didn't jump claims in the twenty-first century, did they?

It was the newness of the situation, she tried to tell herself, not Jake's warnings, that had her listening for every whisper of wind through the brush and turning it into a wolf attack or just a plain thief attack.

She'd tried to act brave when Cooper leveled his dire admonitions. Inside she'd been quaking. The man at the recorder's office yesterday had already informed her that two ranchers in this vicinity had reported jaguars killing their range stock. The friend of Ben's from whom she'd borrowed the shotgun had painted a more gruesome picture. He'd flatly stated that homeless individuals who wandered the hills would certainly kill her and make off with her pickup and trailer.

Inside, the trailer was hot as sin. At first she wasn't willing to open either of the small windows, not even if it meant she baked in this tin can. The screens would be no deterrent, she decided, from any man or beast who chose to break in.

She lay on her back in the close confines of the small alcove and laced her hands across her belly. Talking to her baby helped calm her. "This is our only chance to make a go of things, Junior," she murmured. "Francesca warned me I'd kill us both hauling rocks or blasting ore out of the ground. Hard work never hurt a pregnant woman," she said, more loudly than she intended. "Gramps said my grandmother took care of my mom, planted and maintained a garden, kept house and helped him haul copper out of his first mine."

Sweat beaded Hayley's brow and trickled between her breasts. Breasts that had grown increasingly tender in the past two weeks. She drew up her nightgown and fanned her legs. "It's not the hard work I mind." Her biggest worry was determining the best time to leave here so

Dr. Gerrard could deliver her baby. And would she have found anything worthwhile on this claim?

Hayley couldn't answer those questions. She did know that if she didn't manage to get some rest, she could forgo working tomorrow. Heavens, she ought to be able to stand a little heat tonight. Things would look better in the morning. They always did.

Ten minutes past midnight Hayley gave up suffering and opted for the possibility of a cooling breeze over the threat of death. Soon after she opened the windows, she felt such relief at the breath of fresh air that she began to cry. Unable to stem the flow of tears, she ended up crying herself to sleep.

LIGHT FILTERING in the window woke Hayley before 5:00 a.m. At first it seemed she'd barely gotten to sleep, and she tried to burrow under the pillow. Almost as fast it struck her that she'd successfully spent the first full night in her new home. Not one bad thing had happened. She derived an immense satisfaction from that. Greeting the day seemed far more desirable than lolling about in a hot trailer.

She showered in the cramped hollow carved in rock behind the waterfall. Refreshed, she hummed "Carrying Your Love with Me," a once-popular George Strait tune, as she started a fire and put on water for tea. She ate a bowl of berries and cottage cheese while she waited for the water to boil. In this heat the ice in her cooler would soon be history. "I can't be driving into town too often." She spoke matter-of-factly to her unborn child. "Fresh fruit and veggies are not going to be very plentiful after what I have in my cooler spoils. Maybe some farmer around Arivaca will sell me a milk cow and a few laying hens next time I go to town for supplies. I don't have a lot of the thousand dollars left after laying in prospecting tools and stuff. But if the price is right, junior, it'll be worth the money.''

She patted her stomach. ''Dr. Gerrard said in a few months I can have an ultrasound done at the hospital to show how far along you are. It might also tell us if you're Junior or Juniorette.'' Hayley chuckled, but soon her laughter faded. ''I'm not sure I want to know. Life needs some nice surprises.'' For the first time since learning of her condition, Hayley wondered if Joe would care that he'd left her pregnant. Probably not, but he deserved to know he'd fathered a child. If the law found him, she'd tell him.

Pouring herself a second cup of tea, Hayley firmly rejected further thoughts of Joe and set out to wander the low-lying hills beyond the waterfall. What she hoped to find was a stream that might indicate Gramps had been panning for gold. Swishing water around in a sieve would be much easier on her than blasting rock and hauling heavy ore down from a mountain.

Instead of flattening out into a valley that would support a stream, the terrain beyond the spring grew hillier. There were signs in numerous places that her grandfather had used his rock hammer to split rocks. Since some pieces were missing, Hayley surmised he'd taken sections to assay.

At the top of the second rise, she turned in a tight circle and surveyed the area all the way to her campsite. What had her grandfather expected to find?

Sighing, she hopped from rock to rock and picked her way back to the trailer. This would be a beautiful place to build a home. The trees were green, the water sweet and the sky so blue it hurt her eyes. But Hayley was no stranger to the laws governing mining claims. A miner could throw up a tent or move in a motorhome, but any attempt to erect a permanent structure on land open to claims was illegal. And each year the rules got stickier.

At her camp again, Hayley hauled out a couple of her grandfather's mineralogy books, plus the copies she'd made of his yearly filing papers. Each year he'd listed a different mineral. None were valuable. Mica, pyrite and chalcopyrite, all names for fool's gold. He'd once reported streaks of copper. Not a big deal. The area around this site was rife with small deposits of copper.

"Gramps was nobody's fool," Hayley muttered, pouring herself more tea. He knew that if a person wanted to preserve a claim until he made a big find, it was best to feed the county recorder unimportant facts. His last report included quartz and chalcedony. Totally negative geological findings.

Hayley settled into a chair with her tea, the books and a small journal she'd found in the strongbox. Her grandfather had never been much for writing. In fact, Hayley doubted he'd gone past sixth grade in school. Yet he'd painstakingly cataloged everything he'd found when he worked this claim. She noticed his last entry differed from the report he'd given the county recorder.

Was that significant? Hayley sipped her herb tea and stared into space. He'd written coordinates, and in a shaky hand penned in *hydrous silicon oxide.* Hayley wasn't familiar with the term. Did his unsteady writing mean he was excited, or was it simply a sign that he was growing older?

His death was sudden and unexpected. Hayley, as well as others, assumed he'd recover from his nagging bout of pneumonia. Would he have told her about this spot if he'd had more warning? Hayley liked to think he would've taken her into his confidence. However, the old man really detested Joe, so maybe he wouldn't have breathed a word, after all.

The thought saddened her, but Hayley could only be glad Ben had kept his counsel. Otherwise Joe and Cindy would have converted the truck and trailer to cash and sold this claim to the highest bidder. Probably to Jacob Cooper, if he'd been telling the truth.

To keep from sliding into gloom, Hayley set Ben's mineral books on a low camp stool and opened the first to page one. She might not know what hydrous silicon oxide was, but she had a lot of spare time to find out. If need be, she could drive into Tucson to the library. Although Tombstone was closer, everyone there knew her. The first time any local prospectors suspected she was on to anything, this place would be overrun with scavengers.

The thought had no more than entered her mind when a horse and rider and a black-and-white dog exploded from the trees between Hayley and her trailer. She tried but failed to scramble from the chair. She spilled tea everywhere. Her heart tripped over itself. Darn, she'd meant to keep one of the firearms with her at all times. She'd already forgotten and had left both guns in a closet in the trailer.

Before she could panic or even take a levelheaded look at her situation, a familiar voice rang out. "Don't go for your shotgun until you see what I've brought you." A gunnysack dropped into Hayley's lap, and the fright it gave her slammed her heart up into her throat. The bay gelding she'd only seen in twilight kicked sandy soil all over her fire ring as he danced in front of her. The dog, at least, seemed civilized. He ran up and licked her hand.

"Well, open it. It won't bite," said the man who'd

introduced himself yesterday as Jacob Cooper. Hayley finally caught her breath, although she continued to eye him warily as he dismounted.

Her hands tugged at the string holding the sack closed even as she noted the changes between this man and the stranger from last night. Still dressed in the working clothes of a cowboy, yesterday's saddle bum now wore a clean shirt and jeans. His hat, instead of the battered Stetson was the summer straw variety, and it was as clean as his newly shaven face. The engaging smile he wore exposed a dimple in one cheek and a cleft in his chin.

Jake dropped on his haunches next to her chair. With a quick flip of his wrist, he spilled the sack's contents into Hayley's hands. Four vine-ripened tomatoes, an ear of fresh corn and two thick slices of ham. "It's home-cured," he said of the ham. "My brother, Dillon, has a smokehouse. Smoking ham, bacon and turkey is kind of a hobby for him."

Hayley met the twinkle in the man's gray eyes with a look she knew must reflect her incredulity.

"I know there's a thank-you on the tip of your tongue," Jake said, rising and barely holding back a grin. "It's not so hard once you get the hang of it."

"I do thank you," she finally managed. "It's just…it's more like…you took me by surprise. You don't even know me!" she blurted. "Why bring me food?"

Jake removed his hat and slapped it a few times against his right knee. "No one ever asks why. Neighbors out here share, that's all. Now you're supposed to reciprocate."

This time Hayley clasped the sack to her breasts protectively. She flattened herself tight to the back of the lawn chair.

"Coffee," Jake said softly. "In exchange, you offer me a cup of java. It's a dusty ride over here. I could use something to wet my whistle before I go hunting for strays."

"Oh, coffee. I'll make some. Goodness, where are my manners?" Hayley babbled. Nimbler than before, she untangled herself from the chair and swept up the pot. "I, uh, have coffee grounds in the trailer. I'll go put the things you brought in my cooler and grab a clean mug for you, as well."

"Sure would appreciate it," he drawled. Watching her hurry away, Jake thought she had to be one of the most naturally pretty females in all three of the surrounding counties. Thick corkscrew curls hung past her shoulders, indicating she probably wore braids. Her eyes were huge and expressive. They were more blue than lavender today. She had a generous mouth and even white teeth. Her skin was possibly her best feature. Bronzed a light gold, to Jake it appeared flawless. At least the part he could see. Dang, he'd barely met the woman. He shouldn't be wanting to see more of her skin.

Ha, tell that to a certain part of him!

To keep her from seeing how unsteady his hands were, Jake looped Mojave's reins around a scrub bush and tucked his fingertips into the front pockets of his jeans. No, he decided quickly. That was a bad move.

He snapped his fingers at his dog. When Charcoal dropped panting at his feet, Jake returned his hat to his head and knelt to pet him.

That was the position Hayley found him in when she returned, not only with the coffee grounds and promised mug, but with the shotgun she'd brandished last night.

"Whoa!" Jake tipped his hat to a rakish angle, then held up both hands.

"This isn't for you," she said with a laugh. "But when you rode in, I realized it was pretty stupid of me to be out here alone and unprotected." She leaned the big gun against a boulder and bent to measure coffee grounds.

The seat of her denims pulled snugly over a gently rounded backside. Jake's mouth went dust-dry. For a moment he forgot any objections he had to her walking around with a loaded gun. He swallowed a few times before he could speak again. "So, you haven't had enough of your own company yet?"

Hayley poured his mug full, even though the coffee wasn't much more than colored water at this point.

Jake blew on the liquid to cool it as he waited for her answer.

"I'm planning to stay until December," Hayley said forthrightly.

"December?" Jake scowled. "We're sitting on high desert here."

"Yes." Her tone held an unspoken *So?*

"I don't think you want to camp out when the snow flies."

"Flurries, right? Nothing major. Tombstone and Sierra Vista get a bit of snow. Generally it melts by noon."

"We get more than flurries. If snow happens to fall on the heels of a monsoon, it gives new meaning to the great South*wet*."

"Why are you trying to run me off this claim, Mr. Cooper?"

"I thought we settled last night that you'd call me Jake."

"Either way, I'm not leaving." She gestured with her own mug, clamped firmly in her left hand.

That was when Jake noticed the white band of skin on her finger—the perfect width for a wedding ring, obviously recently removed. It drew him up short to think of her having been married to some faceless man. He let his face match his mood and he frowned again.

Stubborn as she was, no wonder some poor bastard took a powder.

He'd scarcely had the uncharitable thought when he remembered his mother's words, and they kicked in. His mom could be plenty stubborn herself. As could Eden. Both women lived in this valley spring, summer, fall and winter. They made daily trips from the ranch into Tubac, where they shared a shop in the arty community on what had once been the site of Arizona's first mission. The roads in and out weren't great, but their husbands didn't expect them to stop working because of a little bad weather. Jake knew he had no business questioning any of Hayley's decisions.

"Bringing me a few supplies does not give you the right to stick your nose in my business," she said.

Jake was jolted back to the present in the middle of her tart little speech. "You're absolutely correct." He rose to his feet in one rolling motion. "Thanks for the coffee, although it's a mite weak." Moving aside the books spread across a small square table, he set down the nearly full mug. His eyes scanned the pages she'd propped open with a fair-size rock. The chapter was titled: "How to Know Your Minerals and Rocks." Any doubts as to her true intentions were dispelled by her choice of reading material.

"What exactly do you think you're going to find,

hacking around through the rocks and brush, Ms. Ryan?''

"It's Mrs. Ryan."

"Mrs.?" Jake hadn't expected that comeback and it threw him. He recognized that his reaction was equal parts shock and disappointment.

"Yes. Mrs. Joe Ryan." Hayley bit her lip hard and felt guilty for lying. But technically her divorce wouldn't be final for six months. By then, she'd better have uncovered whatever secrets this land held. Meanwhile, claiming to be married might discourage Jacob Cooper from making any more uninvited visits.

But as she saw him climb back on the big gelding, a pang of regret gripped her chest. These past few minutes had been quite pleasant.

Really, though, she'd be foolish to trust him. Since Joe's subterfuge, Hayley had been reluctant to trust any man. She certainly ought to know better than to let one as overtly charming as Jake Cooper get under her skin. She'd landed in this fix because she'd tumbled head over bootstraps for one beguiling frog she'd mistaken for a prince. She didn't plan to let that happen again.

Shading her eyes, Hayley gazed solemnly at Jake Cooper.

"I've got work to do," he muttered. "Can't stay here socializing all day."

"I didn't invite you here in the first place," she snapped. When guilt stabbed again, Hayley dropped her arm and leaned down to pat his dog. "Take care, old fella," she crooned. "Tell your master I'll enjoy my dinner of ham, tomatoes and fresh corn."

Jake glanced down at the straight-arrow part in her hair, and despite himself he smiled. She tried so hard to act tough. Something told Jake she was a lot softer inside. But two could play her go-between game.

"Charcoal, you tell the lady to bury her scraps deep. We'd hate to have her blood spilled by some marauding cougar or one of those Mexican jaguars sighted around here last fall. Honest," he said. "Oh, and tell her to keep an eye out for rattlers. They come out to warm themselves on the rocks by the spring."

That last bit of information stiffened Hayley's spine. "Ick. I hate snakes. I suppose you're telling the truth?" Her hesitancy indicated she hoped he was lying.

"Scout's honor. Ben collected a whole box of fair-size rattles over the years. Promise me you'll take care."

Hayley didn't know why she should promise him anything. But the concern in his deep voice melted her resistance. "Same goes for you," she offered in a whisper. "I mean, you take care around those steers. I noticed you have a scar running along the top of your cheek. Last man I saw with something similar said he'd tangled with a longhorn."

Jake brushed his thumb over the old wound. He tended to forget about it until he went to shave. "This was a present from the last rodeo bull I climbed aboard. My dad said at least the animal knocked some sense into me. And my brother claimed I finally realized a pretty face meant more to me than a trunkful of gold buckles."

Hayley enjoyed the verbal peek at his family. She envied his close relationship with his dad and his brother. But she couldn't allow herself to feel such things, to be anything but resolutely self-sufficient. Swiveling, she grabbed both mugs and hurried to the spring where she knelt to swish the cups.

Jake willed her to look his way again. When it became

clear she didn't intend to and that their visit was at an end, he whistled Charcoal to heel and galloped off through the trees. Hard as it was, he resisted taking a last survey of Hayley Ryan.

CHAPTER THREE

HAYLEY WANTED TO CALL Jacob Cooper back. He, his horse and dog had brought some warmth to her day. She felt a sharp loss when they disappeared from sight. Though she'd never had a lot of close friends, in Tombstone she'd at least interacted with people. Every day she went to the post office, the market and the mine. She'd always thrived on the company of others, preferring it to the solitary life she knew too well. Maybe trying to work this site by herself wasn't such a good idea after all.

What choice did she have? Hayley trudged back to the trailer with the newly washed mugs, thinking it wasn't like Joe had left her any alternative. Here it was mid-July. Christmas wasn't all that far off. By then, she'd have the company she craved. A child. Her child. The thought of holding her baby made Hayley smile.

As she returned to the fireside and picked up her book, she gave herself a good talking-to. She hadn't come to her grandfather's claim to socialize. She'd come to wrest out a living for herself and for her unborn child. She didn't need the distraction of a good-looking, soft-voiced cowpuncher. In her limited experience, men who made nice were after more than a cup of coffee. Jacob Cooper wanted something. It was a cinch he wasn't bowled over by her great beauty or stunning personality.

The notion that he might find her attractive made her

laugh. She looked positively scruffy and she'd acted downright surly. If someone had taken a shot at *her,* she wouldn't be inclined to go back, let alone bring gifts. Not only that, Joe had made it abundantly clear in his note that she had nothing to offer a man—except her grandfather's mine.

So, yes. Jake Cooper had an agenda. He wanted free access to the spring. He'd said his family had plans to buy this chunk of land and all the acreage that adjoined it, if and when her grandfather relinquished his claim.

Well…maybe Cooper had a water agreement with Gramps, and maybe he didn't.

Hayley shook off the uncharitable thoughts that kept crowding in. Jake Cooper had made an effort to be friendly. She needed the fresh produce he'd brought. She needed milk and eggs, too. Why hadn't she asked him if he knew of anyone who might sell her a milk cow or a couple of laying hens? Instead of getting so touchy, she should have made inquiries of her own.

JAKE RETREATED to the top of a rise that overlooked Hayley Ryan's camp. Dismounting, he tied Mojave to a scrub oak and flung himself flat behind a slab of granite. Charcoal whined as Jake peeled off his gloves and trained a pair of binoculars on the Ryan woman.

"It's okay, boy," Jake murmured. "We'll hunt strays in a little while. For now, find a shady spot and rest your bones."

The dog flipped his ears to and fro, then stretched out under a tree. Eventually he settled his nose on his front paws, never taking his eyes off Jake.

Jake wasn't sure what he'd expected Hayley to do once he'd gone. He felt a vague disappointment when she returned to her chair and stuck her nose in one of the books she had piled beside her.

"Crazy woman," he growled. "Acts like she's at a resort, instead of smack-dab in the middle of the wilderness." He watched her read for the better part of an hour. Suddenly she glanced up and straight at his hiding place. Jake found himself yanking off his white hat, lest she spot him and get it into her head to take another shot. This time with her rifle.

Common sense told him he was too well hidden to be seen by the naked eye. *Her* naked eye. And brother, what eyes they were. So dark a blue they were almost purple. Still staring through his powerful binoculars, Jake all but drooled on the bandanna around his neck. He didn't relax until she returned her interest to the book.

That didn't last. She soon tossed it aside, stood and shaded her eyes, staring hard in his direction. She turned slowly as if searching the hills for something in particular. *Or someone.*

Jake realized the sun had shifted and was probably reflecting off the lenses of his binoculars. "Crap." He dropped the glasses and scooted back on his belly until he was safely into the trees. "Why don't I just send up a flare and announce I'm snooping?" he muttered disgustedly.

Lifting his head, Charcoal barked.

"Shh." Jake raised a hand. "Sound carries down these ravines, boy. And we don't want the lady to know the Triple C plans to keep her under surveillance for a while."

The dog cocked his head, gazing at Jake intelligently before slithering to his side.

Grinning, Jake rubbed a hand between the dog's ears. "I know. You think I've taken leave of my senses.

Which is precisely what Dillon will say if I don't hightail it out of here.''

Dillon was expecting him to report the total number of strays between the ranch and Hell's Gate, where they were to meet. He'd been at the number-five line shack all week, moving half the herd into summer pastures. Jake was due to connect with him at three o'clock to exchange head counts and... Jake winced. The produce he'd left with Hayley had been meant to replenish his brother's dwindling supplies. Dillon would have a fit when he learned Jacob had given away the food Eden had fixed for him.

Of course, Dillon would be grumpy, anyway, having spent four nights without his wife. They'd be apart a week all told. Hell, that wasn't Jake's fault. He'd offered to move the herd. It was a chore he used to do with his dad while Dillon oversaw the ranch. Last winter, though, Wade Cooper had tangled with a rogue cow and his bum hip hadn't fully healed. His doctor recommended Wade let the boys handle fall roundup alone. Dillon didn't have a good eye for spotting strays in the canyons. Not like Jake did. As a result, Dillon got stuck driving the steers to pasture.

Taking a last look through his binoculars, just to verify that Hayley Ryan had gone about her business, Jake climbed into the saddle again and set off to complete the job he'd started.

HAYLEY COULDN'T SHAKE the notion she was being watched. She'd closed her book once and let her gaze roam the nearby hills. Nothing moved and nothing appeared to be amiss. Refilling her teacup, she'd returned to her reading. The feeling persisted. Finally she felt so uneasy that she rose and walked to the edge of the clearing. Shading her eyes against the morning sun, she concentrated on a rocky promontory where she thought she'd seen a flash—like the sun reflecting off a mirror.

Hayley stared at the spot so long she became dizzy. Or had she gotten dizzy from self-imposed fright? Her heart was certainly beating fast.

When she could see no sign of any human presence, Hayley gave herself a stern mental shake. She decided that sitting around doing nothing but reading was making her paranoid. Why would anyone skulk around spying on her? No one other than that cowboy even knew she was here. He'd said his piece last night and had made amends today. She'd been perfectly honest about her reasons for being here.

As for the possibility of someone else keeping an eye on her, well, this wasn't exactly a people watcher's paradise. And it was too early for hunters to be combing the hills.

"There, see?" she exclaimed, marching back to her trailer, "You have an overactive imagination, Ms. Ryan. Get over it."

The best way she knew to allay her fears was through physical labor. Rather than digging willy-nilly when she had no information about what to look for or where to search, Hayley elected to conduct a survey of the site. Gramps must have left, if not an open shaft, then at least test holes that might give her an idea of what he was after.

She loaded a day pack with a rock hammer and a cigar box divided into small compartments to serve as a collection box for specimens. She slapped together a peanut-butter-and-jelly sandwich and added sunglasses and a baseball cap to her stash, before she filled a canteen at the spring. Despite the growing heat, the water was cool and sweet.

"This water could be lifeblood to a rancher," she said to no one. No one except two squirrels who frolicked on a nearby branch. Their presence, and the melodious trill of songbirds flitting about, dispelled the last of Hayley's anxiety.

Who needed human companionship when there was all this wonderful wildlife to serve as company and an early-warning system? Hayley took a measure of assurance from the fact that birds squawked and squirrels fled at the mere sound of her footsteps.

She trudged through the trees, walking a blanket of pine needles. For a time she was more interested in the flora and fauna all around her than in settling down to look for test holes in the pockmarked granite hills. She climbed steadily for the better part of two hours before she came to a man-made depression in the facer rock. Bits of broken rock lay strewn about. Hayley paused to inspect the dynamited debris. Quartz and pyrite were all she found. Obviously her grandfather hadn't wasted much time on this spot.

Hayley continued upward. Eventually the trail petered out and the going got tougher. She could tell that Ben hadn't taken his search this high. But now that Hayley had climbed all the way up here, she wanted to examine her claim from the ridge a little above her. Even if getting there appeared more suited to mountain goats than humans.

She was winded by the time she reached the sheared-off granite table. The view was everything she'd anticipated. Spectacular hills and valleys stretched out on all four sides. The binoculars she'd found in Gramps's trailer were old and one lens was scratched; however, they served her purpose and helped her pinpoint his dig sites.

Four were visible to the right and below her. All seemed to follow one deep arroyo. Shedding her backpack, Hayley dusted off a wide flat rock. She clambered onto it, then pulled out her sandwich and a pad and pencil. While she ate, she drew a rough map, sketching in significant trees and boulders and other pertinent features around the test holes, so she could find them again.

As she turned her attention farther afield, a splash of moving color caught her interest. Cattle. The undulations of rock-strewn arroyos were dotted with white-faced steers. Beyond them were square cultivated fields of hay. It seemed strange to see signs of human habitation interspersed with miles of palo verde, ocotillo, yucca and prickly pear. Near the edge of what Hayley judged to be her line of demarcation, were piles of volcanic rock, many with a green tint. Copper. Had her grandfather been drawn to this site by such blatant evidence of copper—before prices plummeted?

A horse and rider came into view over a grassy knoll. The glasses brought him to within seeming arm's length of Hayley. Her breath did a funny hitch. *Jacob Cooper.* He, too, had field glasses raised to his face. For a moment Hayley had the oddest feeling that they were staring at each other. But no, Cooper's head rotated downward. He'd zeroed in on a group of wandering steers. As she studied him, he dragged a pad from his shirt pocket, similar to the one fluttering on her lap. He withdrew a pencil from his pocket and made notations on his pad. Hayley watched until he returned the items to his pocket and let the binoculars swing free around his neck. He nudged the bay's flanks, and as quickly as he'd

appeared, he rode out of sight. The collie trotted com-
placently at his side.

Only then did Hayley realize she'd been holding her
breath. As she let it out, she had to acknowledge that
he'd been a sight worth ogling.

Jacob Cooper's shoulders were wide. His torso ta-
pered to lean hips that melded perfectly to his saddle.
His butt was encased in denim so worn it seemed almost
white in the brilliant sunlight. Having accidentally honed
in on his long legs, Hayley realized why the worn denim
hadn't made an impression before. He wore chaps to
keep from being torn to pieces by cactus thorns. His
chaps met scuffed and spurless boots. Hayley liked that.
She'd always thought spurs were showy, and that the
men who relied on them had little regard for the welfare
of their horses.

A warm ripple ran up Hayley's spine when she realized Jake Cooper was exactly what he'd claimed to be.
A rancher. She couldn't say why she'd felt any doubt
before. Quite possibly because she was guilty of swallowing so many of Joe's lines. Hayley didn't think she'd
ever be quite so trusting again.

She reminded herself that one good thing had come
out of her brief sojourn with Joseph Ryan. A baby. The
reminder brought her crashing back to the present—to
her reason for sitting on a broad rock at the top of a
dusty lonely hill. She'd come here to find the treasure
her grandfather thought was somewhere in this desolate
tract of land. She had no business wasting time salivating
over Mr. Cooper's skinny butt, even if it *was* a nine and
a half on a scale of ten.

Sighing, Hayley folded her empty sandwich bag and
tucked it into her backpack to use another day. Telling
herself she'd probably never see Jacob Cooper again, she

took a long pull from her canteen, then started her down-hill climb.

JAKE HAD GLIMPSED Hayley Ryan seated on a flat rock at the very top of Yellow Jacket Hill. He'd been surprised to see she'd hiked so far since late morning, when he'd observed her scanning the hill from her camp. He'd been more surprised, though, to see her peering at him through binoculars. Jake didn't know whether she'd caught him giving her the once-over. He'd certainly made a show of counting steers to throw her off. His heart had yet to settle into a normal rhythm. Hayley Ryan made quite a picture framed by the rock, a ruff of trees and a cloudless blue sky.

Checking his watch, Jake discovered he'd better put some speed on. He still had to cross the pass into Hell's Gate, where he was meeting Dillon. It was past time he stopped obsessing over a woman he knew little about. One he'd very likely end up fighting with sooner or later.

But as he rode through the arid unfenced range land where the Cooper family had been raising cattle for four generations, Jake's thoughts remained on Hayley. He couldn't identify exactly what piqued his interest about her. He'd been fending off prettier women for years. Not that Mrs. Ryan was hard to look at, by any means. On the contrary, she was well put together. Small, but not so skinny you didn't know she was all woman.

And those eyes. Those changeable eyes that shifted from blue to the color of lavender to a deeper violet, almost purple. He'd never paid so much attention to anyone's eyes before. His own were light gray. Wouldn't it be an interesting experiment to see what color eyes their offspring would have?

"Whoa, dude!" Mojave dutifully stopped dead on the

trail. "Not you," Jacob laughed, bending forward to stroke the bay's neck. When Charcoal trotted back and sat staring up at him, Jake shook his head. "You, too, boy? Too bad you guys can't talk. You'd tell me soon enough how crazy I'm acting over a woman who'd like nothing better than to see my backside trucking down the trail. She may have warmed up after I pulled those veggies out of the bag, but if you noticed, she didn't request our return."

Jake let Mojave amble through the deer grass for a while before they crossed a dry wash and turned north. The sun beat down mercilessly. Jacob thought the humidity had climbed to seventy percent. He shucked off one leather glove, removed his hat and blotted sweat from his brow with the crook of his arm.

"Feels like monsoon weather," he muttered, settling the hat firm and low over his forehead. "I wonder if our Mrs. Ryan is prepared for the big rains that blow in here off the Baja. What do you think, Mojave?"

On hearing his name, the horse whinnied and swished his ears.

"I guess you're right," Jacob continued as if the gelding had spoken. "Better to keep my nose outta her business. She has Ben's truck and trailer. The old guy must've given her directions. If she was stabbing in the dark, she wouldn't have found her way to the Blue Cameo so easily."

The threesome covered another few miles before Jacob spoke again. "There's just something sad looking in the lady's eyes, don't you agree, guys?" Jake urged Mojave into a canter up a long steep incline over the ridge into the valley known as Hell's Gate. "But there's the matter of her calling herself Mrs. Ryan. Where do you suppose Mr. Ryan is? What kind of husband lets his wife prospect all by herself? Even more curious, why isn't she wearing her wedding ring?''

The horse blew out a long breath. Cresting the hill, Mojave automatically quickened his pace. Jake knew why. In the distance Dillon's horse, Wildfire, grazed on a picket. Dillon wasn't yet visible. Jake figured he'd holed up in the shade of a stand of black walnut trees. Likely he was whittling a car or a truck or some part of a train set from the ever-present hardwoods he carried in his saddlebags. Their granddad Cooper had taught both boys to whittle at an early age. Dillon was much more adept at it than Jake. As kids they'd played with wooden toys; now Dillon carved a batch each year, and Eden's church distributed them to needy children at Christmas.

In fact, that was how Dillon and Eden had met. She'd moved to Tubac from Albuquerque to open her own jewelry store, had joined a local church and dived right into community affairs. Small-town churches loved new blood. They'd put Eden to work collecting for the yearly toy drive. One October afternoon she'd arrived at the Triple C, all golden-hair and sweet smiles to beg for a donation of Dillon's toys. Jake recalled wishing he could carve as well as his brother did. Eden Priest was the most beautiful woman Santa Cruz county had seen in a decade. She was nice, too. And talented. Successful in her own right. Both brothers had thrown their hearts at her feet; it was Dillon's she'd picked up.

Jake grinned now, thinking about all the sneaky tricks he and Dillon had pulled trying to get into town without the other knowing. Some women would have strung them both along. It'd happened before. Eden wasn't that sort of woman. She chose Dillon fair and square. She took Jake out for a cup of coffee at the local café and let him down gently.

He remembered feeling lower than a worm's belly all the way home. He hadn't planned to tell anyone in the family. But his mom had either been perceptive or Eden had told her. Nell Cooper arrived home from a long day spent throwing pots to cook her youngest son's favorite meal. Afterward she'd coaxed him into taking a moonlight walk with her, during which she convinced him there'd be a woman in his future as wonderful as Eden. Believing that, Jake had decided to shake Dillon's hand and be happy for him. He vowed to find himself a woman who had both Eden's qualities and his mom's.

It was going on two years now. There were times Jake thought he'd set himself an impossible task.

His brother strode out from under the trees and raised a hand in greeting, even though a half mile still separated them. Unlike the volcanic terrain Jake had recently ridden though, this land was barren of all but an occasional scrub brush or cactus. Distance was hard to measure. It was why so many people who crossed the border illegally, seeking work in the larger Arizona cities, died of exposure or of dehydration. On the desert floor temperatures in the summer and early fall soared upward of 115 degrees—exactly the reason Hayley Ryan's spring was so important to the Triple C. There was precious little hydration in the area. And not a drop of water to spare.

Jacob covered the gap in short order.

"Yo, brother," Dillon called, holding his ground until Jake had galloped all the way into his makeshift camp. "Took your time getting here. I'd about decided we'd got our wires crossed."

"Spoken like a man who's been forced to play the

hermit against his will. You haven't been gone from home a week. Couldn't be you're missing someone special, now could it?'' Jake laughed and jumped back from the teasing punch Dillon threw at his left shoulder.

''You damn well know I'm homesick as hell. How's everything at the Triple C?'' In other words, how was Eden getting along without him?

''You know, Dillon,'' Jake said in a thoughtful voice, ''I think Coronado misses you. Why, it's a crying shame how broke up that parrot's been this week.''

''Very funny. You know the bird hates me.'' Dillon grasped Jake's shirtfront in both hands, nearly lifting him off the ground. Charcoal charged the men, baring his teeth and barking wildly. Dillon lost no time in releasing his brother.

''Tell me about Eden,'' he pleaded. ''What did she send me? And don't hold out. She promised, and Eden never breaks a promise.''

Jake knew when to back off and play it straight. He unbuckled Mojave's cinch, hauled the heavy saddle under the trees and dropped it beside Dillon's. Quickly he extracted a pink envelope from one saddlebag. So maybe he wasn't finished teasing. He passed the scented missive under Dillon's nose, then drew it back and pretended to take a deep whiff himself. ''Mm-mm! I do believe she soaked this in pheromones. Better watch out, or every male in the animal kingdom will be swooping down on us.''

''Give that to me.'' Dillon snatched his letter out of Jake's hand. He promptly put space between them, literally turning his back on his brother while his read it.

Grinning like a crazy man, Jake flopped down with his back against a tree trunk and uncorked his canteen to take a long swallow of the cool water. He'd give

Dillon time to read and reread his message from home. There was a limit to his pranks. But the darned thing was four pages long. Eden must have written a page for every night Dillon had been gone. Though he didn't want to, Jake suffered a stab of jealousy.

He supposed it was understandable. Growing up on an isolated ranch, he and Dillon had gone through all of the normal competitive stages that young boys and then young men developed. At times their poor mother had despaired of their surviving the sibling rivalry. But they had, and had emerged stronger men. They'd ultimately grown to be best friends. So what Jake felt now wasn't personal. He figured it was more that he'd reached the time in his life when the male in any species needed to find a mate and make a nest of his own.

The idea came so clearly that it surprised the heck out of him. He'd believed himself content to drift along, playing the field, so to speak.

He was concentrating on his thoughts and didn't hear Dillon at first.

His brother finished folding the letter and tucking it away. "Jacob, my man, what are you mooning about? Where's the sack of vegetables Eden says she sent me?"

"Oh, that." Jake knew he'd have to account for the missing produce. Suddenly he was reluctant to tell Dillon anything about Hayley Ryan. He didn't want his brother making a big deal over nothing.

"Hand it over, dude. I really don't know how the cowboys of old went for months eating out of cans. Call me spoiled, but I've gotten used to picking stuff out of the garden. Man, I can almost taste those beefsteak tomatoes."

Jake didn't see any way around it. He cleared his throat a couple of times. "Yeah," he muttered. "Well, don't get your mouth too set. I don't have the stuff Eden sent.''

"You left it at home?''

Jake supposed he could delay the inevitable by letting Dillon think he'd ridden off without the package. But he'd always been one to take his punishment rather than lie. It seemed pointless at any rate, since he'd told his dad he'd fill Dillon in on the situation at the spring. He opened his mouth and out poured the story of Ben O'Dell's demise—and Hayley Ryan's appearance.

"Let me get this straight. You and Dad just let that woman squat on the section of land Ben promised would be ours?''

"She isn't exactly squatting, Dillon. She filed legally. Instead of the claim being in Ben's name, now it's in hers.''

"Did she show you the papers?''

"No. But she has Ben's truck and trailer. Why would she lie?''

"Why wouldn't you ask to see proof?'' Dillon's eyes, a shade darker than his brother's, clouded as if heading into a storm.

Jake touched the still-swollen knot over his ear. "She showed me all the proof I needed,'' he said wryly. "The business end of a shotgun.'' Because it seemed almost funny now, Jacob spun that tale, too.

Laughing, Dillon slapped his knee. "What I wouldn't have given to see that.''

"I'm sure. If you know what's good for you, you won't be spreading the story around. It was an accident. Could have happened to anyone. She aimed over my head and hit a damned branch.'' He gingerly fingered the lump on his head again.

"Maybe you won't mind telling me what insanity

possessed you to have a second go at her today. Why in heaven's name would you bring her food? *My* food," he said irritably.

"Regardless of the shotgun incident, she's a woman."

"Yeah, a woman sitting smack alongside the only fresh water for miles around."

"Exactly. Wild animals aren't my only concern. Granted, most illegals crossing the border aren't looking for trouble. But who's to say they'd consider a bitty woman trouble? Some might risk jail for her truck alone. Or a drifter might. Or the occasional homeless guy trying to live off the land."

"You have a point." Dillon ran a hand over his stubbled jaw. His hair wasn't as dark as Jake's. He'd inherited more of Nell Cooper's coppery highlights. When he did start to grow a beard, like now, it was redder still. "What did Dad say?" Dillon asked. "He's not going to let her stay, is he?"

"He and Mom went to Tombstone today. Dad's planning to find out if Ben mentioned our deal to anyone. Then the folks are going on to Tucson. Mom's been chafing to visit a new pottery-supply store she heard about. If Dad doesn't get answers in Tombstone, he said he'd pay a visit to the county recorder. To take a quick gander at the record of claims."

"Makes sense. If the woman's not savvy, she might have slipped up somewhere. Left a loophole or something."

"I wouldn't get my hopes up. She seems knowledgeable about filing issues."

"Well, hell. Did she happen to say what's so all-fired tempting about that twenty acres? Ben worked it for years and he never found diddly squat."

"We don't know that for sure. The old guy was pretty

closemouthed. Oh, he told some tall mining stories, but I can't recall him ever giving away anything personal.''

''He talked a lot about his silver mine. I had the idea it produced all right, didn't you? Why wouldn't that revenue be enough for his granddaughter?''

''Depends on what you mean by 'all right.' Don't you think if it'd been making good money, he'd have stayed home and enjoyed the fruits of his labor a little more?''

''Prospecting gets in some men's blood. It's a lot like gambling. A fellow always thinks his really big strike is over the next rise.''

''I found Ben more down-to-earth than that. I mean, if he had gold fever, he would have spent more than a couple of months a year on his claim. To me it seemed he treated it more like a vacation.''

''Maybe. Gold fever, huh? So you think he was hunting gold?''

''I haven't a clue. I just used that as an example.''

Dillon dug in his shirt pocket and pulled out a toothpick, which he stuck between his teeth. Modern cowboys, especially those who'd once smoked, had switched from tobacco to mint- or cinnamon-dipped toothpicks. Jake had never picked up the smoking habit. Dillon had, but quit at Eden's request. But during serious talks, he sometimes reverted to it. He shifted the toothpick from one side of his mouth to the other as he gazed toward the granite hills under discussion. ''If communing with nature is all the yearly trek was to O'Dell, you gotta wonder why a woman snapped up the claim the minute the old guy cashed in his chips.''

''I don't know when he died. She just said he had. Don't tell me you're getting gold fever, Dillon.'' Jake sounded amused. ''Strikes were never plentiful in this neck of the woods. The Blue Cameo is so remote, nuggets would have to be lying on top of the ground for anyone to convert the ore to cash. Hauling anything out of here over dirt roads takes money and guts.''

''It's not so far to hook up with Interstate 19. No one's ever found reason to lay out the money to improve the road, but that doesn't mean no one would if they turned up something worth big bucks.''

''I'd have to see it to believe it. It's not that I think a woman is less capable than a man of hacking into a ripe vein by accident. But I *am* skeptical of that woman being Hayley Ryan. If you could've seen her poring over elementary mineral and gem books, you'd agree. Plus, she's a flyweight.'' He shook his head. ''I think if we wait a while, she'll eventually give up and go home.''

''She might reach that conclusion faster, Jake, if you didn't supply her with fresh produce. My produce,'' Dillon reminded him.

''I know, I know. But if that was Eden camped there, would you turn your back and walk away, big brother?''

A sudden light dawned in Dillon's eyes. ''Are you saying you've fallen for this stranger?''

''No!'' Jake protested. A bit too fast and much too vociferously. ''We were raised to look out for women. So get off my back. You'd do the same—don't deny it.''

Dillon gazed at his brother narrowly. The staring match lasted only seconds. Dillon capitulated with a shrug. ''Then we'll leave it at that. What's your count of strays? I turned 1,010 head onto our leased grassland. Nine hundred and thirty to open range near Pena Blanca Lake. And twice as many near Hank and Yank's dry spring. By my figuring, we're down roughly five or six hundred head from the number Dad gave me.''

''I can account for roughly half of that in little knots of two or three strays. The missing might have merged with John Westin's herd. I'll ride past his spread and ask if he's seen any of our brand mixed with his."

Dillon gave his brother a playful nudge in the ribs. "This eagerness to volunteer to ride miles out of your way wouldn't have anything to do with Ginalyn Westin, would it? Like, give you a chance to ask her to the fall harvest dance?"

"And have Gordy White punch my lights out? Do I look like a man with a death wish?"

"Gordy's got no claim on Gina. If he did she'd be wearing his ring. But you're so obtuse maybe you haven't seen how the heir to the J & B pants after you, old son."

"You won't catch me in the stampede to her doorstep. John and Bonnie have spoiled her rotten. Can you really see me licking John's boots and jumping through his hoops until he gets damn good and ready to hand over the ranch to his daughter? Her husband will always be a flunky. No, thank you."

"Who mentioned marriage? I only asked if you were inviting her to the dance."

Jake shot Dillon a quelling glance. "Yeah? So sue me for reading between the lines."

Dillon laughed. "I'll concede Gina isn't your type. Hey, how about taking this Ryan woman? That way you can find out what she's really up to."

Jake shook his hand. "Oh, did I forget to say it's *Mrs.* Ryan?"

"I'm afraid you left out that crucial fact. Okay, I'll quit hassling you on that score. Too bad. Okay, go on. Ride out to the J & B. See if John can add to our steer count. You and I will touch base again on Saturday at the ranch. Until then, stay out of trouble."

The brothers slapped each other on the back, saddled

up and rode their separate ways. On the dusty ride to the J & B, Jake couldn't seem to forget the idea of asking Hayley Ryan to the dance. But hell, it was still four months away. He was betting she'd be long gone and only a sweet memory by Labor Day.

CHAPTER FOUR

IT WAS LATE AFTERNOON when Jake rode up the winding path to the Westin ranch. The house itself was far more elaborate than the Coopers' sprawling single-level home. John Westin had not been born into the cattle business as Wade Cooper had. Westin, who'd come from Virginia, was a latecomer to the Santa Cruz basin. A bankroll of family money, coupled with a desire to build an impressive spread, helped him forge a position into the elite establishment of cattle barons. Westin was brash and outspoken—traits that didn't seem to bother some in the valley. Jake, however, preferred his father's easygoing manner and willingness to look at all sides of an issue.

John walked out onto the veranda to light up one of the Cuban cigars he favored just as Jake clattered to a halt in the circular drive. Westin had laid gravel in the area for automobiles, but in deference to the business they were in, he also supplied a watering trough for horses and a hitching rail underneath a stand of shade trees.

"Jacob. Welcome." John puffed out a cloud of smoke. "What brings you to my humble abode?" He leaned negligently against a carved white pillar and guffawed. "As if I didn't know."

Jake glanced at the man's house. The three-storeyed structure looked for all the world like a plantation mansion from the nineteenth century. "'Humble' isn't exactly a word that comes to mind, John, when I see the J & B.''

Westin rolled the cigar around his lips and his laughter deepened. "The place shows well at night. 'Course, my women don't give a damn about the cost of electricity. They turn on every chandelier in the house." He grinned. "I notice you evaded my point. You're here to see Ginalyn. Correct?"

"Nope, though I'll say hello if she's around. Dillon and I came up short on our steer count this week. Thought maybe some Triple C stock might have mixed in with J & B herds. If your hands run across our brand, give us a call, will you? I'll come cut them out."

"Will do. Grass is so dry all the stock's scattered. When's Wade going to wise up and toss that old fool miner off the spring property so we can divvy it up?"

"Dad and Mom are in Tombstone today. We heard Ben O'Dell died."

John's eyes lit. "Excellent. Couldn't happen at a better time. The valley's growing and changing. The Coalition needs free access to that water."

"I expect Dad will work out an equitable agreement if he's able to purchase the property." Jake didn't like the greedy gleam in John's eyes. Or maybe he was touchy about the subject because of the way Dillon had teased him about Hayley Ryan.

"What's to stop him? O'Dell promised Wade first right of option."

"Yeah, but it's come to our attention that someone's refiled Ben's claim."

"You don't say! Now that isn't right. Wade's been far too patient as it is. We ranchers need a show of strength. Did some big mining outfit move in?"

Jake shook his head. "Just a single prospector, like Ben." Jake couldn't say why he was reluctant to tell John more about Ben's granddaughter.

Fortunately he was saved the effort of evasion. The screen door opened and a pretty blond woman strolled out. Ginalyn Westin had her mother's classic beauty but was cursed with her father's arrogance. Though Jake had never seen her make a move that wasn't calculated to put herself in the spotlight, she was still a sight to behold. Shimmering straight blond hair, big blue eyes. She'd perfected the slow sultry drawl of her native Virginia and she had a definite, if practiced charm. Unless a man had seen how those fine attributes changed when things didn't go Ginalyn's way, he'd grovel at her dainty feet, which was what most sons of area ranchers did. Jake might be the only single male in a hundred-mile radius who kept his distance.

Which hadn't escaped the young woman's notice. "Why, I declare," she said, slipping a slender arm through her dad's sturdier one. "If it isn't Jacob Cooper. Let me guess. He's happened to ride in at suppertime, but before the evening's done, he'll get around to inviting me to the harvest dance." She managed to sound bored.

Jake, who'd whipped off his hat the moment she appeared, resettled it low on his brow. "Wrong on both counts, Ginalyn. My business was with your dad. We've concluded it, so now I'll get along home." Jake gave Mojave's cinch a yank. He whistled for Charcoal, who'd drunk his fill at the trough, and swung lithely into the saddle. Touching his hat brim with two fingers, he wheeled the gelding around and cantered down the lane. Not, however, before he heard Ginalyn's indignant sputter.

"Jacob Cooper, just for that I'll accept Gordon

White's invitation. And don't think I'll save you a dance, because I won't!''

Raking his boot heels lightly along Mojave's sides, Jake picked up the pace. He should go back and apologize. She was already complaining to her dad about Jake's rude behavior. The news would make its way to the Triple C. Wade would remind Jake that pretty eligible women didn't grow on trees. Eden and Nell, though more subtle, would find some other approach to get the same point across.

Ginalyn was a beauty and well educated. She just didn't happen to fit Jake's concept of an ideal partner and ranch wife. When his well-meaning family had asked him to spell out what he did want in a wife, he'd failed to put it into clear terms. As a result, the Coopers were exasperated with him. Hell, he was exasperated with himself.

He knew what he *didn't* want. He didn't want a wife whose focus was her looks, her clothes or the next big party. Nor did he want someone who'd set her sights on frequent trips to Phoenix. So many of the valley daughters were given a taste of the city at college, and they made no secret of wanting a man willing to help them escape the hard life.

Jake didn't think it was all that hard. Granted, the money was sometimes iffy and the weather could be the pits. By and large, the freedom a man felt when riding the range was worth far more than the disadvantages. The freedom to call his own shots and be his own man appealed to him.

He tried to understand the situation from a woman's perspective, a wife's, if you will. He certainly didn't object to women pursuing careers. His mother and Eden weren't tied to the ranch. What set them apart from women he'd dated was their ability to combine happiness at home with work. Jake couldn't explain it even to himself. He only knew he'd continue to hold out. No matter how tempting it was when winter rolled around to chuck ideals and simply find someone eager to warm his bed.

Lost in thought, Jake didn't realize he'd unconsciously detoured past the spring until the light from Hayley Ryan's campfire came into sight. It flickered and blinked in the distance, still far enough off that he could change course without her ever knowing he'd been there.

He still had plenty of time to skirt her encampment.

And he did kind of go around it for a few hundred yards. Then he dismounted and covered the remaining distance on foot. All the while his heart slammed against his ribs. For crying out loud, did he want her to shoot at him again—and aim truer this time?

Of course he didn't. He wanted to know if she'd found anything worthwhile in her trek over the hill today. Jake had walked to within shouting distance before he admitted that what he really wanted was to see that she'd made it safely back to camp.

Something shifted ever so slightly in his chest the moment he saw her kneeling next to a blazing fire pit.

"Hayley!" he called. "It's me, Jacob Cooper. I don't mean to scare you. I've been to the Westin ranch and thought I'd stop to say hello before I head home."

Hayley jerked and went white at the sound of a male voice. She'd been a million miles off in her mind, planning tomorrow's assault on the hillside she'd settled on to start her mineral explorations. Jacob Cooper was the last person she'd expected to see again today.

Yet his walking in on her with no warning sent shivers down her spine. He might have been anyone. She shouldn't drop her guard. Especially after the sun had set.

"Mr. Cooper," she said with a hint of unsteadiness in her tone. "Were you this much of a pest to my grandfather?"

Jake laughed as he looped Mojave's reins over a limb. "Ben always had a hot pot of coffee on the fire—and an occasional shot of rum." Thumbing back his hat, Jake moved closer. "If he thought I was a pest, his good manners kept him from mentioning it. I always had the notion that Ben got a kick out of my stopping to talk." Jake bent and patted the collie's heaving sides. He pulled a sack of kibble out of his saddlebag and, after sweeping a clear place on the ground, put out a handful.

Hayley dusted her hands along her thighs to wipe away the sweat dampening her palms. She didn't doubt that Cooper was telling the truth. Her grandfather, like most lonely prospectors, loved a captive audience. He didn't always waste time talking to her, though; he was a man's man. Hayley could well imagine him exploring a wide range of subjects with a local cowboy.

If she were to be honest, she'd admit that she, too, liked her long evenings broken up by lively conversation. Tonight might be the exception. Her stomach had felt queasy for a good part of the day. She'd brewed a pot of chamomile tea to go with her light evening meal, but she didn't know if this was because of the pregnancy or if something she'd eaten for breakfast hadn't set well. At any rate, she didn't feel much like entertaining. She particularly didn't feel like spending time with someone who might see more than she wanted him to see. Jacob Cooper struck her as a man who'd harbor strong opinions about what pregnant women should and should not do.

"You might want to start carrying a thermos, Mr. Cooper. I prefer herb tea to coffee." She slanted her gaze toward the pot sitting on the grate over her fire.

"Tea, huh?" Jake wasn't able to hide his disappointment. "My sister-in-law serves herb tea to her customers. Must be a woman thing." He stripped off his hat and raked a hand through his matted hair.

"Your sister-in-law runs a café?"

Jake shook his head. "She designs jewelry. In Tubac," he added, although he didn't know why. Hayley hadn't given him any reason to think her polite question had been an attempt to strike up a real conversation.

"I've never been there. To Tubac, I mean. Well," she said breezily, though she felt far from breezy as her stomach had begun mixing it up again, "don't let me stop you from going home to supper. I was about to douse my fire and turn in."

Jake's roving gaze lit on a nearly full plate of food she'd left on the small table that had earlier held her mineralogy books. He wasn't usually the type to stick around where he clearly wasn't wanted, but something perverse in him made him dig in his heels. Perhaps it was the tense look that brought an aura of fatigue to the Ryan woman's expressive face.

"Truth of the matter is, anything hot would go down well at this stage in the game. I hate to trouble you for a cup of that tea, but my animals could use a break. While you pour a neighbor a cup, I'll water Mojave and Charcoal at the spring."

Hayley opened her mouth to object. Then she bit back a sigh and reached for the pot, and the mug Jacob had drunk coffee from earlier. "You'll have to take it without milk or sugar. I'm short on some items."

"Plain is fine." Jake led his animals to the spring and

picked a spot where he could watch his reluctant hostess without seeming to. She'd told him she intended to spend several months working this claim. Why, at the outset, was she short on supplies? The story behind her being here intrigued Jake, as did that white strip of skin circling the third finger of her left hand. Maybe he'd do a little discreet probing concerning the whereabouts of Mr. Ryan before he finished that begrudgingly offered cup of tea.

After his first taste, it was all Jake could do to keep a straight face. The stuff was horrid. He didn't know how anyone could drink it for enjoyment.

Hayley must have detected his faint choking sound, or at least noticed the curl of his upper lip. "Something wrong with the tea, Mr. Cooper?" Eyeing him over the rim of her cup, she allowed a tiny smile.

"Uh. No. Say, didn't I ask you to call me Jake?"

She shrugged. "Don't think you have to finish the tea, Jake."

"It's different from what Eden fixes, is all. Mostly she serves stuff with a fruity flavor."

"Eden. What a pretty name. She probably sticks to the commercial berry teas. This one is chamomile—it relaxes."

"Relaxing's a good idea. Why don't we take a load off our feet?" Jake helped himself to one of the two lawn chairs, even though Hayley hadn't invited him to sit. "Go on, eat your supper. Anyone who climbed to the rim and back in one day needs nourishment."

"Have you been spying on me, Mr. Cooper?" Hayley's voice was flat, belying her alarm. As she sat opposite him, she recalled her earlier feeling of being watched.

"Jake," he reminded with laughter in his voice. "Not

spying, exactly,'' he said. ''Hunting strays day after day gets pretty boring.'' He waved a hand, indicating the field glasses slung over his saddle horn. ''About noon I spotted you at the top of the slope. I confess it's more tempting to track a pretty woman's progress than to keep after a bunch of cows. However, my dedication to work eventually won out.''

His candid acknowledgment and the fact that he'd called her pretty brought a surge of color to Hayley's cheeks. This type of casual flirting had never been her forte. Not to mention it had sucked her in and ultimately left her at the mercy of Joe Ryan. ''Some women might fall for flattery,'' she added hastily. ''I'm not one of them.''

Surprising Hayley, the dog loped over, placed a paw on her lap and gazed at her with soulful eyes. She found it disconcerting, but couldn't resist fondling his silky black ears.

''I've never considered it flattery to state a fact.'' Dragging his eyes away from his lucky dog, Jake forced himself to take another swallow of the abominable tea. He'd meant only to make small talk and ease some of the tension between them. His careless statement had obviously had the opposite effect. *Curious.* Jake thought she might be the only woman he'd ever met who took offense at being called pretty. But hell, she *was* pretty. Surely she saw that when she looked in the mirror. On second thought, observing the stiff way she now sat in her chair, Jake decided she might not. The absent husband could have done a real number on her. It made his blood boil to imagine such a thing.

''Eat,'' he said gently. ''I'll change the subject. You know, my mom's scolded me for years about getting too personal too fast. So don't be thinking she's some sort of bad person for not teaching me manners. Poor woman had to raise two irreverent boys. Did the best she could.''

Hayley let her guard slip a bit at that disclosure. ''This isn't the first mention you've made of your mother. She's important to you, I can tell. That's nice, Jake.'' Joe had so rarely mentioned his parents. The few times he had, his remarks hadn't been at all nice.

Jake latched on to a note of sadness he heard in Hayley's voice. ''I'm not an expert on the subject, by any means. It seems to me a mother has about the toughest job in the whole world.''

Hayley's stomach pitched. For a moment she panicked and worried that when her baby came she wouldn't have what it took to be a good mother. In fact, there probably wasn't a woman alive less equipped than she to step into that role.

''Are you all right?'' Jake's words came at her from a yawning distance. ''I seem to stick my foot in my big mouth every time I open it around you. Usually I'm much better at breaking the ice.''

''It's not you,'' she said, clutching her cup between restless fingers. ''I lost both of my parents when I was young. I grew up, well, unconventionally.''

So much was left unsaid, yet a whole range of emotions played across her face. Jake immediately wanted to know more, and at the same time it bothered him immensely that he'd unwittingly chosen yet another distressing topic.

Just how unconventional had her life been?

He took another slug of the tea, then made an inane remark about the brightness of the rising moon.

''More tea?'' Hayley asked, shaking out of an odd mood. She rarely wasted time wishing for things life hadn't seen fit to bestow on her. It wasn't good that a man, literally a stranger, could make her yearn for experiences she'd never known.

"I still have plenty," Jake said in a rush. He so quickly covered the cup with his hand, that they both laughed.

"You really don't have to drink it," Hayley said lightly. "I realize I didn't make you feel very welcome. But I can't help wondering why you'd go out of your way to drop in on me."

The question was direct. Jake saw there were many more unasked ones in her wary eyes. He felt unaccountably guilty and got out of the chair, tossing the contents of his cup on the ground. "It's a mystery to me, too. You've proved you can take care of yourself," he said, pointing ruefully at his head.

"I feel bad about that. I didn't mean—"

"Don't apologize. You have a perfect right to protect yourself."

She shivered and peered uneasily into the surrounding darkness. "I wish you'd stop making reference to vague dangers. I'm staying and that's final."

"Look. I'm not aiming to scare you." Jake set the cup down and jammed his hat on his head. "Water equals life around here. You're sitting next to the only good drinking water for miles. Ben recognized that. He allowed the Triple C and other local ranches to install the valve setup so we could water our herds."

Hayley crossed her arms, studying his suddenly rigid stance. "If that was a satisfactory deal, I can probably go along with it, too."

"It worked reasonably well," Jake said, shifting his gaze from her penetrating stare. "Thing is, there are plans waiting for implementation."

"What plans?"

"A real pumping station and a series of canals following the natural aquifers. The local cattlemen's association is waiting to start construction."

"Waiting for what?"

Jake backed away and unlooped Mojave's reins. "For Ben to relinquish his claim. Any of five other ranches besides the Triple C would give a lot to own this chunk of land. Not all are as community-minded as my dad. Ben picked right up on that. He promised to transfer water and mineral rights to the Triple C when his claim ran out."

"I see. My taking over his claim has thrown a wrench into everyone's plans."

"You could say that." Jake stepped into the stirrup and was soon gazing down on Hayley's worried moonlit face. "Some ranchers are tired of waiting."

"This is the twenty-first century. People don't jump claims anymore. Laws protect them."

"Along the border people write their own laws." Jake tugged on the brim of his hat.

"Are you threatening me?"

"Nope. I'm trying to make you understand the situation you've walked into."

"Are you suggesting... I mean, I said I'd stand by the old agreement."

"That'll help. I'll relay that to my dad. Even then, I hope you'll give this some added thought. The way our deal works is that whenever a rancher passes a herd near here, a vaquero rides in and opens one of the valves. You'd close it after a set time. Follow me. I'll show you how it works."

"That doesn't appear too difficult," she said after two demonstrations.

Jake puffed out a breath. "The men aren't always full-timers. Some are drifters. Ranchers don't ask a lot of personal questions before roundup. Sometimes we scrape the bottom of the barrel.''

Hayley had lived around the mines all her life. It was the same situation. Yet how much difference did any of that make? Her slick-talking husband, for instance, had been employed by a company that prided itself on doing employee background checks. She also had grave reservations about Tilford, the deputy sheriff who'd befriended Joe. ''I'll take my chances,'' she murmured. ''I'm working this claim.''

''All right. By the way, do you have a cell phone? Then you could call me for help if you needed to. I'll leave you my cell number and our number at the ranch.''

Hayley's face broke into a huge grin. ''I'm living on a shoestring. Sorry for laughing, but cell phones aren't in my limited budget.''

Jake walked the restless gelding around in a circle and stopped, facing Hayley again. ''Sometimes it pays to be safe rather than sorry.''

''Sometimes. But if I had extra money, I'd buy a few laying hens and maybe a cow. Tinned milk or recombined doesn't compare to fresh.''

A surge of empathy washed over Jake. Then he brightened. She'd just given him an excuse to keep tabs on her. ''I'll see if I can round up some hens. Cows are harder to come by. We're a long way from grocery stores. Folks tend to prize milk cows.''

''I doubt I can afford one, anyway.''

''If you don't object to my stopping by, I can bring you a quart of milk now and again.''

''I dislike being beholden.''

''No strings attached.'' Jake wanted to snatch back the words the minute they left his mouth. All favors came with strings. He wasn't exactly sure how that related to his confused feelings about this foolishly brave woman who seemed so pitifully alone standing there in the clearing. He only knew he'd find excuses to look in on her.

"In that case—" Hayley flashed another grin "—I'll try to be more gracious next time."

"I'll hold you to it. Well, I've got a ride ahead of me and you still haven't had your supper. Warm up that hash. It's not good for a hardworking woman to go to bed on an empty belly."

Automatically Hayley clutched a belly that was far from empty. Jacob Cooper's odd silver-gray eyes were far too penetrating—as if they could expose all her secrets. Not that she was ashamed of being pregnant. But it wasn't something she felt comfortable disclosing. Not trusting herself to speak, Hayley bent and petted his dog, then lifted her hand to toss Jake a casual wave.

"Take care." His words swirled around Hayley's head in the wake of his leaving. She stood next to the firelight for some time after the sound of hoofbeats had faded. The call of night birds and the singing of cicadas had resumed before Hayley finally took her eyes off the shadowy scrub brush through which Jacob had disappeared.

She didn't understand the wash of emptiness that assailed her whenever this man, a man she barely knew, rode out of her life. As a girl, and then as a woman, she'd spent untold hours left to her own devices. She didn't scare easily. At least, she'd never imagined bogeymen behind every little noise.

Hayley uttered a snort of disgust loud enough to still all the night creatures for a moment. Knowing she had to keep up her strength for the sake of the baby, she deliberately finished the plate of unappetizing hash. Then she banked the fire and went to bed—and pushed aside visions of Jacob Cooper to lay careful plans for her first dig the next morning.

JAKE SET A STRAIGHT COURSE for the Triple C. He felt as if he'd gained some ground with Hayley Ryan with respect to the spring. Now he was interested in finding out what, if anything, his parents had learned about her in Tombstone.

The house was brightly lit when he rode in. Eden's bright red Jeep Cherokee sat next to the front porch. That was good. He could deliver Dillon's message and apologize for having given away the food Eden had lovingly prepared for her husband. Jacob preferred face-to-face repentance to stammering over the telephone; besides, telephone apologies always sounded insincere.

He made short work of Mojave's evening care. Rushed he might be, but he never shirked caring for his horse. Besides, Jake had raised Mojave from a colt. The two had bonded as well as man and beast ever could.

Jake would have liked a shower next. He needed one after a long hot day on the dusty range. Afraid he'd miss Eden if he detoured past his quarters first, Jake marched straight to the kitchen.

Talk stopped. The three seated at the oak table greeted him with smiles.

"Well, it's about time." Eden got up from her chair and tossed back a fall of wheat-gold hair. "Did you see Dillon? Did you give him my letter and the tomatoes I picked? When's he coming home?"

Jake fit two knuckles over her upturned nose and pretended to twist. "Dillon and I met on schedule. He's coming home Saturday as planned. About that letter, my pocket still smells like roses. Poor Dillon had to air out the pages before he read them or risk an allergic reaction.''

"It was gardenia, you doofus. Not roses. No wonder you're still single. A woman likes a man to be able to distinguish between her favorite scent and that of all the other females around.''

Jake blinked, then buried his nose in her hair and sniffed. "Mint, with a hint of rosemary. Am I right?''

His sister-in-law batted his nose away. "Guess there's hope for you yet.''

Nell pulled a pot of stew off the back of the stove and ladled a generous portion into a bowl. Taking a pan of biscuits from the oven, she motioned her younger son into a chair, which he declined for the moment.

Wade tilted his own chair back and tucked his thumbs under his belt. "How's the beef count coming, son? Do the numbers tally?''

After washing and drying his hands, Jake slid in next to his dad. "We came up about five hundred short. Reason I'm late is that I rode over to the J & B to ask John to be on the lookout for strays. I've still got some territory to cover tomorrow, but not enough to make up for such a large discrepancy.''

Eden jammed an elbow in Jake's ribs and rolled her eyes. "It makes a good excuse to visit little Miss Bright Eyes, doesn't it.''

Jake scowled. "Lay off, Eden. Dillon gave me the same song and dance. I'm not interested in Ginalyn Westin, all right?''

His denial sounded so ferocious Eden reared back.

"Sorry for snapping,'' he muttered. "Dillon got in his licks, too. It didn't set well. You'll probably hear in town how rude I was to Ginalyn.''

"Rude? Jacob Cooper? The rangeland Romeo who makes every unattached woman's heart go pitty-pat, pitty-pat with his special line of schmaltz?"

"Come on, Eden. It's been a long day."

She grinned devilishly, but did drop the teasing.

Jake tasted the stew, then broke and buttered a biscuit before he asked his father casually, "What did you and Mom find out about Ben O'Dell in Tombstone?"

"'Bout what we expected. He was a private old duffer. Died unexpectedly. The Ryan woman is his granddaughter."

"So why do you suppose he never mentioned her?" Jake stopped with the spoon halfway to his mouth.

"Could be because there was bad blood between Ben and the girl's husband," Wade said. "At least that would explain why he didn't say anything in the last year or two."

Nell poured coffee all around. "The town was full of her story."

"What *is* her story?" Jake tried to act nonchalant, but tension showed in the grip he maintained on his spoon.

Nell's gaze traveled the table before settling on her son. "Now, Jake, your father and I don't know how much is truth and how much was embellished for our benefit."

"Give it to me straight."

"Mrs. Ryan's husband sold Ben's silver mine and left town with another woman. That much folks agreed on. Whether or not Mrs. Ryan signed papers giving him the Silver Cloud mine was subject to conjecture. It was obvious she didn't tell anyone in Tombstone where she was going or what she planned to do when she left. According to the few people we asked, Hayley Ryan packed up all her worldly possessions one day and disappeared the next.''

''Well, I hope you didn't let on where she went.''

Wade held up a staying hand. ''Jacob, there's no call to snap at your mother. I don't recall anyone asking. But what difference does it make? We checked with the county recorder and she filed right and proper. Her claim to the Blue Cameo is legal.''

Jake would be hard-pressed to say why he felt so protective of a woman he barely knew. Perhaps it was the sadness he'd glimpsed in her eyes. Or the comment she'd let slip about losing her parents. Nor could he discount her being so alone—or the telltale white mark circling her ring finger. Jake did know he wouldn't stand by and let anyone harass her further. Which must have showed on his face when he cut Wade off with a stabbed spoon in the air. ''She's agreed to give us the same water privileges as you negotiated with Ben. You told me to handle it and I did. There's no reason for her to find out we've poked into her private affairs. No reason at all.''

Wade, Nell and Eden all stared at him in bewilderment. Nell was the first to react. She reached across the table and curved cool fingers around her son's taut wrist. ''That's fine news, Jacob. But remember, we still don't know much about Mrs. Ryan, other than that she's Ben's granddaughter.'' Casually tightening her fingers on Jake's arm, she turned to her husband. ''Wade, as head of the Triple C, you'd better ride out to the Blue Cameo tomorrow and firm up the deal Jake made.''

Jake recognized the steel in his mother's voice. It was a tone he'd heard her use for thirty-two years when she wanted things done her way. That same thirty-two years of experience told Jake when to back off and let her think she'd won.

"Sure 'nuff, Mom." He pulled away to help himself to more stew. "I'll be riding out at dawn, checking the draws between here and Ruby for strays. Thought I'd stop by and check on old Ted Mortimer. He's pretty much alone since he retired from ranching. I'll try and make it home in time for supper. This eating warmed-up food every night is getting old."

The tension he'd felt through Nell's fingertips a minute earlier, dissipated, as he'd known it would. A sixth sense made him hold his tongue with regard to the food he'd given Hayley Ryan. The same instinct advised him to skip sharing his idea of taking her a few of his mother's laying hens. Jake quietly finished his meal while Eden said her goodbyes. Shortly thereafter, he tuned into a conversation his mother had begun about finding a fantastic pottery-supply store in Tucson.

"I'm beat," he admitted around a giant yawn. "I'd like to see what you bought, but can you show me later?"

Nell chuckled. "Get off to bed with you. I don't have to be told twice that I'm boring."

Because he loved her very much and wouldn't hurt her for the world, Jacob leaned over and kissed her cheek soundly. "Never boring. I'm proud of you. It's why I'll be hunting until I find a woman like you. And why I lose patience with Dillon and Eden heckling me about the likes of Ginalyn Westin."

Nell exchanged bemused looks with her husband as their youngest son broke off abruptly and left the room.

"I told you to quit worrying about Jake and that Ryan woman," Wade growled. "Boy's got a good head on his shoulders. He's a chip off the old block."

CHAPTER FIVE

THE SUN HADN'T YET RISEN above the mountain peaks when Jacob rode into Hayley's camp, a crate filled with squawking chickens balanced precariously across the broad rump of his mount. Instead of his bay gelding, Jake had chosen Paprika, a placid roan mare with a better disposition for serving as a pack animal. Her gait, however, wasn't nearly as smooth as Mojave's. Already Jake knew he'd pay dearly by nightfall. This trip had been a foolish decision.

"Foolish" was putting it mildly, Jake calculated as he reached the clearing and saw Hayley Ryan emerging from the spring. Though he was afforded little more than a flash of white limbs and womanly curves in the pale gray dawn, it was enough to send a hot corkscrew of blood to his gut. His knees, which gripped Paprika's sides, soon quivered with a different emotion. Anger at Hayley's carelessness replaced his initial masculine response.

"Are you insane?" he bellowed, shattering the serenity of the dawn. Birds flapped excitedly from the trees and a family of rabbits bounded toward previously unseen burrows.

Hayley, who'd wrapped herself in a short cotton robe and now vigorously toweled the ends of her long hair, froze in her tracks. Only the wild rolling of her eyes spoke of her true panic. Then she dived behind a tree trunk and came up holding a rifle, the gleaming barrel pointed at Jake's chest.

That cooled his anger and his ardor. For a moment, as they stared at each other through the hazy mist rising off the spring, Jacob saw his mistake in judging this woman vulnerable.

"Take it easy." He made his voice quiet and even. "It's Jake. I brought those laying hens we talked about last night."

With shaking hands and a disgusted look, Hayley let the gun barrel drop. Her heart still raced madly from the fright. Bending, she retrieved the towel that had fallen from her hair in her haste to protect herself. "Talk about insane," she said at last in barely disguised fury. "What brand of idiot sneaks up on a naked woman?"

"I wasn't sneaking, dammit! I rode straight in off the trail."

"On a strange horse and without your dog," Hayley said, standing the rifle against a tree while she swiftly fashioned a turban around her wet head.

Gritting his teeth, Jake swung down from the saddle. Didn't she know how revealing that damned robe became as the morning light filtered through the canopy of leaves? "You're dead right. I could've been anyone. A desperate man fleeing the border patrol. A deranged war vet wandering these hills trying to live off the land. Or even a no-account drifter riding from ranch to ranch looking for work. We've covered the possibilities before. Thank you for making my point. It's bad enough that you're bunking out here alone. It's pure stupid to be hopping around naked."

"I was not hopping. Well, maybe when I first got out. When you're wet, the air feels cold." She stopped to collect a shell-shaped dish that contained a bar of soap, then stalked over and stoked a bed of coals. "I suppose you'd prefer I slink out in the dead of night to bathe and be eaten by the wild animals you said come here to drink."

Jake untied the ropes holding the cache of chickens to the saddle. He caught the crate seconds before it crashed to the ground. "In my opinion, you shouldn't be bathing at all."

At that, Hayley faced him and arched an amused brow.

He felt a suffusion of heat streak up his neck and into his cheeks. "I mean, not out here in front of God and everyone. Can't you wash up in the trailer?"

"I plan to wash my clothes out here, too. And dry them on that rope I strung between these two trees. Would *you* settle for spit baths if you had this lovely waterfall within reach?"

Still scowling, Jake unwound a roll of wire mesh, took a staple gun out of his saddlebag, and set about stringing the mesh into a reasonable pen for the chickens.

"Well, would you?" Hayley demanded, when the silence stretched out.

"I hardly think it's the same. Even the orneriest scalawag would hesitate before tangling with me. You, on the other hand, are an open invitation." He gestured at the trailer. "Don't let me keep you from going inside to dress."

Hayley, who rarely got her dander up enough to raise her voice, shouted, "Are you accusing me of trying to be provocative?"

"Stop putting words in my mouth. I never said that. But when a man happens on another man skinny-dipping in a wilderness stream, it's no big deal. Let him stumble across a woman in the same situation and…well, there's a lotta guys who'd take advantage.''

The fight went out of Hayley. He was right of course. If she'd been Ben's grandson and not his granddaughter, Joe Ryan would still be peddling mining supplies in the back of beyond. And she'd be unmarried, still living in Tombstone. But then, she wouldn't be looking forward to having a child. A baby of her own.

Holding in thoughts and emotions she couldn't share with anyone, Hayley took a deep breath and gathered her robe tightly under her chin. Then she turned and stomped into the trailer.

Jake had watched the various expressions that crossed her face, including reluctant resignation. He disliked being the one to open her eyes to the harsh realities attached to her present venture. But better him than some guy who thought women had only one role in life—to serve men's baser needs. While most cowboys held women in high regard, he'd met some who didn't. There were men who'd take advantage of rural women who had no sophistication. He didn't know Hayley Ryan well enough to place her in that category. Yet she didn't strike him as particularly worldly.

He released the chickens into the makeshift pen and then dawdled, breaking apart the crate and stacking it carefully near the fire to be used as kindling. The longer it took for Hayley to reappear, the more Jake considered mounting up and leaving her to sulk. After all, he faced a hard day's ride. Why stick around? He'd done his duty, and had even delivered a lecture that would've made his mother proud. What Hayley chose to do with the information wasn't his problem.

Nevertheless, Jake was glad that the door to her trailer

popped open and she stepped out before he could sling a leg over the roan's broad back.

Clean shiny hair curled over delicate shoulders covered in a form-fitting khaki blouse. She'd tied the blouse at the waist of form-hugging denims, worn white in spots from frequent washing.

Jake's breath whooshed out as if he'd been sucker-punched. In a way, maybe he had. His brain backpedaled furiously. It was difficult to know what transformation he'd expected to see. Certainly not this look of innocence, this utter lack of guile. Or the engaging sunny smile she flashed him.

"I'm glad you didn't ride off before I could thank you for bringing me the hens. I started thinking you must consider me the most ungrateful wretch who ever lived."

"Not at all. We got off on the wrong foot today. My fault," Jake mumbled. "For riding in unannounced. For calling on you so early."

A self-conscious laugh fell from her lips. "That's okay. Much later, and I'd have been out digging." She tugged a few loose bills and some change from a tight jeans pocket. "How much do I owe you for the chickens? I'll have to trust you to set a fair price. So far, the only fowl I've ever brought came wrapped in plastic."

Jake grinned at that. "Well, now." He stroked his chin in an exaggerated manner. "I could pad the bill and try to make my day's wages. Then I could skip hunting strays and goof off all day."

Hayley played along. "You could. But I recall you telling me your family owned the ranch. So wouldn't that hurt your profits, too?"

"Smart lady. In any event, I'd be wise to charge you enough to keep me solvent while I hunt for a new job.

I've got a feeling blood won't count for much when my mom discovers I swiped her private stock.''

Hayley's smile disappeared. "You're selling me stolen chickens?''

"Nope. I'm giving them to you. I do have some scruples.''

She looked aghast. "And what do I say if anyone else from your ranch wanders past and happens to recognize these birds?''

Jake laughed. He gathered Paprika's reins in his left hand and swung up into the saddle. Gazing down at Hayley's puckered brow, he knew he should assure her of his mom's generosity. He should make her understand that Nell Cooper would give a neighbor her last dime if need be. But Jacob felt a sudden unexplained need to dig a deep boundary between his home, his family and this woman. He sobered and dropped all pretense of joking. "Give them hens a few days to see if they lay eggs for you. If they do, I'll stop by and collect ten bucks for the lot. I'll even write you up a bill of sale.''

"All right.'' Hayley, who understood that something in their give-and-take had shifted, folded her money and tucked it back in her pocket. "Goodbye until then,'' she said.

Jake, who'd hardened his resolve, who'd argued internally that he couldn't keep riding out of his way to check up on this woman, gave a curt nod. He jerked the mare's reins sharply to the right. The surprised horse wheeled and bolted up the trail. It was all Jacob could do not to turn back and offer a friendly wave, but he kept his shoulders square to the saddle and let the momentum carry him out of sight.

Hayley lifted a hand. Once she realized he wasn't going to return her wave, she curled all four fingers into her palm. She didn't try to gauge how long she stood there smarting at his slight. Longer than she should have, she acknowledged with a grimace. Who was Jacob Cooper to make her feel like an insignificant bug? He was nobody, that was who.

The day she'd filed for divorce from Joe, she'd seen pity on the face of the clerk as she read what Hayley had written: *for reasons of abandonment.* Hayley had promised on the spot that no man would ever make her feel pitiable again. Certainly not an arrogant cowboy. For all she knew, he might be feeding her a line about his relationship to the owner of the Triple C. He could be any old saddle bum.

She would have collected her gear and stomped off into the hills at that moment, if not for the fact that her stomach decided to act finicky again. Very likely because she hadn't eaten breakfast. Hayley chose to place the blame on Cooper's effrontery. "I'll give him back his damned chickens." She fumed aloud as, with jerky movements and roiling insides, she filled a pot of water to heat for tea. After hurrying into the bushes to empty her stomach twice, Hayley dug out the booklet Dr. Gerrard's nurse had given her, outlining what she could expect over the ensuing months of pregnancy. Without the book, she'd probably have panicked over the sudden bout of weakness and flulike symptoms.

Fortunately she'd read the booklet cover to cover before heading into the wilds. Now she had to hope one of the book's recipes—a tincture of horehound, peppermint, ginger and fennel, which she'd bought at a health-food store—would have the promised calming effect on a stomach gone amuck.

The booklet also indicated that staying calm tended to ease many problems associated with pregnancy. Her seeming inability to do so was something else she laid at Jacob Cooper's door. "Insufferable man," she grumbled, sitting down to drink the concoction she'd brewed. As she glared at his morning gift, one of the hens spread her wings and flapped them frantically, then squawked and made gross noises as she burrowed into a pile of dead leaves. When she stood, a pristine white egg lay atop the heap.

Grinning like a fool, Hayley ran to the pen and plucked up the egg. "So, girl," she said, adding a soothing layer to her voice to disarm the bird. "It's high time your new mistress learns to think before she shoots off her mouth. After all, the man went to considerable trouble to cart you ladies here. Maybe I shouldn't be so hasty about throwing you all back in his face."

She promptly soft-boiled the egg, layered it between two halves of a toasted biscuit and ate every morsel. By the time she'd polished off the meal, her nausea had disappeared. With an improved disposition, Hayley gathered her mining tools and set off to coax the rocky hillside into giving up its secrets.

IT WAS STRAIGHT UP NOON when Jake reached the Mortimer ranch that abutted the fenced perimeter of the old ghost town of Ruby. He'd turned up another hundred head of Triple C stock. They looked fat, sassy and content, so he jotted their approximate location in his log; he'd let the wranglers flush them out during roundup.

Ruby was a once-prosperous mining town that had been abandoned for nearly three decades. Its location discouraged all but the most avid ghost-town enthusiasts. Along with other local boys, Jake and Dillon had loved exploring the old buildings, which were still in surprisingly good condition. The mine, originally named Montana Camp, had at one time yielded lead, silver, gold, zinc and copper. Somehow, shortly after Arizona received its statehood, the town's name had changed. According to the story Jake had heard, the owner of the general store and post office had named it after his wife. Currently the town was privately owned. Jake knew the owners hoped to restore Ruby and open it to tourists. But area residents liked the tranquillity its anonymity afforded them. Locals, and Jake included himself, would be happy to see Ruby maintain its status quo.

Ted Mortimer's house overlooked the remains of Ruby. He'd quit ranching after his wife died, but couldn't bring himself to leave the old homestead.

It was time for lunch, and Jake always preferred sharing a meal to eating alone. Besides, catching Ted up on area events would take Jake's mind off Hayley Ryan. He'd meant to forget her after he left her camp. So far it hadn't happened. Visions of her intruded on him all too frequently. He found his mind wandering in her direction when he should have been paying attention to business.

"Yo, the house," Jake called, sliding out of the saddle.

A man appeared from behind a clapboard house. "Well, bless my bones, Jacob. Welcome." He grasped Jake's right hand and squeezed it hard. "Hope you have time to sit a spell. It's been a coon's age since anybody stopped by."

"Isn't Pima College still running field trips to Ruby?"

"Yeah, but them professors and kids have got their own agenda. Between you and me, I think they pity me."

"Pity you? Why?" Jake loosened Paprika's cinch, dropped the saddle on the porch and led the mare to a metal tub brimming with water. Shading his eyes, he gazed over the rolling hills, taking in a hawk soaring against the cloudless sky.

"I get the feeling all those folks from town believe I'm an outcast forced to reside next to a ghost town as punishment."

Jake laughed and followed the man to a shaded side of the porch, where he helped himself to a seat on the soft cushions of a swing glider. "'Course, you don't set 'em straight, do you?"

"You've got my number, boy. But I don't lie. I tell them this is the closest a man gets to paradise without dying. Still, that don't mean I'm a damned recluse. I hope you've got time for a glass of lemonade and a corned-beef sandwich."

Leaning back, Jake swept off his hat. "You know my weakness for corned beef. And lemonade would go down easy. Anything I can do to help?"

"It's ready. I saw you cross over the loop a couple hours ago. You're right on schedule." The man's words were cut off by the bang of a screen door as he went inside. He emerged from the house moments later with a tray of glasses, thick sandwiches on homemade bread and a frosty pitcher of lemonade. Silence settled comfortably around them as the men dug into their lunch. Suddenly the one-time rancher wiped his mouth and said, sounding miffed, "When you see Ben O'Dell next, tell him I'm plenty p.o.'d that he flew past here without bothering to stop by and say howdy. He must be getting close to bringing in a payload to be in such an all-fired hurry."

The corned beef stuck in Jake's throat. When he finally managed to swallow it, he took a big swig of lemonade. "Ben died," he said, rubbing idly at the moisture beading the outside of the glass. "That was Ben's grand-daughter you saw driving his rig. The girl's filed to work his claim."

"A girl miner? Well, don't that beat all!"

Jake saw Hayley Ryan as she'd looked in the early-morning light. "I should have said woman," he corrected himself. "I don't know her age, but I'd guess she's in her twenties."

"When you get to be my age, sonny, any woman under forty-five falls into the category of 'girl.' Tell me about Ben. He stopped here on his way home last fall. Looked hale and hearty then."

"I don't know a lot. All I've heard is that it was pretty sudden. My folks went to Tombstone to check out the girl's story. It isn't any secret that Ben agreed to give us first option on the land. That spring has been the topic of conversation all year at the Cattlemen's Association meetings."

"So now this gal shows up out of the blue with clear claim to your ranch's main water supply. I think I see how the wind blows."

"Well, she said she'd give us the same deal we had with Ben. If she doesn't renege on the bargain, the Triple C, the J & B and probably the Rocking R—that's owned by Marshall Rogers—will still be able to meet the water needs of our summer stock."

"Do I hear a *but* at the end of that statement?"

Jake gave the swing a lazy push with his boot heels. "No. Nothing I can put my finger on."

"I think I understand. This woman's a new unknown player in the game. She could get fed up with digging her fingers bloody in the dirt. If she flies the coop without telling anyone, or if she up and turns loose of her claim, any Tom, Dick or Harry could snap up the land. Including the water and mineral rights.''

"You've got that right enough to ruin my lunch." Jake stopped swinging. "I hadn't got around to putting my fears into words. You summed them up nicely.''

"Is she a looker?''

"Wh-what?'' Jake stammered.

"The woman. Is she pretty? If she is, you might want to marry her. Won't give you automatic rights to her claim. But damn, boy, you'd be in a position to keep tabs on the situation.''

Jake's first inclination was to laugh. Somehow the laugh never materialized. "She's already married,'' he muttered, lavishing an inordinate amount of attention on the uneaten portion of his sandwich. "Or she could be in the process of divorce. According to rumors floating around Tombstone, Mrs. Ryan's hubby took off with another woman after selling Ben's silver mine out from under her.''

"Then you wouldn't want to get tangled up with her if she's already a loser.''

"I wouldn't classify her as a loser.'' Jake didn't realize he'd betrayed his interest in Hayley, until his companion let out a cheeky laugh, winked and jabbed Jake's ribs.

"So, the thought of corralling this filly has already crossed your mind.''

"If you want the continued pleasure of my company, old man, stop deviling me. I get enough of that from Dillon. There's ways to keep tabs on the lady without going to such extremes. I've devised any number of reasons that'll take me past her campsite on a regular basis till roundup starts. If she sticks around that long,'' he added.

"You've got a point there, son. Ben had the know-how and the patience to work a claim. Most folks get discouraged if they don't see any monetary gain. To my knowledge, Ben never took a dime out of the Blue Cameo. Still and all, he seemed mighty sure she'd pay off one day."

"Did he ever mention what he expected to turn up?"

The iron-haired man rocked back in his chair and contemplated. "Can't say that he did. Last year when he stopped by, I thought he seemed reluctant to go back to Tombstone. Hinted about being close to a payload. Hell, I've never met a prospector who isn't just a shovelful of dirt away from riches. I'll think about our last visit. If I remember anything more, I'll give you a jingle at the ranch."

"I'd appreciate that. Frankly I hope there isn't anything. All we need is a big gold strike to bring every hopeful miner from both sides of the border converging on us. Can't think of anything worse." Jake grimaced.

"Ben was right to play his cards close to the vest. Sometimes all it takes is the rumor of a find." He shuddered. "I remember my pa saying that happened once at Lynx Creek. Before scuttlebutt was proved wrong, the rush of miners leached the area clean, destroyed the vegetation and eventually dried up the creek. That area's a wasteland now."

Jake nodded. "Thanks for the warning. I believe I'll mosey back by Mrs. Ryan's camp on my way home and press upon her the need for secrecy."

"Telling a woman not to blab is like waving a red flag at a bull. When you've lived as long as I have, you'll understand the female species makes a point of doing whatever a man tells her not to."

Jake stood and shook hands with his friend before

settling his hat on his head. "Not all women gossip. My mother and Dillon's wife detest the practice."

"I only met your brother's wife at the wedding. Your mother, now, is a rare lady."

"She is at that." In fact, the biggest thing standing in the way of Jake's burgeoning feelings for Hayley Ryan was the reservations his mother seemed to have.

The old man followed Jake and watched him saddle the mare. "One last bit of advice, Jacob. A woman always takes suggestions better from another woman. You might make more headway if you could get Nell to visit your Mrs. Ryan."

Jake made a face as he climbed on the broad-backed horse. "She's not *my* Mrs. Ryan. I hope you remember that. Especially if you cross paths with anyone who works for the Triple C. Or for that matter, the J & B."

"Don't tell me you're sniffing after Westin's little honeybee?"

"I thought you knew me better than that."

"Glad to hear you confirm it. I like John Westin all right. It's a damn shame he's so blind when it comes to his kid."

"People all have their own ways of raising kids. I'm afraid I can't render an opinion until I get some experience. Which isn't likely to be soon." Jake waved goodbye to the man on the porch—whose laughter followed him up the trail. That, as nothing else had, changed his mind about looking in on Hayley Ryan again.

As the mare walked carefully through the brush, flushing a covey of brightly plumed Gambel's quail, Jake's thoughts returned to what he might be like as a father. He'd always assumed he'd have kids someday. Most of his friends in the area, guys he'd gone to school with, were married and had started their families. Bob Verner and his wife had recently had number three.

Link Thompson and his wife, Bev, had four girls. *Four.* Link was two years younger than Jake. Oddly, Jacob found that unsettling. At least Dillon and Eden weren't expecting yet. Jake wondered if they sat around home at night and talked about optimal timing.

"Nah," he said aloud, shaking his head and setting the mare into a trot. "Dillon lives moment to moment. He's not big on long-range plans." Eden, now, was a different story. She organized, saved and kept meticulous books. Building and furnishing the house on Dillon's hundred acres had been her doing. Nesting. Jake would bet Eden did have a baby plotted into her chart somewhere.

It shouldn't matter to him what plans they made. So why did the picture of them sitting around the family Christmas tree, bouncing a laughing infant, stick in his craw?

At that moment Jake spotted a group of steers feeding in a ravine. All wore the Triple C brand. Stopping to take an exact count and write it in his logbook returned his brain to work mode. Not that he considered this *hard* work. Riding the range, even on the back of a horse as uncomfortable as Paprika, hardly fell under the heading of work at all to Jake. His dad used to say he'd been born in the saddle. Ranching was in his blood. Even in the winter when the wind froze a man's nose and any other body part he was unlucky enough to expose, other cowboys bitched and moaned. Jake rarely uttered a complaint. He truly did not understand why so many of his contemporaries couldn't wait to trade the red dust of the Santa Cruz valley for the sizzling concrete of Arizona's cities. Jacob didn't mind wearing white shirts and ties to funerals and weddings. The thought of having to don that getup with regularity sent chills down his spine.

Most women of his generation fawned over jokers wearing suits. Jake saw it at the dances and the singles' bars he frequented when he went to Kansas, Wyoming or Texas to the bull sales. Plenty of women flirted with cowboys. Few committed themselves for the long haul once they had a taste of what it took to carve a home out of earth and rock.

For many of his cowboy buddies who'd gotten married were single again, and looking. Jake would admit cowboying could make a man lonely, and it sure resulted in a few aching muscles. Which was why curling up at night next to a woman's softer body held such appeal. But not just any body, dammit.

When Jake left the Mortimer ranch, he'd set his course for the Triple C. It was a shock to suddenly wake up out of his fog and find himself staring down through a waning sun at Hayley Ryan's camp. *Again...*

He sucked in a huge gulp of air. After all, he'd reversed his decision to pay her a visit. Yet because he was here, he raised his field glasses and scanned the clearing. Just checking to see that all was well. Once satisfied, he'd ride on without her ever being wiser.

Her campfire danced brightly. The chickens Jake had penned earlier scratched contentedly. Her truck and trailer sat untouched. Letting the glasses fall to the end of their strap, Jake gathered Paprika's reins in his left hand, preparing to skirt Hayley's camp. In two seconds he would have been gone. But he happened to catch sight of her. She leapt from her chair beside the fire, bent low, clutching her stomach with crossed arms and made a beeline for the trees.

Jake fumbled with the binoculars again. Sweat popped

out on his own brow when he finally brought her into
focus again. She looked close enough for him to touch.
And touching was what she needed. Her face had turned
a ghastly white. Perspiration dampened the fine dark hair
that framed her oval face. It hurt Jake physically to see
her cling to a sapling and retch violently.

Never giving thought to her wanting or needing privacy at a time like this, Jake snapped the mare into high
gear and galloped full tilt into Hayley's camp. He dismounted on the fly and ran to her side.

"What's wrong?" he demanded, sweeping her up and
into his arms. He babbled the whole time he ran, carrying her to the spring. "Did you catch a flu bug? Or
food poisoning?" Stripping off his dusty neck scarf,
Jake dipped it in the cool water and began to bathe her
face. He forgot to wring out the material and soon
soaked both their shirts.

"Stop," Hayley sputtered. "Where did you come
from? You scared the daylights out of me." Struggling
to get off his lap and out of his arms, she felt her stomach drop and heave. Only the worry on his face eased
her struggles.

"I...I...didn't know anyone was around," she managed. Embarrassment gripped her tongue. She couldn't
tell this man that she was apparently one of the unlucky
women who suffered morning sickness twice a day. According to the book, one in four women endured nausea
both morning and evening. One in ten, the booklet said,
were sick all day. Hayley had counted her blessings to
falling into the one in four category. However, being
tenderly ministered to while languishing by a man not
responsible for her condition, Hayley didn't feel lucky
at all. In fact, she felt about as miserable as she imagined
a woman could feel. She did the only thing she could

do to save face; she forced her roiling stomach into submission, and she lied.

"Thank you for your concern. I wor...worked my claim all day. Got a tad too much sun, I guess." Hayley did separate herself from his muscular arms this time.

Jake's racing heart put on the brakes at last. Now he felt like a fool watching her untie the tail of her blouse and mop at the water he'd all but drowned her with.

"Heatstroke is serious. Didn't you wear a hat?" For some reason he found it easier to sound tough rather than to give in to his desire to gather her in his arms again. She'd fit into the crook of his elbow just fine. Her hair hadn't smelled like that of a woman who'd toiled all day in the sun. A light floral fragrance had tickled his nose, reminding him of the flower shop in town.

Hayley turned away, carefully spreading her laced fingers across her still-shaky stomach. "I wore a hat. A baseball cap. I do have a floppy ghastly straw hat with a big brim. It makes me look like Mother Goose." She would have gone on, but choked and turned clammy when she realized he might get suspicious at her reference to a child's storybook character—or was she totally overreacting. *Damn, damn, damn.* Why didn't Jacob Cooper go away and keep his nose out of her life?

"Women." He expelled the word along with a massive sigh. "You won't find a man letting fashion rule over his good sense."

"You have some nerve." Hayley found the strength to muster indignity. Already the wave of nausea was passing. "You don't know anything about me. Nothing at all."

"Is that so?" Jake let hostility cover his emotions. "You say you're married, but I know your husband really left Tombstone with another woman. Maybe you should ask yourself if she was less vain, less concerned with looks and more mindful of good health.''

The minute the shock registered in her wide eyes, Jake wanted to retract his cruel words. Dishonest words.

''Leave!'' she said through quivering lips. ''I'm going into the trailer to change into dry things. I want you gone when I come out again.''

Jake called himself a million and one foul names as Hayley darted across the clearing and jerked open the trailer's door. The pitifully tiny place she called home. Of course she wasn't vain. He ought to be ashamed.

He was ashamed.

He hung around the fire for twenty minutes, wanting an opportunity to apologize. Jake gazed vacantly at various-size samples of ore she had sitting around in boxes. If she'd dug all of those samples today, no wonder she had a touch of sun fever. Some blue slabs glittered in the firelight. He didn't know enough about rock and minerals to know if she'd found anything worthwhile.

He hoped she had. Jake felt like a rat. Lower than a rat.

After ten more minutes of silence, it became apparent that Hayley wouldn't come out again until he left. He had no doubt that she never wanted to see him again. Shame overwhelmed him and ultimately convinced him to bow to her wishes.

He climbed slowly into Paprika's saddle and then trotted the horse as close to the small side window in the trailer as he could get. ''You can come out,'' he called. ''I'm leaving.''

Waiting, he listened, fully expecting to hear sounds of weeping, which would make him feel terrible—exactly what he deserved. Only silence greeted him. In a way it was worse than tears.

He rode off, keeping one eye trained over his shoulder. If she emerged before he lost sight of her camp, he'd turn back and beg her forgiveness tonight. As she kept stubbornly to herself, Jake knew he'd be riding this trail again in the morning. He only hoped that between now and then, he'd figure out some way to make it up to her.

CHAPTER SIX

WADE COOPER intercepted Jake as he tried to sneak into the house without going through the kitchen, where his parents were sure to be. He was still in a foul mood after the way he'd left things with Hayley. Tonight, food and family chitchat had fallen off his list of priorities.

"You've put in some long days in the saddle lately, son." Wade placed a broad hand on Jake's shoulder and turned him from the dark hallway toward the bright light spilling from the kitchen.

"Yeah," Jake grunted. "I'm bushed. Tell Mom a shower and sleep takes precedence over whatever she might have saved in the oven tonight."

"Oh. Sorry to hear it." Wade looked glum. "We're on our own. Nell is firing kilns tonight. She and Eden are spending the night in town. I waited dinner. Thought you and I could throw together a batch of nachos. I already iced a six-pack of beer."

Jake wavered at the threshold. His dad was so transparent. Since his accident, he wandered the ranch like a lost puppy. The whole family tried to look out for him— keep him occupied so he wouldn't feel useless and start to overdo things. It surprised Jake that his mom had abandoned her shift. He said as much.

"It's the new clay she bought in Tucson. She'd have stayed home, but I know how badly she itched to get her fingers in the new slip. I convinced her I was meeting

John and some of the other ranchers to talk about water.''

"Is that how you spent the day?'' Jake's curiosity carried him into the room. He saw that Wade had already grated cheese and cut up jalapeños, tomatoes, and onions; there was a bowl of black beans, as well as olives and a bag of large corn chips.

The elder Cooper twisted off the caps from two long-necked brews. He handed one to Jake, then set the other aside while he prepared the chips and popped them into the microwave. "John doesn't want to wait for the Ryan woman to get bored. Pearce and Lowell would accept the original agreement if John and Marshall weren't pressuring them to take action.''

"Action? What action?'' Jake turned off the buzzer, grabbed an oven mitt and set the steaming plate between them on a thick pot holder. "Ben's granddaughter filed legally. You checked. As long as she works the claim, we can't force her to sell.''

"No. But John says there's nothing stopping us from giving her money to abandon her claim.''

Jake bit into a jalapeño that made his eyes water. The chili pepper wasn't all that burned. What John Westin proposed sounded like a cheap underhand trick to Jake. "How does John suggest you set fair compensation when no one knows the value of what Hayley's prospecting?''

"Hayley? Pretty familiar aren't you? But then, I suppose a woman might get friendly fast with a guy who took her five laying hens.''

Jake choked on his swig of beer. He should have known his dad would notice. The man had always had a sixth sense when it came to his boys.

"I hoped you planned to tell your mother. Soon as

she figures out those hens are gone, she'll be claiming the gray wolves Fish and Game released last winter got 'em. The way you stood up to the neighbors and backed that release program, I'm sure you don't want to be responsible for its demise. Nell raised that flock from chicks, you know. John's not the only one in the valley who can incite people to riot.''

"You've made your point. I'll talk to Mom soon. And to be clear on another thing, Dad, nothing's going on between me and Hayley. I'm just…well, concerned about her situation. Fool woman's oblivious to what can happen along the border.''

"Then John's plan should appeal to you. Take up a collection and help her move back to Tombstone posthaste.''

It did sound reasonable, Jake allowed. At least it did until he considered how stubborn Hayley was, how intent on self-reliance. "I don't think she'll go for the idea.''

"Why not? Surely she can't enjoy toiling in the sun day after day, digging through rock until her hands bleed. Breaking her back for zip.''

"She's got Ben's pride and more.'' The minute he said it, Jake realized he was making a judgment call. He didn't really know Hayley Ryan, as she'd pointed out tonight. She might well take the money and run. The notion left a bad taste in his mouth. Or maybe it was the beer. He pushed the half-full bottle aside.

Wade licked cheese off his fingers and narrowed his eyes at Jake before he fumbled a napkin from the holder. "O'Dell wouldn't even come to our house for dinner. Said he didn't take handouts. Unlike his granddaughter, he'd never have accepted those chickens.''

Guilty color splashed across Jake's angular cheekbones. "I told her if they produce eggs, she could pay me. Ten dollars for the lot."

Wade choked. "Those prize chicks cost Nell twenty bucks apiece."

Jake didn't respond. He didn't have to. The seed had been planted, and he didn't even know if he should have stuck his neck out. But it was too late. Wade was weighing what he'd do if that was Eden or his wife dug in at the spring. Enough had been said. Unless there was a majority vote to buy Hayley out, Jake bet his dad would vote to leave her be.

Jake rose, rummaged in the fridge, then added slices of roast chicken to the next batch of nachos. He let the hum of the microwave fill the silence.

Both men tucked into the newest platter with gusto. Talk gradually resumed and turned to the beef count and the upcoming roundup. Though Hayley's name didn't surface again, Jake's mind conjured her up. He wondered if he should forewarn her of Westin's plan.

Even though Jake told himself repeatedly that he'd done his part and should keep his nose out of it, he lay in bed that night and worried about the doggedness of the other ranchers. Westin hadn't built an empire by avoiding land grabs. He'd been known to undercut neighbors. People didn't dwell on it, but the truth was there if anyone cared to examine it. Jake had a hunch most partners in the coalition wanted the Triple C to possess the land surrounding the spring rather than letting Westin get his hands on it.

Jake already had his reasons for visiting Hayley in the morning. Technically he didn't owe her anything but an apology, but as sleep continued to evade him, he mulled over ways to put her on guard. What could he say, though, that wouldn't place all the ranchers in a bad light? Including the Coopers. After all, he'd been the first to approach her about leaving her claim—and then about sharing the spring.

By the time the milk cows began to low and the song-birds awakened, Jake had wrestled the problem every which way from Sunday—to no avail. He decided to deliver his apology and ignore the water issue. It was possible nothing would come of John's proposal. Even if it did, Jake needn't be involved. He'd already made up his mind that after today, Hayley Ryan was on her own. He had a job to do for the Triple C, and it didn't include riding herd on a headstrong female.

Decision made, Jake would be hard-pressed to say what prompted him to fill two jugs with fresh milk before he saddled up, whistled Charcoal to heel and then set a straight course for the Blue Cameo mine.

HAYLEY HAD SPENT a sleepless night. By midnight not so much as a breath of wind wafted through her window screens. She'd spent the night thinking about her baby. About how she'd support a child if the mine didn't produce. By law, Joe should pay support. But if he did, maybe he'd demand visitation rights. She couldn't bear the thought of him having even the slightest influence over her child—or her. Support of any kind would make her beholden. By three in the morning she'd decided her only choice was to see that the Blue Cameo gave up its secret cache, whatever that might be.

This morning the air was quite humid and heavy, which added to Hayley's exhaustion. She wondered if it was going to rain.

Jacob Cooper rode into her camp and dismounted in a cloud of red dust as she was trying to decide whether or not to haul yesterday's ore samples inside. Hayley hated to admit she'd kept one eye on the trailhead, expecting, hoping, Jake would appear.

Though it annoyed her no end, her spirits lifted magically when he did.

She was pathetic. Really pathetic. Last night he'd insulted her. Desperate to hide feelings that made no sense, she opened her arms to the black-and-white dog and pretended to ignore his master.

"Morning." Jake had had twelve hours to polish his apology. Hearing Hayley's low alluring laughter, watching his dog lick her face, wiped away any trace of polite conversation. It was all Jake could do to lift down the milk jugs and thrust them wordlessly into her hands. He'd never wanted to kiss any woman as badly as he wanted to kiss Hayley Ryan.

"Milk. So fresh it's still warm," she exclaimed. Her delight over his thoughtful gift blurred any lingering ambivalence. "Of everything I can't pick up daily at the grocery anymore, it's fresh milk I miss the most. Thank you, Jake."

He took the jugs back as he fought the effect of her smile on parts of his body over which he normally had better control. "I'll suspend these under the waterfall so the milk can cool. I hope a few glasses will settle your stomach."

"My stomach?" Hayley went still and grabbed her middle.

Jake had started for the spring. Pausing, he glanced with surprise into her frightened eyes. There was no other word to describe the turbulence he saw there. "The heat, you know. You said it caused you to...well, throw up. I'm sure it's not a pleasant memory. A steady diet of camp food can cause indigestion. Milk soothes the stomach. You can't be sure it was the weather that made you sick,'' he ended lamely.

"Oh. Sure.'' Realizing how silly she must look holding on to her stomach, Hayley dropped her hands.

She was doing it again, looking fragile and...and soft. Shaken, Jake felt the need to say, "I had no right to lay into you last night. For all I know, you kicked your husband out. And he probably deserved it. Anyway, I'm sorry I upset you and then rode off like a jerk without apologizing.''

His contrition was so surprising and complete, Hayley felt as if she'd been thrust backward through a knothole. During their brief marriage, Joe had done a lot of things he should have said he was sorry for. The word hadn't been in his vocabulary. Gramps, too, came from the old school where men lived their lives to suit themselves. Women fit in and adapted, or they lumped it. Jacob Cooper would very likely be shocked to know he'd just atoned for all the men in Hayley's life. She hadn't realized how badly she needed to hear that men could feel regret for the hurt they so often caused women.

She sank into one of the lawn chairs and ran her fingers through the collie's soft fur. "Joe, that's my husband, er, ex. He...he...did leave town with another woman. Which doesn't give me license to take my feelings of inadequacy out on you.''

Jake had met a lot of divorced women. In his experience, a few were willing to share blame for the breakup of their marriages. Most placed the culpability squarely on the man. Hayley's unvarnished statement of fact told Jacob a lot about her character. "Look, I don't want you to think I went out of my way to be nosy. My mom and dad were in Tombstone the day after I met you. They heard all that stuff.''

"Gossip is the lifeblood of mining towns."

"Ranch towns, too."

"I'm sure. How did my name happen to come up? Why?"

Her straightforward questions made Jake uncomfortable. "It wasn't that we doubted you had a good claim. But…well, Dad hoped Ben had told someone about his deal with the Triple C. We should have known if he'd told anyone, it'd be his next of kin."

Hayley's fingers clutched convulsively in the dog's fur. "There you go, making assumptions again. Gramps's poker partner knew this claim existed. I didn't."

"Wh-where did you think he went for months at a time every year?"

"Prospecting. When I was little, he took me along. After I reached school age, he left me with a friend who taught me sewing, cooking and such."

"He wandered off for months on end and left you alone? That must have been rough."

"I'm not complaining," she said lightly. Too lightly.

"So if you weren't aware the Blue Cameo existed, I guess you really don't know what Ben was after." Jake started to wave a hand and realized he still hadn't submerged the milk in the water. Worried that he was prying again, he told her she didn't owe him an answer. He hurried to the spring.

Wanting to make amends, Hayley stood up and brushed the dog hair from her hands. "Are you any good at reading streak plates?"

Jake made a half hitch in the rope he'd threaded through the jug handles. "Excuse me?"

"You know. The color of powder left behind when any given mineral is rubbed over the cut edge of an unfinished tile or unglazed porcelain streak plate defines what's been found." It sounded as if she was reciting a definition from a textbook. Which, essentially, she was.

"Is that all there is to prospecting for, say, diamonds or gold?"

"There's the Moh scale, too," she said matter-of-factly. When Jake shrugged, she went into a little detail. "For hardness. The scale indicates what mineral scratches another mineral. Talc is number one. Diamond is number ten. Gypsum, calcite, feldspar, quartz and to-paz and corundum are a few that fall in between. The Moh is a novice prospector's Bible. Someone experienced, like Gramps, identifies minerals from the way they break. I have to run all the tests." She sighed. "These are the samples I dug yesterday."

"Sounds like a lot of work for maybe no reward," Jake ventured.

Her chin shot up to the angle he'd begun to recognize as determination. "There'll be a big reward," she insisted.

Jake tucked his hands in his back pockets and headed for his horse. He'd ridden Mojave again today, and the bay gelding looked up with interest and began to move toward him. Freeing a hand, Jake grabbed the reins. "I wish you luck, Hayley. I'll try to stay out of your hair from now on. Next week we start roundup. From time to time we'll send a man to open the valves to the ditches." He pulled a piece of paper out of his shirt pocket. "These are the brands you'll deal with from now to November. If a horse carries any of these brands, please don't shoot the rider." His eyes teased as he handed her the list.

"This sounds like goodbye." Hayley almost dropped the paper.

Gazing at a spot beyond her right shoulder, he removed and resettled his hat a couple of times. "Busy time of year for the Triple C. About the only socializing I'll do for the next few months is with ornery cows."

Hayley's chest felt suddenly hollow. A few months sounded interminable. By then, her pregnancy would show. Because she didn't know how to introduce that subject, she donned a bright smile instead. "I trust you'll spread the word that anyone showing up on a horse *without* these brands is courting danger."

"I surely will. I showed you how to close the valves to the various ditches. To keep traffic in your camp to a minimum, let the water flow for six hours, then shut her down."

"Right. I'm not planning on going anywhere. Oh…unless I need to replenish supplies. So if my truck isn't here, I've gone to Tubac. I assume the water system will do its thing if I'm gone. I don't foresee ever spending a night away from camp."

"Does that pickup have a radio? The road between here and the highway can turn into a quagmire during our August monsoons. Sometimes a road washes out. Usually we fix it within a day or so, but you need to stay alert."

"I have a portable radio and cases of batteries. The truck also has a radio."

"Good. Then I guess you're set. I took the liberty of drawing a map to the Triple C on the back of that paper showing the brands. If you need anything, anything at all, someone will most likely be around our place or Dillon's. I marked his house on the map, too."

"Thanks. Don't worry that I'll wear out my welcome. I've got a lot of ground to cover right here. Anyway, I'm not a big mingler."

It was on the tip of Jake's tongue to ask if she liked to dance. What Dillon had said about inviting her to the Harvest Dance ricocheted inside his skull. But the decision he'd made before he left the house—to keep his distance from Hayley Ryan—loomed larger. Jake tipped his hat, whistled for Charcoal and climbed into the saddle.

Hayley moved beside his shifting horse. "It's really humid today. I don't have to worry about storms yet, do I? Because July isn't over?"

Jake squinted at the sky. Clouds had rolled in and covered the sun without his noticing. That showed how much this woman confused him. He was dead right to cut the self-imposed ties and go on about his business. "We've had gully washers in July before and we've been a spell without rain." He took some time to study her camp. "You're laid out the same way Ben used to be. He weathered a few humdingers. I expect this'll blow over, but if the spring should fill and overflow, open the valve marked *one* for a while."

"Thanks. Well, I won't keep you." This time the smile she pasted on didn't feel so bright. It must have fooled Jake. He galloped off without a wave.

Hayley didn't budge until an attack of nausea drove her into the bushes to empty her stomach of breakfast. Darn, this couldn't be good for the baby. Not even if the book said it was fairly normal.

Alone, lonely and vaguely out of sorts, Hayley grouped her ore samples around the fire pit. Telling herself that she didn't need anyone's company but her own, that she was happy to be rid of Jacob Cooper and his constant interruptions, Hayley hunched over her boxes doing streak-plate tests until her fingers bled. Eventually the roll of thunder and the crack of lightning drove her inside. At least she could blame her wet cheeks on the rain that had begun to spit.

HUDDLED IN A NARROW CAVE with a wet smelly horse and dog, Jake stared out at the storm he'd wrongly told Hayley would blow over. Since the clouds started dumping, he'd wager two inches of rain had hit the ground. Arroyos filled and there were tumbling rivers where hours ago none existed.

But Hayley Ryan wasn't his problem.

What if she forgets how to open the valve? What if it sticks?

Against his better judgment, Jake nudged Mojave into the downpour. He simply wouldn't draw an easy breath until he was satisfied Hayley's camp hadn't washed away. That didn't mean he planned to let her know he was checking up, however.

At the same vantage point he'd used the other day, Jake lay spread-eagle in the wet saw grass. He scanned the clearing below, gnashing his teeth until he could determine that she was snug in her tin can of a trailer and that water flowed through the valve merrily, keeping the spring at an acceptable level.

Two days later Jake came down with a doozy of a summer cold. For three days after that, when the high desert heat had once again set in, he was grumpy as a rank bull. Everyone but his mother maintained a discreet distance. She brought soup to his room. *Chicken* soup. And casually mentioned her missing hens.

"I planned to tell you," Jake mumbled. "It slipped my mind. So I guess Dad ratted."

Nell Cooper met the challenging gaze of her handsome personable tenderhearted youngest son. "What sort of woman has a man thieving from his own family?

You're sick because of her, too,'' she accused. She held up a palm when Jake's head came off the pillow and his eyes blazed. "Don't deny it. A mother knows these things.''

"Mom, no. I played good neighbor a time or two. That's the extent of it. She's out there digging her damned rocks. Soon as I'm well, I'll be joining the roundup on the north range.''

Nell hesitated at the door. "Since Dillon and Eden's wedding, I've watched you change, grow restless. The right woman will come along, I know it. Someone as nice as Eden.''

Jake sneezed four times. Dropping his chin to his chest, he muttered, "My soup's getting cold.''

"So eat. I'll have my say and then I'll leave. This phase will pass. You don't have to settle for a…a divorced nomad, Jacob.''

He rallied to Hayley Ryan's defense. Too late. His mother had said her piece and gone, slamming his bedroom door. Well, hell! He didn't plan on seeing Hayley again, anyhow.

Still, his mother's words grated. He was a grown man. One capable of making his own decisions where women were concerned. His mom loved him and meant well. But she was a potter, not a damned psychologist.

By the middle of the following week his cold had cleared up, but Jake was still angry when he rode off to the roundup. The crew sensed his mood and left him to his own devices. They probably figured hard work and the elements would take it out of him soon enough.

And they were right. A blistering sun rolled up every morning, soon drying every trace of that one brief monsoon. The few pockets of water that remained after the sandy soil had sucked in the excess simply evaporated as the earth baked to a hard clay. Slowly plodding steers kicked up clouds of dust. Jake ate his share. Yet every night, when the majority of the wranglers knocked off for dinner break, he'd take a fresh mount and ride out to check on Hayley. He did that for several weeks.

The first day that Dillon let the herd rest for a full twenty-four hours, Jake cut a small surefooted pinto from the remuda, saddled her and presented her to Hayley.

"I can't take such an elaborate gift." She had, by chance, cooked extra macaroni and cheese, and handed Jake a full plate. "What makes you think I can even ride?"

"Can you?"

"Yes." Her cheeks burned as she glanced away.

"I heard your pickup stalled twice on your drive into town to replenish supplies. Graze the mare regularly and she won't break down."

Hayley laughed. Jacob couldn't know that the gift of his visit meant more to her than anything tangible. Including the chickens and the rock sled he'd sent last week with the man who'd opened the valve. The sled helped make removal of the ore she blasted out much easier. She'd had the wrangler take a look at her pickup's engine while he was there, as well. He must have been the one who told Jacob about its stalling.

"Jake. This morning two men, ranchers, came to visit me."

His fork stilled. "Who? What did they want? I hope you showed them your shotgun."

"No. They were gentlemen. Checking on the spring." She unfolded the sheet of brands and tapped a skinned finger with a broken nail on the intertwined J & B.

"Westin and his foreman, Gordy White," Jake breathed after she'd finished describing the two.

"The older man tried to give me five thousand dollars to quit what I'm doing here. Before he left he was up to fifteen thousand."

Jake made mush of the steaming macaroni. He tensed, prepared to hear, but hoping he wouldn't, she'd accepted John's offer.

A frown settled between her brows. "I expected you to act surprised. I thought they were trying to pull a fast one on your family. You know, go behind your back and buy this parcel out from under you. But I can see you knew about it," she said, sounding hurt.

"I'd heard rumors. John's the Cattlemen's Association president. Almanac predictions that we're heading into a long drought probably spooked him. He owns a huge thirsty herd."

"Well, I'm not dropping my claim."

"Look at your hands," Jake said gently. "Do you really think whatever's under the quartz and granite hill is worth killing yourself for?"

"I thought you were in my corner, Jacob." Her eyes, suddenly sad and serious, seemed to assess him.

"I think you're crazy," he muttered, heaving himself up to scrape his plate into the fire. She kept it burning even though the heat was almost 110, even this late in the day. Earlier, when they'd been talking, she'd confessed to having seen mangy coyotes and several rooting families of javelina at the spring. The Southwest pigs were ugly razor-backed animals. Jake had seen them turn nasty; he worried they might attack Hayley if the drought got really bad.

"Thank you." Now her eyes snapped. "Thank you so much for the vote of confidence. I didn't ask you to hang around. And I don't need any of your sneaky bribes. Take back your chickens and the mare. Stop plying me with vegetables and milk.'' This last fell reluctantly from her lips. But he'd called her crazy, and that hurt. Jacob Cooper had sneaked past her defenses, reminding her acutely of how swiftly and easily she'd been duped by Joe Ryan, too.

"Hayley, dang it! I'm not part of that extortion party.''

"Can't prove it by me. Go, Jacob Cooper. I can take care of myself.''

Without another word, Jake gathered Mojave's reins, mounted smoothly and left, taking the pinto with him. He felt frustrated by her attitude. And darn, he'd hated watching Hayley's complexion go from lightly tanned to sunburned to scaly brown. His mother's hands and Eden's, too, bore the calluses of their work. Neither had cracked skin and horribly broken fingernails the way Hayley did. If, on occasion, Eden burned a finger with her jewelry soldering iron, a Band-Aid took care of the problem. Jake doubted a normal first-aid kit contained enough bandages for Hayley's cuts and scrapes.

Once again, as he covered the punishing miles back to the roundup, Jacob vowed that Hayley Ryan wasn't his problem. Let her mummify, for all he cared.

He managed to stick to his guns for the rest of August—three weeks spent branding and moving a third of the herd to the rail cars. Then he rejoined the crew. The first afternoon back, he had occasion to object to the wrangler Dillon had chosen to send to Hayley's camp to open the valves.

"Send Julio, instead,'' Jake barked, indicating a wrangler with nearly white hair.

"It's my decision.'' Dillon rounded on Jake. "If I ask

Ray, you want Alonzo. Miguel, instead of Orleans. What in hell is wrong with sending Emilio?''

''He's new. What do we really know about him?''

''That he gives us a full day's work for a day's pay.''

''You're always riding point so you don't hear the men talk like I do. The others joke about him being a ladies' man.''

''Exactly what half the valley says about you.''

Jake crowded Mojave close to Dillon's mount. ''I've never forced myself on a woman. Besides, you feed into that hype, and you damn well know it.''

Dillon studied Jake's smoldering eyes and cocked jaw. Backing his big black gelding up a couple of steps, Dillon placed two fingers between his lips and issued an earsplitting whistle. ''Hold up, Emilio,'' he shouted. ''Take a load off your horse and go get some chow. Jake'll go open the valves tonight.''

The young stud, Emilio, galloped up to his boss. It was obvious he was too disciplined and too in need of the job to argue. But the mockery brimming in his dark eyes let Jake and Dillon both know he'd figured out the score.

When Emilio wheeled his tired piebald mare around and proceeded to ride to the chuck wagon as he'd been ordered, Dillon curled a hand around his brother's hard forearm. ''Maybe I should go. Honestly, dude, I've never seen you in this state over a woman.''

''I'm not in any state. That punk Emilio thinks he's hot stuff. The Triple C doesn't need the reputation of hiring guys who can't keep a lock on their zippers.''

''Sounds as if what you've got in mind is the same thing you're accusing him of.''

''Bull puckey! I'll be glad to let you bust *your* butt making the round trip to release the water.''

Dillon laid an arm across his saddle horn while his horse nibbled the sparse dry grass. "Maybe you're far too willing at that. I guess the hots you had for the Ryan woman have cooled. Hope you don't mind if I relay that bit of news to Mom and Eden. They've had their heads together, plotting to import a woman the two of them met at the last craft show. A quilter. Mom's gung ho, but Eden thinks the woman's too old for you. She's thirty-nine," Dillon said slyly.

The smile Jake forced more closely resembled a grimace, but he knew what Dillon was trying to do. Shake him up and make him admit he still had a yen for Hayley Ryan. "I've dated older women," he said, determined to keep his brother guessing.

Dillon stroked his stubbled jaw. "You trust the judgment of those two in picking you a woman? If I were you, I'd hurry up and ask someone to the harvest dance."

For the first time in a lot of years, Jake considered skipping the dance. He wasn't fool enough to tell Dillon. He'd never hear the end of the razzing.

"The older you get, Jacob, the slimmer the pickings in the valley. Ask Dad to let you attend more stock shows. I hear there's an abundance of pretty, well-heeled ranch widows looking to find second husbands there."

"Or I'll just build my house and live out my days as a bachelor. What's it going to be, Dillon? Are you riding out to open the valves or am I?"

"Aw, go on. Seniority has its privilege. I'm happy to let you get saddle sore."

In answer, Jake whistled for Charcoal. He nudged Mojave forward and let him pick his way around the herd. The minute they cleared the hill, out of sight of Dillon, Jake urged the gelding into a gallop. Damn, he didn't want his mom and Eden importing some designing woman. He'd ask Hayley Ryan to the dance. It'd serve those sneaky matchmakers right.

Jake rode at a steady clip, eager to see her. He wondered if the weeks had passed as slowly for her as they had for him. It made no earthly sense, but he'd missed sparring with her—and missed other tings about her, too.

He couldn't resist spying on her camp when he landed within field-glass range. Not that he'd see her if she wasn't seated by her campfire. The days had grown shorter. Ten minutes ago the sun had dropped behind Bella Vista Point.

Raising the binoculars, he fiddled with the central focus. Suddenly Hayley's camp loomed right beyond the tips of Mojave's ears. "What in blazes?" Jake kneed the horse forward. Was the woman having a party?

No! A hiss escaped Jake's strangled lungs. Two men, a woman holding a baby and four other kids were sitting cross-legged near her fire. She wove between them, scooping food out of a metal pot. Every one of the ragtag group seemed nervous and ill at ease. "Damn! She's got herself visitors from across the border."

His heart leapt half out of his chest. Were they armed? If Jake hadn't been so panic-stricken, he might have watched longer and thought through his actions a little more clearly. All he could imagine was Hayley lying bloodied and battered, her meager possessions appropriated by the crooks who promised to guide illegals through the desert.

He let out a rebel yell guaranteed to raise the dead. And he rode Mojave hell-bent for election into her camp, sliding the shocked horse to his haunches a foot from the crackling fire. Ashes scattered, and so did Hayley's visitors.

Charcoal, loving the unexpected chase, ran hither and yon, setting up a din that drove every animal in the countryside wild.

Within seconds of Jake's making his grand entrance, all that remained of the wanderers was six cracked plates and an unholy silence. Even the animals who'd been drinking from the stream went quickly to ground.

"Jacob Cooper, are you drunk?" Hayley braced her hands on her hips. Hips that had broadened an inch or two since the last time he'd seen her. In fact, there were other changes in her appearance. Her hair had grown. It now swirled about her waist. Instead of the ever-present blue jeans, she wore a long loose print jumper over a round-necked T-shirt. In the center of her jumper, below where her waist should be, Jake noticed a bulge—like a misplaced pillow.

His eyes nearly popped out of his head. Hayley Ryan was pregnant, or Jacob Barrett Cooper had not been raised on a ranch where the procreation of God's creatures was a cyclic fact of life.

Hayley stopped yelling at him the minute she saw where Jake's eyes were trained. Nervously she smoothed a hand over the secret she'd kept from him. Then she caught herself and carefully shook her jumper loose so that nothing showed. As if she believed that, once hidden from prying eyes, her condition no longer existed.

Jake went hot, then cold, then hot again. He stumbled over two of the plates dropped by the fleeing family. As the night creatures began to stir, he slumped heavily into the closest lawn chair. Instantly the webbed seating gave way with a loud rip, dumping Jake in the dirt. But his pain and humiliation seemed minor compared to the turmoil in his gut. *Pregnant. The woman he hankered after was going to have some other man's baby.*

CHAPTER SEVEN

"MY STARS, JACOB! Are you hurt?" Hayley ran to his side and extended a hand to help him up from the tangle of metal tubing that had been a chair. "This belonged to Gramps. I knew the webbing was frayed. Honestly, I never dreamed it would give way," she babbled, hovering over him anxiously.

Almost in a daze, Jake watched Hayley's cotton jumper flow from her shoulders, draping the tops of her boots in a shapeless mass. He wondered if he'd imagined her condition. Yes. The light from the fire pit must have been playing tricks. Her face hadn't changed. It was the same narrow oval. Her arms were still slender, although darkly tanned now from her work in the sun. The wind must have billowed out her dress. After all, he was used to seeing her in jeans.

Clambering to his feet—with the only real injury to his pride—Jake dismissed what he thought he'd seen. Instead, he tackled the subject that had brought him roaring into her camp. "Those people you were feeding. I hope you knew them."

"We didn't get around to exchanging names. The children...the entire family was hungry. You barged in here like some demented warrior and scared them witless." She walked to the outer edge of the clearing and peered into the darkness. "It's all right," she called softly in Spanish. "He's a friend. Please come back and eat. The baby didn't finish his milk."

"Hayley, for God's sake." Jake vaulted the dog to reach her. Gripping her shoulders, he yanked her out of the shadows. "It's okay if they milk our cows at the Triple C or butcher an occasional steer. There are men around to handle anything that might get out of hand. But you're alone, for crying out loud. I guarantee one guy in that outfit is being paid a lot of money to illegally get those folks into Arizona. It's a huge racket. A dangerous one for the families and for you. You simply can't put out the welcome mat. You're damn lucky I arrived when I did. The instigator might have stolen everything you owned, or worse, left you dead in the process."

"You are so cynical, Jacob Cooper. They were polite and appreciative. Down on their luck, but since when is that a crime? Oh, I'm wasting my breath. I doubt you've ever not known where your next meal is coming from."

"I understand the problems. We hire as many family men with temporary work permits as we possibly can. The people who traffic in humans for money are bastards. Con men. They charge exorbitant fees and as often as not dump *la familia* in a blistering desert without resources of any kind. It's less the family I'm trying to warn you about than the guy in the Panama hat who was with them. He's probably a ringleader."

Hayley released a sigh of resignation. *"Abuelo,* the little boy called him. Grandfather. The mother's younger than me. Her dream is to provide a better life for her kids. Is that so wrong?"

She spoke with such passion while unconsciously cradling her stomach that Jake's heart collided with his own churning stomach. His first impression had been correct.

He had no notion how far along she was, but Hayley
Ryan was definitely going to have a baby. That made it
a thousand times more foolish for her to be out here.
"You're pregnant," he said simply. "Why didn't you
tell me that right off the bat? It puts a different spin on
everything. You can't stay here. When's the baby due,
anyway?"

Hayley, who'd hoped Jake had missed her new
rounder shape, wheeled away from him and extended
shaking hands toward the fire. She felt suddenly cold.
Not stay here? She *had* to. The makeup of ore she'd dug
the past few days had changed dramatically. She wasn't
altogether sure what the changes meant, but felt in her
bones that she was on the verge of discovering something that would make a difference in her baby's life.
"It's for me to say what I do, Jacob," she said with
renewed ferocity. "Go away and leave me alone."

"Damn, Hayley. I worried when I thought it was just
you." Jake flung an arm wide. Mojave shied and Charcoal paced between the two humans, whining as he
looked at each. "But you and a baby... It's craziness for
a pregnant woman to be this far from a good road. You
need to be close to town, where there's adequate medical
care and decent doctors."

"Thank you very much for your flattering opinion of
my capabilities. I've seen a doctor. He gave me a book
describing all the stages of pregnancy. I plan to be out
of here and back in Tombstone long before it's time to
deliver my baby. Anyway, I don't answer to you. It's
my baby. My responsibility. My decision." Her eyes
flared as she crossed her arms protectively over the gentle slope of her abdomen.

"Oh? So the kid doesn't have a father? I'll bet he'd

have plenty to say about how you're jeopardizing his child's life.''

Hayley's face crumpled. Her lips trembled and her eyes filled with pain. Long seconds ticked by before she seemed to get a grip on her emotions. "You're wrong. Joe didn't care about me. He's not the type to be a husband or father. Besides, he forfeited all rights when he walked out on me.''

"I didn't mean to open old wounds. It's just…if it was me, I'd want to know I had a baby in the works. A man deserves a chance to do right by his child.''

A haunting smile came and went. "Not all men have your sense of responsibility, Jake. Believe me, the last thing Joe Ryan wants is to be tied down.''

"He married you. I'd say that represents a tying down of sorts.''

A harsh broken sound emerged from her throat. "You don't know the facts.''

"So tell me.'' He walked over and shackled Hayley's restless fingers in his larger hands. "I want to understand why you're willing to take such risks.''

Hayley kept her eyes averted. A second sound, this one more like a sob, worked its way to the surface. No words or explanations followed.

Jake felt the pain that obviously racked her body. Releasing her wrists, he gathered her against his chest. It was impossible not to notice the slight framework of her bones. Hell, her head didn't even reach his chin. Despite everything Jake knew about her tenacity, her determination to tough it out on her own, she seemed fragile enough to break.

He wasn't in the habit of kissing women to comfort them. Especially not women who were pregnant with another man's child. But something about the stoic way

Hayley tried to hold back tears suggested she believed this pregnancy was solely *her* obligation. Jake didn't know why her husband had chosen to leave with another woman. He didn't care, except that Hayley had clearly decided it was because she wasn't desirable. Which was hogwash. Outwardly, though, she put on a good show. Inside, she was like a raft breaking apart in high seas. She needed to be shown there was nothing wrong with her in the desirability department.

He could tell her in so many words, but Jake didn't think she'd listen. Or if she did listen, she wouldn't believe him.

Kisses were harder to dispute. And kissing Hayley Ryan was far from a hardship.

Yet he didn't want to scare her. He took care to slide his hands to the nape of her neck. Tunneling his fingers beneath her heavy hair, he slowly tilted her face toward his. He lowered his lips even more slowly, leaving a decorous space between their bodies, making sure, however, to meet her eyes. He didn't want her mistaking his intentions. No way did he want her misconstruing this as a pity kiss. He had to be honest—he was doing this for him as much as for her. Kissing Hayley had been on his mind for some time. And damned if he didn't intend to do it right.

The campfire popped and shot sparks. Hayley's heart cartwheeled, and she gave a start—a move plastering her to Jake's body. Even with her belly slightly rounded, she felt, and instantly recognized, the hard ridge pressing against her from behind his jeans zipper. She was assailed first by panic and then shock as his lips covered hers. But as his kiss grew more demanding, she felt herself responding. Her eyes drifted closed, and soon she ceased to think at all. She let the human contact soothe a desperately lonely ache that resided deep inside her. An ache Joe Ryan had done nothing to assuage.

Jake's mouth was soft, mobile. His tongue warm and coaxing. His body hard and urgent. Everything around her receded. The campfire, her trailer, his animals. Vanished, as did the night noises beyond the perimeter of the dancing flames. Scary sounds that too often pulled Hayley from sleep and set her heart pounding in fright—the way it did now.

No, it wasn't the same. She felt nothing of the dread that inevitably followed the sudden stark awakenings. Those black moments of pure terror that forced her to face facts. She had only herself to rely on now.

She was all the tiny life inside her had, too.

Yet...in holding her close, in kissing her, Jacob Cooper offered solace. Solace and something more. He offered hope.

Hope for what? Some part of Hayley's befogged brain struggled to make sense of why she stood here, her lips locked to a virtual stranger's. A series of flutter kicks low in her stomach served as a potent reminder. She was pathetic. This wasn't the first time she'd been blinded by that lonely vacant feeling. A need to be held, comforted and loved. The very need that had confused her and made her fall for Joe's lies.

He'd never wanted her. Not really. He'd only wanted the easy profits from the Silver Cloud mine. And Joe had been unscrupulous enough to walk her down the aisle to get them.

What did Jacob Cooper want?

Hayley's baby kicked again, a sobering reminder. The Blue Cameo. Of course. Or rather, the water—the natural spring that was on this site. For a second Hayley was sorely tempted to grab whatever fleeting comfort she could derive from Jake's kisses and the strong arms in which he cocooned her—until she remembered that *fleeting* wasn't what she wanted for the child growing inside her. In a hailstorm of regret, she began shutting down her senses and started to withdraw.

Jake was vaguely aware of faint movements beating feebly against him. At first he was too engrossed in the pleasure of kissing Hayley to realize he was feeling her baby. When she arched her back to gain leverage to push him away, it dawned on him how tightly their lower bodies fit together. That flutter he'd felt was a tiny human being.

Sensations raced through him. Awe, mixed with heat and lust and outright possessiveness. As he paused to catch his breath and stroke his thumbs lightly over Hayley's kiss-dampened lips, he was suffused with a blinding desire to safeguard something precious. Hayley and her unborn child.

Shaken by such intense feelings he let her go and took a stumbling step backward.

Freedom from the threat of Jake's closeness was what Hayley wanted. And yet she reeled from their sudden separation. But when he reached out a hand to support her, she shrank away, telegraphing a touch-me-not warning. She hauled in the next breath, her breasts rising and falling rapidly, then clutched her stomach and began retching. "Just...leave," she choked out, moments before she lurched into a nearby thicket.

"Like hell!" Jake shouted, not fully understanding her rapid transformation. "I'm taking you to the Triple C. Go sit by the fire while I hitch up your truck and trailer."

Hayley poked a white face out from a network of shrubs. "Don't you dare lay a finger on anything that belongs to me." Racked by the nausea that chose indiscriminate times to strike, she bent double into the bushes again, and this time emptied the meager contents of her stomach.

Darn, but she hated having Jake see this. Over the past three or four weeks, she'd discovered that her morning sickness, which had gotten a late start according to the pregnancy-advice booklet, descended at any time of day or night.

"Hayley…" Jake's tentative voice battered her ringing ears. The bouts were always followed by cold sweats. She clung to a sapling, waiting for the waves to pass. And pass they always did.

Jake stripped off the neck scarf he wore to protect his face from the dust kicked up by plodding steers. He ran to the spring, wet the material thoroughly and, though his knees weren't steady, bulldozed his way to Hayley's side. "Here," he said gruffly. "Let me wipe your face. Do you have a cup out there? I'll get you some water."

"Go away," she said weakly. "I'm fine."

"Yeah, you sound fine. Just great. How long has this been going on?"

She pressed her face into the cool fabric of his bandanna, willing him to leave her to her misery. Even in the darkness afforded her by the trees, Hayley felt his concern. From what little she knew of Jake, she doubted he'd walk off and abandon her in this condition. But maybe she could shake him with a lie.

"I have an aversion to being grabbed and kissed," she said, trying to sound angry and disgusted, instead of merely weak. "That's why I'm sick. I'm sure it's not a reaction you're used to getting, since you probably have your choice of women in this valley. Collect your horse and ride out. Forget me, Jake."

His brows shot up. Dammit, he'd *felt* her react with desire to that kiss. Not for one minute did he buy into this claim that kissing her made her sick. However, a lot had happened in the past few minutes and he saw the need to give them both some space. "I reckon we can set aside this contest of wills while I deal with the business at hand. Make yourself comfortable in your remaining chair while I turn on the water."

Sometimes Hayley could will the bouts of nausea away. She tried now, taking deep breaths as she patted the damp cloth to her face and neck. "There," she breathed. "All better." That was an out-and-out fib she thought as she led the way out of the thicket on wobbly legs. The booklet said it was rare for vomiting to stretch beyond three months. On the other hand, at the end of each discussion of possible side effects were exceptions to the rule. Hayley figured she was exception number four. Four being her unlucky number. After all, she'd married Joe Ryan on the fourth day of the fourth month. A double whammy if ever she'd encountered one. And exception number four in the booklet said a few women experienced nausea and vomiting for all nine months of their pregnancy.

Falling into step with her, Jake slid a supporting arm around her thickening waistline.

If she hadn't felt so rocky, she'd have never allowed his help. "Really, these spells pass quickly," she said in a matter-of-fact voice. "It's common for pregnant women to suffer some vomiting. Stress adds to the frequency."

"Mm," he said noncommittally. He saw her firmly seated before he left to open the valves. "I'll bet you all four of those women live within a ten-minute drive of their doctors," he muttered.

Starting to shrug, Hayley looked guilty, instead. But she wasn't going to let him draw her into an argument over something that wasn't his business. She clamped down on her tongue just in time. The minute he was out of sight, she got up and put on the kettle to heat water for tea. Peppermint generally calmed her stomach.

Jake hadn't missed the stubborn light that flicked on inside Hayley's eyes. And it made him worry that he wouldn't be able to persuade her to leave the Blue Cameo's site. Well, first things first. Going out into the desert with Charcoal, he rounded up her family of strays. He spoke to them in fluent Spanish and quickly determined they weren't part of a larger illegal ring. Best of all, the men possessed work permits. He made them understand that he lived on the Triple C, and that if the two men in the unit knew cows, they were hired for roundup.

He led them back to the campfire, and they resumed their meal with many expressions of gratitude. Then Jake gave them directions and told them about another migrant family living in the valley who would give the wife and kids temporary shelter.

Hayley thanked him quietly and fervently.

Only later, after he'd collected and washed the dishes left by her visitors and he'd again broached the subject of towing her trailer to the Triple C, did Jake accept that her refusal didn't mean *maybe*. She had every intention of remaining right in this spot.

"Look, you *can't* stay here," he said, stomping angrily around the fire for about the hundredth time in the past hour.

If she hadn't been so weary of going over the same ground, Hayley might have smiled at his seriousness. Setting aside her now-cold cup of peppermint tea, she formed her fingers into a tent in front of her chin. "You warn me not to take in strays. Yet it's precisely what you'd be asking your family to do. Not only wouldn't they appreciate you dragging home a pregnant stranger, Jacob, it doesn't sound to me as if the Triple C is all that much closer to town. Anyway, it's irrelevant. I'm not going."

Frustrated by her logic, Jake raked a hand through his hair. "I'll admit this is a busy period for us. Right now is when my mother and Eden replenish their stock—you know, for their shop. Mom's a potter and Eden makes jewelry. And it's roundup, which keeps Dillon and me hopping. But you'd have access to phones at the ranch. A telephone could make all the difference if something went wrong."

Jake carefully avoided making any comment about his family welcoming her. He thought they would. Or rather, he thought that, given time, he could talk them into it—although he suspected his mother might object to his taking a more-than-neighborly interest in a pregnant woman.

Be that as it may, he couldn't tolerate the thought that Hayley might be risking her safety and her baby's if she stayed here. Her stubbornness exasperated him beyond belief. "Look," he shouted, pushing his face close to hers, "I don't have time for this. I have to get back to help with the herd."

"Then go. Who's stopping you?" Hayley bolted upright, clenching her fists. "I survived without a man before. I certainly don't need one calling the shots now."

Jake let his anger drain. "This isn't about me ordering you around because you're a woman and I'm a man."

"No? Then what is it about?"

Jake's thoughts and feelings were so jumbled he

couldn't honestly answer her. In a lot of ways he barely knew her—as his family kept telling him. He certainly didn't know her well enough to stake any claim. Yet he felt in his soul this was about more than principle. More than the chivalrous values his parents had instilled in him. He hesitated and finally stuttered, "It's because I'm worried about you. I can't completely explain it. The baby, I guess. And I admit that what you said earlier is true—I'd never have questioned Ben's decision to stay out here alone."

For a minute there Hayley thought Jake was going to blurt out something more personal. Her breath had even stalled in her throat as he wrestled with his words. In that teetering moment she realized she'd have capitulated and followed him like a pitiful puppy if he'd offered so much as a token reason suggesting that she might, in any way, be special to him.

The moment passed for both of them. Jake felt flushed and ineffective.

Hayley's resolve doubled right before his eyes. She built a bulwark of strength around her. Nevertheless, he made one last stab. "I'll leave Charcoal with you. If you need me for any reason, tell him to find me."

"That's very kind," Hayley said in a brittle voice. "But I can't...won't accept. He's a cow dog. He deserves to do what he's trained for. Besides, what if he wandered off or got hurt? No. You take him."

As Jake tightened the girth on his saddle and prepared to mount, he searched for reasons to stick around longer. Clearly, though, Hayley was anxious for him to go. "You're sure..." he began once his knees gripped the leather.

"I'm positive." Hayley plastered a confident smile on her lips. It remained in place until he was gone and there was no way the occluding darkness would allow him to see it slip.

Jake rode slowly and methodically away from the clearing. Away from Hayley. Many times he hauled on the reins and stopped. Half of those times he turned Mojave and almost went back. He did send Charcoal in his stead, continuing on his way to rejoin Dillon only after he'd verified from a vantage point on the ridge that Hayley had emerged from her trailer and discovered the dog. Though not as satisfactory as having Hayley parked at the ranch, he guessed it'd do until he found a way to change her mind.

"YO, LITTLE BROTHER." Dillon rode out to meet Jacob ahead of the meandering herd. "What's happening up at the spring? Is she going dry?"

Jake reined in sharply.

Dillon snapped his fingers in Jake's face. "Earth to Jacob. Did that woman chase you off with a shotgun again?"

Jake finally sorted through his brother's barrage of questions. "I released the water. It ran a couple of hours. Should have filled the ditch."

"Made a thin stream of red mud, is all. Half the herd went without a taste. We've pushed them hard since yesterday. Their tongues are hanging out. If they don't get more water by morning, we could be in trouble."

"I didn't follow the ditch back to the stream. It must be blocked somewhere." Jake shifted in his saddle, making the leather creak. "I suppose I'd better ride back and find the problem area. I sent two men to see you. Did they get here?"

"Yes. I took 'em on. And Dad showed up an hour ago. He says the doctor cleared him to help us finish roundup. You know he'll overdo it if he takes it into his head to beat the arroyos for strays. And I need a break. So Dad and I will check the route to the spring. We'll meet up with you at Lark's Meadow tomorrow."

"Sure." Jake stripped off the high-powered binoculars that hung around his neck. "I doubt you'll have to ride all the way into Mrs. Ryan's camp to find the blockage." He paused. "There are several places where you'll overlook her camp. Would you mind making sure she's all right?"

Dillon gave his brother the once-over out of lazy-lidded eyes.

Jake tightened his jaw. "Just do it, all right? A woman's got no business digging rock. It's plain damn foolish for her to be out there doing it alone—as I told her."

"I take it she didn't appreciate your opinion. Guess I haven't taught you anything about handling women, ch, Jake? You gotta sweet-talk 'em. You can't just throw out orders."

Jake snorted. He recalled vividly the feel of Hayley's lips under his. He'd always thought kissing worked better than sweet talk, and he'd never needed Dillon's instructions when it came to dealing with women.

Wade Cooper rode up on a brown-and-white pinto gelding. His appearance effectively put an end to Dillon's teasing. Talk turned to water, or the lack thereof. "Dammit, we need full control of that spring," Wade fumed. "I'll bet Ben's grandkid hasn't found a nickel's worth of assayable ore. You were there, Jake. Did she show any signs of capitulating?"

Jake shook his head. Personally, knowing her condition, he figured she'd have to stop sooner than later. He kept her secret, though. She'd seemed so desperate to stay in spite of being pregnant. And he'd seen her boxes of rocks. She hadn't sat idle. If there was something valuable in that claim, Jake wanted Hayley to find it. He shook himself out of a stupor to hear his father talking again.

"John Westin's pressing the co-op to use their collective muscle to commandeer that plot. I'd feel a whole lot better if he'd shut up."

Dillon leaned an arm across his saddle horn. "Me, too. Westin's been growing too fast. Eden heard rumors in town that he's overgrazed his fields. He's leased to the maximum on government range."

"Yeah," Wade put in. "Yesterday I heard even more disturbing news. Link Thompson said John bought Ginalyn the old Naylor spread out on Cougar Flats. He's leased from there to the Arivaca junction in her name. Link said if anyone thinks Ginalyn's going to be out there punching cows, he has some swampland to sell them."

Dillon swore. "The only water for Cougar Flats would have to come from our spring."

"Except," Wade pointed out, "it isn't ours."

"Ain't that the truth," Dillon said. "Hey, Jacob. Where's Charcoal?" he asked suddenly, shading his eyes to gaze around.

"I, uh…" Jake stuttered. "I left him with Hayley." When Wade lifted a brow, Jake explained again about the illegals Hayley had fed.

"I hope you don't mind if we mosey on into her camp and pick up your dog," Wade said. "The object here is to get her to abandon that mine, not facilitate her stay."

"I do mind," Jake growled. His comment drew surprised glances from both Dillon and Wade. "Hayley's determined to work that claim, even though it's not safe.''

Dillon laughed as Wade continued looking troubled. ''Come on, Dad. I think it's high time we took a gander at this woman who's got the valley's most eligible bachelor dancing at the end of a short rope.''

''I'm not dancing on anybody's rope!'' Jake shouted. ''Mom used to send pickles and bread to Ben,'' he said more quietly. ''Tell me how this is any big-deal different?''

Grinning lecherously, Dillon appeared ready to try. Wade called a halt by glowering at both his sons. ''Jake, take the herd on to the Triple C. Dillon and I will ride ahead and set up the grain feeders and the branding pens when we finish inspecting the stream. I figure we'll all be too busy over the next week or so to worry about acting neighborly.''

His statement severed any further conversation about Hayley Ryan. Jake recognized his father's method of manipulation. As far back as Jake could remember, his dad had piled on the chores to keep his two sons walking the straight-and-narrow path he'd decided they ought to take. Never before had Jake felt the resentment he experienced now in watching Wade ride off, complacent that his edict would be obeyed.

Jake's anger flared. He was no longer a boy. He didn't appreciate his father's heavyhanded tactics. He'd choose what women to date. And he'd fit them into his work schedule. *Not them, her. Hayley Ryan.* If he wanted to see her badly enough to give up his sleep time, he damn well would.

But Jake hadn't allowed for his father's breakneck pace. The first twelve days of September passed in a blur of hard work before he found time to do more than stare at the dusty horizon, wondering how Hayley was doing. On the thirteenth day, after the whole weary crew packed the last beef into the cattle train headed for market, Wade gave everyone two days off before starting the entire process again on the south range.

Jake, who'd ridden into Tubac with Dillon that morning, saw a woman on the street whose hair color reminded him of Hayley. He was struck by an acute need to visit her. "Hey, Dillon. I've got better things to do than hang out in town. If you're going to stick around and bug your wife, I'll take the truck home and let you snag a ride with her."

"What do you have to do that's so all-fired important?"

Jake grinned disarmingly. "Catch up on my sleep. Dad's a slavedriver. I liked it better when the doc made him stay off a horse."

"I hear you." Mistakenly Jake assumed Dillon had bought his story. He dismissed that notion when Dillon punched his arm and said, "When you drop my pickup at the house, go on inside. There's a package of soup bones on the second shelf of the fridge. Charcoal will be right happy to get one."

Jake swung around, his guilty gaze colliding with Dillon's mischievous grin.

"You never could lie worth shit, little brother. Frankly, the Ryan woman didn't strike me as anything to write home about. But deny a man access and he'll never find that out for himself."

Jake bristled, then rotated his shoulders and sighed. "I can't explain the attraction myself, Dillon. It won't do me any good to try defending it to you."

Dillon pulled up next to the curb outside Eden's jewelry store. He left the pickup running as he climbed out.

"It's only fair to tell you that your lady ran Dad and me off at shotgun point. Dad was apoplectic all the way home. He's definitely going to need time before he greets your friend with open arms."

"What made Hayley go for her gun? Never mind." Jake slid under the wheel and released the parking brake. "I want to hear her version first." He slammed the door on whatever Dillon had to say.

HAYLEY BENT HIS EAR plenty when he rode into her camp and interrupted her as she washed screen-bottomed trays filled with some blue-streaked stone.

"I don't need you bringing me bribes, Jacob Cooper. Much as I liked having Charcoal here for company, you can take him home, too. Tell your father and brother I *have* discovered something worthwhile." She gestured at an array of oddly lustrous rocks.

"Doesn't look like precious metal to me," Jake said, going on one knee to examine the collection more closely. "What is it? And why should it make any difference to my dad and Dillon?"

"Ha!" She loomed over him, hands on her hips. "As if you didn't know they stormed in here the day after you left and gave me an ultimatum. They said if I didn't discover something of value in two weeks, they'd file a petition with the state recorder's office to have my claim revoked. Well, I've found an opal deposit!"

Jake didn't hear her at first. He was furious to think that a man of his father's gentle nature would bully any woman, let alone one so obviously pregnant. For Hayley was no longer able to hide her condition in the folds of her loose jumper. The roundness of her stomach was quite prominent now.

"I guess you're speechless, huh?" she demanded.

"On second thought," she said, wagging a finger in his face, "I'd rather you didn't spread the news around town. I don't want a stampede of gem-hunters crowding me."

"Gem-hunters?" Jake shifted his eyes from her stomach to stare blankly at her flushed face.

"Honestly! Haven't you heard a word I said?" she asked as he rose to his feet. Too happy not to share her joy with somebody, Hayley flung her arms around Jake's neck. "I hit a vein of opal! I'm not sure of the grade, but I've positively identified my find. A lower grade only means the difference between my baby and me surviving and being comfortably rich." Her delighted laughter was muffled against Jake's chest as she tightened her arms and buried her face in his shirtfront.

He didn't even realize that his heart had kicked into overdrive or that he'd flattened his palms across her narrow back. Once again Jake felt the wriggle of new life when Hayley's stomach pressed tight to his. "I've missed you," he said simply, bringing her against him. "Missed you a lot. Now that you've made your discovery, you can hire someone to dig this stuff. You can supervise from the Triple C." He unwound her arms and held her at arm's length, then yanked her close to hug her again. "I can't explain what's going on inside my head—and my heart," he said, raining kisses on the top of her head. "I only know I want you where I can take care of you and your baby."

"What are you talking about?" She freed an arm and then wrenched out of his grasp. "I can't leave my claim. I have to stay here and dig as much ore as I can. Enough to sell and tide us over until my baby's old enough to bring here with me. "I can't afford a crew, Jake. Even if I could, I wouldn't trust them not to steal me blind.

Please, if you want to do what's best for me, go home and forget what I've found." Her voice broke with emotion. "I shouldn't have told anyone."

Jake didn't like to hear her beg. "I won't tell," he promised gruffly, feeling sick inside as he clasped her hands and found them chapped and bleeding. "Just because I've agreed to go along with your harebrained scheme doesn't mean I'm giving up trying to get you to leave. If I have to ride out here every night after roundup and help you dig this stuff by moonlight until you have what you consider *enough,* then that's what I'll do."

She looked at him oddly. "I'm not sharing this find."

"Who asked you to?" He sounded as annoyed as hell.

"I just wanted to be clear up front. Joe walked away with the proceeds from Gramps's silver mine. He also stole a blue cameo that belonged to my mom. The only thing I had of hers. I was gullible once. I won't be twice."

"Hey—not every man is a scumbucket like your crummy ex." Jake could see from the distrust in her eyes that Hayley didn't believe him. *Too bad.* He didn't like being painted with the same brush as the jerk who'd let her and his baby go.

Striding to his horse, Jake yanked the cinch tight. Climbing on, he whistled for Charcoal to heel. "If you ever wake up and discover that people are worth more than money, you can find me at the Triple C."

She looked very small and alone standing in the middle of those rock trays she wanted so fiercely to protect. Jake figured she must not have heard that opals were supposed to be bad-luck gems. However, that wasn't something he'd ever mention, since it would only diminish her delight in her find.

The bottom-line truth—he might be peeved enough to

leave her to her stubborn pride for now, but he would never do anything to hurt her.

He hadn't ridden far before he gained control over his anger. He'd been unwilling to admit to Dillon or anyone—not even himself—that Hayley had gotten under his skin. He could no longer deny that she had. She was entrenched good and deep. At the moment he didn't know how to go about convincing her of that. It nagged at him the entire ride home.

CHAPTER EIGHT

WHEN JAKE ARRIVED home, he discovered that his mother had left work early to barbecue for the family. "To celebrate midpoint in the fall roundup," she informed him as she urged him to hurry and unsaddle Mojave. His dad, brother and sister-in-law were already gathered outside around the barbecue pit.

"I see you got Charcoal back," Dillon observed after Jake had showered, changed clothes and joined his family.

Jake, who'd stewed all the way home about the shabby way his dad and Dillon had treated Hayley, grabbed his brother by the shirtfront. "I'm sorry my dog didn't bite you at Hayley's camp, you sorry son of a bitch. Those bully tactics you guys used on her don't set well with me."

Ever the self-righteous older brother, Dillon roughly broke Jake's hold. "Watch it. This is a new shirt Eden bought me."

"Boys! What in heaven's name is wrong?" Nell's gaze skipped from her older son to her younger. "Stop squabbling this instant."

"We're not boys," Jake snapped, never taking his eyes off Dillon. "And men don't run roughshod over women."

Looking confused, Nell sent a silent appeal for help to her husband.

He popped the lids off two beers and shoved one into each of his son's hands. "Cool off, Jacob. That was Triple C business and I handled it as tactfully as possible. So happens, it's just as well I did. Westin formed a committee to go meet with the governor. If he endorses their proposal to seize the land, I foresee bigger problems than we have now. John talks a good game, but he's splitting the co-op. I have some pull with state environmentalists, and I'll call on them if necessary. I thought it only fair to give Ben's granddaughter a neighborly warning."

"She said you gave her a two-week ultimatum to come up with a strike or else. That sounds stronger than a neighborly warning."

Wade shrugged, but he denied nothing as Nell stuck a long-handled fork in his hand and asked him to turn the steaks. "Could we forget about water and mining claims for tonight and enjoy one another's company? You men are heading into phase two of the roundup, and by next week, Eden and I will be inundated at the shop with the start of tourist season. Who knows when we'll get time together again?"

Eden slipped her arm through Dillon's. Smiling at Jake, she edged her husband toward the screened porch that held a table set for six.

Dillon poked Jake. "Looks like these sneaky women have found you a date for tonight," he chortled. "Who'll it be, I wonder? My money is on the unknown quilter."

"Mom!" Jake counted the table settings twice before he strode toward his mother.

Eden gave Dillon a rap on his arm. "It's nothing, Jacob. Lisa Clover is someone Nell and I met and liked.

She's in town for the arts-and-crafts fair. We wanted to show her some Southwestern hospitality, that's all.''

''Uh-huh!'' Jake didn't buy into Eden's too-pat explanation. But it was too late to beg off. Twin headlights turned into the lane, slicing through the gathering dusk.

''Be nice,'' cautioned Nell as she and Eden headed around the house to greet their guest.

''You're in for it now, brother.'' Snickering, Dillon ducked the foamy beer bath Jake attempted to douse him with from a well-shaken bottle.

The women returned. Nell introduced her friend. Lisa had shoulder-length auburn hair and direct blue eyes. She wore layers of loose clothing—obviously an artsy type. She'd brought a cold twelve-pack of beer and a set of handmade coasters for Nell. Cleverly quilted ranch scenes. A thoughtful gesture, Jake decided. But he wouldn't have sat next to her at the table if the choosing had been up to him. Eden had handled seating arrangements, and Jake didn't feel like making a fuss that would hurt her or their guest.

As it turned out, Lisa was easy to talk to. Partway through the meal, though, Jake started to think about Hayley spending the evening alone at her camp. At least he *hoped* she was alone and that she wasn't entertaining iffy visitors. He grew quiet once he'd dispensed with the usual opening subjects. He found himself picturing Hayley in place of Lisa at tonight's gathering. She wouldn't be nearly as confident or as chatty.

The others at the table began to notice his one-word responses. Nell and Eden shot puzzled looks his way. Nell finally rose and tapped him on the shoulder.

''Come help me serve up the apple pie and coffee, Jake.''

Eden and Lisa both offered to lend a hand. ''No, no.''

Nell stayed them with a glance. "I haven't seen Jacob lately. We'll get in a few private words while we're preparing dessert plates."

Dillon waggled his eyebrows, announcing at large, "Uh-oh. Jake's in for it now. Mom's about to deliver lecture number 199 on company etiquette." Eden silenced him with a kick under the table, but not before their guest followed Jake's departure with bewildered eyes.

Inside the kitchen Jake waited for the lecture to begin. He knew he'd dropped the ball out there. All his mother and Eden had expected of him was that he'd make this friend of theirs feel welcome. It wasn't that there was anything wrong with Lisa Clover; it was just that his mind happened to be stuck on another woman.

Nell moved the pies to the table, found a knife and plates. Jake had played out this routine enough times in his life to automatically cut slices of cheddar for the top of each pie slice. That accomplished, he counted out forks.

"Lisa is considering renting the vacant shop next to ours permanently after the craft fair."

"So she said." Jake popped the first two pie wedges in the microwave and turned it on low, long enough to soften the cheese.

Nell sighed loudly. "She's nice, don't you think?"

Jake turned and caught her looking exasperated. "You and Eden must've already determined that or you wouldn't have invited her to dinner."

"Jacob Cooper, why are you being so obstinate?"

"I'll give our guest the first piece of pie." Jake whipped the two plates out of the microwave, added forks and hurried out to the patio. His mother was slapping slices of pie on the remaining plates when he returned for another batch.

"You know perfectly well I wasn't talking about your company manners, Jacob."

"Maybe you ought to quit pussyfooting around and spell out what you mean, Ma."

"All right. Lisa is bright and funny and talented. She'd settle here with a bit of encouragement. And don't call me Ma. You know I detest it."

Jake didn't say anything. He delivered the next two pieces of pie. As he made his way back, his mother busily covered the leftovers in the pie tins with foil. Their two slices sat awaiting cheese. Clearly he hadn't heard everything she had on her mind.

"Dillon said you haven't asked anyone to the harvest dance yet. Lisa happened to tell Eden that she loves to dance."

"I haven't asked anyone, but I have someone picked out."

"Who?" Nell wouldn't be put off. "Eden and I hear all the gossip in town. All the single girls are already spoken for."

Jake turned his back. He studied the number pad on the microwave as the carousel went around. "I'm going to ask Hayley Ryan."

"A stranger? Why, Jacob? She's frustrating your father and the others in the co-op over her silly mining claim."

Jake leveled a glare over his shoulder. "What she's digging out there isn't silly to her. It's important. She has no family left, Mom. And...and...Hayley's pregnant."

Nell stifled a tiny gasp. "Pregnant? Where's her husband?"

"He walked out on her, remember?" Jake's jaw tightened. "She shouldn't be there alone in her condition. Near as I can tell, she hasn't got a thing for the baby. I intended to ask you to visit her. She claims she's consulted a doctor in Tombstone and is following the advice in some booklet he gave her. I thought you might talk to her. Find out if she's overdoing things, what she needs—you know."

The carousel had stopped rotating, but neither Nell nor Jake made a move to retrieve the pie. Nell's throat worked. At last she croaked out, "Jake…I…you…we really shouldn't get involved. We don't know anything about this woman."

Jake hooked his thumbs in his belt, his stance belligerent. "I'm not hungry for pie, after all. See if Dillon wants an extra piece. I'm hitting the sack early."

He was crossing the living room by the time Nell rallied. She stepped to the center of the arch and called out, "Jake, this is foolish, arguing over an outsider like this. Think about what you're doing. Ben worked that claim every summer. He never found anything of value. Besides, Hayley Ryan will leave at the first frost. Jake, you're opening yourself up to get hurt."

"I just asked you to be neighborly. *She's* the one who's hurt. Good Lord, her ex even stole the one thing she loved most, a blue cameo that belonged to her mother. And you're wrong. Hayley's made a strike. She doesn't want it spread around, but she found opals."

Nell digested that as he disappeared and the door behind her opened.

Eden joined her mother-in-law. "We're almost finished with our dessert. What's keeping you and Jake? Why were you two shouting? And who found opals? Are they jewelry quality?"

Pursing her lips, Nell spun and plucked the last pie wedges from the microwave. "That woman at the spring has apparently led Jake to believe she's unearthed something at Ben's old claim."

"Jake's so gullible. I've never heard of opals being mined in Arizona."

Nell gazed toward the door through which Jake had escaped. Her eyes went soft. "Maybe not. But I've suddenly decided I want to meet this Hayley Ryan. You don't know Jake like I do, Eden. For years I've watched girls and women chase him. This is the first time I've detected more than a superficial interest on his part. Since he and Dillon fought over you, that is," she added with an affectionate grin. "Because I tend to see both my boys through a mother's prejudiced eyes, I'd welcome a second opinion. What do you say? If we can break away early one day, would you run out to the spring with me to check out the Ryan woman?"

"Certainly. If for no other reason than to debunk her phony claim. Although there *have* been veins of opal found in Mexico," Eden mused thoughtfully.

"Jake said to keep the news under wraps. I know you share everything with Dillon. But until we know for sure what we're talking about, I'd like to respect Jake's wishes and keep this between us. I have a feeling Wade would try to talk me out of going."

"Sure. Okay, I have no problem honoring Jake's request for secrecy. And, Nell—I didn't mean any disrespect in calling him gullible."

"I know. I prefer to think of him as tenderhearted. In this case, however, gullible just might be a better word. Eden, he told me Hayley Ryan is going to have a baby."

"What? Not his?"

"No. She's Mrs. Ryan, but her husband took a powder."

"Wow. This is heavy-duty stuff. Is she looking for a sucker, you think?"

"I don't know. At this point I'm willing to give her the benefit of the doubt. From what Wade's said, Jake's invited her to the ranch and she's refused to leave her mine. That doesn't sound like someone trying to take advantage."

Eden swiveled toward the door as Dillon pushed it open. "Hey, ladies. What's the holdup? Your guest is making noises about going home." He withdrew, leaving Nell and Eden to exchange frowns.

"I'd planned to suggest Lisa spend the night," Eden murmured. "Probably pointless, huh, given how we've struck out with Jake?"

"Seems like it. However, she doesn't know the roads and they can be quite confusing at night. I do feel responsible for her."

"Dillon and I'll lead her out. We can stay at the shop tonight. He might be late for the second phase of roundup is all." Eden's eyes turned sensual.

Nell smiled. "Then Jake will have to oversee things until Dillon puts in an appearance. It'll do him good. Maybe take his mind off Mrs. Ryan. I might put a bug in Wade's ear about giving Jake more work to keep him occupied, too."

"Roadblocks, Nell? Did you do stuff like that to slow down Dillon's romance with me?"

"Not at all. The way he and Jacob quarreled, I knew one way or the other you'd end up in the family. In fact, I counted on it."

"Jake was never serious," Eden said.

"No, but he thought he was. Which is why I'm sticking my nose into this Ryan situation. Jake's getting antsy about living under our roof. He's going to build on his acreage. When a man's that ready to settle down, he doesn't always make his choices with a clear mind. And he sure seems obsessed with this Mrs. Ryan.''

"Darn. Lisa would have been so perfect. You with your pots, me with my jewelry, and her making quilts.'' She sighed. ''You're right. We need to find time soon to visit Mrs. Ryan. If Jake's in the nesting mode, he'll completely forget about family compatibility.''

"My fear exactly.'' Nell collected the two plates. "So it's set. Next week we scope out the enemy camp.''

MONDAY, AFTER DILLON had left the shop and headed for the ranch, Nell announced to Eden that she was going to knit a baby blanket before they called on Jake's pregnant nomad.

"Aren't you afraid that'll give her the wrong idea? I thought you wanted to discourage her involvement with Jake.''

"I don't know what's gotten into me, Eden. I woke up in the middle of the night thinking how Jake said she didn't have a thing for her baby. I remembered some of the stuff we learned about her when Wade and I went to Tombstone. She lost both her parents at an early age. Ben took her in, but he was gone prospecting a lot. And her husband absconded with her inheritance. Knitting her one blanket is not like I'm giving her a key to the ranch or anything. Call it a goodwill gesture. I think I can finish one by Friday, if I knit while my kilns are firing.''

"I'll keep Friday afternoon open. I hope we don't run into Jake while we're there. What if he rides in off the range to pay her a visit?''

"He won't. Wade put him in charge of branding strays. The south range is a catacomb of arroyos. He'll be tied up well into September finding them. I intend to get a handle on this woman way before then."

Eden nodded and started back through the connecting door into her shop. "So is the baby a boy or a girl?"

"I don't have any idea. If Jacob knew, he didn't say. I plan to buy a soft pastel-green yarn. Why are you asking?"

"I love buying baby gifts. I can never resist those cute outfits. Maybe I'll pick up a couple of terry sleepers."

Nell smiled. "Now who's a softie?"

"Actually there's method to my madness. If she really did discover some decent opals—and granted, that's a big if—I wouldn't mind having first crack at buying them."

"Yes—she'd need an outlet. But don't get your hopes up, Eden. She may have been trying to buy time. You know Wade and Dillon issued an ultimatum. Either she strikes a vein worth further exploration or they'd petition the state claims agent to force her to trade this site for another."

"In that case maybe we should ride in waving a white flag of truce."

"The thought has crossed my mind. I'm not forgetting she took a shot at Jake and brandished a shotgun at Wade. Of course, Jake did blunder into her camp at sunset. We'll go in daylight and carry our gifts in plain sight."

"You know," Eden said, "add up all we know about this woman and she doesn't sound very appealing. What do you suppose Jake sees in her?"

"That, my dear Watson, we won't know till Friday. Let's go early, shall we?"

NELL STOPPED her four-wheel-drive Range Rover outside Eden's house at the time they'd agreed on. A gaily wrapped package lay on the back seat. In a box on the floor behind the seat sat a hot crock filled with a mild tortilla soup.

Before Nell could climb out and go to the door, it opened and Eden came out juggling a wrapped gift, another foil-wrapped package and a small covered dish.

"What's that you're bringing?" Nell asked, hurrying around the car's hood to take one of the items so that Eden could lock her house.

"I baked bread last night. And churned butter. I get domestic when Dillon's gone."

"Ah," Nell said. "You couldn't sleep, huh?"

Eden, who would never admit such a weakness to her mother-in-law, denied it. "Actually I started thinking it wouldn't hurt to butter up the Ryan woman." She giggled. "So to speak."

Nell chuckled. "I stayed up and cooked up a batch of Grandmother Cooper's tortilla soup. I craved that stuff when I was carrying Dillon."

"No wonder he cajoles me into making it whenever he can. But isn't it too spicy for someone who's pregnant?"

"I used chicken and the mild chilies I grow to pickle and make into relish. She must be in fair health if she's out there chopping holes in the hills."

Eden set her things on the back seat, climbed into the passenger side and buckled her seat belt. "Makes sense. Of course, we don't know if she'll break bread with us or not. We're assuming a lot."

As Nell eased into the lane that led up and over a ridge that cut the ranch off from Hayley Ryan's camp, she looked doubtful for a moment. Then she said, "I owe it to Jake to go once. He's worried about her pregnancy and asked me to pay her a call. Men think having babies is something to worry about, although most are too embarrassed to broach the topic.''

''Aren't ranchers matter-of-fact about life and death? At least, Dillon acts like our getting pregnant is an inevitable evolutionary process.''

Nell's face erupted in a smile. ''Are you two…well, are Wade and I going to be grandparents?''

Eden blanched. ''Uh…no. Sorry, Nell. I shouldn't talk behind Dillon's back, but having a baby is the only thing we've argued about. To him, it's no big deal. I *want* it to be a big deal, dammit. I want my carrying his baby to be special.''

Patting Eden's tightly fisted hand, Nell said gently, ''It will be. Wade is ten times more pragmatic than either of his sons. But with both of my pregnancies, he was a basket case from the minute I started to show.''

''He always treats you like a queen.''

''Yeah, but that didn't come without a lot of reminders that I wasn't just part of the stock.''

''You're kidding?'' Eden gave a little laugh. ''Dillon's not as unromantic as that.''

''He'd better not be. I hope I raised both my sons to be caring men. I expect them to remember birthdays and anniversaries. Their father was notoriously lax the first few years of our married life. When he forgot our third anniversary in a row, I ordered myself the biggest bouquet the florist could stuff in one vase and had the flowers delivered all the way out here from town. I also had the credit-card statement sent to Wade, so he opened it along with the feed bills.''

''What did he do?''

''He's never forgotten another special date.''

"I feel guilty for complaining about Dillon," Eden said. "He's forever buying me little gifts." She donned a complacent smile and wore it all the way to Hayley Ryan's camp.

Hayley was in the clearing washing rocks when the dusty vehicle bounced to a stop next to her pickup. Her jumper was streaked with water, her boots caked with mud. She wore an out-of-shape khaki bush hat to hide her tangled hair. Even though she hadn't talked to another human being for more than a week, she was wary enough to retrieve the shotgun braced against a nearby log.

Expecting men to emerge from the range vehicle, Hayley let her mouth fall agape when two women climbed out, instead. She was even more surprised to see their hands filled with what looked like wrapped packages and food containers. Both women wore fashionable boots, jeans and pretty blouses tucked under leather belts that spanned narrow waists. Hayley felt dowdy by comparison—and a little intimidated. For that reason, she didn't offer a welcome. Not even when the older of the two women—and they both looked energetically young to Hayley—greeted her with a winsome, somehow familiar smile. Hayley was quite certain she'd never met either woman before. They weren't the forgettable type.

"Hello. I'm Nell Cooper and this is Eden." Nell inclined her head toward her daughter-in-law, never taking her eyes off the restless fingers clamped around the shotgun. "You've met my husband, Wade and Eden's husband, Dillon. But it was my son Jake who suggested you might enjoy a woman's company. Sorry if we've come at an awkward time. We know how it is to have your work interrupted. I throw pots and Eden designs jewelry.

Neither of us likes to leave in the middle of tasks. We did bring lunch on the off chance you'd take a midday break. If it's not convenient, we can leave soup, bread and fresh butter. Oh, and a couple of things for the baby. Jacob mentioned that you were expecting.''

Hayley ran a tongue over lips gone suddenly dry. ''You brought things for my baby?'' Letting the gun slide through her fingers, Hayley blinked rapidly in an effort to halt the tears that fell without warning.

Nell quickly covered the ground separating her from the crying woman. ''Oh, my dear, you haven't lost the baby, have you?'' It was impossible to tell, given the shapeless cotton jumper Hayley wore.

''No,'' Hayley said through chattering teeth. Her bottom lip quivered badly. ''I...I...I don't know what to say. Food and gifts. I...well, Jake and I argued last time he was here. He even took Charcoal with him. Not a day's gone by that I haven't regretted my words. Lord, I should be used to my own company. But the days get long and the nights even longer when a body has only squirrels to talk to.''

''And chickens,'' Nell said, her attention drawn to the pen filled with her fat laying hens. She set the things she carried on the small table next to a single lawn chair and slid her arms around Hayley. ''I shouldn't kid, you poor thing. Solitude is great up to a point, but no one can survive a steady diet of it. Come, sit down and open your presents while Eden and I heat up the soup and slice the bread.''

Hayley pulled away and ran her hands nervously over the front of her jumper. ''You shouldn't touch me. I'm a mess. I've been working. Did I get your nice clothes dirty?''

''I'm not afraid of a little dirt. Neither is Eden. We

work up to our elbows in clay and silver dust. I don't think either of us buys clothing that isn't washable. Relax."

Hayley tried to blot her eyes. She didn't know why she was crying when her heart felt lighter than it had in days. "I...I can't seem to stop these pesky tears," she admitted, burying her face in the crook of her arm.

"It's part and parcel of being pregnant. Weeping over nothing comes with the territory." Nell ran a soothing hand over Hayley's hunched shoulders. She felt the sharp outline of a narrow backbone. Something shifted inside Nell's breast. Her heart went out to this waif her son had befriended. She was probably working too hard and not eating right. At least not eating regular meals.

Hayley's teary eyes widened and locked with Nell's. "The booklet my doctor gave me mentions mood swings. But not crying jags. This past week I've found myself sobbing over nothing. You're saying that's normal?" She let her unsure gaze drift toward the younger woman, Eden, as if wanting her concurrence.

Eden placed her offering on the seat of the lawn chair. "I've never had the PG experience. Too newly married," she said with a shrug. "But my best friend cried from about the sixth month on if anyone so much as looked at her cross-eyed. She was weepy up until her baby was a month old. So if she's any example of what's normal..."

"That's often the way it goes," Nell agreed. "Would you prefer we heat this soup inside your trailer or out here over the open fire?"

"It's like an oven during the day in my trailer," Hayley said, again acting uncomfortable in the presence of strangers. "I live pretty primitively. Jake probably told you he disapproves. We had words over him wanting me to move my trailer to the Triple C."

"He didn't say that, no," Nell admitted. "However, it sounds like something I'd expect of him. Of the Cooper men in general. You'll find they speak their minds."

"That's certainly true of your husband and hers, Mrs. Cooper," Hayley said, her expression suddenly cool. "Is that what's really at the bottom of this visit? Did they send you to softsoap me into giving up my claim?"

"Goodness, no! And call me, Nell. When Eden and I are together, it's too hard to figure out which Mrs. Cooper a person means. Anyway, I doubt Wade and Dillon will follow up on what they said last week. It depended on your failure to find anything of value. According to Jacob, you've made a significant find."

Hayley dusted her hands. "I haven't had a formal chemical or mineral assay done yet," she said as if afraid to predict good things.

Eden went down on one knee next to a tray of robin's-egg-blue rocks. "You've done preliminary testing, haven't you? These samples look like tectosilicate."

Hayley used a toe to push the tray out of Eden's reach. "Nothing's official."

Nell clasped Eden under the arm and raised her to her feet. "Why don't we sample the goodies we brought? Talking business on a full stomach is more palatable, don't you think?"

"So this *isn't* a social visit?" Now Hayley's eyes turned positively flinty.

"It *is* a social visit," Nell insisted. "Eden sets her silver designs with local turquoise, citrine and tourmaline. Her antennae went on alert when she heard Jake mention opal to me. But I insist we table any work-related discussion until after we've eaten and you've opened your presents. The soup will only take a few minutes to heat. Eden, I'll hang this crock over the fire. Why don't you slice the bread? Hayley, if I may call you that, have a seat. We'll put this together in a jiffy.''

"Oh, but I only have one chair!" Hayley exclaimed, once again worried about her ability to play hostess.

"Not a problem," Nell assured. "I have two or three folding stools in my Range Rover. I use them at craft fairs."

"I'll get them." Eden headed to the vehicle immediately.

Nell bustled about. She hung the soup crock over the fire, brought water from the spring and poured it into a washbasin Hayley already had sitting on a stand. "The spring is getting low. We could do with another rain. Rainstorms have bypassed us this season."

Hayley squinted at the blue skies overhead. "It won't hurt my feelings if the rain holds off another month or two." She clasped her hands over her stomach. "I don't have any idea how much rock I need to earn enough to pay for the delivery and then get the baby and me through until next summer, when I can dig again. I figure I'll need to spend every day until the end of my eighth month just digging ore."

"How far along are you?" Eden asked as she opened the two stools she'd carried over and set them next to the chair.

"I'm due around Christmas."

Nell looked concerned. "Have you allowed time to close up here, get out and still buy the supplies you'll need once the baby's born? You certainly don't want to risk hauling heavy rock and bringing on premature labor."

"I don't want to, no. This is just what I have to do." Hayley lifted her chin.

"Of course. I didn't mean to meddle." Nell bent and stirred the soup a bit more vigorously than necessary.

"That sure smells good." Hayley had finished washing her hands and now sniffed the air. "I appreciate your thoughtfulness. I've been hungrier than normal lately, and I've got to make my supplies last."

"Nell and I both have gardens," Eden said. "The veggies are spoiling on the vines faster than I can pick them. You're welcome to come get all you'd like. It'll be the end of them soon. Or Jake can bring by a sackful. But he might not be free until roundup's over. That could be three or four weeks yet."

"Since no one's come to open the valves recently, I assumed roundup was over."

Eden shook her head. "Only the north range. They're working the south sections now. Here," she said, thrusting two packages into Hayley's hands. "Open these. I don't know how you've resisted. I can't stand to let wrapped packages alone."

Hayley hugged the gifts a moment before she sat and patiently untied the bow on the gift from Nell.

"You can rip the paper," Eden said dryly. "Honestly, I'd have torn it apart by now." She'd no more than said it than Hayley parted the outer paper, then the tissue.

"Oh!" she cried. "This is beautiful. Did you…? It looks handmade."

Nell shrugged it off as nothing.

Hayley lifted the soft folds, then jumped up and ran to wash her hands again. She washed twice before she was satisfied her hands and fingernails were clean of the red clay. All the while, tears rolled unchecked down her cheeks, leaving the other two women at a loss as to what to do.

"This is so beautiful," she crooned over and over. "Mint-green is my favorite color. Oh, but I can't let it touch my dress. I need to go change. My jumper is gritty with ore." She carefully set the blanket on the chair and ran to her trailer.

Eden paced the clearing. "Will she be gone long enough for me to get a look at those stones? I'm not an expert on opal, but blue ones are rare. If the stone doesn't shatter when it's scratched, she may have stumbled on a real find. I'd pay her a fair price. A good price. Do you think she'd trust me to do that?"

"I don't know, Eden," Nell said impatiently. "How can you focus on rock when what we need to do is talk her into getting good prenatal care? Think how much effort it takes to dig this much rock." She gestured at the ore Hayley had spread out. It's backbreaking labor. And speaking of labor, what if she's out here alone when her labor starts?"

Eden shook her head. "There's enough Coopers to keep tabs on her. She sounded pretty adamant to me about staying and following this through." She shrugged. "It is her life, after all."

Hayley returned then to open her other package. Eden fell silent, letting Hayley exclaim over the sleepers and cap and sweater she'd purchased at a local baby store.

"You don't even know me, and look what you've done! My baby will come home from the hospital in style. Thank you both so much. Jake said nice things about you two. I think he understated the case." Hayley seemed reluctant to put the baby gifts aside and accept the bowl of fragrant soup Nell handed her.

Hayley had her teeth sunk in a thick buttered slice of

bread when Eden again brought up the subject of her gems. "If these samples are opal, Hayley, I can do more for you than a few baby items are worth. Should it cut, polish and set well, I'd be willing to buy all the raw material you can provide. Even discarding the potch or matrix to get to the usable stone, I'd like to purchase what you have here." Eden figured in her head a moment and came up with an amount.

Hayley gasped. "So much? I...thought maybe half that amount...in my wildest dreams."

"That's conservative, depending on the grade. If you'd trust me with a slab to take back to my shop, I'd know better by the end of next week. Are you familiar with how consignment works? If the ore is high-grade, I'd advance more as my jewelry sells."

"And," Nell broke in, "to keep tabs on what she's doing, you could come and spend a few weeks at the Triple C, Hayley."

"Now I *know* you're related to Jake." Hayley smiled, but she kept shaking her head. "If the ore isn't high-grade, I'll have to dig twice as much. I appreciate your wanting to help, but I'm not going anywhere. Take a sample or two, Eden. All I ask is that you don't let anyone know where you got it."

"That's the least I can do," Eden murmured. "A good jewelry designer never reveals the source of his or her materials. I'd like to nail down an exclusive contract, but in all fairness, I have to tell you that you're free to sell to any market."

"To save us all a major disappointment," Hayley said, "Why don't we wait for the assay results?"

"Fair enough." Eden stood and collected the soup bowls. "I don't want to rush you, Nell, but you know how I am when I face the prospect of working with a new stone.''

''Yes. You're as obsessed as I am when I discover a new clay or dye. Are you sure you won't reconsider, Hayley? We'd make you comfortable at the ranch.''

''Thanks, but no. Maybe I'll drive over at the end of next week for those vegetables. And if you could spare a gallon of milk—I'll buy one,'' she added quickly.

''Nonsense. It's a gift. That's settled, then,'' Nell said, clasping Hayley's work-roughened hands between her own callused palms. ''If I see Jacob in the interim, shall I tell him you've had a change of heart and would welcome Charcoal back?''

''Would I ever.'' Hayley's eyes brimmed again. Because she wasn't used to so much kindness, she hugged each of the women awkwardly, then stepped back and waved while they climbed into the Range Rover. Her campsite seemed twice as lonely after they'd gone. Yet Hayley knew her decision to stay and extract additional ore was the right one.

A memory of Jake's kiss taunted her. She wondered if his mother would be so chummy if she knew about that—and the way he'd touched her.

CHAPTER NINE

JAKE DIDN'T KNOW about his mother and sister-in-law's visit to Hayley when he rode in on Wednesday of the next week to turn water into the southern ditches. He arrived at approximately four in the afternoon and found Hayley up to her knees in mud as she washed ore. Piles of blue-streaked rock, some boxed and some not, all sorted by size, made it difficult for him to navigate the clearing on horseback.

Charcoal ran through the piles, sniffing each one. He barked and wagged his tail enthusiastically when he finally reached Hayley. She let him lick her face, but tried not to pet him with her muddy hands. The blood coursing through her veins gushed like water through a broken dam the moment she'd identified Jake. Darn it, she didn't want to admit how much she'd missed his visits. She did her best to appear nonchalant.

Frankly, she was surprised to see him after what Eden had said concerning the timetable for roundup. Content to watch the easy way he sat a horse, Hayley stopped work and waited for Jake to speak first. He said nothing, only swung from the saddle, inspecting her from the top of her wind-tousled hair to the muddy soles of her boots. She returned the favor, shading her eyes with a dirty forearm. "You look exhausted," she said, shocked to see that it was true. "There's no coffee made, but I'll fix a pot. Give me a minute to wash up." She got to her feet, and at her first step, tripped on a large speckled rock.

Jake vaulted two rock heaps in succession to steady her. "I don't look half as tired as you do," he growled. "Sit. I'll fix the coffee."

"You haven't been here five minutes and already you're bossing me around." It made her nervous the way Jake zeroed in on every tiny detail. Gazing into his hungry eyes, she felt an urgent need to keep him at arm's length. "I'll knock off when these samples are clean. Anyway, I'm not drinking coffee, remember? Caffeine isn't good for babies." She thought a reminder wouldn't hurt, in case he'd forgotten her condition. Although he could hardly miss the changes in her body. This week she'd begun to feel as if she waddled rather than walked. Straightening, Hayley rubbed the heel of her palm on a spot that had ached constantly since she'd started hauling ore by hand again.

Jake thought she'd been doing that a lot—rubbing a place low on her spine. Mud caked the back pleats of a jumper that appeared sun-streaked from frequent laundering. She'd worn a T-shirt under the jumper the last time he'd seen her, but today her brown arms were bare and coated in dust. She also had dirt streaks on the brim of her hat and on her forehead, where she'd wiped away perspiration. It was hot. A hundred and five. It'd been that temperature for more than a week, and it felt twice that in the rocky canyons Jake had explored to hunt for strays. It must be worse digging ore from a hillside with the sun blistering down. "Now that we've agreed we both pretty much look like hell," he said, removing his hat and hanging it on a limb, "let's see what a hug will do to improve our sorry state of affairs." Giving her no time to object, Jake enfolded her in his arms. The minute he felt her warmth, it was as if his tiredness disappeared.

Hayley's hat tumbled from her head during a brief struggle for release. Then as Jake's hands slid to the base of her spine and began to massage away the dull ache lodged there, she relaxed against his chest and sighed. While her head told her she shouldn't let him touch her so intimately, her body dissolved under the motion of his hands. Almost before she knew it, her fingers had curved over his shoulders and she began to stroke his tight shoulder muscles.

Closing his eyes, he practically purred. They both did. And no words passed between them as they gave and took pleasure from the simplest touches. Jake didn't know when his body passed the basic need for comfort and slammed sexual desire through him, instead. It hadn't been his intent when he reached for her. Or maybe it had. She'd been on his mind constantly, day and night. At night, as he lay looking up at the same starry sky that covered her, his thoughts had been quite graphic.

Touching her ceased being enough. He wanted to taste her and watch the change in her eyes as he slowly worked up to burying himself deep inside her.

Hayley felt his transformation at about the same time as he recognized exactly where they were headed. Jake had started at the neck of her jumper, unbuttoning the long row of buttons that traversed the length. Though her cheeks grew hot, Hayley tried to ease from his hold without making a big deal of it. "You have magic hands," she murmured, catching them before he exposed her breasts. Breasts swollen and more tender in recent weeks. She'd had to dispense with wearing bras.

Jake brought her scraped fingers to his lips. He tasted

his way up the inside of her arm, pausing at the elbow.
"I saw you rubbing your back. Come stand under the
waterfall with me. The water's warm and it'll help me
do a better job of getting the kinks out. I'll lend a hand
washing your hair, too," he said, swishing her long braid
around to the front where she could see the bits of dried
mud clinging to the ends. A chunk fell off and went
down the open front of her jumper.

She pulled back, wadding the gaping edges of material
into one hand. "We can't get naked together, Jake."

"Mind telling me why not?" His liquid gaze heated
another trail up her body.

"Because...because it's still daylight, for one thing,"
she sputtered.

"Yeah. So...?" He smiled crookedly as he ran his
index finger down her cherry-red cheek and over the
indignant quiver of her lower lip. Bending, he let his
tongue trace the path his finger had taken. "A guy kind
of likes to see the woman he loves looking the way
nature made her," he said huskily, his breath tickling
her skin.

Hayley sucked in a hot puff of air so fast she choked
as it seared her lungs. "Have you...have you been drinking?" she asked in a strangled voice.

"You're the one acting weird." Frowning, he
thumped her solidly on the back.

Indeed, she probably was, Hayley thought as her head
reeled and spun, and her legs went rubbery, forcing her
to flop into the lawn chair. "You might have heatstroke," she muttered under her breath. "Or else you
accidentally chewed locoweed."

Jake knelt in front of her and spanned her hips with
both hands. "It just dawned on me what I said. I swear
I'm not in the habit of tossing the *L*-word around, Hay-

ley. I wouldn't say it just to get you out of your clothes.
You've gotta believe me, it's what I feel. I want to go
to bed with you at night, yes, and wake up with you in
the morning. Now, and when you're eighty. But that's
only part of it. Damn, I'm not good with words.''

She scooted her chair out of his reach. With fingers
that shook, she tried restoring her buttons.

One look at the pale cleavage, creamier by far than
her exposed suntanned skin, made Jake hard again. It
didn't seem to matter—to him, anyway—that he obviously had stronger feelings for Hayley than she had for
him. He must be in love or he wouldn't have made that
declaration she'd refuted. He'd lusted after other women.
Never had he mistaken those feelings for love. Jake was
reasonably sure this was the real thing.

A thought struck him as he watched her fumble with
the button just below her breasts. Scrambling closer on
his knees, he batted her fingers away and slipped the
button carefully through the buttonhole. "Is it the
baby?'' he asked earnestly.

"Is what the baby?'' Hayley shivered, although sweat
popped out on her forehead. She wished he'd stop this
assault on her senses.

"I can love another man's baby. It won't make any
difference, I swear. I know I didn't mention the baby
when I said I wanted to be with you. I assumed you'd
understand it went without saying that I want you both.''
As if to prove the point, Jake caressed her stomach and
kissed it. He was surprised to discover how much the
bulge had expanded in the weeks he'd been away. As
he marveled, a tiny foot or elbow smacked him in the
nose. Amazement spread through them both, bringing
them closer for a moment. They stared at each other and

enjoyed the interlude, neither remembering that four buttons of Hayley's jumper remained open.

Which wouldn't have made a difference if Eden Cooper hadn't wheeled into the clearing in her gleaming Cherokee and hopped out in a cloud of dust. Her precipitous appearance caught them disheveled and flustered.

She skirted boxes and jumped over piles of stone, breathing fast when she finally arrived at their side. "What happened? Did Hayley faint? Oh, God, she hasn't gone into early labor, has she?"

By the time his sister-in-law loomed over them, Jake and Hayley had sprung apart. Their faces had gone pale. It wasn't until a minute later, when no one jumped in with answers, that Eden recognized the expressions they wore as guilt. She slapped a flat palm to her forehead. "I, ah, I'm interrupting, aren't I?"

Jake saw a blushing Hayley fumbling to fix her jumper. He rose and quickly placed himself between the two women, allowing Hayley her privacy. "What in hell are you doing here, Eden? Has something gone wrong at the ranch? Did Dad get hurt again?" he thundered.

"No. Didn't Hayley tell you about Nell's and my visit? Or that I took some of her ore samples to have them assayed?"

He acted as if she was speaking a foreign language. Eden snapped her fingers in front of his face. "Hel-lo. Nell said you asked her to visit Hayley. I realize I wasn't part of the equation." Her lips twitched in a grin. "I heard you mention opals before you made your grand exit the night of the barbecue. You should know it's like waving a red flag at a bull. I had to see her discovery for myself."

Hayley struggled to rise from the low-slung chair.

"This is only Wednesday. We'd set Friday as the day you might have news. I planned to drive over to the Triple C in the afternoon. You have bad news, don't you?" She looked stricken. Accepting Jake's help, she'd finally managed to stand, but her pinched lips reflected her disappointment.

"Not bad news at all," Eden declared, reaching to grip Hayley's arm. "The news is good. Great, in fact. All the tests show the opal to be a good grade. The most important test was one I had to farm out to a geologist I know—which is why I'm here early. He knew from the makeup of the dirt and surrounding rock attached to the sample that the ore was mined locally. I'm afraid he'll stir up interest among local gem-hunters, even though I asked him not to say anything. It might only be a process of elimination before someone connects these opals to your recorded site."

"Why should it matter?" Jake and Hayley asked in unison.

"Hayley needs to go to the recorder's office and list the discovery of valuable mineral deposits on her claim. Then if anyone accidentally or purposely crosses her vein, she can legally prosecute them." She turned to Hayley. "You don't have to use the term *opal.* Call it cristobalite. It's a term for opals rarely used outside of Australia. A person would have to be a seasoned opal hunter to recognize what you had."

Hayley sat again, hard, and feeling dazed, she looped her arms around the dog's neck. She remained mute until he bathed her cheek with his rough tongue. "I can't seem to comprehend anything beyond the fact that you verified the legitimacy of my find. I hate to sound mercenary, but I have to think about feeding and clothing my baby this winter. Is my opal worth anywhere near the amount you mentioned during your last visit?'' An outflung arm encompassed her collection of rocks.

''More.'' A smiling Eden leaned down so she could meet Hayley's eyes. ''The stone is so high-grade that even if you sell only to me and come here to dig once a year, you and your baby will be able to live comfortably for years. Probably until the field plays out. As opals typically form over quite a large radius in areas that were once basin lakes, it might behoove you to do some research and extend your claim.''

''Great!'' Jake yanked Eden upright. ''The Cattlemen's Association is hunting ways to kick her off this land, and you're recommending she encroach on Westin's leased range.''

Eden presented a stubborn jaw. ''He's leasing the land for grazing, not mining. But if word gets out before Hayley files the appropriate changes, I wouldn't put it past Westin to file his own mineral claim ''

''It doesn't matter,'' Hayley broke in. ''To make a trip to the recorder's, I'd have to leave what I'm doing. Someone could jump my claim while I'm gone.''

Jake's brows drew together. ''I wasn't suggesting you not protect what's already yours. I just don't want you to face off against guys like Westin and maybe get yourself hurt. Hell, I'll stay here and guard the place. Let Eden drive you to the courthouse in the morning. Fast as she drives, you ought to be back before noon.''

''Are you insinuating I have a lead foot?'' Eden punched his arm.

''Dillon's the one who told me you have a drawerful of speeding tickets and you got a letter from Motor Vehicles asking you to come to Phoenix to review your driving record.''

''That was a long time ago. Right after I got my

driver's license. My dad, bless his heart, felt that if Dillon was going to marry me, he deserved to know all my faults. Of course, he'll tell you he was trying to scare Dillon off.''

"Could be true. As I recall, your dad wasn't keen on your dating cowboys.''

"The very same man who griped about me graduating with an art degree. He insisted that all artists starve.''

Jake turned to Hayley. "Did I tell you Eden has jewelers all over the world fighting to sell her designs? You couldn't have found a better outlet for your opals.''

"You're the one who made it all possible. Heaven only knows how long it would've taken me to find a market if you hadn't asked your mom to drop by. Why did you, by the way?'' She gave him a blank stare.

"Because I...well, you wouldn't listen when I said you shouldn't be out here by yourself. I thought she might be more convincing. Boy, was I wrong. She and Eden set you on a breakneck course to become a millionaire.'' He glared at his sister-in-law.

She arched a brow and smiled wickedly. "So what were *you* offering her, Jacob?''

His eyes glittered darkly. "What do you mean, what was I offering her?''

Eden inspected a polished fingernail. "A little bird told me you're pressing Wade about building a house on your acreage. It occurs to me that a woman and baby need a solid roof over their heads.''

Jake knew very well that Eden was trying to provoke him into revealing the extent of his involvement with Hayley. Even though the idea of marriage had planted itself in his mind, he hadn't reached the point of discussing it with her. Jake would be damned if he'd let her learn something so important secondhand—or in front of an audience.

"You're on a fishing expedition, Mrs. Nosybody, and it'll get you nowhere. I hate to think what label you'd paste on me if I didn't show a little concern for a woman stuck out on her own here. More than once I suggested she use the ranch as home base. Ask her what she thought of *that* idea."

Hayley wrinkled her nose. "Don't argue, you two." It was plain that Eden assumed she and Jake had a romantic relationship. And equally plain that Jake was backpedaling for all he was worth. Hayley felt a yawning pit opening in the bottom of her stomach. She shouldn't let it affect her, she'd known Jake hadn't meant it when he said he loved her. How could he mean it? He barely knew her. Besides, it'd be a few months before her divorce from Joe was final. Hadn't jumping into that marriage been the lesson of a lifetime for her?

Jake stood by silently and watched steely resolve replace the vulnerability in Hayley's beautiful eyes. He felt helpless to try to rectify her misconceptions here in front of his sister-in-law. For one thing, he wasn't that sure of himself around Hayley. She'd rebuffed all his offers so far. Even if she seemed to fall under his spell when he kissed her, she got over it quickly enough when the kissing ended. While there was a lot to be said for physical compatibility, Jake didn't fool himself into thinking it could hold a marriage together. A good marriage needed more substantial glue, like friendship and respect, as well as good sex.

"You ladies go ahead and take off," he said. "Spend the night in Tubac and hit the recorder's office in Nogales tomorrow. Eden, if you wouldn't mind swinging past the ranch, would you roust Dillon on the mobile

phone? Tell him what's going on. I promised I'd turn
the water into the spillway, then scour Vulture's Roost
for strays tomorrow morning. Tell him it'll be afternoon.''

"It'd be better if you went with Hayley," Eden told
him. "I'll ride Mojave to the ranch. Bright and early
tomorrow I'll get Nell to bring me back. The two of us
can load the bed of her Range Rover with this ore. That
way, if anyone does chance by, there'll be nothing to
show you've found anything worthwhile. I'll weigh it at
the shop and write Hayley a check. Then I can start
cutting and polishing. Which is what I really want to
do.''

Jake deferred to Hayley. "It's your call." Seeing Hayley hesitate, Jake pulled her aside and lowered his voice.
"Is Eden moving too fast? She has a tendency to run in
high gear, especially in matters related to her jewelry
designs.''

Eden, who'd overheard her brother-in-law, looked
chagrined for all of two seconds. "We're approaching
the main tourist season. The sooner I get some opal
pieces on the market, the sooner we'll know if I'm right
about this venture making a profit for both Hayley and
me. But if you don't trust me to weigh this without
you—''

"It's not that." Hayley cut her off. "I wondered if I
could help polish the stones. My grandfather left some
lapidary equipment with a friend. If whoever takes me
will circle through Tombstone, I could collect the tumbler. If I dug ore during the day and polished stones at
night, it'd speed up the process.''

Eden paced among the piles of ore, inspecting indi-
vidual pieces here and there. "I'd need to run a few
additional tests. The early samples stood up well and

didn't fracture or crumble. But opal's delicate. Some jewelry-makers fill the cracks with a type of silicone. That reduces the value of a piece. And it won't stand up under the scrutiny of a well-trained appraiser. I'd never use fill. My signature on a piece means quality. If this opal is touchy, I'll have to handle the polishing phase myself.''

"Of course." Hayley linked her hands and dropped her gaze. "I wasn't suggesting that we cut corners. Forget I said anything."

Eden swung round. "No, don't apologize. I'm amenable to your offer. In fact, I've been considering hiring an apprentice, someone I'd teach cutting and polishing. My time is better spent designing and working with the silver and platinum settings. If you decide to stay around here, Hayley, you may fit the bill."

"Stay around here, how? You mean live in Tubac? I don't know I've heard it's a really expensive place to rent or buy property. Tombstone or Bisbee would be less expensive"

Eden wasn't subtle about jamming her elbow in Jake's ribs. "I meant…like settle on the Triple C."

Hayley's face colored. So did Jake's. He recovered first and hissed, "Mind your own business, Eden."

Jumpier than a frog on a hot skillet, Hayley set about dousing her campfire. "It's getting late. Hadn't we better go, Eden? I don't know anyone who'd put us up for the night, and motels in Tombstone fill up fast this time of year. Oh, if we're making the circle trip, would you mind swinging by Dr. Gerrard's office?" Her gaze remained on Eden.

"Is something wrong?" Jake and Eden asked together.

"Not that I know of," Hayley mumbled. "If it's too much trouble, I'll skip it."

"No, you won't." Jake made the decision and then, declared he'd be the one escorting Hayley. "Eden, tell Dillon I'm taking the whole day off. The doctor will need to work Hayley in."

"Gerrard's winding down his practice," Hayley said. "He's never that busy. Old-timers in the area still go to him. Newcomers prefer the younger doctors. Dr. Gerrard delivered me—and my mother. He knew Tombstone in its heyday."

"Is he competent?" Jake asked.

"What? You think he bounced me on my head?" Hayley laughed.

"Very funny. Not all deliveries are routine. Ask me," Jake said. "I've run into some dicey situations during calving season."

Hayley flexed her arm. "I'm healthier than a horse."

"And more stubborn than a mule," Jake said wryly. "Come on, grab a change of clothes and climb into Eden's rig. Let's get this show on the road. Eden, you'll feed Mojave and Charcoal, I presume?"

She nodded on her way to adjust the stirrups.

The minute they buckled in and drove off, Hayley felt tongue-tied. Where bantering had seemed easy around the campfire, now Jake was too close and seemed far too male. She cast about for a safe subject. "The Cooper men must be so proud of Eden and your mom."

"Why is that?" Jake asked, unexpectedly ejected from thoughts centering on the woman seated beside him. He enjoyed the feel of them driving off together— as if they were already a married couple.

"Are you kidding? They're talented and intelligent and beautiful."

"So are you."

Jake glanced up from the washboard tracks he was doing his best to take slowly. "You sound as though you think they're something you're not."

Her eyes met his ever so briefly, then she paid an inordinate amount of interest to the passing scenery, shadowed by the lowering sun. "I appreciate your trying to bolster my ego, Jake. But I'm nowhere near their league."

"Hogwash!"

Hayley shook her head. "As nice as your mother was to come visit and knit me a gorgeous baby blanket, she'd just as soon I disappeared. Please assure her I have no intention of inveigling my way into the Cooper family circle."

"Did my mom hurt your feelings? It was about the harvest dance, wasn't it? She wants me to take that quilter, Lisa. I said I was inviting you. It's a big event, weekend before Thanksgiving. To celebrate cutting the winter wheat. Say you'll go with me."

"I don't dance. I never learned how." Hayley was embarrassed to admit it. "That's what I'm trying to tell you, Jake. I have no talent. I barely finished high school. Look at the way I dress, compared to your mom and Eden. I'd never fit into their crowd. Or yours. Ask someone to the dance who does."

Her jaw was so tense Jake knew arguing served no purpose. They talked little after that. It was quite late by the time they reached Tombstone.

When he'd first thought about accompanying her, Jake had imagined them sharing a room. He stopped at the first motel with a vacancy sign and without asking booked them each a single. She thanked him and refused his offer to take her out for a meal. "I'm exhausted," was her excuse.

"Dammit," he growled. "You need nourishment."

"I was tired before we left. Bracing myself against that unpaved road sapped any energy I had. Let's meet for breakfast at seven. We'll go to the café where Dr. Gerrard eats every morning. That way, we'll know early if he can see me, and when."

Jake didn't like her edict, but she did look weary and he hadn't the heart to make a fuss. He skipped eating, too. And slept poorly, thanks to all the thoughts that kept running through his head.

Nor was he in the best of moods when they met in the lobby the next morning and he discovered Hayley had canceled his credit card for her room. "Why?" he demanded. "It's no crime to be short of cash. If you feel you have to pay me back, by the time the bill comes, you'll have money from your mine."

"Shh." She put a finger to her lips as the motel clerk stopped what he was doing and cocked an ear.

Jake gave the clerk a dirty look before he led Hayley out to the car. He thought she seemed more rested today—and really pretty in a violet maternity jumper he'd never seen her wear. It brought out the lavender flecks in her eyes. He was on the verge of complimenting her, but the moment passed as she scolded him for mentioning her mine.

Clamming up, Jake drove the few blocks to the café. Their entry into the establishment stopped talk. Hayley paused beside Dr. Gerrard, who was seated at the counter. She got her appointment—and some unwelcome news.

The doctor wadded his napkin as he spoke in hushed tones. "Joe blew back into town last week." The old doctor trained suspicious eyes on Jake, who hovered near Hayley, a proprietary hand settled low on her back.

He felt the ripple of alarm that shook Hayley. Jake thought for a minute that she was going to bolt. Instead, she took a deep breath and let it out slowly. She seemed calmer after Jake had moved his hand to her shoulder and squeezed.

"Joe's whereabouts don't concern me," she told Gerrard. "Our divorce will be final soon." Catching Jake's hand, she led him to the center of the room, to the only open table. But in a few minutes the buzz of normal conversation resumed around them and he relaxed.

The waitress added to the news about Ryan when she took their orders. "You'd probably like to know what I heard on good authority—Cindy Trent fleeced Joe after she hooked up with some guy she knew from Vegas. Joe showed up here, figuring you'd take him back. Ha! As if you would, considering what he did." The woman flashed Jake an admiring grin. "Looks like you've done all right, honey," she said, nudging Hayley. "Serves Joe right. But you take care. That man's trouble. He's hanging out with Deputy Dawg again. You know who I mean, Shad Tilford." The waitress ripped the order off her pad and started away. Suddenly her steps faltered. "Speak of the devil and his sidekick. Look who walked in and lowered the caliber of our clientele."

Jake, who sat facing the door, saw two men threading their way through the tables. One had greasy black hair and beady eyes. He wore a badge and a holstered weapon. The other had blond hair. His unshaven upper lip needed more hair to pass as a mustache. In Jake's estimation, Ryan could use a beard to hide a weak chin.

His stomach took a drop when Hayley turned, spotted

the duo, and looked as if she'd faint. "Steady," he murmured, holding one of her hands tightly.

It was Joe who hitched up his pants and swaggered over to confront Hayley. "Well, well. Rafferty over at the Holiday Inn said you'd found yourself a new stud. What's this about another mine?" The pale blue eyes were nasty. "That kid they say you're carrying can't be mine. Hell, I didn't hardly snap my fingers and you fell into my bed. But by law, babe, we're still married. If ol' Ben left you another mine, half belongs to me."

Jake would have punched Joe Ryan before he finished spreading his bullshit if he hadn't wanted to know more about the bastard's plans concerning Hayley. But he felt bad for waiting, because Hayley gave a low keening sound, like a wounded animal.

Leaping from his chair, Jake's knuckles crunched against the sparse hairs of Joe's mustache, meeting resistance at feral white teeth.

Hayley screamed and slumped forward as Joe went airborne and landed two feet away, crumpled at the feet of a fast-stepping waitress who dropped two orders of eggs and one of pancakes over the felled man.

Shad Tilford lunged for Jake but crashed to the floor as he tripped over a size-twelve boot someone slid across his path. Spitting and fuming, he made dire threats about arresting Jake for assault. "I'll throw your ass in jail!" he bellowed.

Dr. Gerrard moved fast for an old man. He sidestepped Joe's prone form and in a low authoritative voice ordered Jake to bring Hayley to his office. Her friends in the room cleared a pathway to the door. Jake wasn't sure if it was by accident or design that patrons formed a body blockade to keep the furious deputy inside the café.

In the doctor's waiting room, Jake paced. Gerrard's receptionist, Esther, provided Jake with the whole story of the Ryan courtship and subsequent marriage, and Joe's infidelity with the woman from the nail-painting place. What could Jake do but listen?

Esther hinted that Joe was responsible for Ben O'Dell's early demise. Even then, she wasn't quite finished. "That no-good Joe Ryan wouldn't have found out a thing about Hayley's new mine if that snake, Shad Tilford, hadn't strong-armed good folks in town to notify him if she ever showed up. Since Joe's return, he and Shad have been thick as thieves. Too bad you brought Hayley to town, young man. Might be best if you skedaddled out the back way. Shad's watching the front. I doubt he knows the clinic has a back exit. I'll call a couple of miners who used to work for Ben. They'll create a diversion long enough for me to pull your Cherokee into the alley."

Jake declined her offer. It tasted like cowardice. Slinking off with his tail tucked between his legs wasn't how he operated. But one look at Hayley's wan face and huge eyes bruised with pain, and he changed his mind. He gave Esther the okay. Within twenty minutes he and Hayley were burning up the highway out of town.

Hayley sat so quiet and withdrawn Jake felt a shiver of apprehension. "The doctor didn't find anything wrong with the baby, did he?"

She idly smoothed a hand over her stomach. "The doctor said everything's on track."

"That's good. Why aren't you happier?"

Fear choked the life from Hayley's eyes. "Someone provided Dr. Gerrard with a running commentary on what Joe said after he came to. He's going to sue me for half the mine. If he files before our divorce is final, all my work will be in vain. I'll just get shafted again.''

"I won't let that happen!" Jake exploded. "It's my fault for mentioning it at the motel. Anyway, he's got to find the Blue Cameo first. That ought to give us time to bleed the damned vein dry. I'll skip the rest of roundup and help you dig.''

"Like your dad'll let you do that. He already wants me gone. I wouldn't put it past him and your brother to lead Joe straight to me so they can make a deal with him for the land.''

"I guarantee that they wouldn't. Not that it matters, since the claim is solely in your name. In the eyes of the state, there's not a damn thing that asshole you married can do about it. Free claims transfer to family by different rules than mines on land a person actually owns.''

She sat for a minute and studied the rhythmic flexing of Jake's stubborn jaw. "I'll fight my own battles, Jake. I want you to stay out of it.''

A numbness invaded his chest. Eden's Cherokee weaved from side to side as he left the two-lane highway and merged onto the freeway.

"Slow down, Jake! My life may not be the best, but I'm not ready to die.''

"Can't prove it by me," Jake snapped, mostly because she'd hurt him with her curt reply. "The danger you're in—staying out in the middle of nowhere all alone—hasn't changed.''

"I *am* alone," she raged back.

"You don't have to be. I said I want to be there for you, Hayley.''

Her resolve wavered for a second. Not long enough to give Jake hope. In a gritty passionate voice, she lashed out, "I trusted a man's promises once. They turned out to be silver-plated lies."

"If you mean Joe Ryan, he's no man." Jake's denouncement of her ex-husband rang out bitterly. The truth didn't seem to matter, at least not when it came to healing the rift between him and Hayley. She only looked scornful, and her comparison of him to that bastard felt worse to Jake than a slap. All he wanted at the moment was to get shut of her. He wished now that he'd let Eden do the honors and make this trip with Hayley.

CHAPTER TEN

UPDATING HAYLEY'S CLAIM report went without a hitch. The clerk at the recorder's office was more interested in popping her gum and talking on the phone than in paying attention to what Hayley put down as her most recent findings. Not wanting to take any chances, Hayley used the term Eden had suggested rather than mentioning opals by name. If Joe did hunt for her mine, she wanted to make it hard for him to figure out what she'd found at the Blue Cameo. Hayley couldn't shake the fear that he'd do everything in his power to claim what he'd already declared was his rightful share.

Even though talk between Jake and Hayley was still strained, he insisted they eat lunch in Nogales before returning to her camp. "We missed dinner last night and breakfast today, thanks to your ex. My stomach is near caved into my backbone. I'm not driving another mile without eating."

"That suits me. I'm famished, too. Have been since we left Tombstone. But you looked so grim I didn't want to ask any favors."

"If I'm grim, it's because I don't appreciate being lumped in the same category as that SOB you married."

"When did I do any such thing? You're nothing like him. I screamed when you hit him, but he had the local law backing him up. I was afraid Tilford would shoot you."

"I'm talking about later. It sure sounded like that's what you meant when you said that jerk fed you lies and now you won't trust *me*."

"I'm sorry," she said, lowering her lashes as Jake got into the drive-through line at a fast-food restaurant. "I guess it makes no sense to say my comments weren't aimed at you, but more at the promises you keep tossing around."

"You're right. It makes no sense." Jake drummed his fingers on the steering wheel.

Hayley bristled. "Look, Joe made the right promises, too. He just didn't keep them."

"So we're back to that. I'll have you know my word is good."

"I don't want to argue with you, Jake. Are you going to order? We've reached the speakerphone."

"You always make me forget what I'm doing," he said irritably. "What would you like?" She made her selections. Jake got huffy again when she pulled out her money and tried to pay her portion of the bill.

"Would you buy Eden's lunch?" she said, throwing the money down on the seat between them.

"Not as a rule. If Dillon's there, he pays for them. Times I'm in town by myself and I meet my mom and Eden for lunch, we go dutch. Generally those two carry more cash than I do." A dimple appeared in one of his cheeks.

"See." Hayley opened her milk carton and drank from it. "You admit to allowing them equal power. You don't assume they need to be cared for. Well, neither do I. I'm just as capable of providing for myself and my baby. I don't need anyone."

"Dammit, Hayley, if you don't beat all at twisting words to suit your purpose. Oh, never mind." Jake bit into his burger and muttered something dark and unrecognizable around the mouthful of beef and cheese. The milk painting Hayley's upper lip begged to be licked off. It was all he could do to look away.

She barely nibbled at the chicken she'd ordered, even after proclaiming to be famished. "Jeez, just eat," Jake said with a sigh. "Consider the subject closed."

Proving he was a man of his word, he steered their conversation to impersonal things. On the drive he pointed out a series of sun-blistered fields belonging to ranches bordering the Triple C. Jake lamented the ever-increasing need for measurable rainfall.

"I've noticed the spring isn't refilling as fast now as it did when you showed me how to open the valves. Has it ever gone completely dry?" Hayley asked worriedly.

"Five years ago it came close. The monsoons weren't just late, they blew past Arizona altogether. That year the J & B doubled their herd—a move that prompted Dad to speak to Ben about eventually acquiring his site. Ben agreed, but said he felt in his bones that the Blue Cameo would produce. He was the one who suggested the valve system. At the time it seemed the best and cheapest compromise."

"Isn't it still?" At Jake's arched brow, Hayley elaborated. "The men from the Cattlemen's Association who paid me a visit were antsy even before it became apparent there'd be a shortage of rain. Weren't they crying wolf? I mean, you said the system's been in place and working for five years."

"Yes, but all the valley ranchers have added to their herds. They had to or go under, the way beef prices have fallen these last few years."

Hayley sighed. "Everything always boils down to dollars and cents."

''My theory is there's enough to go around if no one ranch gets greedy.'' Jake's thoughts centered on John Westin and the rumor that he'd expanded his operation yet again. This time through leasing land in his daughter's name.

Hayley murmured agreement, her mind pulsing with Joe's threat to sue for half of her mine. Joe Ryan was lazy and greedy. A dangerous combination. ''I suppose I should be happier with the news that Cindy Trent fleeced Joe. Turnabout is fair play, and he deserved it. Except that doesn't help me gain restitution. If Shad Tilford tracks Cindy down, he and Joe will split any money that's left.'' She paused. ''You know what hurts worse than losing the proceeds from Gramps's mine? Joe telling people in Tombstone this isn't his baby.''

She looked so downcast that Jake rallied, ''Boy, we sure know how to pick depressing subjects. All this started because I mentioned a lack of rain. And I've seen some wet Novembers in the past.''

''If that's the case, I'd better speed up the digging. The vein of opal is situated in a ravine I suspect feeds the waterfall during heavy rains. The more rough opal I stockpile, the more secure I'll feel.''

Looking at her sitting there so small yet so determined to go it alone and beat the odds tripped a chord in Jake. A chord relighting the flame of desire he'd thought snuffed out during their earlier argument. Only this time he wasn't going to announce his feelings or restate his promise to help her dig. It could take a few days to clear things with his dad and Dillon, and he didn't want Hayley thinking he'd made a promise he wouldn't keep. No, what he'd do was show up and pitch in after he had his arrangements in place.

He knew exactly how he felt about her now. And he

knew he'd have another chat with his dad about clearing the property where he planned to build a house—for Hayley and for him. Of course he'd have to chip away at her barriers a little at a time. Perhaps, though, she'd believe he was serious if she actually saw progress on the building, and knew he really wanted to provide a home for her and the baby.

"Goodness, the clearing looks naked!" Hayley exclaimed as Jake topped the rise above her campsite.

He jammed on the brake, ripped headlong out of his plans for the future. "Were you robbed, you mean?"

Hayley gripped the dash with both hands. "No, silly. Eden and your mom must have transported all my samples. Oh, look. They left Charcoal to guard the place. How sweet. Would you consider letting him stay with me, Jake? I feel safer when he's here." With a guilty expression, she stammered, "I'll understand if you refuse. After all, I said I didn't need anything from anybody. I know you're still angry with me."

Jake let the vehicle roll down the slope. Killing the engine, he unsnapped his belt and moved toward Hayley. While she was confined by her belt, he leaned close and feathered kisses over both of her eyes and the tip of her nose. Then he gently nipped her bottom lip. "Something you need to know about the Coopers. We have a low flashpoint, but we're not ones to hold grudges."

She sighed, opening her eyes and lifting a hand to touch his cheek. "I'd feel horrid if I ruined our friendship, Jake. I'll need friends if I'm to consider staying in the area and apprenticing to Eden as she suggested."

Jake's breath caught. His heart clenched. He wanted more than mere friendship, dammit. But as he gazed into her still-wary eyes, he realized that this was a significant step. Asking to keep his dog was a start, however miserly. And he'd have to go slow if he ever hoped to win her love.

"Friends it is. Shall we cut our wrists and bind them together?" He grinned lazily.

His teasing apparently hit the right tone.

"The sight of blood makes me sick, Jacob. I doubt that comes as any great surprise, considering how fast I blacked out when you slugged Joe and blood spurted from his nose." She unbuckled her seat belt, picked up the satchel that held her dirty clothes and slid out of the Cherokee. "I cheered you on, even if I don't hold with violence."

Jake blocked her from closing the door. "This from the lady who took a potshot at me?"

"Are you blaming me for protecting myself? Men think they have a right to use muscles or kisses to overpower a woman. Well, they don't. *You* don't."

"I backed off, Hayley. There are men, of course, who wouldn't. Those same men might turn your gun on you. Sometimes it's smarter to hide or just plain climb in your truck and flee. Promise me you'll do that if need be."

"You mean if Joe shows up to jump my claim, don't you? I'm supposed to tuck my tail between my legs and let him take it? No, Jake, I won't."

"Dammit, Hayley. No amount of opals is worth putting your life or your baby's life in danger. You've recorded your find. There are legal avenues to beat Joe."

"Tell that to someone who believes in fairy tales. He forged my name on the sale papers for the Silver Cloud. He walked off with seven-eighths of the money. The law said it was his right as my husband. So much for your legal avenues."

"Shad Tilford does not speak for the real law in this

state. You have my word, Hayley. Joe won't get away with stealing from you again.''

Hayley wanted to believe him. The thought of Joe playing her for a fool twice frightened her. A rare sliver of luck had allowed her to land on her feet. But luck and Hayley Ryan weren't best buddies. ''Here we are, Jake, arguing over something that may never come to pass. I have work to do before the sun sets. As do you. So long, and stop worrying. I'll be fine. You said yourself it won't be easy for Joe to find the Blue Cameo even if he stumbles onto the recorder's files.''

''I said that, yes.'' Jake only wished he was as sure of that fact as he'd let on.

''Well, then.'' Hayley smiled softly as she circled a palm over her swollen belly. ''Junior and I will be right as rain. Speaking of rain, aren't there a lot of black clouds moving in?'' She squinted up at the darkening sky.

Hunching down to peer out the windshield, Jake saw she'd spoken the truth. ''Damn, I wish I didn't have to leave you alone. Heed your own advice and stop digging if those clouds do open up and dump on us.''

''I will. Jake, if you're headed to the Triple C to collect Mojave, would you mind taking a minute to call Eden and let her know I'm back?''

''Will do. I'm telling her to buy us tickets to the harvest dance, too. I don't care if you can't dance—I'm taking you.'' Jake shut the door, buckled himself in and threw the Cherokee into reverse.

He didn't want to admit that Hayley had scared him, talking about Joe's criminal traits. Jake intended to do more than notify Eden of their return and ask her to buy dance tickets. He planned to speak with his father about releasing him from his duties at the roundup. In view of Joe's threat, Hayley needed a full-time bodyguard.

The dark clouds had begun to roll with thunder and dance with heat lightning by the time Jake drove the Cherokee through the gates of the Triple C.

Wade Cooper glanced up from tying a tan slicker over a bedroll that spanned the broad rump of his favorite mare. He waited impatiently for Jake to alight. "About time you quit fiddledee-fartin' around the countryside with that fool woman and remembered it's getting our steers to market that pays your bills, as well as ours."

Jake froze, his hackles instantly raised. "Actually I came by to tell you I'm going back to help Hayley dig as many opals as possible before bad weather sets in. Dock my share of the profits from this sale, if it'll make you feel better. I already rounded up more than half the damned strays."

"Now they're *all* strays," his father roared. "I just got off the mobile with Dillon. A big clap of thunder spooked the herd. They scattered nine ways from Sunday. We need every hand we have to track them down. That includes you." He jabbed a finger in Jake's chest.

"A stampede?" Jake's jaw went slack.

"Has playing Romeo made you deaf? Throw a leg over Mojave and let's make tracks."

"You go on ahead. I promised Hayley I'd phone Eden."

"The hell with that. I already called your mom. Jacob, quit letting that little bloodsucker lead you by the nose. Before you know it, she'll have you convinced to move her lock, stock and barrel into our house."

Eyes narrowed dangerously, Jake cut his gelding out of the corral. As he slung a saddle on Mojave's back and cinched it tight, he said in a deadly quiet voice, "I'll thank you to keep a civil tongue any time you mention the woman I plan to marry.'' His sudden glimpse into the future shocked even Jake. An idea took shape in his head. He clearly knew his next step. "I won't be bringing Hayley to the Triple C. After I round up the herd, I'm coming home and calling Carl Brown, that architect who designed Dillon's house. I want my own finished by December. I want to marry Hayley before she has the baby.''

"December? Holy hell!'' Wade almost spooked his own mount with his shout. His face turned beet-red as he hopped around with one foot in his stirrup. By the time he finally managed to drag himself into the saddle, his scowl was more formidable than the low-riding clouds. "I told Nell not to visit that Ryan woman, I knew it'd only encourage your foolish interest in her. Marry her? You hardly know the woman. Do you hear what you're saying? It wasn't six months ago everyone in the valley laid bets on how soon you and John Westin's daughter would be booking a church.''

"I dated Ginalyn twice. Maybe three times,'' Jake said, getting as red in the face as his father. "She's spoiled as sin. Hayley Ryan is a hundred—no, a thousand times more woman.'' Vaulting into his saddle, Jake clattered off without waiting for Wade to chew on his ear any longer.

Jake had the faster stronger horse. He managed to stay ahead of Wade until they got into rough terrain. Then the surefooted mare came into her own and drew abreast of Mojave. Together, father and son flushed eight or so bewildered-looking steers bearing the Triple C brand from a thicket of greasewood. Jake unlooped a lariat and swung it back and forth to try to head the cattle in the right direction.

Hearing steers bawling in the distance, Wade rode over the next rise. He had ten more head on the move when Jake rejoined him.

"Where's that cow dog of yours?" Wade asked. "He'd keep these strays on track and leave you and me free to hunt down the remaining delinquents."

"I left Charcoal with Hayley. By the way," he added, changing the subject. "Did you know Eden's offered to buy everything Hayley's mine can produce?"

"The lot of you encouraged her. If you'd let things be and hadn't taken her milk and garden greens, likely the little gal would've pulled up stakes by now. But no, my own family facilitated her operation, even though every last one of you knew I've been dickering for years to acquire that property."

"Don't forget the chickens I gave her."

Wade seared his son with a scowl.

"I was being facetious," Jake informed his dad. "But what's the big deal? Hayley's agreed to the same water arrangement you negotiated with Ben."

"Hell, Jake. I didn't want to spout off out of turn. All I have is an unsubstantiated rumor. When I collected our last stock check, Charlie Goodall, a rancher I know from Phoenix, asked what we thought down here of John Westin hobnobbing with developers."

"Developers?" To a rancher, *developer* was a scary word, too often synonymous with resorts and golf courses. It generally meant the demise of the government land ranchers leased to graze large herds. "Are you sure this Goodall didn't mistake John's chat with the governor on behalf of the co-op's water interests as a move to develop?"

Wade rubbed a thumb over a stubbled jaw. "Charlie sat near John's party at lunch. He knows who attended that meeting and what he heard. He'd have no reason to lie. Marshall Rogers from the Rocking R was hip-deep in it, too. I know for a fact that for the last two years he's made noises about selling out.''

''Are you going to confront John at the next cattlemen's meeting?''

''Not knowing the extent of his backing, I'm almost afraid to. What I need is control over the spring. Without a water source, the developers will back out.''

''Right now Hayley controls the water. So I can't understand why you aren't treating her more nicely.''

''She controls the mineral rights. Not water. Westin could make a case to the governor that the valley ranchers need the water rights split off from the mineral rights. It could happen as fast as that.'' He snapped his fingers.

Jake finished his father's thought. ''And if John's convinced a majority of our neighbors to go along with his scheme, he's nabbed a pot of gold. The Triple C either capitulates and sells to the developer, or we're eventually squeezed out.''

''That's about the size of it.''

''I can't believe John would be so sneaky. If he's of a mind to sell the J & B, why set Ginalyn up with a spread of her own?''

Wade scrammed three steers out of a thicket of mesquite. ''I figure it's a smokescreen for those of us not in on his racket. Think about it. A few of us have been on John's case for bringing in too much new stock and overgrazing the leased rangeland. I always suspected the guy was a wheeler-dealer out to make big bucks.''

''So you're saying Westin's depleted the rangeland and now plans to sell and make an even bigger killing on the property?''

''Much as I hate it, that's my theory.''

Jake charged off after a stubborn yearling bull who objected to being brought into the small herd they'd mustered. "Then it seems to me," he said, out of breath when he returned, "that'd be in the best interests of the Triple C for me to stick close to Hayley's operation. Won't John think twice about pulling any shenanigans if I'm on-site?"

They rounded up several more strays before Wade responded. "My druthers, plain and simple, is for you to talk that gal into revoking her claim so we can purchase the acreage fair and square. That would stonewall John."

"The mine is Hayley's insurance policy. Her ex swindled her out of Ben's property in Tombstone. I don't want her thinking we're shysters, as well."

Wade looked at Jake long and hard. "Don't talk to me again, boy, until you make up your mind where your loyalty lies. With your family or with that woman." Reining his mare sharply to the left, he kicked her into a gallop. Horse and rider soon disappeared over a rise, leaving Jake to swear at the steers they'd already rounded up.

His herd grew in size during the long grueling afternoon. Night had fallen by the time Jake merged his group of stampeded runaways with the main body of steers captured by Dillon and the vaqueros. Again the storm had rolled over the Santa Cruz Valley without dropping any rain. The milling bawling cattle were winded from their run and they were dry. The added humidity left herd and wranglers cranky.

Dillon rode out to meet Jake, who pivoted in the saddle, expecting his dad to be bearing down on him, too. Jake had been ganged up on by family more than once.

This time, apparently, Dillon was alone. Which was a relief.

Until Dillon skidded his mount to a stop, dropped his reins, dismounted and grabbed Jake right out of his saddle. Their noses inches apart, Dillon shook his younger brother hard enough to rattle Jake's teeth.

"It's not enough that you have Mom and Dad arguing over that little tramp you've befriended. Now she's got you turning your back on the blood, sweat and tears we've all put into the Triple C."

Jake broke Dillon's grip on his shirt. Seeing red from the moment his brother called Hayley a tramp, Jake lowered his head and rammed it hard into Dillon's midriff. With a huge *oof,* the two began punching wildly. Locked together, they rolled down a rocky incline. Furious though he was, Jake was the first to hear the cattle lowing in alarm. He stiffened an arm against Dillon's throat. "Listen, you dumb shit, maybe you like blistering your butt in the saddle all day digging these cows out twice. Once is enough for me." Though his chest heaved from the exertion, Jake stood and jerked his brother to his feet.

Dillon dusted off his hat and jammed it on. "I don't need your help, you—"

"Shoot your mouth off about Hayley again, and I'll say the hell with us causing a second stampede. Hayley's no more tramp than Eden is. Anyway, I don't believe Hayley caused an argument between Mom and Dad. They never fight."

"They are now. Dad fired Ernesto Torres for coming back drunk between the north- and south-area roundups."

"What does that have to do with Hayley?"

"Mrs. Torres is a midwife. Mom told Dad right in front of the crew to give Ernesto back his job because she'd already talked to Mrs. Torres about moving out to Hayley's camp in case her baby comes early. I guess you'd know she's pregnant.''

"Mom did that?" Jake relaxed his shoulders. "She's brilliant."

"Well, Dad didn't think so. The vaqueros wouldn't respect him again if he reversed his decision. You know we can't condone drinking on the job."

"Ernesto has worked roundup on the Triple C for ten years. That ought to be reason enough to consider letting him dry out and stay on the crew."

"Exactly what Mom said. But she didn't let up. Dad finally blew his cork. They put on quite a show for the hands." Dillon sounded disgusted.

"So how did it end?"

"Dad won. Mom is pissed off. They're barely speaking. As if losing Ernesto isn't bad enough, according to Dad you're leaving us even shorter-handed while you go help that woman dig her damned opals."

"He never mentioned losing Ernesto. If you're in a bind, I'll ride back and forth, helping Hayley whenever I can—unless you badmouth her again. Then the deal's off."

Dillon stuck his fingers into his back pockets and leaned close to Jake. "You're serious. I can't believe it. Some days it'll be a two-hour ride each way. You'd give up sleep and stretch yourself thin for this woman?"

"I would," Jake said, his face stony.

Dillon bit back an oath and wrapped his reins around one hand. He mounted fluidly, the stiff set of his shoulders conveying his disapproval. "I certainly hope you're not expecting me to like a woman who'd pit husband against wife, son against father and brother against brother." He wheeled his star-faced gelding off into the darkness before Jake could formulate a comeback. Probably just as well, though. He was too angry now. And someday in the not-too-distant future, after he'd finished building his house and installed Hayley in it, Dillon would be forced to eat his words. Once she was no longer Hayley Ryan but Hayley Cooper, they'd return to being one big happy family.

Jake's good fortune continued. His path never crossed either Dillon's or their dad's over the next two days. Every last hand extended himself to help bring the herd's count to what it'd been before the stampede. The heat and dust, which had seemed to double after the passing of the rainless storm, sapped any will the cowboys might have had for bickering.

Jake didn't bother to check out with anyone at noon on the third day after he'd driven the last six strays he'd found into the main herd. Mopping sweat from his brow, he refilled his canteen from the water barrel and lit out for the Blue Cameo.

An hour later his heart did a fast jig as he rode into Hayley's camp. The fire was out, her camp empty of the ever-present piles of ore. Jake panicked.

But her pickup was there, so she hadn't taken a load of ore to Tubac. Then where was she? He called himself all kinds of fool for leaving her alone, unprotected.

Wait! He hadn't left her totally unprotected. Charcoal. Where was that dog?

Swinging down from his horse, Jake unsaddled the big bay and tied him to a tree near a patch of grass that wasn't completely brown. Though Jake hadn't the vaguest idea where Hayley's mine was located, he set off on foot to search the foothills. She'd said she was digging in a ravine that, if it rained, would feed the waterfall.

Considering how much ore she'd already gathered, Jake didn't think she could be hauling it far.

The longer he walked and the more barren his uphill ascent became, the greater his worry. His stomach bottomed out when he heard the muffled blast of dynamite.

He ran blindly and pulled up panting under the shade of a gnarled piñon. Placing a shaking thumb and forefinger against his teeth, Jake whistled for Charcoal. He was rewarded by a far-off but recognizable bark. At first delighted, then concerned that Hayley might be lying ahead somewhere hurt or disabled, Jake charged up the rocky cliff in the direction of the still-vibrating cloud of dust.

His boots slipped on the slick granite. He cursed the steep grade, but didn't slow down. Not until a shot rang out, coming so close it knocked the hat from his head. His heart slammed against his chest as he dived for cover behind clumps of desert bloom that wouldn't hide a flea. As his throat tightened convulsively, Jake's immediate thought was that someone had jumped Hayley's claim. The shot had come from a higher-powered rifle than she owned.

Sweat poured down his neck in rivulets. He buried his face in broken bits of shale and wondered how he'd let himself get pinned down so neatly.

No other shots followed, but it wasn't long before Jake felt eyes boring into his back. He had little choice but to raise his arms slowly. Maybe it would buy him time with the claim-jumpers.

He didn't even get one hand up before he felt a cold nose sniff his ear.

"Jake? Is that you?" Hayley shrieked. By then, Charcoal had all but deafened him, barking in his ear.

"What are you doing sneaking up on me when I'm

blasting?'' Hayley demanded, ejecting an unused shell from the chamber of a deer rifle Jake recognized as his own.

"Hey." He muzzled the Border collie with both hands and warned him to cease barking. "That's my old rifle. I can't believe you almost killed me with my own gun. How did *you* get hold of it?"

Hayley, who'd turned pale in spite of her tan, set the worn gunstock on the narrow trail and leaned on it as she massaged her protruding belly. "Your mother left it when she stopped by this morning to pick up another batch of ore. She heard from an attendant where she buys gas that two men, strangers, were asking questions about any new gold or silver mines in the area. Oh, Jake, I'm so afraid it's Joe and Shad. They don't know it's opals I've found, but..." She dropped the rifle, skidded down the sidehill and threw herself into Jake's arms.

It felt wonderful to hold her. To feel the ridges of her backbone. To breathe in the flowery scent of her shampoo.

Jake had no compunction about pushing the dog aside to fill his arms with the woman he loved.

"You scared the hell out of me, lady. I thought someone jumped your claim." Jake nuzzled her ear. Groaning, he tightened his hold and trailed damp kisses along her throat, down to a jutting collarbone that peeked out from under her sleeveless denim jumper.

"No wonder you were scared," Hayley murmured. "I shouldn't have shot without knowing who you were. But you shouldn't have sneaked up on me, either. Not while I was still half-deaf from the blast. I can't use a jackhammer because of the baby, and the ore's running deeper. The only way I can widen the vein is with dynamite."

"That blast scared me even more than riding in and finding your camp empty. I thought something had happened to you." His hands roamed her back.

Hayley drew back. "Oh, right," she drawled. "I haven't seen you for days. You must've been really worried."

"Didn't Mom tell you the storm stampeded our herd?"

"No. In fact, she never said the rifle was yours, either."

"Wow, I hope she's not mad at me, as well as my dad."

Hayley managed to regain her feet, although it wasn't easy given the incline and her pregnancy. "Look, I need to go back and dig. Nell said she or Eden will drive out here every morning to pick up whatever ore I've managed to haul out. That way, if Joe does show up, he'll have less to steal."

Jake's control snapped. "I suppose it never dawned on any of you that he'd be mad as a hornet if he comes up empty-handed? Why didn't Mom call on the mobile and let me know Joe was closing in? Dillon has a phone at our base camp."

"It's not your fight, Jake. It's mine. I thought I made that clear."

"Oh? Then why did you throw yourself into my arms?"

Hayley stomped up the hill. "My mistake," she said, stooping to grab a pickax. "A reaction to having shot at you. Relief I didn't kill you. Go on back to your roundup. If Joe shows up, I'll take care of him."

Jake's anger crumbled in the face of her courage. "I've come to help, and you need me whether you admit it or not. I learned there's more people than Joe who'd like to see you gone. John Westin of the J & B promised developers access to the spring if they buy him out. They'd turn this area into a resort.''

She gasped, then swore they'd get it over her dead body.

Jake hesitated mentioning his dad and Dillon's wishes. Because when it came right down to it, he was one-third of the Triple C. Jake didn't see how he could allude to his family's interest in obtaining rights to the spring without implicating himself. He decided not to involve his dad and brother at this point.

''Until John pays you another visit, there's no sense trying to second-guess him. In the meantime I'm here to help you dig. Why don't we get to it?''

''Maybe it'd be better if you didn't know the exact location of my mine.''

Jake stared into her eyes, his own refusing to let her get away with questioning his integrity.

Eventually Hayley expelled an uneven breath. ''I take that back, Jake. I know you're a hundred percent in my corner. It's because of you that I have an outlet for my opals. I owe you a lot already.''

''No. I can't take the credit. That all goes to Eden. She overheard me asking my mother to visit you. Hayley,'' he said earnestly, ''I want you to trust me because I care about you. A lot.''

''We did agree to be friends. Come on. I'll show you the mine. And we'll see how fast you beg to go back to chasing cows.'' Her laughter trilled.

Jake followed her swaying skirt up the rocky trail. It was evident she still didn't trust him as fully as he wanted to be trusted. He tried not to let that matter. He'd known he'd have to win her over slowly. And once she saw that he was sticking around for the long haul, it might not be so hard for her to agree that the next logical step was marriage.

Coming to a halt behind her, Jake stared into a yawning pit of dynamited rock and wondered how on earth a man made himself indispensable to a woman capable of blowing up a hill and packing it out a piece at a time—all while she was seven months pregnant.

CHAPTER ELEVEN

JAKE HAD DUG plenty of fence-post holes in this unrelenting ground. He knew how much muscle it took. He soon discovered that layers of blue stone Hayley sought were embedded in a tougher thicker clay she called bentonite. His hammer and chisel bounced ineffectively off the stuff five times for every bite he made into pay dirt. If he hadn't had respect for Hayley before, he sure did now. In plain speaking, mining was damned hard work for a strong man, let alone a small pregnant woman.

The two of them were wedged in a cut in the ground barely big enough to move around in. As the sun fell in its westward journey, it beat down on them without mercy.

Hayley seemed oblivious to the hardship. She chipped away steadily, pausing now and again to drink from a canteen she'd hung over a sturdy tree limb. Each time, she refilled the dog's cracked bowl, too. He whined, lapped up every drop of water and flopped down again in a narrow strip of shade that kept moving.

Jake took a long pull from his own canteen. He'd fetched it from his saddle when he'd gone after the jackhammer she hadn't been able to use, plus an extra set of mining tools she'd stored in her trailer. He'd never been inside her sleeping quarters before, so he'd spent a few minutes measuring what he was up against in trying to pry her away from here.

Her bedroom was little more than a cubbyhole. Her bed was a hard narrow mattress on a piece of solid plywood. A small clock sat on the floor beside a battery-operated radio. The cupboards above and below the bed must be where she stored her clothes, although Jake refrained from opening any doors.

The bathroom, which didn't look as if it had ever been used, was approximately the size of his mother's broom closet. Jake liked space; he found Hayley's present home claustrophobic. The tiny area that served as her living room and kitchen was uncluttered except for geological and mineral books piled behind a small rocker. The stack also included a few outdated western novels. A handknit baby blanket that Jake recognized as his mother's work and two terry-cloth infant sleepers occupied a prominent place on one of the built-ins. Other than that, no personal mementos sat among furnishings more masculine than feminine. This was probably the way Ben had left it.

Jake felt strongly that Hayley deserved to have a real home where she could hang pictures and decorate a nursery to suit her tastes.

And she deserved a soft wide comfortable bed. One where a man lay next to her every night and made her feel safe, made her feel loved. And not just any man. *Him.*

That last intimate thought had ended Jake's examination of Hayley's private space. On the way out, however, he'd tripped over a freestanding gem cutter and a barrel tumbler of the type Eden used at home and in her shop. It reminded Jake that he'd come for a hammer, chisel and spade, and made him feel less as if he'd snooped.

Now, while wedged tightly in a pit mindlessly hacking rock, he found himself thinking about Hayley's easy ac-

ceptance of hardship. He'd long since removed his shirt
and was still sweating like a hog. Hayley wore a long
denim jumper and seemed oblivious to the heat.

She'd sewn bags from canvas—to facilitate transport-
ing of the rocks, she'd explained—and wore one now
draped over her left shoulder. Nearly full, it hung past
her knees. Jake didn't doubt that it bruised her calves.

"You ought to have something with wheels to haul
this ore back to camp." he said, pausing to blot sweat
from his face. "Like a wagon. The kind with wooden
sides. We have one stored in the garage. I'll stop there
tomorrow and bring it when I come."

"A wagon?" Hayley blinked as if drawn back from
far away.

"Yes, a kid's toy. Mom saved a lot of Dillon's and
my old stuff. For her grandchildren." Jake threw that
out deliberately. It was time Hayley began to picture the
Coopers not just in their work environments but as a
family.

The rhythm of Hayley's hammer never faltered.
"Thanks, but I don't want to leave any tracks to and
from the mine that anyone could follow. That's why I
quit using the sled you built. Well, it also put a lot of
strain on my back."

"The ground at this level is too hard for a rubber-
wheeled wagon to leave tracks. And below, through the
trees, it's a bed of pine needles."

"The bags are fine."

"When they're full, they weigh a ton. Doesn't being
pregnant already hurt your back?"

"I'm okay, Jake." Even as she said it, Hayley adjusted the canvas sack and without realizing it, stopped
a moment to massage her lower back.

Jake didn't have to say a word. She followed the line

of his intent gaze, quickly yanking her hand away as she gave a short laugh. "Bring the wagon." She sighed. "I could probably carry two or three times the ore that fits in one bag. When I first sewed these, I lifted two at a time. Lately I've had to cut down to one."

"Lord, Hayley! Don't apologize as if you're shirking," he said gruffly. "Don't most pregnant women slow down before they're as far along as you are?"

"Dr. Gerrard said the majority of his patients continue normal lives throughout their pregnancy. I'll bet your mom never coddled herself."

Jake laughed. "Not having been around at the time, I'm afraid I can't say. On second thought, you're probably right. My mom's a doer."

"So am I. If you're going to stay and help me, Jake, you have to quit trying to pamper me."

"To an extent, I'll agree. While I'm on board, I want you to take regular breaks, though. I'll carry all loads of ore down the hill or wheel them once I bring the wagon."

Hayley might have argued, but the low nagging pain in her back had taken its toll. She'd awakened with it this morning, and it hadn't abated even a little. "Okay. How often are you going to be here?" she asked breathlessly. "Are you done with roundup?"

"No. For a few weeks I'm only available half days."

"It's too much, Jake. I'll pay you," she burst out. Almost at once her eyes filled with concern. She knew what miners earned an hour. Until Eden set and sold some of the polished gems, Hayley's income wouldn't cover what she needed for a hospital delivery, let alone the funds to tide her and the baby over until she could dig again next summer. How in the world could she pay Jake?

"I'm going to pretend you didn't make that ridiculous offer. Friends—" he emphasized the word "—don't pay one another for favors."

"Thank you, then." Those were perhaps the hardest three words she'd ever spoken.

"You're welcome. Now, about your breaks. It's time for the first one."

Hayley had been feeling shaky. It seemed hotter today, or was that her imagination? Without offering a single argument, she crawled out of the ditch and uncapped the canteen. She filled Charcoal's bowl and sank down beside him in the narrow band of shade, resting against the tree trunk.

Jake continued to chip away, breaking out chunks of colored stone. "I suspect you've been at this far too long today," he said. "Why don't you knock off and go back to camp where it's cooler under the pines? I'll fill both our bags and bring them down when I finish."

"I shouldn't." The way she lingered over the word said she was tempted.

"I saw a rock tumbler in the trailer. Start it, why don't you?"

"Can't. When I jumped at the chance to apprentice with Eden, I didn't think about needing electricity. I can't even watch the videos on cutting and polishing she sent with your mom."

"See? You ought to move your operation to the Triple C." He'd no more than said it when he could have bitten his tongue. Especially after recalling his dad's snide comment about moving Hayley lock, stock and barrel into their home.

"That's not necessary," she said stiffly. "Nell's going to talk to Eden. She thinks there are polishers that run off battery packs. If not, my training can wait until after I have the baby.''

"Did the doctor do an ultrasound?'' Jake's question came out of the blue because he'd found himself wondering if Hayley was going to have a boy or a girl. Not that it mattered either way; he was just curious.

"No. Dr. Gerrard is a real country doctor. He doesn't do them routinely for women my age. And they don't always tell you if it's a boy or a girl, anyway. But that's okay. The prospect of learning my baby's sex after nine months of wondering may make the labor easier to handle.''

"Do you have a preference? Boy over girl or vice versa?''

"That's an odd question.''

"Why? Don't some women lean toward one or the other? Have you already picked names?''

Hayley grinned. "How about Opal if it's a girl?''

Jake shook his head. "Uh-uh. Too old-fashioned. She'd hate you when she landed in first grade with all the Ashleys, Nicoles and Caitlins.''

"Dr. Gerrard's receptionist said I can get a book of names from the library. I'll add that to my list of things to do after I leave here and go to Tombstone for the birth.''

"When's the baby due? Apparently Dillon arrived late and I showed up early. This isn't an exact science, you know.''

"The doctor said around Christmas.''

"So it could be Thanksgiving or New Year's?''

"I hope not. By New Year's Day, I'd be the size of an elephant. And I'm counting on being able to do Christmasy stuff after Thanksgiving, like trim a tree.''

Jake detected homesickness in her wistful words. He

felt badly about being the cause of her nostalgia, but she'd given him a better idea of when he'd need to have his house ready for occupation. The stab-in-the-dark date he'd thrown out to his dad for completion of the house was pretty much on target. Jake pictured cutting a tree and helping Hayley trim it. "I like real trees," he said. "How about you? You don't strike me as a person who goes for fakes."

"We never had a tree. I enjoyed the ones in the stores and Francesca's, although hers was plastic. I realize now that she probably bought the artificial tree out of concern for my grandfather's asthma."

"Who's Francesca?"

Hayley blushed and rose to her feet, concentrating on dusting off the seat of her jumper. "I never know what to call her. She and Gramps were, uh, lovers."

Jake thought about bowlegged old Ben O'Dell. Though generally clean, he rarely got a haircut and his clothes tended to be well washed and frequently patched. He'd shown virtually no interest in his appearance. Somehow, Jake would never have linked the old guy with a woman named Francesca.

"Does that shock you?" Hayley asked, looking back at him before she started down the hill.

"Shock? No. I just find it odd that Ben had two important women in his life, and all the times we sat and talked, he never mentioned either of you."

Hayley's fingers curled into her sides. "That's because prospecting was the most important thing in his life. Francesca accepted it. I was the one who always wanted more than he could give."

Jake's temper fired. "A relationship doesn't have to be that way, where one always gives and the other takes."

"Really? How should it be?" Her tone was...not sarcastic, but cynical. Unbelieving.

Damn, he'd stuck his foot in it now. Hayley nailed him with a look that said, *Go ahead, lie. Tell me life is beautiful.*

She waited, so he had to say something. Jake cleared his throat. "I can only explain my own views. All relationships have ups and downs. Ideally, more ups than downs."

Hayley snapped her fingers for Charcoal to follow her down the narrow path. "Funny," she called back. "I thought only girls believed in fairy tales."

It wasn't until Jake hit his thumb with the hammer, swore viciously, then dropped the heavy chisel on his knee, that he discovered how profoundly her defeatist attitude had affected him. Jaded as Hayley was, talking her around to accepting marriage presented a bigger hurdle than he'd first imagined.

Patience, Jacob. The admonition came out of nowhere. As a kid he'd never been known to have any. It was a phrase he'd heard from his grandfather and his parents as far back as he could remember. Grandpa Cooper used to say, "Hot will cool if greedy will let it." Not true, Jake thought now. At least not when it came to his desire for Hayley.

He'd prove to her that he could stick like a firefly to a screen door. Others had let her down. He planned to keep showing up until she learned to count on him. That was the answer, plain and simple. He'd outwait her.

Jake whistled a popular ballad as he filled his knapsack and then loaded Hayley's. The sun's face had disappeared behind the horizon by the time both bags were filled. The day was still far from cool. The humidity, which had risen the day of the stampede, had yet to

subside. It might be a while before it did, Jake figured
as he trudged toward Hayley's now-crackling campfire.

Charcoal whined a welcome and bounded out to meet
Jake. After licking his hand, the dog ran back and
flopped at Hayley's feet.

Reaching the lawn chair, Jake saw that Hayley had
fallen asleep. A book titled *The Opal Challenge* lay open
across her rounded stomach. Something that smelled like
stick-to-your-ribs food bubbled in a pot hanging over the
fire. Jake realized he hadn't eaten since five that morning. He'd grabbed a pancake rolled around a sausage
before riding off to flush out strays, and he hadn't even
gone back for coffee later because he was hoarding the
time to spend with Hayley.

Jake wasn't sure he ought to wake her. She probably
needed the sleep. He should saddle up and take off so
he could catch a few winks himself before he had to do
his part in the roundup again.

He set the bags of ore near her chair as soundlessly
as possible. Looking at her, so tuckered out, Jake suffered a barrage of conflicting emotions. He was torn between leaving her to go uphold his obligations to the
Triple C and skipping out on them to give her a few full
days of relief.

While he debated, her eyes flew open. She sat up fast,
tumbling the book into the red dust. Charcoal leapt to
his feet and began a frenzied barking.

"Whoa, there." Jake caught Hayley's arm with one
hand and Charcoal's collar with the other. "I didn't
mean to scare you. It's late. It got too dark to see what
I was digging. I left the tools in the ditch and covered
them with a tarp." He jerked a thumb toward the mountain. "I'm glad you're awake," he said, dusting off her
book. "I was about to saddle up."

"But...but..." Hayley stuttered. Gripping the chair arms, she heaved herself up. She made her way to the fire and stirred what was in the pot. "How long did I sleep? The stew is sticking. Give me a minute to make biscuits. I won't hear of you leaving without my feeding you first."

"Believe me, I'd rather stay." Jake meant it. "But I have the midnight shift riding circle on the herd. If I leave now, maybe I'll be able to snag an hour's sack time before I trade places with Dillon."

It dawned on Hayley, the sacrifices he was making for her. It was *why* he put himself out that worried her. Frowning, she moved the pot off the center of the heat. "Then by all means, don't let me keep you. You've done far too much already. It's silly for you to ride back and forth every day. There's simply no need, Jake."

"There *is* need," he said, removing his hat to rake his fingers through sweat-matted hair. "You have no idea how my gut churns and burns at the thought of you out here alone while I'm doing nothing but rousting the same stupid steers again. The thunder stampeded them. Regrouping set us back two weeks or more."

"All the more reason you should stay there and tend to your own affairs."

"You may not want to be my affair, Hayley," Jake said, walking up behind her and gently pulling her back against his chest, "but you are." When she stiffened, so did he. "A poor choice of words," he acknowledged, brushing light kisses over her temple. "Nothing you say will make me stay away. You may as well save your breath."

"Why, Jake?" She pushed ineffectually at his grasp. "Look at me. I'm big as a barn with another man's child. I'm virtually homeless. This mining claim is all I have that someone like you could possibly want. Well, I won't abandon it, Jacob. I won't, and that's final.''

Jake tried hard not to let her accusation wipe the hope from his heart. The hope that she'd take a second look at herself and revise her opinion. She might be technically correct in what she'd said—except the part about the mine being all she had of value. God, no. To him, her mine was irrelevant. It was *her*. And her baby.

Turning her to face him, he stood quietly until she was forced to lift her eyes. Jake did his best to pour everything he was feeling into the loving look he bestowed. He eased her toward him by inches. The minute their bellies bumped, he leaned forward and put everything left inside him into a goodbye kiss. She tasted warm and inviting and honeyed. How could she not want this forever and ever?

Maybe she did. He thought they were connecting, at least on the physical level, when her mouth softened and her tongue explored the contours of his. And when she grabbed his belt, then his waist, and hung on for dear life as her knees wobbled and banged against his legs.

Her weight, or rather the imbalance caused by the baby's weight, dragged him forward until he opened his eyes and saw they were nearly horizontal to the ground. Afraid he'd drop Hayley accidentally and hurt her, he broke the kiss and righted them swiftly. ''I promise we could have a good life together, Hayley.''

Hayley blinked at him. Her heart beat madly like an orchestra of kettledrums. It annoyed her that the shame she wanted to feel wasn't there, even though by now it couldn't be a secret that Jacob's kisses made her totally forget her scruples. There were people in Tombstone who would claim she'd done the same with Joe. It wasn't true, of course. Joe's kisses didn't compare to Jake's.

Joe had sabotaged her with promises she'd naively believed.

But she was no longer naive. At least she shouldn't be, Hayley reminded herself as Jake released her. Crossing her arms, she rubbed away the goose bumps peppering her bare skin. She willed her voice to be cool, her words methodical. "According to my booklet, during pregnancy women sometimes start to dislike kissing, touching and the like." She moved out of his reach. "I think it's obvious. A woman in this shape isn't exactly desirable. I'm sorry, Jake. I don't feel anything when you kiss me. Now, please leave and take Charcoal with you. Our goodbye tonight is final. I tried to tell you earlier. There's nothing here for you, Jake."

He scooped up his hat, which had fallen off without his knowing, and settled it far enough down his forehead to hide the firestorm of desire his eyes must surely reveal. It cost him dearly to keep his tone as flat as hers. "The pooch stays. And I'll be back tomorrow." He hoisted the heavy saddle and cinched it solidly around his horse. Hayley's back remained toward him as he cantered off. She'd delivered a nice little speech. One that might have discouraged a less-determined man. A man who could ride out of sight and put her out of his mind. That wasn't him. He saw Hayley's face every minute of every hour, whether or not she was around.

For some time after the clip-clop of Mojave's hoof-beats faded, Hayley did her best to feel bad that she'd failed to convince Jake to stay away. But some rebellious portion of her heart refused to fall in line and insisted on looking forward to seeing him tomorrow. "Where is my backbone?" she asked Charcoal as she fed him. He tilted his head, wagged his tail and whined. His empathy, if that was what his actions meant, was short-lived. He almost knocked her down diving for his bowl.

She watched him wolf his kibble and lick the bowl clean after she'd dished up her own stew and sat toying listlessly with her spoon.

She was nothing more than kibble to the whole Cooper clan. Or rather, opals to Eden. An avenue to the springwater for Jake and his dad. Nell was still a puzzle.

Hayley performed her nightly chores and went to bed, unable to get a fix on what Jake's mother wanted from her. Eventually, she guessed it would become clear. Meanwhile the analogy she'd drawn put Jake's persistence into perspective. Hayley drifted off to sleep feeling stronger and more able to rebuff his many charms.

THREE MEN RODE into her clearing the next morning while Hayley tidied her breakfast dishes. This time she didn't question Charcoal's loyalty when he edged between her and the riders, and bared his teeth. Grateful for his presence, she kept a hand on his furry head.

John Westin climbed off a long-legged palomino.

Hayley tensed when she recognized him. His last visit had been to represent the cattlemen's concerns. She supposed he'd come here now to give her dates and instructions on opening the valves for his roundup.

Westin tipped his hat before introducing his companions. "Little lady, the tall drink of water is Marshall Rogers, owner of the Rocking R ranch that sits due east of my spread. The shy dude is Tully Mack. He owns the Eagle's Nest, directly south as the crow flies." Westin laughed at his own joke.

Hayley noticed the other men seemed nervous. They

barely cracked smiles. "I'm Hayley Ryan," she said. "I don't own anything but the claim you're standing on."

Westin's laughter cooled. His ice-blue eyes honed in on Hayley's protruding stomach. "Now, me and the boys want to discuss your claim. It appears to me that your mining days are about over."

"I'll be pulling out after Thanksgiving. Expect to be back next July."

The man confronting her exchanged an unreadable look with his pals. Slapping his reins against a gloved palm, Westin took a couple of steps closer to Hayley. Charcoal checked his forward motion by nipping at his ankles.

"Ouch! Damned dog bit me! Say, is that pup kin to Jacob Cooper's cow dog? The two look enough alike to be from the same litter."

While Westin was distracted, Hayley walked over to a log and picked up Jake's deer rifle, which she'd left there earlier. She threw a shell in the chamber. "He's a guard dog, Mr. Westin. Prospectors have to be careful. Why don't you gentlemen state your business?"

"Put that down before you shoot somebody, little lady." Westin scowled, but he moved out of range.

Marshall Rogers nudged him with a foot. "Tell her our deal, John. I don't mind saying a woman with a gun makes me skittish."

Westin snatched off his hat, a high-crowned, broad-brimmed monstrosity like Hayley had seen Hoss Cartwright wear in TV reruns of "Bonanza." She wanted to laugh, which wasn't a good idea when faced with three men who had no legal right to try to pitch her any kind of a deal.

"I'll get right to the point," Westin said. "You need

money or you wouldn't be out here, alone, pregnant and scratching for nothing in this godforsaken land.''

In Hayley's opinion, he paused a little too long on the words *alone* and *pregnant*. Obviously news of her opal discovery hadn't yet reached the ears of this trio. She could make a couple of deductions from that. One, the Coopers kept their own counsel, and two, Joe and Shad weren't behind Westin's deal, whatever it was.

''Last offer I made you was fifteen grand. We're prepared to fork over eighteen right this minute. All you have to do is stop by the county recorder's office on your way out of town and rescind your current claim. We'll even help you hitch up the trailer. A woman in your condition shouldn't be lifting that heavy trailer tongue.''

''Eighteen thousand dollars?'' Haylcy smiled at that.

Westin pulled out a wallet he had chained to one of his belt loops. ''Twenty-one, then. Come on, Mrs. Ryan,'' he snapped, when the increase didn't appear to move Hayley. ''Twenty-one thousand dollars is a lot of money for nothing. If you're frugal, it should get you through confinement and maybe give you time to find a sitter and a job.''

''I have a job,'' Hayley said mildly. ''Mining. And you're trespassing.'' She didn't exactly threaten them with the gun, but her hold on the rifle tightened, and she might have shifted and brought the barrel in line with John Westin's heart. If he had a heart.

Hayley would never know if her show of bravado could have dissuaded the men from turning surly because that was when Nell Cooper appeared. She bounced and jounced into the clearing in her dusty Range Rover. Westin's wallet disappeared into his pocket, and he'd mounted up by the time Nell set her brake and climbed out of her vehicle.

"Morning John, Marsh and Tully," she said cheerfully. "Guess you three are about to wind up your tallies and are heading into roundup. I suppose you stopped by to coordinate the valve-release schedule with Hayley."

Hayley wondered if she was the only one there, except for maybe Charcoal, to notice that Nell's easy banter belied her tension.

John leaned an elbow on his saddle horn. "Is that why you're here? Did Wade and the boys send you to release water? Tell 'em I said shame on them. That old valve wheel is rusty. Too tough for a lady to unscrew. Lucky for you I happened to be around to help." John started again to swing out of the saddle.

"Actually Jacob's been handling our water needs." The look she shot Hayley asked her to play along. "Wade suffered a setback. Thunder from that last storm caused a stampede. I came to tell Hayley they're running a few days behind the schedule they'd originally planned."

"They wouldn't cut into *my* water schedule, would they?" Westin danced his big palomino across the clearing until he loomed over Nell. "Tell Wade I said this parceling out the water is damn crazy." He shook a ham-size fist at Hayley. "And while you're here, Nell, convince this little lady it's dangerous to think she can turn back ranchers with that peashooter." Dragging on the reins, he wheeled the palomino around. Then he gestured to his companions and the lot of them disappeared up and over the ridge.

It was several minutes before either of the women moved or relaxed her guard. Nell did first. Walking toward Hayley, she wore a smile on her face, even though she never took her eyes off the grip Hayley maintained on the rifle. "Whew. What was that all about?"

"One-upmanship. Your husband's friends offered me cash again to clear out."

Nell gave a subtle shrug. "Unfortunately they're friends no longer. John, Marshall and, I suppose, Tully, since he was here, are undercutting the Cattlemen's Association. They want this spring so they can sell out to developers. You need to be careful of them, Hayley. Wade doesn't know what they might do to gain their objective."

"Ah, but your menfolk were prepared to have the state revoke my mining permit."

Nell's lips parted. "That was before you found opals."

"Which Eden wants. So now I'm supposed to believe the Triple C no longer cares to purchase this property? Did your cattle stop drinking water?"

"Of course not. But you agreed to give us access to the spring, the same as your grandfather did." Nell smiled easily again. "By the way, Jake rang through on the mobile unit. He asked me to deliver a wagon. It's in the back of the Range Rover. Let me open the tailgate, and I'll trade the wagon for your latest batch of ore."

"You and Jake are making all these trips to my site out of the goodness of your hearts? Neither of you expects a payback?" Hayley felt nasty saying it, but once the words were out, there was nothing she could do.

Nell wrestled the cumbersome wagon over the tailgate and set it on the ground, the friendly light extinguished from her eyes. "My son with the big heart has it in his head that you're a nice young woman who needs rescuing. Period."

"I'm not. I don't. I *am* nice," Hayley sputtered, "but

I don't need rescuing. Why would he choose me? A man like Jake must have an oceanful of women to choose from."

Nell looked startled, then tipped back her head and laughed. "I must remember that to tell Eden. I suppose if you're likening women to fish in the sea, I'd have to say that while many swam by, both my sons are picky fishermen."

Hayley realized she still had a tight grip on the rifle. She pumped the shell out of the chamber and returned the gun to its place on the log. Mulling over Nell's comments, she carried the first box of ore to the pickup.

"Let me do that," Nell demanded. "Honestly, Hayley, I can see why Jacob worries. If I didn't think you'd accuse me of having an ulterior motive, I'd invite you again to come stay at the ranch. Pregnancies aren't always smooth. Unpredictable things happen. When they do, you need to be within reach of a phone."

"I'm sorry if I sounded bitchy, Nell." Hayley hugged the older woman. "I don't want you to worry. After my experience with Joe Ryan, it's hard to trust anyone. I can't even trust my own judgment. I'll work on the attitude, okay?"

Nell brushed Hayley's dark hair back from her face. "I confess that before I dragged Eden over here to meet you, my biggest concern was that you'd break Jake's heart. Now...I'm just as concerned about you and the baby."

Tears seeped from Hayley's eyes. "I've been as honest as I know how to be with Jake. I'm feeling well— really I am. I promise that in approximately two months I'll be out of here, and Jacob will forget all about me."

"Hmm." Nell handed her handkerchief to Hayley before she loaded the remaining ore. She made no further comment, and the women waved gaily to each other as Nell drove off.

Hayley kept a bright smile on her face until she could no longer hear the crunch of Nell's tires. Nell Cooper had a good heart. Kindness and generosity were part of her makeup. But deep inside her ran an implacable need to protect her family—her son—from the Hayley Ryans of the world. Hayley felt it, and Lord only knew she accepted the strikes against her. For very soon she'd be a mother who'd go to any lengths to protect her own child. Unconsciously Hayley rubbed her stomach.

If—no—*when* Jake showed up this afternoon, she'd have to work that much harder at convincing him to stay away.

CHAPTER TWELVE

HAYLEY'S VOW to treat Jake in such a cavalier manner that he'd stop slipping around every afternoon lasted ten minutes, tops. She wouldn't have found it so blasted hard to give him the cold shoulder if he hadn't blown in each day wearing one of his impossible-to-resist grins.

Jake had called out from the bottom of the steep grade to announce his arrival today, but Hayley already knew he was there. Charcoal, roused from doggie sleep, had lunged awake to sniff the air. His whine of recognition was pitched differently from his earlier growl.

"Good dog," Hayley praised him. She doubted if her compliment made any impression. His joyful barks drowned her out as he leapt a foot in the air to lick Jake's face. Charcoal wriggled all over and poked his nose into Jake's shirt pocket.

"Ha! Smart dog. You know I swiped some bacon from the chuck wagon." Jake dug out the treat he'd wrapped in a bandanna. Instead of wolfing it down, Charcoal closed his eyes and almost daintily savored each morsel.

That was when Hayley's indifference flew out the window. She laughed in spite of herself. "I've seen him lick his lips before, but never smack them. He must not like bacon the way I fix it."

"You probably don't burn it. Manny burns almost everything. That's how Charcoal got his name. I took him to roundup right after I got him. Manny was new then, too. The crew tore off the charred edges of their meat and tried to discreetly toss them in the fire, but the pup kept catching them in midair. At that point I hadn't named him. The wranglers called him the charcoal mooch, and the charcoal part stuck.''

"You still have the same cook? I would've thought you'd fire him.''

"Don't kid yourself. Cooks are in big demand with so many ranchers shipping beef to market at the same time. We're lucky to get anyone who wants the job.''

"I thought you staggered roundups. At least, I think that's what the men who came by this morning said.'' Hayley dislodged a blue-layered rock and reached out of the open ditch to set it in the wagon.

Jake's gaze had narrowed to a frown at her announcement. "Mom delivered the wagon. Who came with her?''

"They weren't together.'' Hayley coughed. She hadn't intended to tell Jake. Now that she'd let it slip, she grudgingly gave him details.

"I don't like Westin's bully tactics. Why would Mom tell him we're on to his development scheme?''

"She didn't. It's okay, Jacob. The men left. Everything's fine.''

Not mollified in spite of her assurance, Jake yanked on a pair of leather gloves and climbed into the hole he'd made with the jackhammer the day before. "I think you ought to shut down this site until next summer. Like right now. After we finish today.''

"I'll do nothing of the sort.''

"It'll be two weeks, maybe more, before I can give you full days. When Ryan and Deputy Dawg were your only threat, it was bad enough. I figured they'd have to hunt long and hard to locate you. But Westin and his cronies know where you are and they know you're alone most of the time. That makes two threats too many.''

"Oh, not three?'' Hayley grit her teeth and drove her chisel deep. Now she was back on track. It wasn't hard to spurn Jake's advances when he provided an opening like this. "Haven't you conveniently forgotten that the Coopers tried to weasel me out of this twenty acres? Funny how everyone else is the bad guy for wanting me gone, but *your* intentions are so pure.''

Jake wanted to fly out of the shaft and refute her every word. But his family *was* guilty. And so was he. Not just guilt by association, either. All night, as he circled the restless herd, he'd hatched a plan of his own to halt her digging. Even though his motives were based on love, that wouldn't matter to Hayley. She still didn't trust him. Until he overcame that obstacle, one plan to displace her would probably sound pretty much like another.

Hayley more than half expected Jake to make excuses, or at least object to the way she'd lumped his family in with a bunch of thugs. The longer the silence drew out between them, the more she battled a cold sweat. Each time he whacked hammer to chisel, a knot in her stomach clenched tighter. Pretty soon she wanted to scream at him to deny her accusation. He had before. Why not now? She felt hot and cold. Nauseated. Sick. She crawled from the trench, wanting to blame her symptoms on her pregnancy. Hayley hated the need to give Jake the benefit of doubt.

"Break time?'' he asked, poking his head above the fissure. Though he was glad she hadn't continued her indictment, the fact that she was taking a break without his pressuring to told Jake he ought to step up the time-table for closing down her operation.

She didn't answer his question, and Jake noticed that her face was pale under a sheen of sweat. Her grip was so unstable she almost dropped her canteen.

Flinging down his tools, Jake vaulted out of the hole. "Are you ill?" He scrambled to her side. His boots slipped on loose rock, knocking two large pieces into the shaft where she'd been working.

"It's nothing." *As if she'd admit the real problem,* she thought.

"Not a breath of air gets into these troughs. How long have you been working today? Since first light, I'll bet." He planted a flat palm to her forehead, then pressed it softly against her stomach. "I'm glad Mom brought the wagon, but dammit, Hayley, you were supposed to fill it and leave it for me to truck back to camp. How many loads have you hauled down the mountain today?"

His devotion and solicitude seemed to contradict his earlier silence. Maybe he hadn't heard her question before…. Spurred by hope, Hayley smoothed a finger over the worry lines bracketing his lips.

A shudder coursed through his body. Turning his head slightly, Jake buried his mouth in her palm and planted a kiss. "Hayley, dammit, honey, you scare me to death. It's plain foolishness for you to keep at this. To stay out here alone."

She felt the reverberations all the way to her toes. From his admission and the brief touch of his tongue to her palm. It produced a string of tiny contractions—low, where the baby was forever doing somersaults. *Or it could be the baby.* Hayley quickly snatched her hand from Jake's.

His grave gray eyes assessed her. "I realize I'm

crowding you. Last night, riding back to the roundup, I promised myself I'd quit rushing you. I just did it again. I want to start over. Take things slower. Next time I swear I'll let *you* say when you're ready to be kissed.'' He made an exaggerated cross over his heart.

She was ready. Hayley hitched in a long ragged breath, which Jake misread.

He stepped back to give her some space. ''No dice, huh?'' he said gloomily.

Hayley grabbed her canteen. ''Does starting over mean that we'll start off equal?'' she ventured in a shaken voice. ''You won't give me orders?''

''Promise.'' Jake leaned forward and urged her free hand up for a limp high-five. He felt a whole lot better, glad to be given another chance. ''I'm asking, not ordering, okay? But would you like to play hooky this afternoon?'' He capped her canteen and traced a finger over her dusty nose. ''We could use your truck and go into town. You've never seen Eden's store or her design room where, with any luck, she's going to make you a rich woman.'' A dimple flashed in Jake's cheek.

Hayley shook her head, yet smiled tentatively. She thought he was kidding, but wasn't altogether positive. ''I can't just quit work in the middle of the day.''

''Sure you can. You're the boss, aren't you?''

She ran nervous fingers down the front of her dirty jumper. ''It's impossible. I'd need to take a bath and change clothes.''

Jake could tell the idea appealed. ''A quick shower under the waterfall and throw on a clean dress. Meanwhile, I'll finish loading the wagon. We can be on the road in, oh, twenty minutes.'' He made a show of checking his watch.

''It's tempting.'' The frown that had settled on her

forehead began to fade. "I want to see Eden's shop. I should bank the check she gave me. I hate to leave it lying around the trailer." She paused suddenly. "We'll get back here late. Aren't you riding herd tonight?"

"Nope. Not till tomorrow night. We'll have time to take my mom and Eden to dinner. Tubac has this great Mexican restaurant. Wait...will that upset Junior?"

"I don't know. I haven't thrown up in a while." A new sparkle lit her eyes. "I shouldn't listen to you. But...oh, I want to go."

"All right. Go shower. Take Charcoal in case anyone rides in unexpectedly."

"What about him?" Her face fell. "We can't leave him here."

"He can stay to guard the place if you prefer. But he loves trips to town."

"Let's take him. I'm afraid he might tangle with the wolves if he's here by himself. I've heard some close by the last few nights."

"Probably the Mexican grays the state reintroduced along the border last year. They were released south and west of here. The drought is driving wild animals from their natural habitats to look for water. I hope you're not bathing at the spring after dark. It's not safe, Hayley. One of our vaqueros sighted jaguar tracks again."

"Still safer than during the day when two-legged animals are on the prowl."

Jake started to say something, thought better of it and offered a hand to help her up. She climbed to her feet, obviously embarrassed by her awkwardness. "Easy, easy," he cautioned. "Your center of gravity is off. You need to lean backward a little to compensate."

"I refuse to waddle like a duck, Jacob Cooper. It's bad enough that I have to get patterns from Omar the

Tentmaker for these jumpers.'' Calling to Charcoal, she marched off down the hill with her shoulders squared and her chin high.

After she'd disappeared, Jake let a small whistle escape his lips. He hadn't had a lot of experience with pregnant women. He'd heard from married friends that pregnancy was a touchy time. Hayley looked fine to him. Damned fine. But she'd probably bite his head off if he told her so.

Once he, too, had washed up and they were ensconced in her battered pickup, he decided to compliment her, anyway. The plum-colored maternity top she wore with denim pants brought out the lavender in her eyes. ''You're very pretty in that outfit, Hayley,'' Jake said lightly as he turned the key and stepped on the gas pedal.

''It makes me look as round as I am high,'' she grumbled.

''It does not. What's wrong with this damn truck? Does it always growl like it's on its last legs?''

''What do you expect? It's older than dirt.''

Jake gave up and closed his eyes. ''Great. For God's sake, Hayley. You need reliable transportation. What if you went into labor early and needed to get to the hospital fast? Not only doesn't this beast have air conditioning, it's cantankerous starting.''

Charcoal, who sat between them, barked as if in agreement.

''The baby isn't due for ten weeks. I'm going to leave here the first week of December. I'm sure the truck will last that long. Gramps drove it for years without incident. Pop it into gear and pump the foot feed. That's generally all it takes.''

Jake muttered things best not repeated. He did as she suggested, and the engine caught. Except for an occasional miss, it ran smoothly after that. They made it into town without further malfunction.

Edging forward, Hayley craned her neck around the dog to see out both side windows. "So this is Tubac? I've never been past the general store out on the highway."

"In that case I wish we had more time to explore. Anthropologists call Tubac the City of Nine Lives. It's been a lot of things. Indian village, Presidio, boomtown, ghost town, mining town and now an art community that lives its motto, Where Art and History Meet."

"It's charming. Did anyone ever tell you you'd make a good spokesman for the Chamber of Commerce?"

His laughter filled the cab. "As kids, Dillon and I pretended we were Juan Bautista de Anza, Presidio commander, and Fray Francisco Garces, the Spanish explorer who established the fort. I could impress you with my knowledge of Tubac's history, but I won't. I'll leave the hard sell to my mother and Eden."

"I'm already sold," Hayley said around a nervous laugh. "It's more a matter of being able to afford to live here. And Francesca's in Tombstone to help me with the baby."

If Jake hadn't promised to back off and give her space, this would be the time to tell her about his house, the one he wanted her to share. With Hayley, though, he was beginning to see the importance of laying solid groundwork first. So he merely pointed out Eden and Nell's combined shop, then found a place to park.

"Jacob. Hayley." Nell poked her head out from a back room as the bell over the front door tinkled. "What are you doing in town? Nothing's wrong with the baby, I hope?" She hurried to meet them.

"I'm fine," Hayley assured her. "Jake came to help

me dig, but talked me into goofing off, instead. Don't ask me how.'' Glancing at him, she smiled.

Eden appeared in the doorway Nell had just vacated. She wore goggles and held a small bright torch. ''My brother-in-law is a smooth-tongued devil.'' She grinned wolfishly. ''This time he did good. Come see the pendant I'm making. The first of your opals, Hayley. I hate to brag, but it's beautiful. Only fine opals are cut into cabochons.''

Hayley and Jake followed Eden. ''I'll have a look,'' Hayley murmured. ''However, you may as well be speaking Greek.''

''Stick with me and you'll learn gem terminology. Opal is so fragile it sometimes has to be underlaid. Depending on the number of layers, those are known as doublets or triplets. Substantially less valuable than cabochons, like the one I cut from your ore. It looks like the sky with a trace of clouds,'' she finished rhapsodically.

Jake slid his hand over Hayley's shoulder and squeezed. ''I think Eden's trying to say your opals are top quality.''

''Thank you, Jacob, for interpreting,'' Eden drawled. ''Why are you off playing when you should be helping my husband with roundup so he can get home faster?''

''I've been pulling my weight out there and then some. I had business in town. Carl Brown has my blueprints ready. Could you or Mom give Charcoal a bowl of water and show Hayley around while I dash over to Carl's office? And if you lose that nasty tongue, I'll take all you ladies out to dinner.''

''Nasty, is it?'' Eden hissed the acetylene in the torch in his direction before she shoved up her goggles and shut off the flame. "But far be it from me to turn down a free meal. Can you get away, Nell?"

Nell's hands and arms were covered in clay. "Sounds good. The pot I'm working on is a lost cause, anyway." She folded the clay together and shut down the wheel. "Eden, give Hayley the grand tour. I need a word with Jacob. I'll walk him to the door," she said, shucking her apron.

He clutched his heart with both hands. "What did I do now? If you've lost more of your prize chickens, my fingerprints aren't on them this time."

"You really did steal those laying hens you sold me!" Hayley yelped.

Jake gave a helpless shrug as Nell marched him toward the front door. "I fessed up to Mom—and I didn't take your money," he declared firmly.

Eden and Hayley could be heard giggling. Jake noticed that his mother looked serious, however. She trailed him outside the shop before she spoke, and when she did, her voice was furtive. "Andrea Sheldon, who sells my pottery at her gift shop in Arivaca, came by today to pick up a new supply. She said two men were in town, one flashing a badge. They mentioned you by name and had a picture of a woman resembling Hayley."

Jake lost his teasing manner. "Did anyone direct them here? Damn, obviously Ryan and Tilford meant what they said. I thought they were all talk."

"Andrea said they knew she handled my pottery. She told them all roads leading out of Arivaca dead-ended on private land. Which is true. She also said she sold my work, but didn't know me personally. I thanked her for fibbing."

"Hayley won't listen to reason. I don't know what to

do, Mom. It'll be mid-November before I can hang around her mine full days. This roundup isn't going well."

"Big as that baby's getting, Hayley shouldn't be out there digging anymore."

"You tell her. It won't do any good. Eden told her you worked right up until the day both Dillon and I were born."

"At home. Sitting on a stool, moving my foot up and down to turn the pot carousel, doesn't compare to crawling in and out of holes, shoveling tons of dirt."

"Don't get huffy with me. She's not ready to accept what I'm offering. Every time I think I'm making headway, she pulls back." He sighed. "She's been badly burned, and she's afraid to trust another man."

Nell reached for his arm, saw the clay caked on her hand and let her hand drop. "Jake, maybe you ought to give up. Stop knocking yourself out."

He looked her square in the eye and put his feelings into words. "I can't, Mom. I love her."

"I know you think you do. But are you sure that when the chips all fall, she won't go back to Ryan? It's his baby she's carrying. That's a powerful tie."

"She's smarter than that. I'm sure of it. Hayley's like an injured rabbit. One who doesn't know who to trust or which way to run. Eventually she'll see that I'm not going to let her down."

"Oh, Jacob. I hope you're right, son." Nell's troubled gaze remained on Jake's broad shoulders as he zigzagged across the street to Brown & Brown architectural offices.

He returned with a spring in his step, whistling a chipper tune. "Mom, you and Eden head on over to the restaurant and snag a table on the patio. Hayley wants to stop at the bank. We'll walk through the plaza—that way she can see some of the other shops in town."

"Okay, but where are your house plans?" Eden asked. "Carl said you're interested in the hacienda he first designed for Dillon and me."

"You guys turned it down. It's exactly what I want. I initialed the blueprints and sent them to the builder. Art Wahl's going to break ground on Monday."

"So soon?" Both Eden and Nell gave a start. Hayley had wandered over to inspect one of Eden's display cases. If she was curious about Jake's house plans, she didn't show it. His pensive gaze tracked her every move.

Eden, who'd been unsure of the real situation up to now, let her mouth form a soundless "oh." Even then she turned to Nell for confirmation. "I'll fill you in on the way to the restaurant," her mother-in-law whispered. "Let's go, everyone!" Nell said aloud.

The four went out, leaving Charcoal behind. Nell locked up while Jake took Hayley's hand and crossed the street. He didn't let go as they sauntered past one of the art galleries and paused to look at the paintings in the window. He released her at the bank while she opened an account, but recaptured her hand as they left.

She'd relaxed by then and was laughing at something he said when he shoved open the door to the restaurant where they were meeting the others. Jake slipped an arm around her waist as they stepped aside to let a boisterous trio of young women make their way out of the building.

"Well, I declare. Jacob Cooper." A well-made-up blonde stopped and gushed his name. Her attention faltered on the woman he had tucked under his left arm. The blonde's expression changed. "Oh, look, Tina. I do believe this is the shabby little gold digger. Daddy said she plans to turn our valley into a wasteland. With Wade Cooper's help,'' she added, pouting at Jake.

Hayley tried to duck out from under Jake's arm, but he tightened his grip. "Ginalyn, apologize to Mrs. Ryan." Jake momentarily blocked the women's exit.

"Mrs.?" Ginalyn Westin cooed, her eyes firmly locked on Hayley's stomach. "Gosh, Jacob, maybe the girls and I ought to add up the months you've been out of circulation." All three women snickered.

A muscle jumped along Jake's jaw. "Spread whatever dirty rumors you'd like about me. But apologize to Hayley."

Ginalyn, who'd probably mastered the coy look at age two, ran her gaze over Hayley's home-sewn outfit. Ginalyn and her friends were wearing designer jeans and silk blouses tucked into narrow waistbands. "I'm positive I didn't misunderstand Daddy. Isn't she digging for gold out by the springs where we used to go skinny-dipping?" This time Ginalyn made no attempt to soften the derogatory twist of her lips.

Hayley finally broke free of Jake's suddenly lax grasp. Midflight she ran into Eden, who'd evidently come to see what was keeping them. Eden had only caught the tail end of the conversation, but she, who had a stature in town equal to Ginalyn's, caught Hayley's arm. "Actually," Eden exclaimed loudly enough for everyone to hear, "Gordy White told me Jake's the only guy in the old crowd Ginalyn hasn't been able to coerce into skinny-dipping with her."

Smiling sweetly, Eden faced Jake. "Nell's ordered a pitcher of iced tea. I hate to break up this reunion, but I'd like to finalize my contract with Hayley for her next shipment of ore."

Jake knew he ought to thank Eden for bailing him

out, but he felt like strangling her, instead. Ginalyn would rush right home and report to her dad; John would think Hayley had found gold on her claim. The minute they sat down at their table, Jake unloaded his fears on Eden.

"I'm sorry, Jake. Blame the devil in me. Ginalyn Westin is a bitch. Someone should have given her a taste of her own medicine long before this."

Nell shushed them. "Could you keep it down? The Triple C still has to do business with the J & B. I thought you two had more finesse." She waggled her brows toward the surrounding tables filled with interested onlookers.

"It's my fault." Clearly stricken, Hayley started to rise.

Jake stopped her. "It's not your fault. You didn't say a word. Let's order. We have a long drive ahead of us in a pickup that's iffy at best."

Hayley watched him bury his nose in a menu. Of course, he had to regret the unfortunate encounter with those women, who obviously knew him well. While it was true she'd forgotten who she was for a minute and had begun to dream of fitting in here, the exchange at the door had opened her eyes. Jake's attention came with conditions attached. His family and all the ranchers in the valley wanted the spring. Hayley supposed that eventually he'd get around to asking her in his own words; it was foolish of her to pretend otherwise. She should have put a stop to his visits from the beginning. But Lord help her, for all her big stubborn talk, she—who ought to know better—had fallen head over heels in love with Jacob Cooper.

Dinner was strained. Nell remained miffed at Jake and Eden, who'd let themselves be drawn into a catfight in the foyer of a restaurant where half the people in town could hear. Eden was irked at Jake for scolding her when she'd only come to his rescue. And Jake hated watching Hayley pull back into her shell. He cursed himself for bringing her to town and exposing her to spiteful women like Ginalyn Westin and her friends.

He'd planned to talk to Hayley about his house on the drive back to her camp. But from the minute they'd collected Charcoal, she huddled into a corner of the cab with the dog and feigned sleep. Jake didn't know how to scale this latest barrier she'd thrown up.

Her old truck sputtered for most of the trip. It up and died at the top of the incline overlooking her clearing. All Jake's efforts to restart the engine failed.

Hayley roused, rubbed her eyes and yawned. "Are we there?"

"Did Ben keep a tool kit behind the seat? The engine coughed for the last twenty miles. Now it's stopped. The carburetor may need an adjustment." He opened the door. Charcoal bounded out into the trees.

"There was a box of tools—but the truck doors don't lock. After you said transients might steal me blind, I put the toolbox inside my trailer."

"That's great! I suppose the flashlight's in the toolbox, too."

"No. In the glove compartment."

Jake reached past her to open the catch, but she admitted meekly, "The batteries are dead. I've been meaning to replace them. They're larger than the ones I bought for my radio."

Jake's temper erupted, then quickly fizzled. One look at her, sleepy, disheveled and contrite, and his heart spiraled into a free fall. He'd promised both of them he wouldn't touch her again until she issued an invitation.

But she seemed so forlorn he couldn't help himself. Cupping her chin, he lightly drew a thumb over her softly protruding lower lip and bent to steal the kiss he'd been wanting all day.

The kiss felt right to Hayley. Right enough that he didn't have to beg her to come into his arms. Nor did he steam the windows alone. She was a willing participant.

Jake went wild. He wanted to do more than kiss her. Kisses weren't enough. Had never been enough. From the noises she made in her throat and from the way she moved against him, it was evident she wanted more, too. "Hayley, honey, I've never made love to a pregnant woman," Jake murmured as he kissed her ear. "Did Gerrard cover that subject? Is it safe?" He ran his hands underneath her maternity top and choked on a groan as he realized she wasn't wearing a bra. For a minute Jake thought the shear joy of feeling her beaded nipples against his palms would make him explode prematurely. He kissed her again hard, hoping to regain control.

Hayley stirred. The little contractions she'd experienced in the midst of their last kiss had brought dampness between her legs. "The book has a chapter," she moaned, pulling away from his warmth. "I skipped it. Why would I need to know what it said?"

Jake dropped his head to her forehead and sighed. "Why indeed?" He'd hiked up her top. Unconsciously his thumbs circled and scraped her swollen nipples.

"Oh. Ohh. Jake, stop."

He did, pulling his hands away. "Sorry, you must be tender. I didn't mean to hurt you."

The cool air striking her bare breasts hurt more than the curl of heat winding tight inside her. Here she was—falling apart in Jake's arms again—dreaming of the ecstacy they might share, not in a truck, but in a real bed. She'd been ready to lead him to hers in the trailer. Would still do it, if only she could be sure he didn't have an underlying agenda.

Hayley struggled to sit up straight and breathe normally. Her top fell back into place. "Jake." She reached for his hands, needing the connection because he'd turned off the lights and the cab was pitch-black. "I deserve to know what plans you have for the spring. Not knowing is making me crazy. It's driving a wedge between us."

Jake's heart sped up. He did have a plan. One he'd fashioned last night as he idly blew his harmonica to calm the herd. How could she know? He'd told no one. Maybe Hayley was beginning to trust him.

Hayley held her breath. If there was a God and he heard her prayers, Jake would keep quiet or categorically deny giving her any reason not to trust him with her heart.

Jake combed his fingers through her hair. "I've chewed on this idea since your ex and his partner threatened to find your mine." He didn't mention what his mother had said about Joe and Shad showing up in Arivaca. Jake hated to complicate matters or add to Hayley's worries. If she agreed to his plan, her troubles with Joe would be over.

"All we have to do to get Joe off your back is go to the county recorder and switch your claim to my name. It's brilliant, really. You get the ore, but Joe loses his leverage." Jake started to add that as soon as her divorce was final, he and she could get married and there wouldn't be any further need for these machinations, but Hayley reared back and planted a fist in his left eye before he got that far.

"Ow! What was *that* for?" Jake strove to see her through the dark.

"I don't like getting the shaft."

"Shaft? What? I said the ore is all yours. This would be a transfer in name only—for your own protection."

Hayley fought with the stubborn door until it finally creaked open. Fuming, she got out and slammed it on Jake's sputters. With the Blue Cameo in his name, he'd have everything his father needed to purchase the property. Maybe he'd give her the opals and maybe he wouldn't. Did he really think that because she went weak in the knees when he kissed her it also made her weak in the head? She might have fallen for him like a nitwit, but she'd get over it. She'd once thought she loved Joe Ryan, too.

Damn him. Damn Jake. Damn them all.

"Oh, Charcoal," she moaned as the dog loped up and pressed against her legs. "Lead me home, boy. Then go with your master."

Jake heard Hayley talking to Charcoal. He stumbled after her through the darkness, making so much noise he couldn't hear what she'd said. Why was she so mad? She'd asked for his help, hadn't she?

He figured out pretty fast, after he reached the clearing and heard her go into the trailer and slam and lock the door, that he'd said something wrong. Dead wrong.

"Hayley. Come out here. We need to discuss this rationally."

"I'm not rational. Go away and don't come back."

"I damn well will be back. I don't want your stupid opals. Is that what you think? That I'd gyp you?"

Charcoal sat on the top wooden step leading into Hayley's trailer. He raised one paw and scratched the metal door, whining.

"Just because you're mad at me, don't take it out on the dog." Jake heard her moving around inside the trailer, but she didn't answer.

"Well, hell! Stay, boy," he said sternly, patting the wood. "I'm riding out to the herd. You guard the lady. Hanged if I know why I don't give up," Jake grumbled, now petting the dog's head. "But I swear," he said through gritted teeth, "she's going to be my wife one day and your mistress."

Though Jake hated leaving Hayley virtually stranded, he left the old truck at the top of the hill. Lacking proper light and tools, he had no other choice.

THE NEXT AFTERNOON he brought tools and tinkered with the engine until he got it running.

"It might only be temporary," he explained after he'd climbed the sidehill to continue helping Hayley dig. "That engine can't be trusted. I wish you'd wind down here."

She gave him the silent treatment.

Not only that day, but every day thereafter for the next week. She spoke only when spoken to. She was a damn stubborn woman.

But Jacob Cooper was stubborn, too.

He knew that his parents suspected Hayley was at the bottom of his surliness, and that the whole family talked behind his back. The day they'd corralled the last steer, Wade approached his son. "Dillon deserves time with his wife now. Jake, you're taking our beeves to market."

"No. I'd have to be gone too long. I can't—won't— leave Hayley alone. She's too far along in her pregnancy to be doing what she's doing."

"A break will do you both good," Nell advised

gently. "Go on up to Phoenix. Buy Hayley a present while you're there. Or get her something for the baby."

His face lit up for the first time in a week. "A cradle. Early on she talked about wanting a cradle. I'd hoped to build her one. I haven't had time. I'll buy one. And a really nice maternity dress. One suitable for the harvest dance."

Wade grunted and stomped off. Nell hid her concern. "I'll go see her a few times while you're gone, Jacob. I'll take her some acorn squash."

"And milk," Jake reminded her, heading to his room to pack. "She's looking so peaked. Dammit, Mom, she's got it in her head that all I want is access to the spring. I've told her I love her a hundred times. She doesn't call me a liar, but she might as well. Her eyes say it loud and clear."

"I wish I could advise you, son. Hayley's distanced herself from Eden and me, too. She's never had a family, Jake. Maybe we overwhelm her."

"I don't think it's that. But I'm telling you right now, so clue Dad in. When I get back, I'm pitching a tent at her site until she's ready to stop and go have the baby. I'll pay Dillon to do my chores and keep an eye on Art Wahl. I want that house finished in time to bring Hayley and the baby home from the hospital."

"Oh, Jacob. Seeing you like this breaks my heart. I'll talk to her. Plead with her. There'll be frost soon. Maybe by the time you get back, she'll be ready to give up. At least move her trailer to the Triple C."

"Or not," Nell whispered to the four walls after Jake left.

CHAPTER THIRTEEN

BEEF BIDS WENT SMOOTHLY. Jake managed to shave three days off his trip; instead of a week, he'd been gone four days. Though he was eager to get home and shed the trappings required for wheeling and dealing in the stockyard, he took the time to swing by his mother's shop. She and Eden were both busy with customers. Although he was anxious to hear about Hayley and also to see her, he nevertheless cooled his heels until one of the women was free to talk.

He'd gone into the back room and helped himself to coffee, and now stood over Eden's workbench, studying her latest designs, when his mother joined him.

"Isn't that ring gorgeous? Too bad it's presold, or I'd buy it for myself. Eden's having the time of her life with Hayley's opals. I heard her tell a dealer yesterday that the fire and the passion of these stones inspires her creativity."

"I'm glad for Eden and for Hayley. How is she, Mom?"

"Still at the site and not at the Triple C, if that tells you anything. I tried, Jacob. So did Eden. Art Wahl phoned Dillon. He said it's impossible to finish your house before late January. Over the weekend Eden helped me paint Dillon's old room. We papered one wall in a nursery print. The antique store down the street had a crib and chest they'd taken on consignment. Solid ma-

ple. Fabulous condition. I hauled them home. Wade
helped me wrestle the pieces into the house. He only
grumbled a little." Nell smiled, then sobered. "Hayley
cried when I told her what I'd done. But she kept saying
I shouldn't have and refused to even come back with
me to look at the room."

Jake's expanded lungs deflated like a pierced balloon.
He pressed the heels of his palms to his forehead, shut
his eyes and massaged the deep furrows away. "Why is
she being so stubborn if Eden's sales are taking off? I
know she was fretting about not having enough money
to take proper care of the baby until she can open the
mine again—but that shouldn't be a problem now." He
shook his head. "She can't seem to trust anyone but
herself to provide for them."

"You told her you love her. I said we'd welcome her
at the ranch. Dillon's old room is ready and waiting. I
hate to say it, honey, but the rest is up to Hayley."

"I know." Jake turned bleak eyes her way. "I'm going home to change out of this suit and give Dad the
check from the sale. Then I'm going to see her."

"Did you find a cradle?"

"Yes. That's one less item she needs to save up for.
I bought other stuff for the baby, too. Two of everything
a kid needs in the first week of life, or so the clerk at
the store said."

"Oh, Jake. That was sweet of you." Nell smiled at
her son through misty eyes. "I wish your love was re-
ciprocated. Over the years I've watched so many local
girls toss their hearts at your feet. I never thought I'd be
sorry you hadn't caught and held on to one. Now I am.
If you'd chosen one of them, you wouldn't be going
through this heartache."

Jake hugged her awkwardly. "I distinctly remember

you telling me hearts go their own way—regardless of what the mind says.''

Nell slipped out of his arms and blotted her eyes with the sleeve of her blouse. ''That was when Eden chose Dillon and I knew you were dreadfully hurt.''

''I got over Eden. She and Dillon are right for each other. Hayley...'' He tried to articulate how this was different, but words failed him.

Nell's every feature conveyed sympathy.

Eden bounced into the room and stopped inside the door, darting a puzzled glance between the two. ''Oops. Sorry if I'm interrupting.''

''You're not. I'm headed home,'' Jake said briskly. ''Then on to see Hayley.''

''Tell her the customer who just left ordered an opal pendant for each of her five sisters.'' Flinging her arms aloft, she danced around the room. ''Our winter visitors are really going for the opal jewelry. Wait until I exhibit at the gem show this spring. Will you ask Hayley if she's still interested in becoming my apprentice? If not, I'll place an ad in next month's *Rock and Gem* magazine. At the rate I'm selling, I'll need to start training someone soon.''

Jake stroked his chin. ''Before Hayley has the baby? I know she wants the job, but she's facing so many big decisions all at once, I don't think she knows which way to turn. She's sort of hung up on the cost of living here, too. If it wouldn't put you in a bind, could you cut her some slack?''

''Sure.'' A puzzled look settled between her brows as Eden looked at Nell. ''What's with the cost of living? Are you going to charge her rent?''

''Hayley turned down my offer of a room. I was disappointed, to say the least. I didn't let you know because I'm still hoping Jake can change her mind.''

"Don't count on it." He heaved a sigh. "She's one stubborn lady. But if Dillon and Dad can spare me around the ranch between now and the harvest dance next weekend, maybe I can help Hayley dig enough ore to satisfy her. That's a couple of weeks earlier than she intended to shut down. As far as I'm concerned, any days she lops off would make me worry less about her health and welfare.''

"You've got to admire her guts," Eden said. "She's out to here." Eden linked her fingers approximately eighteen inches away from her flat belly. "Most women would have called it quits already.''

Totally in agreement, Jake turned to go. "Oh, hey," he said, poised at the door. "I take it there's been no further evidence of Hayley's ex?"

"He's still out there bumbling around." Nell combed a hand through her short curls. "Link Thompson bought a bull in Nogales on Saturday. He told Dillon there were two men in the café attempting to throw some official weight around. They mentioned Ben O'Dell and you in the same breath. Link's ears perked up. He said he didn't like the way they acted, so he kept his mouth shut.''

"Nogales, huh? How long before they stop at the recorder's? Don't those dudes have jobs? How can they afford to keep searching?"

"People with vengeance on their minds make the time, Jake. I don't like them including you in this. It's not your fight," his mother reminded him. "There's plenty to keep you busy at the ranch. But I suppose any hope of getting you to stay at the Triple C is just wishful thinking.''

Jake didn't even bother to reiterate his decision to

devote his days to Hayley; he knew his mother had read his intentions in his wry smile. She'd know where to find him during the hours he wasn't asleep. If he thought Hayley wouldn't pitch a royal fit, he'd roll out a sleeping bag in front of her door and spend his nights at the Blue Cameo, too. But he was positive she'd never go for that.

Jake missed the days he'd been out of the saddle. He'd have preferred to ride Mojave to Hayley's, were it not for the gifts he'd bought. This once, he'd drive his pickup over the longer bone-jarring route. After today, he'd ride his horse.

The sun was on the wane by the time he actually pulled in and parked next to Hayley's truck. Jake was surprised to see her in camp rather than up the mountain digging. She appeared to be sitting in her lawn chair, staring into the fire, one hand aimlessly stroking Charcoal.

In spite of her added bulk, she'd moved fast enough to grab the shotgun before Jake even got out of his vehicle. He recognized her gun as the weapon with which she'd first greeted him. This time, though, even his dog stayed close to Hayley and snarled.

Jake approached with his hands up and laughter in his voice. "Except for the fact that I'm not riding Mojave, this is déjà vu."

"Jake! I didn't realize it was you."

Was that relief he heard in her voice? Maybe absence *had* made her heart grow fonder.

"Your truck's hidden by mine. I didn't know who or what to expect. I suppose this is like the first day you rode in and surprised me. I was looking smack into the sun then, too. Could hardly see you."

Jake could see her well enough, though. She looked beautiful, but more tired than when he'd last seen her.

"Knocked off early, huh? Is that a case of while the cat's away the mouse, play?" he joked.

Charcoal, having identified Jake, raced around in circles, wagging his tail.

Hayley set aside the gun and raked twitchy fingers through her hair. "About an hour ago Charcoal alerted me to another visitor. One of your co-op cops. I wasn't sure if he was gone or not. I left my tools at the mine and decided to light a fire and sit a spell. I thought you might be him sneaking back."

"Co-op cops? You mean Westin?" At first Jake's gut tightened. Then he relaxed and dropped to his haunches beside the fire. "John and Marsh Rogers would be into their roundups. I imagine they needed to open the valves to release water."

"That, and to dispense advice."

"Such as?" Jake brushed dog hair off his hands.

She settled gingerly down on the chair, taking care not to meet Jake's eyes. "Nothing. His message was personal."

The light dawned on Jake. "So Ginalyn got around to complaining to her daddy about that night at the restaurant. I'm sure she bent his ear good. I hope you told him to buzz off. Dammit, Hayley, you don't have to take guff from them."

She laced her fingers across her stomach. "I'm the gate-crasher. Your Ginalyn belongs here. I understand why Mr. Westin would take up for his daughter."

"Piss on him," Jake said savagely. "John's the outsider, if you want to get technical. You were at least born in Arizona. Westin blew in a few years ago from Virginia. And we know how much he cares about this land. He's after a fast buck."

"Jake!" Hayley sounded shocked.

He sliced a hand through the air as if to say the conversation was finished as far as he was concerned. Rising smoothly, he leaned over and dropped a kiss on the tip of her nose. "I brought you some stuff from Phoenix."

She tried to keep a childish anticipation in check. Few people in her life had ever brought her gifts. She couldn't contain her curiosity and finally capitulated. "What? What did you bring? It wouldn't be milk. Not from Phoenix." She clapped her palms soundlessly, at last pressing her fingertips, prayerlike, against a quivering bottom lip. "I know, a new drill bit. You said mine is hopelessly dull."

When Jake straightened and grinned, she started to rise. "Wait," he told her. "Sit and relax. I'll bring everything to you."

"Everything? You bought more than one thing?" Sudden wariness extinguished the excitement from her eyes. "You shouldn't spend money on me, Jake."

He ho-ho'd merrily. "If I hadn't shaved, you'd call me Santa."

Hayley giggled in spite of herself. Before she could again deny his right to buy her presents, he jogged off. During their chatter, darkness had cloaked the area in and around the clearing. Both Jake and Charcoal blended with the evening shadows.

Hayley strained to see what Jake carried a few minutes later as he walked toward her again. Slowly. He'd brought something large, judging by the way he staggered under the weight. What on earth…?

"Close your eyes," he ordered, still several feet from the fire.

"Honestly, Jake. Oh, all right," she agreed when it became obvious that he intended to stay out of sight until she complied with his request. "Hurry. The suspense is killing me."

One-handed, he untied the old quilt he'd wrapped around the cradle to keep it safe from dust. The layette had needed three department-store sacks, and they'd all been stuffed into the cradle. Still in his truck, inside a box from a Phoenix maternity store, was the dress he'd bought her to wear to the harvest dance. But that could wait.

"Can I look yet?" Hayley eyed him through splayed fingers.

"Okay, now." Jake had removed the baby clothes from their bags and arranged them on the cradle mattress. He wished he'd taken time to tie on the bumper pads and put the brightly patterned sheet over the mattress. He gazed at the hodgepodge, wondering how it would look to Hayley. As if in answer, she suddenly burst into tears.

"Hayley, oh, God! You hate it. The cradle's nothing like what you wanted."

"Noooo." She kept shaking her head and wiping her cheeks. "I *love* it, Jake. In my whole entire life no one's ever given me such a wonderful surprise."

"Then why are you crying?" Jake was genuinely perplexed.

She ran a finger tentatively over the maple spindles. The cradle didn't sway.

"There's a metal pin at the foot." Jake pointed to a ring. "Slide it out and you can rock the baby. Shove it in and it remains stationary. A good feature, I thought."

She nodded, not trusting herself to speak. Hayley swallowed around the huge lump in her throat and picked up a tiny pastel undershirt. Refolding it carefully, she brushed at the front of her jumper. "I need to wash before I touch anything more. Jake, you bought too much. I'm only having one baby, you know."

He knelt at her feet and solemnly tucked a stray curl behind her ear. "The clerk said this is barely enough to get started. Otherwise, you'll be doing laundry every day. And that's just for the baby, she said."

She clamped her teeth over her bottom lip. "I know so little about caring for a baby. You must think I'll be a horrid mother."

"You're going to be a great mother. Parents can't do more than put their child's welfare before their own. That's what I see you doing, Hayley."

Without warning, Hayley flung her arms around Jake's neck. She kissed him soundly on his lips. As tears trickled down her cheeks, she peppered his face with soft damp kisses.

"Hey." He wobbled backward, dangerously unsteady. "We'll be in a real mess if you tumble out of that chair and flatten me." He laughed.

Smiling at last, she turned him loose. "Is that a nice way of saying you'd rather not have a hippopotamus land on you?"

"No way." Jake scowled. "Will you quit putting yourself down? The only weight you've gained is baby. I don't know where you get these notions. To me, you're perfect exactly the way you are."

Hayley blushed. "I've never met a man as intense over little things as you are, Jacob Cooper. You don't really know me."

"I know all I need to know." Rising fluidly, Jake started for his truck again. "I have another package. If you want to wash up, do it while I'm gone."

"More gifts?" She blinked. "Oh, Jake, no more, please. I'll be indebted to you until I'm a hundred."

"Gifts don't come with strings, Hayley."

He'd stopped in the deeper shadows to deliver the rebuke. Hayley couldn't see his eyes, but she imagined they burned like liquid silver. She'd noticed they did that whenever he was serious, angry or trying to make a point. "All right. No strings," she agreed. "You've made me so happy I couldn't possibly pay you back properly if I tried."

Jake shifted restlessly from one foot to the other. It was on the tip of his tongue to tell again that he loved her. But it would sound too much as if he was trying to extract payback, after all. He wanted her to love him not because of the comforts he could provide, but because life itself would be bleak without him. Fearing he wanted what could never be, he retrieved the last package.

He had to wait for Hayley to return from the spring. And then she made him wait while she held up and exclaimed over each item in the layette. Disposable diapers. Shirts, sleep sacks, receiving blankets, bibs and booties. At the bottom of the stack, Hayley discovered a rattle and a plush yellow squeaky duck.

She cried again, harder. She'd been weepier than usual. But Dr. Gerrard's pamphlet warned that might be a side effect of pregnancy. Jake tugged her upright into his arms, and he held her patiently until her tears dried. "Come on," he wheedled, fanning his hands across her back. "Open the last box. This one will make you smile. Especially when I tell you how ill equipped I was to buy it. The saleslady asked me fifty questions I couldn't answer. In the end I picked it because I could picture you wearing it. So if it doesn't fit or you really hate it, you've got to promise to tell me. Eden's going to Phoenix tomorrow. She can return it and replace it with something you'd rather wear to the harvest dance."

"Jake, I told you I don't dance!" Hayley gasped. "Look at me. Do I look like someone able to dip and swing?" She stepped away, drawing his attention to her misshapen form.

"So? You can sit around and look pretty with the best of them, Hayley."

"Sure," she croaked. "Tell that to Ginalyn Westin and her fashion-plate pals. I suppose she's going to the dance," Hayley muttered.

Jake ran his hands from Hayley's elbows to her shoulders and back again without commenting.

"I thought as much." Hayley withdrew again and took a deep breath before picking up the gaily wrapped present. "The bad thing about this is that I know automatically I'm going to love whatever you bought. You can't imagine how tired I am of wearing these sacky jumpers. I sewed them up fast before I left Tombstone. I had the material and the pattern was easy. I'd make something more fashionable, but my machine needs electricity."

"Mom would let you set up your machine in one of our guest bedrooms," Jake said as she dropped into the chair again and untied the big pink bow.

Her fingers stilled. "I know, Jake. But I'm not going to impose. And I'm reasonably sure your dad would hate to have me hanging around. How would it look to the members of the Cattlemen's Association, anyway?"

"What do they have to do with who we invite to the Triple C?"

Hayley pried the lid off the box and rested one hand on the thick folds of tissue paper. "Are you kidding? I saw how upset you were when you found out that Mr. Westin tried to deal with me behind your dad's back. Don't you think that's precisely the view other association members would have if I took up residence at your house?''

"The difference is that Dad wants the spring so *all* the ranchers can share the water equally. Westin plans to stab us in the back by selling his spread—*and* the spring property—to developers. Without water rights, all the valley ranchers will go under. So you're absolutely right. I wasn't pleased about Westin dickering with you.''

"How do I know your dad's on the up-and-up? Maybe he asked you and Nell and Eden to treat me nice just to throw me off guard.''

The hiss Jake made in his throat brought Charcoal to his feet. ''What kind of person can't tell who's lying and who's telling the truth?'' Jake's stance was belligerent. Charcoal edged closer to Hayley and bared his teeth at Jake.

"Obviously not me!'' she snapped, becoming as agitated as Jake appeared. "Otherwise I wouldn't have been so gullible as to believe Joe's big fat lies. I even believed Shad Tilford when he told me he'd bring Joe in for questioning. I know I'm a sucker. And I attract con men. So why wouldn't *you* have an ulterior motive to hang around me, too?''

Jake did more than hiss. He couldn't get the words out and practically choked as he tried. Giving up, he threw his hands in the air and stalked toward his truck. "This is getting us nowhere. I intended to come back tomorrow and help you dig. Although I'm sorely tempted to let you sit here for a few days to realize how idiotic your off-kilter analogy sounds to a rational human being.''

It took three tries for Hayley to heave her pregnant body out of the low-slung chair. "Ha! As if the way *you're* acting is rational." She crushed the partially open gift to her fast-beating heart. Seeing him continue to stride away, she said with less fervor, "Please don't go, Jake. I *want* to trust you. If you only knew how much..." He didn't turn, but climbed into his truck.

He drove off, and Hayley didn't understand why the fear of abandonment overtook her unpredictably and at random. It twisted her tongue and her thoughts. Only a person who'd been through such an experience could possibly sympathize. Which wasn't Jake. Just the opposite, in fact. He knew nothing of betrayal or real loss.

It was just as well she'd driven him off. He belonged with someone pretty and rich and confident. Hayley got sick every time she thought about Jake matched with someone like Ginalyn Westin, but she had to admit they were better suited than the two of them.

She could imagine the whispers Jake and Eden and Nell would have to endure if he took a pregnant guppy like her to the harvest dance. Nell herself described the event as the biggest one of the year for all the local ranchers. No, it was better to make Jake mad than have him end up the talk of the town.

Hayley's hand strayed to the dress box. She had no right to even look. But she couldn't resist. Peeling back the tissue carefully, she exposed a beautiful red dress. Made of silk crepe, it rustled when she held it up and let it drift over her lumpy body in a perfect A. The collar and cuffs of the long sleeves were pristine white satin, and there was a white satin rose at the neck. It was by far the finest dress Hayley had ever owned.

She quickly folded it back into the box, not wanting a new flow of tears to stain the material.

How could she have tears left? As she made neat piles of the baby things, placed them on the mattress and dragged the cradle and its contents into her trailer, Hayley knew she'd cry buckets of tears over losing Jake. She had missed him terribly during the four days he'd been in Phoenix. She'd never missed Joe as much. Never.

Sitting on her bed, calling herself all kinds of names for not leveling with Jake about the truth of John Westin's visit, Hayley dried her tears. Westin had said he was aware that her *husband* was trying to find her. Westin said if she didn't take his offer and turn over the mine, he'd direct Joe to the Blue Cameo.

The threat was still very much on Hayley's mind when Jake showed up lavishing her with gifts. But Joe Ryan was her albatross, not Jake's. Hayley knew that if Jake had any idea Westin had threatened her, he'd take it upon himself to shoulder her burdens—and that chilled her to the bone. Jake was too kind. Too sweet and decent a guy to ruin his life fighting with scum like Shad and Joe. If she could hold out another three weeks, Joe would legally be her ex. Then he'd no longer have any claim on property that belonged to her. Anyway, Westin might have been bluffing. Joe was probably off hitting on some other woman. He had the attention span of a gnat.

JAKE ARRIVED at the breakfast table looking like a thundercloud. When Nell and Wade greeted him, he grunted something unrecognizable.

Nell rose and removed a check from her purse. "Eden wonders if you'll give this to Hayley today when you go to help her dig. If Hayley asks why it's more than the previous amount, Eden said it's because sales have increased considerably."

"You take it to her," Jake said, staring at the check as if it might bite him. "I'm riding fence today. I talked to Dillon last night. He said we had a report of several miles down. Apparently he promised to plow Eden's garden to get it ready to replant, so that leaves me.''

"Yes," Nell said. "When he's finished with hers, he's going to plow mine. I can't visit Hayley today. Business at the store is booming."

"She won't die without these funds," Jake said nastily. "I doubt she'll take time out from stockpiling ore to go and bank them."

Nell dabbed her lips with a napkin. "Did Hayley refuse the cradle and layette?"

"She didn't have a choice. I left them. We didn't argue over that."

"But you did argue?" Surprisingly it was Wade who asked.

Jake snorted. "She thinks you're a bogeyman. Has herself convinced the Coopers will use treachery to get clear title to the spring."

Wade looked shocked. "I've only met the woman once. I had my say and I listened to her. Yes, I want the water rights, but when you and Nell and Eden took up for Mrs. Ryan, I backed off."

"I know. Hayley sees enemies at every turn. Do you mind if we change the subject? It'll give me an ulcer if I keep thinking about it."

Nell curled her hand over Jake's. "I'm sorry, Jacob. I like Hayley. I prayed it would work out for you two. But some things will never be. I guess I'd better take the crib and chest I bought back to the store. I'd hate them to be a sad reminder each time you pass Dillon's old room."

"Keep them, Mom." Jake rose and plucked his hat off a rack by the door. "One of these days Dillon and Eden will give you grandkids. Undoubtedly they'll ask you to baby-sit. Anyway, in a couple of months I'll be in my own house.''

"Yes.'' Her eyes remained troubled. "A home you built for her. I know it's probably too soon for me to say this. But, Jake, the right woman is out there somewhere. Give it time. You'll find her.''

"Hayley's the right woman. The only woman, Mother. Aren't you the one who's always said that when a Cooper falls in love, it's forever?'' Stalking through the kitchen door, he tried not to slam it shut. He wasn't giving up, dammit. Oh, he'd stay away a few days. Maybe all week. Call him a glutton for punishment, but he *would* go back. He worried too much about Hayley being out there alone, working like a stevedore, with her due date so close.

By Wednesday Jake had blisters on his hands from setting posts and stringing wire. The project required another day, but he needed a break. He decided to ride over to check on Hayley from the top of the ridge, if nothing else. Before he could head in that direction, his general contractor called, asking him to take a look at the location of the kitchen and living-room fireplaces. They were back-to-back, and Wahl thought the nook on the living room side would be perfect for built-in bookshelves. If Jake approved, his men wanted to rough in the change today.

The decision didn't take five minutes after Jake had driven the ten miles out to his property. On his return to the house, he saddled Mojave, deciding he'd just go finish the fence project, after all. While Jake had been gone, his brother had unloaded a tractor to plow Nell's garden.

The two men exchanged waves. As Jake started to ride past, Dillon killed the tractor's engine. ''Are you going out to Hayley's?''

Jake tugged on his hat brim. "North pasture. Why?"

"Didn't Mom reach you? She phoned me looking for you. She didn't leave a message, but I gathered it had something to do with Hayley."

Jake's heart took a dive. Icy sweat slid down his backbone. "Do you have your cell phone on you? I'll ring Mom. Save me going back and unlocking the house."

"Sure." Dillon dug the phone out of his shirt pocket and handed it over. Jake connected with Nell on the first try.

"What's up? Dillon said you'd phoned. Regarding Hayley?"

"It may be nothing," Nell said, unable to keep the worry from her voice. "I find it hard to believe, but according to Eden, Ginalyn told friends her dad had met with Joe Ryan this morning. She indicated the men made some deal involving the spring. Like I said, it may be rumor, nothing more."

"Hellfire! Westin just might be that underhanded. I'll ride out and take a look-see. If you hear anything else—or if Ryan shows up in town—leave a message on the recorder. At this point I won't say anything to Hayley. In fact, I may look things over and not let her know I'm there. Whatever I decide, I won't stay. I'll be home in time for dinner. We'll touch base then."

"Trouble?" Dillon asked as he accepted his phone.

"Maybe. Maybe not. It concerns Hayley's ex. He's a jackass. A jackass with an ax to grind. They're the most dangerous kind."

Dillon stared silently as Jake wheeled his horse around. "Take care, little brother. If you're not back by suppertime, shall we send the dog with the brandy?"

Jake laughed at that. "Hayley already has Charcoal," he said. "So you can go ahead and drink the brandy."

He wasn't one to ride a horse into a lather. But something had a grip on Jake's spine and it wouldn't let go. He rode hard and fast. Where he'd planned to nose around quietly, the sight of a dirt-spattered Jeep parked up against Hayley's pickup changed everything. Jabbing his heels into Mojave's flanks, Jake galloped down the incline like a madman.

It was a good thing, too. Joe Ryan and Shad Tilford were shoving Hayley back and forth between them. Her face was ghost-white, except for a trickle of bright red blood running from one edge of her upper lip.

Charcoal barked and ran in frenzied circles. Shad kept trying to kick him.

The two men evidently heard Mojave's hoofbeats. Both turned. Jake could see Tilford's shiny badge. Too damn bad. That badge bought him nothing in this territory. Not one damned thing.

Jake rode past the trio, sprang from his saddle and scooped up Hayley's gun, which leaned against the log where she kept it. "Touch her again and I'll fill both of you full of lead." At the time Jake fully intended to follow through. His face must have reflected his intentions.

"Jake, no!" Hayley's voice caught in a sob as Joe backhanded her hard and sent her flying across the rough ground. She landed against a jagged boulder. Though her face twisted into a mask of pain, she threw a protective arm over her swollen stomach, and the other she flung out to block Jake. "Don't shoot them, Jake. They aren't worth spending your life in jail." He voice caught in an agony of shuddering breaths.

Jake didn't agree. However, the truth was, he could never kill anyone. He wasn't the one on the ranch who dealt with putting down horses who'd broken their legs or cows mired in sandy bogs. He knew that. These bastards didn't.

Pumping shells into the double chambers, he laid a row of shot so close to Ryan's boots the man danced back and back until he smacked into Shad.

"I'll have your ass in jail for attempted assault so fast you won't know what hit you," the deputy screamed.

"The authorities will have to find your bodies first," Jake snarled back. "You're forgetting this is my territory. And it's awfully remote. I can dump your remains in Mexico." He slammed the butt of his rifle into Ryan's soft gut. "Who'd be the wiser?"

Something like fear entered the men's eyes. Turning, they ran as fast as they could toward the Jeep. Jake sailed another smattering of lead past their ears. Bounding after them, Charcoal tore at their pant legs, growling ferociously.

From the safety of the Jeep, Ryan and Tilford shouted obscenities at Jake and his dog. They made a series of dire threats that he countered with a single one of his own. "You're dead if I ever see you near Hayley again."

Tilford, the driver, laid rubber out of the clearing and left a rooster tail of red dust behind. Not before Joe threatened to sue Jake for attempted murder and Hayley for the mine. One hundred percent of it.

Trusting they'd gone and wouldn't risk returning without backup, Jake rushed to Hayley's side and dropped to his knees. His heart slammed erratically.

She was curled into a ball and made terrible sounds. It scared the hell out of him. Especially as the lower part of her jumper and one of her boots was wet.

"Jacob, my water broke," she sobbed, tears mixing with the dust on her face. "It's too early. More'n a month too early. Oh, God, my baby. I'm going to lose my baby.'' Her fingers clawed at Jake's shirt.

"Hold on, honey. Let me start your truck. Then I'll come and carry you up the hill. We'll get you to a hospital.'' His hands shook so hard Jake had difficulty grabbing the key off the hook inside her trailer. Charcoal barked sharply and punctuated it with howls, as if to hurry him along.

The ignition clicked once, then twice. Not a shred of a spark reached the engine. Swearing, Jake tried it six times and almost lost his lunch when each attempt failed. Her battery was dead as a doornail.

Racing back to Hayley, he lifted her gently into his arms and tried to put on a confident face. "Dead battery,'' he informed her. "I'm taking you to the trailer.''

"Jake, no! I need a doctor. This baby is coming.''

"Listen, woman,'' he growled softly. "I've delivered hundreds of cows and a few horses. Hell, I delivered Charcoal. There's nothing going to happen to you or your baby. Not while I'm around.''

His speech seemed to calm her. It did nothing to settle the tennis tournament going on inside his own stomach. Nor did it help that the inside of the trailer was hot as an oven. And Jake had zero room to manipulate in the cubbyhole she called a bedroom. He ended up placing her in a chair while he dragged her mattress out into the living space, where it was only marginally cooler. It was eighty outside, but it felt like a hundred in the closed-up trailer.

Hayley was too shaky to remove the wet jumper by herself. Jake helped her, then gave her privacy to don a soft cotton nightgown. He really hoped that when she lay down, the contractions would stop.

They didn't.

He timed them and noted they were ten minutes apart. Then eight. As they continued, it became obvious that he was indeed going to have to deliver the baby. At her request, he placed a makeshift waterproof pad underneath her, then began gathering supplies. A basin for water. A pair of scissors. Towels.

All the while he prayed, and prayed hard, for the skill he'd need.

CHAPTER FOURTEEN

AFTER SEEING to Hayley's comfort, Jake took a quick turn around camp. Mostly to satisfy himself that Joe and Shad hadn't parked somewhere and sneaked back. Jake carefully dusted away any wagon prints leading to Hayley's mine. Then he collected his rifle and Hayley's shotgun, stationed Charcoal by the trailer door, and inside the cramped trailer again, he closed and locked the door.

Hayley watched his deliberate actions. "You think they'll come back?" she asked.

"I never should have left you alone," he said tightly. "I knew they hadn't given up. Last I heard, they were hanging around Nogales. God, Hayley." Jake slid to his knees and clasped her hands. "What if I'd gone off to mend fence and hadn't come here?"

"You're not to blame, Jacob."

"I sure as hell am." He stared down at her in anguish, not looking for absolution. "If I'd been more vigilant, you wouldn't be lying here in early labor."

Hayley moved restlessly on the mattress. "No, Jake. The day Westin and his friend stopped by, he said if I refused to leave the property, he'd tell Joe where I was."

"Why in hell didn't you tell me that? I'd have stayed with you. I wouldn't have gone off in a huff."

"If I can't take care of myself, how can I care for a child?" Even as she finished saying the words, a contraction left her breathless and moaning in pain.

Jake turned her and massaged her lower back until her muscles stopped their siege of spasms.

"Better?" He took note of the time between this spell and the last. He felt self-conscious about asking to check Hayley's progress, yet the contractions had been six minutes apart for an hour. Jake worried that something might be wrong. If she lost this baby because he was too squeamish to do the job, he'd never forgive himself.

He avoided looking squarely into her pain-clouded eyes as he smoothed back strands of sweaty hair and brought one of her clenched fists to his lips. "I need to check to see how far dilated you are, sweetheart. Can you let me do that?"

"Check? You mean, like a doctor would?"

Jake saw that her cheeks had gone from white to pink to a blaze of red. "I, ah, don't know any other way to measure your progress," he stammered.

"Jake, I wasn't thinking straight when you offered to deliver my baby. I can't let you...well, I mean, I won't embarrass you like that. Leave me. Ride to the ranch and get a vehicle to drive me to the hospital. I'm sure I can last that long."

"Hayley, I love you. What kind of man would I be if I left you to deal with this alone?" Jake collected both her hands, and this time he met her panicked expression with a warm assured smile.

Another contraction struck. Hayley was swept away by the pain, and as a result was saved from having to respond to Jake's declaration. One he'd made before, but she'd steadfastly refused to give it credence.

Nor did she really believe him now. Quite frankly, she hurt too much to think about anything beyond the pain. The booklet Dr. Gerrard's receptionist had given her said that when the time came to deliver, she should pant like a puppy and ride through the wave of contractions. She tried. Amazingly it did help. When the latest paroxysm loosened its grip, Hayley was too tired to argue with Jake. "If you insist on staying," she muttered weakly, "I won't argue. I'm scared to death of having my baby early."

Jake wiped her face with a cool washcloth he'd prepared. "You're what? Just over four weeks early?"

She nodded, catching his hand and squeezing it in fear.

"Is there any possibility the doctor could've been off in figuring the date?"

"I didn't know I was pregnant. I thought I had the flu. Dr. Gerrard set the date after his exam. I think he's right. Joe...well, he'd found someone else. The doctor's prediction works out to the last time Joe joined me in bed. Not that he did *that* very often."

Jake brushed her cheek with the back of one hand. "Don't you act guilty. Joe was the fool."

Hayley smiled. "You do know how to make a lady feel better. Do whatever needs doing, Jake. I'll try not to be prudish."

He checked her as discreetly as possible and saw she probably still had a few hours to go at the present rate. "All systems are go," he said lightly, pulling her gown down over her knees. "I remember hearing a friend who had a new baby say her doctor sped up the process by having her walk the hospital halls."

Hayley rolled her head from side to side. She could easily see from one end of the trailer to the other. "I might manage walking in circles." Pursing her lips, she levered herself up on an elbow.

Jake helped her to her feet and steadied her when she

bent double and clutched her abdomen. "Another contraction?" he asked, glancing at his watch.

"No." She blushed. "Standing feels funny. It's ridiculous, I know, but I'm sort of afraid the baby will fall out on its head." Deliberately standing erect, Hayley moved away from Jake's support. Her grimace confirmed what the effort cost her.

"Birth is an awesome process," he murmured. "In all honesty, though, I'm glad God gave the chore to women. Cross my heart, I won't make fun of a single thing you say or do. If you want to scream or cuss at me, go right ahead."

"I hope I can be more reserved. Now that I'm up and about, shall we get the cradle ready? If you hand me the mattress and a sheet, I'll fix it while you tie on the bumper pads. Please? It'll take my mind off what's happening."

Jake jumped at the chance to do something worthwhile to help pass the time. "Pick out what you'd like the baby to wear. I'll find a place to store the rest of this stuff."

"Good luck. There's not an empty drawer in the place. I had to leave everything in the cradle." She shuffled across the room toward him.

"I'll put everything back in the sacks, at least."

"When I first looked at these, they seemed so tiny. If my baby is premature, he or she may swim in these." She held aloft a nightgown with bears on it and started to cry. "Darn." She hiccuped, swiping at the tears. "I hate crying and that's all I've done lately. It doesn't do any good. Why can't I just accept that I've botched my life again?"

"You didn't botch anything. It's just the changing hormones." Jake gave up trying to keep his hands to

himself. He slipped his arms around her and swayed to
and fro until the rough hitches in her breathing began to
subside.

"Oh, Jake," she said quietly, twisting the wet sections
of his shirtfront in her hands. "This is above and beyond
the limits of friendship."

"Yes, it is," he agreed dryly, taking care to cradle
her face against the hollow of his shoulder. "But it's
easily within the bonds of love." He let the simple statement stand. He was through tiptoeing around her silly
objections. If ever he hoped to convince Hayley how
much he cared for her, he had a ready-made situation at
hand. If he hadn't gotten through to her by the time the
birth was said and done, he probably never would.

Hayley fell silent and hobbled through several more
contractions, letting Jake assemble the cradle alone.
When her pains became harder and closer together, he
helped her lie down. Pulling a harmonica out of his
pocket, he began to blow softly.

"I never knew you played harmonica," she said, pil-
lowing her head in the crook of her arm.

Taking it from his lips, Jake grinned at her. "Some
of our hands play guitar when we're circling a big herd.
I couldn't seem to get my fingers on the right strings.
Any idiot can blow a harmonica."

Smiling, Hayley tugged on the hem of his jeans.
"You're too modest, Jake. Play me a lullaby and calm
this baby down." She rubbed her taut stomach.

He leaned forward on the straight-backed chair.
"Calming isn't the object, Hayley. Now that the little
rascal's started, we want a swift appearance."

"Speak for yourself. I'm not ready." Tears welled in
her eyes again. "I thought I was so smart setting a time-
table for everything. I shouldn't have argued with Joe

this afternoon when he demanded I sign over half the mine. In retrospect it would've been the smart thing to have done. I honestly never dreamed he'd hit me.''

''He'd better never lay a hand on you again.'' Jake scowled fiercely.

''I'm sorry for involving you, Jake. I heard Shad say you'd be sorry for interfering, that the local sheriff would back Joe's claim.''

''Our local sheriff should have retired years ago. He's up for reelection next month, but he's going to lose. It's the case of another jerk like Tilford throwing his weight around. He can't hurt you.''

''I wish I was as certain. Whoever thought Joe could forge my name to my grandfather's papers and get away with it? He did it slick as you please. Oh, oh, oh!'' she cried, curling into a tight fetal position.

Jake tossed his harmonica aside and went down on his knees beside Hayley. He gripped her hand tightly as she gasped and panted like a puppy.

''A rough one?'' he whispered consolingly, again sponging her feverish cheeks with the cool cloth.

She barely had time to straighten out before the next hard pain hit. By the third one, Hayley uttered some words she'd never used in her life. Gritting her teeth, she swore like a miner and ordered Jake to leave. ''No, don't you dare go,'' she proclaimed in the next breath, grabbing for his hand.

''Easy, easy, honey.'' Jake smoothed the fingers she'd clamped around his wrist. ''Wild horses couldn't drag me away. Here, hug this pillow. Don't let go, no matter what. I think Junior is about ready to put in his appearance.''

''Oh, help!'' she cried in increasingly jerkier sounds.

"Names. I haven't thought of names. Jake, I need to push. Oh, Lord, what shall I do?"

Jake had hurriedly washed his hands in the basin and moved to the foot of the mattress to rearrange her nightgown and allow him room to work. He smiled at her. "Our kidlet has crowned, so push away. Whatever you're having, Hayley, boy or girl, this kid has a mop of black hair."

The next rolling cramp brought out the full head and shoulders. A heartbeat later, the baby was born.

"We have a girl!" Jake proclaimed excitedly, holding a wizened red-faced infant, who waved skinny arms and wailed feebly. There were tears in Jake's eyes as he cut the cord, tied it off in an economy of motion. Lifting the baby from Hayley's stomach, he wrapped her in a thin blanket and placed her in her mom's shaking arms.

Outside, Charcoal howled a long mournful howl, as if announcing the new arrival to the outside world.

"Uh-oh, is she all right? Jacob, she's so tiny. And homely." Hayley burst into tears even as she rained kisses over her baby's furrowed brow.

Jake, busy with matters that came after the birth, stopped and moved in closer. He cradled mother and child tenderly. "She's beautiful," he said, his voice husky with emotion. "When she gets a little food in her tummy, she'll start to fill out and she'll be as beautiful as her mother." Jake touched Hayley's face reverently.

Through a curtain of tears, she gazed first at Jake, then at her new daughter. "I've waited so long," she sobbed. "I was afraid Joe had hurt her. Oh, she's gorgeous. Simply gorgeous." Hayley smoothed fingertips over the red wrinkled cheeks and wiped away the tears that had fallen on a matted shock of dark hair.

Jake curved a palm tenderly around the baby's perfect

skull. "Prettier by far than the calves I've delivered. And Charcoal…well, he was runt of the litter. This little miss will clean up just fine. Speaking of which, I'll do that as soon as I make sure Mom is A-OK. Why don't you count her fingers and toes?" he suggested, wanting to make Hayley less self-conscious about the final phase of the birthing process.

His method of distraction worked.

"Look how long her fingers are," Hayley said when Jake came to take the bundle away for a wash in the warm bath he'd prepared. "Maybe she'll play the piano. I always wanted to learn," she added softly.

Jake responded to her wistful tone. "Why didn't you? Don't they have piano teachers in Tombstone?"

"Yes. But music wasn't high on Gramps's list. To him, even radios and TVs were frivolous."

"Well, then, you and the little miss here will have to take lessons together." He opened a clean towel and stood where Hayley could watch him dry the baby.

She shifted awkwardly and curled one arm under her head. "You handle her so easily, Jake. Aren't you afraid of dropping her?"

He grinned. "I've had a lot of practice throwing and branding calves."

"Branding. That's like naming, in a way." Hayley yawned and struggled to partially sit. "What do you think of naming her Cameo, after the mine? With a middle name of Joy because…well, having her is a joyous occasion, and I feel so wonderfully incredibly happy."

"Listen to your mom," he said, crooning to the baby as he patted her dry and put a diaper on her before tucking her into a cheery yellow night sack. "Your mother certainly wasn't saying such nice things half an hour ago, as I recall," he teased.

Hayley made a face. "So much for not poking fun at me. You promised."

"That's right, I did. Okay, no more jokes. As for the name, Cammy's a lot more appealing than Opal." He handed Hayley the baby and then arranged several pillows behind her back. Already it seemed the redness was fading from the infant's tiny cheeks.

Sitting cross-legged beside Hayley, Jake curled the baby's thick damp hair over his forefinger in one long sausage curl.

Hayley touched it and smiled. "You did that like a pro. Are you sure you don't have a wife and six kids stashed away at the Triple C?"

Jake gazed at her so seriously Hayley wished she hadn't given in to the urge to tease him. Especially after he said, "You've had plenty of offers to see the ranch and everything there, Hayley. You can take the grand tour anytime."

To cover her uneasiness at this turn of the conversation, Hayley focused on the baby, who'd begun to root around the front of her nightgown. "Cammy acts hungry. Could she be this soon?"

"It's hard work being born. Uses up a lot of calories. You need to try her at the breast. Get her into the habit of sucking. She's not likely to get much at first. I boiled water and it's cooling in a bottle in case she's too fussy."

Hayley pulled uncomfortably at her gown. "Obviously I wasn't thinking about breastfeeding when I bought this." A hot blush colored her cheeks.

Jake knew she was back to feeling ill at ease around him. Which he thought was silly. What could be more intimate than assisting someone you loved through childbirth? But he didn't want her to feel awkward. "I have a clean shirt or two out in my saddlebags,'' he offered. ''I carry them in case I unexpectedly have to spend the night at one of our line shacks. My shirt will hang to your knees, but it buttons down the front.''

''Thank you. That's thoughtful, Jake.''

He didn't like her stiff tone of voice. Or maybe he just felt like an outsider, watching her gaze at Cammy with her heart in her eyes. He remembered that his married pals sometimes complained of feeling shut out from the mother-infant bond. And they were attached to their offspring in ways he wasn't attached to Cameo. Rather than risk sounding jealous, Jake went out to get the shirt.

Charcoal greeted him with a miffed expression and an uncomprehending whine. ''Ah, you're a lot like me, old boy. Except you were truly exiled. Still…Hayley lets you sleep in her house. Hell, in her bed. I've only had that privilege in my dreams.''

Returning with the shirt, Jake left the dog outside again. ''While you change,'' he told Hayley, ''I'll feed Charcoal. After that, I'll rustle us up some food. It's getting late. Past suppertime.''

He took the mewling baby from Hayley's arms and placed her in the cradle. ''Do you need help?'' he asked her. Frowning, Jake watched Hayley gingerly pull herself upright with the aid of a chair.

''You've done more than enough already. Pioneer women didn't have men waiting on them hand and foot. Thank you for—for everything. You probably want to get on home. Don't worry about me. I'll mail your shirt back from Tombstone. I'll loaf around here a couple of days and then hitch up the trailer and leave. I want Dr. Gerrard to check Cammy as soon as possible.''

Jake's frown grew darker. ''Apparently you didn't hear me say your truck has a dead battery. That's why

you didn't deliver Cameo in the nearest hospital. And I
don't give a good goddamn what pioneer men did—I'm
not letting you fend for yourself. Got that?''

Her shoulders slumped as the baby started to wail.
Darn it all, she was trying to show responsibility for her
life and that of her baby. But her legs were shaking and
she was more tired than she'd ever been. She really
didn't want Jake to go off and leave her alone. After
struggling to get up off the mattress, she sank to her
knees and bawled in a very unladylike manner.

Jake didn't know whether to try to comfort her or not.
Eventually his need to hold her won out over having her
possibly bite his head off. He gathered her fully onto his
lap and rocked her in a chair that wasn't a rocker.

"I'm tired," she mumbled into his neck. "I didn't
even dig today, yet every muscle in my body aches.
And…and the slightest decision seems overwhelming.''

Jake resisted reminding her that a short time ago she'd
said she felt incredibly happy. "Shh," he whispered,
instead. "Why do you think they refer to giving birth as
labor? It's hard work. I know you want to be in command of your life, honey. You will be again in a few
days. Please, let me help you through this rough patch.''

"All right." She snuggled closer before drying her
eyes. It felt good to be held. Her grandfather had never
been much for dispensing hugs. Nor had Joe. But touching came easily to Jake.

"I'm okay now." Hayley eased off his lap. "Feed
Charcoal while I change. When he's finished eating, why
don't you bring him inside? I've liked having a pet. If I
can swing getting an apartment where they allow pets,
I'd like to have a dog." Hayley made a stab at smiling.

Jake didn't have to be asked twice to go. It bothered
him the way she talked about living on her own. Was

he a fool to keep beating his head against a stone wall? If he hadn't witnessed moments where Hayley lowered her guard and showed him a vulnerable side, he'd give up. But he'd seen her melt into his arms almost as often as she'd shoved him away. Somehow she had to figure out that he was nothing like the men she'd known, that he wouldn't turn on her or let her down. To convince her, he had to find a way to keep her from going back to Tombstone.

Cammy was wailing by the time he returned to the trailer carrying a steaming pot of beef barley soup. "Hey, hey, what's the trouble?" He set the pot on the tiny stove and hurried to Hayley's side.

"The baby acts hungry, but she just cries, instead of trying to nurse. Maybe I don't have what it takes to do this. Where did you put the bottle of water?"

"Nursing is better for her," Jake declared. "Maybe you're too tense."

"I am not," Hayley declared. She'd barely said it than both she and Jake recognized the fallacy of her words. Their shared laughter vented the pressure that had built between them. And Cammy finally latched on to Hayley's nipple.

"Ohh." Hayley dragged out the sound. She gazed down in wonder at the tugging rosebud mouth. Lightly she ran a finger over the baby's soft cheek.

Jake was blinded by the love that sprang instantly into Hayley's eyes. This was the woman who'd said in so many ways that she was incapable of love. Now he had proof it wasn't true. The moment bolstered his spirits and renewed his patience. His goal was to be a husband and a daddy-by-choice. Someday—and he hoped it was soon—Hayley Ryan would become Hayley Cooper. She'd gaze lovingly not only at Cammy but at him.

Cammy fell asleep suckling. Jake hated to disturb them, but Hayley needed nourishment. Her eyes had begun to droop. "I'll put the baby in the cradle and bring you a bowl of soup," he said. "Then you ought to nap for a while. From what the new parents of my acquaintance say, the adults need to grab some sleep when the baby naps."

"How will I ever get anything done?"

Jake smiled. "It won't be that way forever. I doubt you'll feel like dashing out to dig opals in the next few weeks."

She stared into the bowl of soup Jake had placed in her hands as if it were a crystal ball that held all the answers. "You're right. How will I accomplish the things on my list, Jacob? I can't drag Cammy around while I hunt for housing. Even if I find a furnished apartment I can afford, I'll need to stock it with groceries. Go ahead, say I didn't plan very well. I should have closed down earlier like you said."

Jake curved the fingers of her right hand around a spoon. He checked on the baby and let Charcoal in before he sat down to his own soup. "Eat, Hayley. There's nothing you can do tonight. Unless I miss my guess, by tomorrow part of your problem will be solved. Mom will come roaring in here to see why I didn't come home. She'll go all crazy over Cammy, like all women do with babies. Unless I don't know her as well as I think, you and the baby will be installed at the Triple C before you can say Winnie the Pooh. That's how she and Eden decorated the nursery, you know?"

Hayley stopped with the spoon halfway to her mouth. "Jacob, I can't impose on your parents like that. It's out of the question. I already explained to Nell."

"Okay, so you explained. I know Eden has another

check for you. That should make you feel better. Now, eat," he said again, feeling sorry about her distress. He and his dad and brother had been bulldozed by his mother's decisions more times than he could count. Even Eden had succumbed. That was how she and Nell had ended up sharing a work space. However, his mom's intentions had been good—they normally were—and she'd been hurt when Hayley refused to so much as look at the room. Jake didn't want to take sides. But he would if his family tried in any way to strong-arm Hayley.

After they ate and he washed the dishes, he moved the mattress back into the cubbyhole. Charcoal, who couldn't seem to understand the changes, sniffed the cradle once, then flopped down under it. After Jake helped Hayley into bed, Charcoal hopped onto the foot, and dog and woman slept.

Jake was reluctant to awaken either of them when an hour later he heard the crunch of approaching tires. The night was so dark he couldn't see a vehicle out of the small trailer windows.

"Hayley." Jake tiptoed up to her and shook her gently. "We've got company. In case Joe and Shad have come back with the sheriff, I need you awake enough to stand watch over Cammy. If it's me they're after, I'll go peacefully. But only if they swear to leave you alone and let me notify my folks to look after you and the baby."

Too sleepy to comprehend all he'd said, Hayley crawled out of bed. "Someone's coming? Why isn't Charcoal barking? He's always warned me before." She stared in confusion at the collie, who'd blinked awake in a massive yawn.

"Beats me. Maybe it's because I'm here. At any rate,

I'm leaving him inside as protection for you and the baby.''

Hayley bit her bottom lip. "Stay, Jacob. I'm scared. Make them come to the door.'' Though Hayley moved slowly, she managed to insert herself between Jake and the door.

He was torn between doing as she asked or keeping danger as far from her and Cammy as was humanly possible.

He'd let the time for decision pass. The vehicle had apparently been closer to the clearing than he'd judged. The next thing Jake knew, there was a series of loud raps on the door.

Startled, Cammy awoke with a scream that became a long high-pitched wail. "See to her and stay out of sight,'' hissed Jake, motioning Hayley away from the door. He picked up the shotgun and quickly checked to see that it was loaded.

Charcoal padded to the door, sniffed along the threshold and whimpered. Jake had no ready answer for his pet's unusual behavior. Not until he threw open the door and thrust the muzzle of the gun into his father's ashen face. Wade jumped backward off the makeshift step and landed on his wife's foot.

Nell cried, "Watch what you're doing, Wade. Jacob? Why in heaven's name are you pointing a gun at your father?'' In the next breath she covered her mouth with both hands. "Oh, dear. Tell me that's not a baby crying.'' Tears glistened in her eyes.

He ejected unspent shells from the shotgun. "Yes, it's a baby. Now suppose you tell me why in hell you two are creeping around Hayley's place in the dead of night.''

"Ask your mother,'' Wade growled. "She came unglued when you missed supper. As if you weren't full-grown and never missed a meal before. She was hell-bent on driving out here. Would've come alone if I hadn't pulled my boots back on and driven her.''

Nell shoved past Wade while he was still explaining. She zeroed in on the crying baby. ''How precious! Hayley, she's an absolute doll. But she's early. Oh, I knew something was wrong. See, Wade? I had a premonition, didn't I?''

Jake's father stepped inside, filling the doorway with his stocky frame. He was a big imposing man, but looked less so when he snatched off his hat and gazed at his wife, pure adoration darkening his eyes. ''I learned to listen to your mother's hunches, son. Nine times out of ten she's right on the money.''

''Ten out of ten,'' Nell chided, rubbing her hands to warm them before she scooped the tiny squalling bundle from Hayley's arms.

Jake had never heard his mother talk baby talk. He found it humorous. Yet something indefinable clogged his throat and impeded his breathing when his dad got into the act. Wade Cooper tickled the baby's tummy with a big work-roughened forefinger and did his own version of cootshy-coos.

Jake could tell that Hayley didn't know what to make of them. She'd never had a family.

Afraid she'd tear Cammy away from his parents, Jake shut the door, then casually slipped his arms around Hayley.

''Cammy's only a few hours old,'' he informed his folks. In low tones he followed that news with a condensed account of the scene when he'd ridden in. He mentioned the failure of Hayley's pickup to start and ended by saying the baby had decided to put in an early appearance.

"That horrid man hit you?" Nell glanced up at Hayley with fire in her eyes. She touched the purplish bruise marring Hayley's cheek and chin. "He ought to be jailed for assault. Wade, you and Dillon take care of that right after we get Hayley and this little sugar pie settled at home. Jacob, you and Dillon can come back tomorrow with whatever parts you need to fix Hayley's pickup. We'll store it and her trailer in one of the vacant barns until she needs it again."

Jake watched the play of emotions across Hayley's face. "Mom," he said earnestly, "Dad and I are used to you arranging our lives. Hayley calls the shots when it comes to Cameo Joy."

"Cameo?" Nell beamed at Hayley. "You named her after the mine. It's perfect. And she's beautiful. But she *is* premature, and the nights are beginning to get colder. Wouldn't you rather have her in a heated room? Oh, and there's a retired pediatrician who bought a small farm east of the Triple C. We'll ask him and his wife by for coffee tomorrow. I'm sure he'll be happy to give this sweet child a quick exam."

Jake sensed the minute Hayley lost the battle to his mother. "It's all right," he whispered close to her ear. "Her heart is as big as the whole outdoors. Cammy couldn't be in better hands."

"I know. And I'm too tired to make a fuss. Not only that, she's right—it is getting colder at night." As if to punctuate her words, she shivered. Hesitantly she said, "Thank you. I guess it won't hurt to spend a day or two at the ranch."

Hayley had no sooner agreed than Nell began to bark orders. She rebundled the baby to travel. Jake did the same with Hayley and carried her to the Range Rover. Wade collected the cradle and the layette Jake had purchased. Spotting the blanket she'd knitted, Nell covered Cammy with it before dashing to the vehicle.

In less time than it had taken Jake to fix their evening soup, he'd saddled Mojave and was trailing behind the precious cargo being transported at a crawl over the bumpy unpaved path. Smiling, Jake wondered how many times his mother cautioned his dad to drive more slowly. Wade Cooper wasn't one to go easy on the gas— except that he'd do anything his wife asked.

Once they'd reached the house, Jake hovered while Nell settled Hayley and the baby in their rooms. Instead of placing Cammy in the nursery, Nell directed Jake to set the cradle next to the bed, where Hayley now lay wearing one of Nell's frilly silk nightgowns.

"The warm shower felt like heaven," Hayley murmured, her eyes drifting closed. "Funny, but I hardly missed the convenience before."

Smiling, Nell fussed with the covers. "If you need any help with the baby during the night, just yell. Promise me you will, child. I won't hear of this notion that you're imposing. You must think of us as family." Stepping back, Nell nudged Jake forward.

Family. The word had a nice ring. Hayley glanced up and saw Jake.

"I sleep light," he said. "Mom, too. When Cammy cries, it'll be a stampede to the cradle. Don't you worry. You need to rest."

Wade stuck his shaggy head around the door. "Make that three light sleepers. I'll probably lead the stampede. It's been too long since I rocked a baby at night."

Hayley gazed from one smiling face to the other. The fear that had clutched at her heart since Joe blew into her camp began to unravel. She smiled at Jake as he ambled over to take a last peek at Cammy. And she didn't act embarrassed or push him away when he turned and kissed her good-night. She slid fully beneath the warm covers in a room that felt totally secure. Her heart accepted Jake and his family—even if her brain was slower to come around.

CHAPTER FIFTEEN

AT MIDNIGHT, again at two and sometime after four, Hayley awakened to Cammy's crying, only to have Jake or Nell or Wade place a freshly diapered baby in her arms for nursing. Now it was almost nine-thirty. Jake stood over her bed, smiling and holding a breakfast tray.

Hayley cast a sleep-fogged glance at an empty cradle. Panicking, she bolted upright and threw aside her covers.

"Whoa! Mom has Cammy in the kitchen. The pediatrician has come and gone—Cammy got a clean bill of health. The doctor left you a note. Mom sent the tray. The doctor ordered a healthy breakfast to, uh, help produce milk," Jake stammered. "Cammy was slugging down a two-ounce bottle of water when I left them," he said, his voice growing stronger. "Can you manage the tray by yourself?"

Hayley fluffed two pillows and eased back against them, taking care to restore the quilt, although she couldn't say why she'd suddenly be self-conscious around a man who'd seen her all. She focused on the stack of toast, bowl of cereal and tall glass of milk, but those blasted tears plagued her again.

"Don't you like toast and cereal? Why are you crying?" With his hands full, Jake felt at a loss to console her.

Unable to speak through a constricted throat, Hayley

staved him off with a hand. "I...I... No one's ever served me breakfast in bed before."

"Then you'd better eat, before it gets cold," Jake urged gently. "In the Cooper family, it's a treat reserved for special occasions, like anniversaries or Mother's Day."

Hayley let him settle the tray across her lap. "I feel like such an impostor. You're all doing so much for me, and I'm not a Cooper."

"Not yet." Jake left her to digest that, along with her breakfast.

As Hayley ate, she studied the sunny room with its hand-rubbed oak furniture and oval braided rug. There were watercolor paintings on the walls and knickknacks on the dresser. Grandpa Ben had never owned a home; he'd always rented. Only now did Hayley realize how long they'd lived with secondhand junk.

She wished Francesca could see this room and the nursery Nell had let Hayley peek at last night. Francesca insisted no one lived in homes like the ones that were pictured in the magazines Hayley collected. They were just for show, she'd said. But the Coopers' house was beautiful yet obviously well lived in. Hayley understood in a way she never had before that expensive furnishings and lush carpets and shining oak floors didn't make a home; the people who lived there did. The Coopers had created a place of beauty and shelter and love. A home.

Wade himself came in to take her tray. He seemed incongruous in the elegant feminine room, Hayley still felt ill at ease in his presence. She sat very quietly, expecting him to try to harass her into revoking her mining claim.

"Nell's busy playing grandma," he told Hayley with a huge grin. "I'm relegated to being your waiter. Jake and Dillon have gone to put a new battery in your pickup. They'll have your truck and trailer here by noon.''

"Good. Tomorrow or the next day I can be on my way to Tombstone.''

"What's the rush? And why Tombstone? I thought Eden said you were going to learn the jewelry business by starting out as her apprentice. Isn't Tombstone a far piece to travel?''

"Oh.'' Hayley inspected her ragged fingernails. "Yes, we discussed an apprenticeship. I realize now, with the baby and all, I wasn't being very realistic.''

"I expect Eden will change your mind when she gets here. She and Nell are already conspiring on where to fit a crib and a playpen in their office.'' A fond look softened his craggy face. "Nell and I always took the boys to work with us. That's the best thing about being your own boss—setting the rules.''

Hayley weighed what he'd said as he left and Nell breezed through the door, bringing Cammy for a feeding. "I'll leave you two to your privacy. Eden just drove in, and right behind her is the county sheriff. Jake told his dad that no-good ex of yours threatened to file a lawsuit to gain half your mine. Don't you worry. If that's why the sheriff's here, Wade will set him straight in a hurry.''

"I can't ask you to fight my battles, Nell.'' Hayley shifted Cammy so she could wriggle out of bed. But the baby set up a howl.

"You didn't ask us. It's become a family matter. Get your body back in bed and feed that poor starving child.'' Nell grinned and winked as she leaned down and kissed Cammy's nose.

The baby quieted enough to blink unfocused blue

eyes. Hayley sank back into the pillows. She really ought to object more vigorously to all this pampering. "On the other hand, cupcake," she whispered to the baby after Nell had gone, "let's wallow in it while we can. They're all so darn nice, how can we *not* love them?"

Hayley was asleep when Jake tiptoed into the room two hours later. Cammy had begun to stir in her cradle. He lifted her and carried her into the nursery next door for a diaper change. Returning, he sat in the rocking chair in Hayley's room.

It was there that Hayley saw him when some small noise happened to wake her. He was concentrating so hard on singing to the baby he obviously didn't realize Hayley had opened her eyes. Which suited her. She liked looking at the way Jake's big strong hands tenderly swayed the small bundle, as if he held something precious.

Hayley couldn't recall the size or shape of her father's hands. Or if he'd ever held her like that. But he must have. Ben said she'd been her parents' pride and joy.

Hayley had always intended that her children would have the love of two parents. Sadly that wasn't to be. A hole seemed to open in her heart and left her feeling drained and empty.

"Well, hello, sleepyhead." Jake stopped rocking and bestowed a loving smile on the rumpled woman in the bed. "Your daughter was just telling me her tummy's growling and I should interrupt your nap."

Hayley scrambled into a sitting position, hoping Jake hadn't been able to read her dark thoughts. As he leaned over her and placed Cammy in her arms, another wave of emotion swamped her. Jake smelled like sunshine and soil and car grease. Earthy scents Hayley associated with good memories. It shook her to realize she still did have good memories of men. Her dad. Gramps. And now Jake Cooper.

"Before you get started feeding the wee one," Jake said, straightening to slide a hand into his snug jeans pocket, "I have something for you."

"Jake, you can't keep buying me things." Even as she said it, Hayley was curious to know what kind of gift would fit in his pocket.

He pressed a pendant into her hand. A white-gold modern bas-relief sculpture of the Madonna and child. Where their faces should have been were two ovals of pale blue. *Her opals.*

"I asked Eden to specially make it for you," Jake murmured. "I know it'll never replace your mother's cameo, but I wanted you to have something to commemorate Cammy's birth and your opal discovery."

Hayley's tears began to flow. They fell like rain, wetting Cammy's blanket.

Jake, who was better prepared for Hayley's tears this time, kissed them away while he fastened the chain around her neck. "It has a safety catch on the back of the pendant if you'd rather pin it on a jacket."

His smile held more than warmth and friendship. Hayley recognized love in the depths of his eyes. Her trembling fingers blindly sought and found the smooth pendant. Clutching it, she stammered out a wholly inadequate thank-you. Twisting to stare at the delicate piece, she whispered, "I've never told a soul, but Joe…didn't buy me a wedding ring. At the JP's, I gave him a gold band. He refused to wear it. I saved out of my grocery money and bought myself a band. He got mad. Said it was a waste of money. Oh, I don't know why I'm telling you this. It's just…your mom said the sheriff came by. If Joe knows I have anything this nice,

Jacob—'' her voice turned to a sob ''—he'll find a way
to take it away.''

''Shh.'' Jake tipped her tear-streaked face up and
kissed her lips. ''I'm not going to let Joe near you. Dad's
phoned our lawyer. He said for you not to worry. Joe's
bogus lawsuit will be laughed out of court.''

Eden knocked on the open door. ''Excuse me. I hate
to interrupt this touching scene, but I'm dying to know
what Hayley thinks of the pendant.''

Hayley could do little more than telegraph Eden a wet
radiant smile.

''I told Jake it was a bad idea, that you'd hate it.''
Eden entered the room, nudged Jake and winked. ''I
guess you won't mind if I steal this precious lamb while
you pull yourself together,'' she teased Hayley. ''Oh, I
can see now she's a future Miss America,'' Eden
breathed, gazing reverently at the baby.

Still with a death grip on the pendant, Hayley tried
again to articulate her deep appreciation.

Eden brushed off Hayley's gratitude. ''It's a simple
design. Jake sketched what he wanted. The hardest part
was finding matched opals. The stone is a joy to cut and
polish, as you'll soon learn. Well, not too soon,'' she
added, smiling into the infant's sweet face. ''Some time
this spring. How does March sound? By then, you guys
will be settled in Jake's new house. Besides, if you bring
Cammy to work too soon, I'll be tempted to badger Dillon into starting our family a year earlier than we've
planned.''

Hayley clutched the Madonna so tightly her knuckles
turned white and she almost snapped the slender chain.
''I...I'm not moving in with Jake.''

Eden shot her brother-in-law an apologetic glance.
''Oops. Nell and I thought we'd given you time enough

to pop the question. Shall I call Dillon? Do you need a script?''

Jake closed his eyes. ''Scram, Eden,'' he muttered gruffly.

''Sure. But get on the stick, Jacob. Nell and I are itching to decorate for a holiday wedding.''

''Eden!'' Jake roared. His harsh voice startled Cammy. She screwed up her small face and let out a cry. Rising, Jake relieved his sister-in-law of the baby. Holding Cammy on his shoulder with one hand, he used the other to hustle Eden out.

She muscled her way back into the room and grinned at Hayley. ''I'm counting on being your matron of honor. I've got a new bronze-colored dress just begging for such an event. And Nell reminded me that the boutique across the street from the shop has a gorgeous, pale-peach empire-waist dress that would go great with your coloring. With Nell's pearls, it'd make a perfect wedding—''

Jake shut the door. He stood, facing away from Hayley a moment, catching his breath before he found the courage to turn and look at her. When he did, he felt awful. She'd turned white as the sheet clenched in one hand. ''Well,'' he said lamely, ''now that Eden's let the cat out of the bag, I guess I'll have to hold you prisoner until you agree to marry me.'' He kissed the baby, who'd quieted.

''Dammit, Hayley, I was going to soften you up with the pendant and then drag out the big guns.'' Fishing in his shirt pocket, Jake produced a flat velvet pouch. He sat on the edge of her bed and laid it in Hayley's lap while he pried her cold fingers open. It wasn't easy, but he eventually managed with one hand to dump out a pair of wide gold bands studded with diamonds and opals.

"If you'd rather have a set with an engagement ring, I'll have Eden trade yours. Unlike Joe Ryan, Hayley, I want the world to know I have a wife. I want everyone to know we're a matched set."

She picked up the smaller of the two bands. Her lower lip quivered, but this time she was determined not to cry. "I love you, Jake. But I've been so afraid to let that happen. I don't need fancy rings or houses. Only regular hugs from someone who'll love me and Cammy unconditionally."

"I know," he said, tears springing to his eyes as he moved closer and urged her to share his grip on the baby. "What I need is for you to trust me completely."

"I do. I think I have from the beginning."

"It's done, then. And there'll be no more doubts, Hayley. From here on, you and Cammy are part of the Cooper family." He kissed her and drew back. "Feed this hungry child while I go alleviate everyone's anxiety. Mom, Dad, Dillon and Eden are all in the kitchen waiting for your answer."

Hayley detained him a moment, stealing another kiss. Jake backed from the room, wearing a goofy grin. "Hold that thought," he said.

THE WEDDING WAS SMALL, but more lavish than the harvest dance, which not one of the Coopers had attended. They'd had too much going on. Their ranch house rang with the laughter of family and close friends.

Hayley wore the peach dress, but she refused Nell's pearls. The opal Madonna-and-child pendant and her new wedding band were the only jewelry she wanted.

The minister christened Cammy at the same time— Cameo Joy Cooper. Jake had tracked down Joe Ryan— in jail—and convinced him to relinquish his rights to

Hayley's daughter. It hadn't been difficult. Adding to his sleaziness, Joe couldn't wait to sign away any responsibility. Of course, he wasn't in any position to offer support. Mere days after the incident at Hayley's camp, Joe and Shad Tilford had been arrested for smuggling illegal substances across the border. Cammy would be ready for college before Joe finished serving his sentence. And Hayley's opals would more than pay her way through.

Following the wedding ceremony and before Jake spirited Hayley away for a one-night honeymoon at a bed-and-breakfast in Tubac, Nell and Eden took Hayley aside. "Come into the kitchen," Nell urged. Eden proudly displayed a new sign for their shop. "Wade carved it," Nell said, tracing the letters spelling out Triple C Southwest Art Gallery.

Eden gave Hayley a spontaneous hug. "Wade renamed the ranch the Triple C when Dillon and Jacob became his partners. We three Cooper women are partners, too. It's only fitting we trade on such a distinguished name, don't you think?"

"I promised myself I wouldn't cry tonight," Hayley said, sniffling. "Darn, I lied." She broke down completely as Nell thrust a tissue into her hands.

The Cooper men crowded into the doorway. Their eyes weren't exactly dry. Jake covered his tears fairly well by twice repeating instructions to his mother for taking care of Cammy while he and Hayley went away for the night.

Dillon broke the tension. He walked over and clapped Jake on the back. "When you get back, I have a housewarming gift. It's a sacrifice, but what are brothers for? I'm giving you guys Coronado."

"What?" Eden shrieked. "Give them my parrot? No

way! You should be ashamed. The poor bird just needs more attention.''

"I was kidding. Only kidding." Dillon captured Eden and kissed her silent, making everyone smile. "Believe it or not, I've made peace with that fowl."

"Wait." Hayley hung back as Jake dropped her new wool coat around her shoulders and eagerly shepherded toward the door. "I have a gift, too."

The group eyed Jake, all assuming it was some sort of bride's gift to her groom. What Hayley pulled from her purse was a bill of sale for the twenty acres on which her mine, and the spring, were located. "I asked your lawyer to handle everything, Wade," she said shyly. "I wanted to make sure the land belongs irrevocably to the Triple C."

No one knew quite what to say. "The opals from the mine are all yours, Hayley," Jake said, cupping her face softly as he turned up her collar. "I'll help you dig the ore, but everything earned goes into your private bank account."

Dillon and Wade quickly seconded Jake's promise.

Rising on tiptoe, Hayley pressed a lingering kiss to her husband's lips. "Last week when Eden drove me into town to try on the dress, I had the bank move everything from my account into the joint one you established for us, Jake. Cammy and I are Coopers now. It's share and share alike."

Jake almost didn't get out of the house to go on their honeymoon, although Dr. Gerrard had given Hayley the okay to resume all normal activity a few days before the ceremony. And Jake had been counting the minutes until they could consummate their marriage. Her announcement came as a shock. Trusting him with the nest egg that had for so long spelled her independence and

Cammy's future was like announcing to the world that she embraced his love fully and completely.

"Come on, Mrs. Cooper," Jake whispered, tracing her lips with his tongue. "Tonight we share a bed, setting a precedent for the rest of our lives."

Eden, Dillon, Wade and the remaining guests followed the couple outside into the cool night, pelting them with laughter and birdseed. Charcoal raced around trying to catch the seed in midair.

A smiling Nell Cooper stood framed in the living-room window, her first grandchild cradled in her arms.

"Look, Jake." Hayley stopped him before he backed the new reliable Land Cruiser he'd bought her out of the drive. "With the lamp shining behind Nell, she and Cammy could be models for my pendant."

"Mom wasn't my model, Hayley. Even before Cammy was born, it's how I pictured the two of you. My wife and my child." Straining against a seat belt that held him fast, Jake kissed her fully and deeply. A kiss that brimmed with love.

"I love you, Jacob Cooper. I'm about the luckiest woman alive," Hayley murmured in a husky whisper.

"Likewise," he returned. "I'll show you exactly how much after we check in tonight." Jake framed her lovely face with his hands momentarily before drawing away. "But I'm the lucky one. No man could ask for more than a wife like you to make his house a home. You and Cammy complete my life, Mrs. Cooper."

Hayley snuggled happily against his shoulder. "And you, Mr. Cooper, are the fulfillment of all my dreams."

THREE FOR THE ROAD

Shannon Waverly

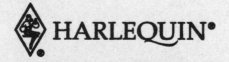

TORONTO • NEW YORK • LONDON
AMSTERDAM • PARIS • SYDNEY • HAMBURG
STOCKHOLM • ATHENS • TOKYO • MILAN • MADRID
PRAGUE • WARSAW • BUDAPEST • AUCKLAND

PROLOGUE

CHARLES DRUMMOND STARED at his daughter over his reading glasses. "How far along are you?"

Mary Elizabeth swallowed. "Nearly three months."

"Nearly three months," he echoed, his long patrician face set in distaste.

"I'm sorry," she said on a broken whisper.

Removing his glasses and tossing them onto the desk, he got to his feet and began to pace. "How could you do this, Mary Elizabeth?" He didn't raise his voice. A Drummond never did. "How could you bring such disgrace to this house?"

Above his meticulously groomed gray head hung a family portrait painted seventeen years earlier, one year after he'd been named president of the Deerfield Institution for Savings and two years before his wife's death. The five Drummonds presented as perfect a family image as ever there was, even to the extent that the artist had inadvertently painted Mary Elizabeth's eyes blue instead of brown, to match everyone else's.

"But no one cares about such things anymore." Mary Elizabeth spread her hands. "Times have changed."

Charles stopped pacing. A muscle jumped in his cheek. "If you believe that, you're more a fool than I thought."

She flinched.

"People talk, Mary Elizabeth, especially about families like ours. And they never forget. Ten years from now, twenty, they'll still remember you as the Drummond girl who got pregnant before she was married.''

This wasn't the way she'd envisioned their conversation. She'd entered this library hoping they'd discuss her situation like two rational, enlightened adults. She hadn't come looking for easy answers; all she'd wanted was his love and support during a difficult time. When would she ever learn?

Charles reseated himself in his leather chair with a long disgruntled sigh. ''Have you set a date?''

''For what?''

''A wedding, of course. Have you and Roger set a date?''

Her breath stalled. ''No. Roger doesn't even know.''

''Well, what are you waiting for? Are you afraid he'll refuse to marry you? He won't. He's an extraordinarily decent young man.''

''Father, we broke up seven weeks ago. It's over between us.''

Charles breathed out a bitter laugh. ''Apparently not.''

''But I don't want to marry Roger. We don't love each other.''

''You made your bed, Mary Elizabeth…or do you think you're so extraordinary you should be excused from doing what's morally right?''

''No, of course not, but I don't see the point of raising a child in a loveless home.''

''You should be grateful to be so lucky. Roger has a good job and a secure future at the bank. He doesn't have any vices that I can see…well, any *other* vices.'' His hard blue eyes flicked briefly to her waist. ''He comes from a pleasant family.…''

But Mary Elizabeth was still shaking her head. ''Marrying under these circumstances, he'd feel trapped. He'd resent me and the baby. I don't want that."

"What do you intend to do, then, have it out of wedlock?"

"I…yes, that's an option."

Charles shot her a crippling look. "Over my dead body."

"But—"

"I don't care if certain segments of society have relaxed their standards, or that unmarried mothers are as common these days as the married variety. Drummonds do not belong to that vulgar trash."

Mary Elizabeth glanced at the painting, blinking away tears. It seemed she'd been receiving lectures all her life on how Drummonds did or did not behave. Once again, she didn't measure up.

"Tell me, what sort of social life do you expect to have, burdened with a child?"

She misunderstood his remark as rising from concern and was about to reassure him when he added, "Who do you think is going to be interested in you now?"

A piercing pain sliced right through her.

"It isn't merely that you're pregnant, although Lord knows that's a formidable enough reason for any man to avoid getting involved with you. After all, who wants to take on another man's child?"

Mary Elizabeth's breathing had become so labored it felt as if someone had stuffed a rag down her throat.

"It's also the fact that you've obviously had intimate relations, and by remaining unmarried, you're all but announcing to the world that those relations were meaningless. From there, I'm afraid, it's an easy leap for people to see you as indiscriminate and promiscuous. In plain English, Mary Elizabeth, they'll see you as cheap."

With each word he leveled at her, Mary Elizabeth felt

smaller and dirtier. She sensed she ought to say something in her defense, but her will to act seemed to have deserted her. On a level she hadn't wanted to acknowledge, she knew her father made sense.

"I hope you realize I'm saying these things only because I'm concerned about your future happiness. I want to see you settled, with a family, in your own home. But if you continue to follow this path, I don't see how that's possible." Charles smoothed a palm over the desk blotter, wiping away imaginary dust. "Now, you might argue there are lots of broad-minded men out there who'd be interested in you, but don't kid yourself, Mary Elizabeth. Most decent men still want to marry a 'nice' girl, no matter how liberal they claim to be, and I hate to say this, but the label that's usually attached to the sort of woman you aspire to being is—" he cleared his throat "—'used goods.'"

In a mature, detached part of her brain, Mary Elizabeth marveled at her father's ability to manipulate her emotions. Equally astonishing was her inability to stand up to him. But it wasn't really such a mystery; they'd had a lifetime of this sort of confrontation to perfect the pattern.

Unfortunately, knowing what was happening still didn't prevent her from being reduced to a helpless bundle of shame and guilt. She could only lower her eyes and hope she didn't break down before she reached her room.

Charles folded his hands on the desk blotter. "Have you considered terminating the situation?"

Mary Elizabeth blinked, rising out of her pain. "No."

"And why not?"

She reared back in sheer incredulity. Her father had been a pro-lifer as long as she could remember. But apparently the "morally right thing to do" existed on a sliding scale, depending on how close to home an unpleasant situation struck.

"I just can't."

He shook his head. "Ah, Mary Elizabeth. You've always been a burden."

She looked down at the Persian carpet, remembering other times, other lectures, when she'd stood just so. Yes, she'd been a burden to him, not as studious as his two other children, not as well-groomed, never as well-behaved. She'd tried. Lord, how she'd tried. But evidently there was simply something inherently wrong with her.

Charles pinned her with a look of renewed determination. "Tell Roger."

She shook her head.

"If you don't, I will."

Panic engulfed her. "You can't."

"I most certainly can. If you insist on having this baby, then, by God, you'll have it married. You'll give no one reason to gossip." Not for a second did he doubt his ability to persuade Roger to marry her. Neither did Mary Elizabeth. Apart from the fact that Roger idolized Charles, he enjoyed his job far too much to cross his employer.

For one brief moment, Mary Elizabeth regained her normal adult perspective and saw her father's attitude as absurd and archaic. She was twenty-seven years old, for heaven's sake. She was an educated, accomplished woman in a professional career. He had no business dictating her decisions, especially one that was so important. And that was why, when he offered her one last alternative—the choice to go away, have the child and give it up for adoption, a choice she was already leaning heavily toward herself—she said no.

"No?" Charles jerked his head, as if her impudence had struck him a physical blow.

"No."

In a most uncharacteristic loss of control, he flung a

priceless paperweight across the room. It hit a plaster bust of Winston Churchill, leaving the statesman without a chin. "Damn you, Mary Elizabeth! You're just like your mother."

Mary Elizabeth frowned. She didn't understand his comment and would have let it go—if he just hadn't turned so red.

"What do you mean, I'm just like my mother?"

He continued to stare at her, saying nothing, but a look came into his eyes, an angry determination she thought she'd seen over the years now and again, a look almost too fleeting for her to be sure it had been there before it moved on, always leaving her trembling and relieved when it did.

"Tell me." She shot forward, gripping the edge of his desk, challenging him, finally.

This time the look in his eyes didn't pass. It settled in and focused, like the cross hairs on a rifle.

"Why am I like my mother?" she persisted. "Tell me." And he did.

CHAPTER ONE

KEEP MOVING, DRUMMOND. Don't think. Just pick up the carton and go!

Mary Elizabeth obeyed her own command, ignoring her fatigue and mounting anxiety, and carried the last of her bedroom things down the wide, elegantly turned stairs.

But at the open front door, a surge of sadness blindsided her and caused her to hesitate. Outside, at the top of the circular brick driveway, basking in the golden September sun, was what might appear to be an ordinary eighteen-foot motor home. To Mary Elizabeth, however, it was her future.

Behind her rose the dignified, twelve-room Georgian where she'd lived all her life—her past. Her very definite, no-coming-back past. Her throat tightened and her eyes threatened to well up again.

Fortunately, Mrs. Pidgin chose that moment to come lumbering down the hall from the kitchen. The poor woman was already upset enough and didn't need to see Mary Elizabeth breaking down, too. She pulled in a fortifying breath and smiled before turning.

The short, sixty-year-old housekeeper was carrying two plastic grocery bags by their straining handles, their weight seeming to tip her blocky form side to side as she walked. Like a windup toy, Mary Elizabeth thought with painfully deep affection. She only hoped the woman didn't end up like most of those toys, overbalanced and on her side.

"What's all this?" she asked. They'd already packed the RV with more than enough food to get her through her trip from Maine to Florida.

"Just a little extra. You never know."

Mary Elizabeth suppressed a smile. Mrs. Pidgin was fussing over her as if she were setting off on a months-long journey in a covered wagon instead of a three-day zip down the interstate.

"Thanks, Mrs. P. But I wish you'd stop worrying. I'm going to be fine."

"Of course you will. Of course."

They both looked at the foyer floor, unable to hold each other's gaze, then hastily headed out to the motor home.

Inside the vehicle, Mary Elizabeth threaded her way through the kitchen, down the short passageway with the bathroom on one side and storage cupboards on the other, to the bedroom at the rear. With a grunt of relief, she dropped the box she was carrying onto one of the two twin beds—already overburdened with her belongings.

The motor home was a marvel of storage compartments, but in her haste she hadn't packed as efficiently as she could have. She'd do that later, when she had more time. Right now she felt compelled to hurry. Charles had gone to the bank this morning, giving no indication he'd be returning to see her off, but Mary Elizabeth didn't trust him anymore. She especially didn't trust him to keep from speaking to Roger.

Although Charles abhorred the idea of her staying in town, pregnant and unmarried, he didn't like her going away so abruptly, either. People were bound to wonder what had happened here to cause such unseemly behavior, he said. He also worried about her accidentally running into people they knew during her pregnancy. And what if she decided to return with the baby some day? His lack of control over the situation bothered him, and she knew he'd started thinking of telling Roger again. To Charles, marriage was still the best solution to the problem.

Mrs. Pidgin was fitting a package of six single-serving quiches in the freezer compartment of the refrigerator when Mary Elizabeth emerged from the bedroom.

"Here, let me help." She dipped into the bag, pulled out a deli container of lobster salad and tossed it into the refrigerator.

Mrs. Pidgin closed the freezer. "I don't suppose there's anything I can say that'll make you change your mind." It was a question, a last-ditch hope. She was the only person other than Charles who knew why Mary Elizabeth was leaving. She was the only person, period, who knew where she was going. Mary Elizabeth had told Charles Chicago, in case he decided to come looking for her, but she didn't want to drop off the map entirely. She wanted someone here to know where she was if a family emergency arose.

"Change my mind? Afraid not, Mrs. P."

The housekeeper's face looked pained. "Well, I can't really say as I blame you. Your father's behavior this past week has been unforgivable."

Mary Elizabeth worked at keeping her expression set. The past week had been difficult, that was for sure. Charles had found a reason to make each day hurtful and exhausting. He'd continued to harp on her pregnancy and denounce her choices, and always he wondered what people would say if they knew. The barbs that especially dug in, though, probably because she was already frightened and insecure, were the ones regarding her ability to survive on her own.

Charles accused her of having no real job skills or practical experience, and said the only reason she'd landed the curatorship at the local museum five years ago was that he had used his influence with the board. She'd never find another position like it, he said, just as she'd never find another man like Roger whom, coincidentally, Charles had also "provided" since he'd arranged their first date.

Mary Elizabeth didn't know what she would have done without Mrs. Pidgin. The woman had always been an ally and a comfort, but never more so than this past week.

Mrs. Pidgin had accidentally overheard the tail end of the conversation between Mary Elizabeth and Charles in the library, the part about Eliza Drummond's affair and Mary Elizabeth's true parentage, and had followed Mary Elizabeth up to her room afterward. There a shattered Mary Elizabeth had broken down, letting the shock of Charles's revelation give way to grief.

When she'd eventually brought her tears under control, she'd filled Mrs. Pidgin in on the rest of the conversation and the full scope of her dilemma. Mrs. Pidgin had been shaken when she learned of Mary Elizabeth's pregnancy, but she'd controlled her reaction well, better than Mary Elizabeth had when she learned the housekeeper had known all along about Eliza's illicit romance. Despite Charles's order not to tell anyone, Eliza had confided in Mrs. Pidgin. Mary Elizabeth could understand why. In time of trouble, a more loyal and nonjudgmental friend couldn't be found.

At present, that friend was folding the empty grocery bag with exaggerated care, distracted by her continuing worries.

"I just wish you weren't taking the camper," she said, frowning. "Such a big, difficult thing to drive." She tucked the folded bag into a drawer crammed full of embroidered tea towels and cutwork napkins. "It would be a lot easier if you left it here and let my Alfred sell it for you. You could take a plane then, have a moving truck transport your things. That way you could relax, take more things with you, too."

With a sigh, Mary Elizabeth reached into the second grocery bag. "I thought you understood, moving vans are expensive. So are plane tickets. Besides, I don't need any more things." She wasn't sure of much these days, but she was certain that taking the RV was the right choice. Not only would it get her and her possessions to Sarasota economically, but it would also become her home once she got there.

Chloe, her old college roommate, lived in Sarasota, and when Mary Elizabeth made the decision to move away from the northeast, she'd immediately called Chloe. Her friend had said she knew of a trailer park a few miles from her house that might take her in. Mary Elizabeth hoped so. She didn't want to impose on Chloe, who was a newlywed. Neither did she want to encumber herself with the expenses of an apartment until she was secure in a well-paying job, and that might be a while. In addition, things might not work out for her in the Sarasota area, and what better way to move on than to simply turn an ignition key?

With the groceries finally put away, she started for the door, eager to get the last of her belongings and be on her way.

"Stop a minute, will you please?" Mrs. Pidgin grasped Mary Elizabeth's wrist. "I won't keep you long, I promise." The housekeeper tugged her gently toward the front of the RV. Mary Elizabeth took the driver's seat, swiveling it to face the other.

"All right, so you're going, then."

Such a note of finality, Mary Elizabeth thought. She looked down at her clenched hands. A faint band of white skin, left by Roger's engagement ring, was still discernible against her light tan. "Yes," she said softly.

Mrs. Pidgin sighed. "You have to promise me you'll be careful on the road. Florida is so far away, and you haven't had that much experience driving or being on your own."

It was useless to remind Mrs. Pidgin that she'd had her license for eleven years and never been in an accident. The woman worried as only a person could who'd never driven or traveled—irrationally.

Besides, there was a grain of truth to what Mrs. Pidgin said. Mary Elizabeth hadn't traveled much. She'd bought the motor home a full year ago, but since then had taken only four weekend trips, all within New England.

"Please don't worry. The trip takes only three days, four if I drive very slow, and it's major highway all the way. What could possibly go wrong?"

The older woman stared deep into her eyes. "A lot," she said, her voice grave.

"Don't talk like that," Mary Elizabeth chided mildly. "You're scaring me."

"Good. That's good. The crime rate being what it is, you should be scared." The housekeeper tipped to one side so she could slip her hand into the right pocket of her blue cotton housedress. "I have something I want to give you." She pulled out a small plastic figure and set it on the dash.

"A St. Christopher?" Mary Elizabeth bit off a laugh.

"Ayeh."

"But he was kicked off the saint roster almost thirty years ago."

The woman's look said she didn't want to hear it. Mary Elizabeth closed her mouth and gave the icon, protector of travelers, a welcoming nod.

Mrs. Pidgin pulled a second item from her pocket, a square blue envelope. "I have something else."

Mary Elizabeth gazed at the envelope. "What is it?"

"Something from your mother. She gave it to me before she died. She told me I was to give it to you only if Charles did something like he did this week and you found out he wasn't your real father."

Mary Elizabeth's fine-boned jaw hardened. "What makes you think I want anything from her?"

"She was your mother,· Mary Elizabeth, and no matter how upset you are with her now, you still love her. I know you do." Mrs. Pidgin placed the envelope on Mary Elizabeth's knee. "Here. It isn't much, but it belongs with you now."

Giving in to curiosity, Mary Elizabeth opened the envelope and pulled out a yellowed photograph. "Oh." The sound she made was barely audible.

"Ayeh, that's him, your real father. A handsome fella, wasn't he. You have his eyes."

Mary Elizabeth gazed at the man in the photo with a mixture of fascination and denial. He was slim, good-looking, young. A carpenter's belt, heavy with tools, hung around his hips. Behind him rose the Drummond house with its sun room under construction.

Swallowing, she slipped the photograph into her open purse on the floor. "Thank you," she said quietly.

"Wait. I have something else." Mrs. Pidgin grunted as she tipped to the right, pushing her hand into her left pocket this time.

Mary Elizabeth's eyes popped when she saw what the woman pulled out. "Where did you get such a thing?"

"Oh, it isn't a real gun."

Mary Elizabeth looked at her skeptically.

"Believe it or not, this is only a toy, a water pistol. My Alfred bought it for our grandson, but Judy wouldn't allow him to keep it."

"I can see why. It looks so real." Mary Elizabeth gazed at the lethal-looking toy. She'd heard such things existed. She'd even read about them being used in robberies, but she'd never actually seen one before. "And you want me to..."

"Yes, take it. Here." The housekeeper placed the water pistol in Mary Elizabeth's lap. "I wish I had a real weapon to give you, but—" she shrugged "—this might work if you're ever in a bind."

Mary Elizabeth stifled the urge to laugh. She thought Mrs. Pidgin's fear of traveling had put her over the edge, but she said a polite thank-you, anyway, and slipped the gun into her purse.

Mrs. Pidgin breathed a sigh of relief. "Good. Now, another thing…" She dug into the pocket again. Mary Elizabeth was beginning to feel decidedly like a knight in a medieval tale, being given magical gifts before setting off on a quest.

"Here's my cousin's phone number in Orlando and my sister's in Gainesville. If you ever need help, anything whatsoever…"

Mary Elizabeth nodded. "I'll call. I promise I will." She took the slip of paper and filed that in her bag, as well.

"You have enough money?"

"Yes, and my credit cards, too. Don't worry."

Mrs. Pidgin took Mary Elizabeth's smooth, slender hands in her plump, work-reddened ones. "I have only one more thing to ask." Her voice lowered. "If things don't work out for you, you've got to promise me you won't let pride prevent you from coming back."

Mary Elizabeth turned her head and gazed out the windshield toward the perfectly sheared shrubs gracing the perfectly manicured lawn that surrounded Charles Drummond's perfectly perfect house.

"I can't promise that," she replied hollowly.

"I know it hurts now but—"

"Hurts? Learning you aren't who you always thought you were doesn't 'hurt.' It's more like having your entire world turned inside out." Or maybe, she thought, like discovering that gravity doesn't work anymore. Your footing is gone and you're spinning away from everything that's familiar, out of control, with nothing to hold you safe.

Turning, she saw that the housekeeper's red-rimmed eyes had filled again.

"But such a big step."

Mary Elizabeth pulled her hands away and placed them tentatively on the steering wheel. There was nothing tentative about her voice, however, when she said, "I have no choice. I have to go. There's nothing left for me here. Charlie's in London doing graduate work, and Susan has her own family to keep her busy. We were never close, anyway. All I have, really, is you."

Mrs. Pidgin wiped her eyes and rasped a string of curses, all directed at Charles Drummond.

"Don't be angry with him, Mrs. P. It couldn't have been easy for him all these years, either. Every time he looked at me, he must've been reminded of my mother's infidelity. Actually, he did more for me than anyone in his position was obligated to do."

"Ayeh," Mrs. Pidgin affirmed bitterly. "All those insulting lectures, all that criticism... and the restrictions he imposed! It's a wonder you didn't choke on all he did for you."

Mary Elizabeth shook her head. "He was instilling values, Mrs. P. Punctuality, neatness, frugality. I have no complaints. Just the opposite. I led a privileged life here. Just look at the house where I was raised. I had the best clothes, went to the best schools...."

"Only because he was afraid. If he didn't give you those things, same as he gave your sister and brother, people might wonder why he'd singled you out. And if there's one thing your...Charles can't abide, it's having folks think anything's wrong here. He's the proudest fool I ever met."

"You're right. And that's the reason—one of the reasons—I'm leaving. I don't want him feeling shamed or unable to hold up his head in town just because I refuse to get married."

"Just? There's no 'just' about it."

"Right again. Getting married is hardly a trivial step." Mary Elizabeth smiled, trying to shift the conversation onto a more cheerful path. "Besides, it's past time for me to leave the nest. I'm practically ancient, Mrs. P." But the brightness slid from her voice when she said, "I need my independence. I want to finally be free."

The two women fell quiet. Outside the motor home, birds chirped noisily in the maples that bordered the property. The foliage looked played out, even a little tired. The calendar might say it was still summer, but the sky was too blue, too dry and clear. Change was in the air.

Finally, the older woman said softly, "You'll call me when you reach your friend's, won't you?"

"Of course. And you won't tell Charles where I've really gone until I tell you it's safe?"

"Ayeh." Mrs. Pidgin gazed at her a long, worried moment. "Well, I can't think of anything else, so maybe we should get on with your packing. Is there much more?"

"Only the rocker from my room and the cat." Mary Elizabeth rose and the woman followed. But at the door of the RV, Mary Elizabeth turned. "Before I go, I'd like you to know…" She fidgeted self-consciously with the buttons on her jacket. "I mean, what I want to say is…" She swallowed, and then simply wrapped Mrs. Pidgin in a fierce hug. The woman patted her consolingly while tears streamed down her wrinkled cheeks.

"I know. I love you, too, Mary Elizabeth."

EVEN THE PHONE BOOTH brought a smile to Pete Mitchell's eyes. You just didn't see those things anymore, only the open half-shells that looked like something out of *Star Trek* and didn't exactly encourage a guy to linger or say anything personal.

The glass bi-fold door closed with a familiar squeak-thump, recalling hot summer nights, cheap after-shave, and dialing Sue Ellen Carlisle's number while friends serenaded him with cat calls and whistles from the drugstore corner.

Pete lifted the receiver, noted the rotary dial and got the urge to call everybody he knew. He called his office.

Outside the booth, morning sunshine glittered over the dewy, deep green lawn in front of the Rest E-Z Motel. Old Adirondack chairs, ignorant of the fact that they had become a hot new item in backyard furniture, dozed under a stand of maples and birches.

Pete lowered himself to the booth's small metal bench as the call went through. He tried to cross his legs, rest his right ankle over his left knee, but his long limbs kept knocking into things.

He heard a click, and then, ''Mitchell Construction.''

''Brad?'' he said, surprised to hear his brother's voice.

''Pete?''

''Yeah.''

''Hey. How ya doin', man?''

''Great. What are you doing answering the phone?''

''Oh, I thought I'd goof off, sit around and drink coffee. My boss is gone for ten days.''

Pete knew Brad was kidding, at least he hoped he did, but that didn't stop his stomach from tightening. They were already two weeks behind on the McKenna house.

''Did the shipment of drywall come in?''

''Hey, you're on vacation. You're not supposed to be thinking about work. Remember?''

Pete sent a daddy longlegs flying off his boot with a flick of a finger. "So, did the drywall come in?"

His brother chuckled. "No. I just called, though—that's what I'm doing here at the office—and it's on its way. Should be here tomorrow."

"Good. Get the men on it right away, as many as you can spare."

"I will." After a short pause Brad said, "So, did you get it?" His voice contained a smile.

As did Pete's when he replied, "Get what?"

"The measles. Jeez Louise! You know what."

Pete laughed. "Yeah, I got it."

Brad whooped. "Oh, man! That's great. So, tell me about it. Is she as sweet as the ad promised?"

"Sweeter. What a beauty, Brad. I even brought her into my motel room with me last night. Couldn't get enough of looking at her."

"Good price?"

"For a mint-condition '53 Triumph, the exact same model Brando rode in *The Wild One*? Yeah, it was a good price. Well, a little steep. The old man knew what he had. But she's worth it."

"I can't wait to see it. Where are you now?"

"Still in New Hampshire, west side of Lake Winni-pesukee, about forty miles south of where I bought the bike, although I must've put a hundred and forty on it yesterday up in the mountains." He paused, his sharp builder's eye sweeping the grounds.

"I wish you could see the motel I stayed in last night, Brad. Separate cabins, each about the size of a garden shed, painted this bright fifties aqua. It's the genuine article, too, not some fake retro setup with an eye on the nostalgia buck. I'm calling from a phone booth outside the motel office 'cause there aren't any phones in the rooms."

"And you're having a good time?"

"The best." He hadn't taken a vacation like this in so long he'd forgotten how much he enjoyed being on the road, totally alone and freewheeling—how much he needed it. His construction business had thrived this past year, and he'd been working full-tilt all that time, unaware of the wear and tear on his body as well as his spirit. But already he felt better, and he'd been gone from home a mere two days.

"Only you, Pete. Only you." Brad laughed. "So, are you still going to ride her home?"

"That's the plan." That had always been the plan. Pete had flown up from Tampa on a one-way ticket, with only a duffel bag and a certainty of his luck.

"What I'd like to know is," Brad said, "what are you gonna do with one more antique motorcycle?"

"Love her, cherish her, till the road runs out for either one of us, what else?"

Brad chuckled. "That reminds me, somebody stopped by the apartment yesterday who maybe wishes you'd think about *her* in those terms."

Pete was glad his brother couldn't see his face. He suspected it had fallen to somewhere around his knees. "Sue Ellen?" he asked, trying not to hesitate. Hesitation might give his brother the impression he cared more than he did.

"Uh-huh."

"What did she want?"

"Came by to hand-deliver her reply to our wedding invitation."

"Cutting it close, wasn't she?"

"Sure was. Jill had to call the country club last night with a final count."

Pete swallowed. "So, is she coming?"

"Of course. She is Jill's cousin, after all."

Pete got to his feet and moved around the phone booth like an agitated tiger in a too-small cage. Two teenage girls, walking slowly in his direction and trying to pretend they weren't checking him out, giggled.

Brad said, "I'm reluctant to give people advice, especially my older and so-much-wiser brother, but now that her divorce is finalized, this might be a good opportunity for you to explore the possibility of getting back with her. She's a gorgeous lady, Pete, and if you ask me she's still real interested in you."

"No, she isn't."

"No? Then how come she's been calling you three times a week? How come she's been coming by the office?"

"She's thinking of renovating her house, dummy."

"A house that was built only six years ago? Come on, Pete, open your eyes."

Brad was getting a real kick out of this. So were their sisters, Pam and Lindy. They saw it as the ultimate romance, Pete and Sue Ellen, high school sweethearts, getting back together after fifteen years of unfortunate separation.

Pete saw it as a good time to hit the road.

"Listen, kid, I'm not interested in getting back with Sue Ellen, and I don't want any matchmaking going on at your wedding, hear?"

"Yeah, I hear."

No, he didn't. Pete could tell his brother was smirking.

"Look, just because you're getting married doesn't mean everybody around you should do the same. Hell, you're getting as bad as your sisters."

"It might not be a bad idea to start thinking about settling down, too, Pete. I think I saw a few gray hairs on your head the other day."

"Yeah, well, they're my gray hairs and I'll thank you not to worry about them. Hell, I'm never going that route again. Once was enough for a lifetime. For several life-times.''

A few seconds of uneasy silence followed, then Brad said, ''Not to change the subject, but when can I expect my best man to get home?'' The reminder of Pete's disastrous marriage had effectively killed the discussion. Pete felt his equanimity return.

''Do you need me sooner than Friday? Not this Friday. The one before the wedding, I mean.''

''Of course I need you. I'm getting as nervous as a turkey in November.''

Grinning, Pete picked at a small tear on the right knee of his jeans. ''Well, hell, I'm hardly the guy to have around if what you're looking for's support. My advice would be to give up this deranged idea of marriage and come on the road with me.''

''You just haven't met the right girl yet,'' Brad replied righteously. ''Wait till you do. You'll be eating your words.''

''Don't hold your breath.''

''And don't you go sounding so sure of yourself. But to answer your question—no, I don't need you. Just be here the day before the wedding. We have to pick up our tuxes and go to the rehearsal.''

''Sure enough. How's the rest of the family holding up?''

''Good. Pam has decided to have the rehearsal dinner at her house.''

''That isn't necessary. You know I offered to take everybody to The Sand Dollar.''

''You've done enough, Pete. Besides, she really wants to do this.''

''Well, in that case... Has Lindy's husband made it into work this week?''

"So far."

Pete sniffed. He didn't like his brother-in-law a helluva lot. The guy had a serious drinking problem. But he was family, and so, when he said he needed a job, Pete gave him a job.

"How are Abby's tonsils?"

"Pete, will you stop worrying about the family, already!"

Pete almost said he didn't know how. He'd been at it too long. But that might come out sounding like a complaint, which it wasn't, so he just shut up.

The two teenage girls were nearly abreast of the phone booth now, walking stiffly, eyes straight ahead. Pete slouched a little—enough to look disreputable, yet not so much that he'd slide off the bench—and sent them his sexiest half smile and a slow nod hello. Their eyes rounded and their faces turned red as thermometers about to pop. As soon as they'd passed, he sat up, laughing to himself.

"So," Brad said, "what are you going to do with the rest of your vacation?"

Pete felt a warmth like new love melt over him. "I plan to hit the back roads, do my Jack Kerouac thing, look for America in the slow lane."

"Man, do I envy you."

"You should. I don't have to shave or change my socks for the next nine days if I don't feel like it."

"Have fun, but do me a favor? Take a shower before crossing the town line, okay? I'm not sure even I could stand you that ripe."

"I'll think about it. Take care, Brad."

"Hey, you will be here by Friday, right?"

"Yes, I'll be there. Have I ever let you down?"

When Brad answered, his voice held more emotion than Pete had intended to elicit. "Never, big brother. Never."

"So, okay." Pete uncoiled from the seat. "Till then, hang tough. Jill is worth it."

"I know."

"I hope so." Pete ran callused fingers over the heart-enclosed initials someone had scratched into the black paint of the phone. "Don't let this get around, it'll kill my image, but I'm the one with every reason to be envious."

Brad was quiet awhile before mumbling, "Thanks, Pete."

"For what? See you Friday."

He hung up quickly, but continued to stand there staring at the phone. He'd added that remark about envying Brad merely to bolster his brother's confidence and get him through the prewedding jitters. But just for a second...

In general, he was happy with his life. He liked his work, enjoyed his freedom, wasn't looking for any more responsibility than he already had, certainly not the kind you got saddled with in marriage.

But just for a second he thought he'd felt something, like a faint pang of hunger, an intimation there could be more.

He gave his head a little shake. Well, of course he knew there could be more. He always had. That was why he'd asked Sue Ellen to marry him when they were just eighteen. As things turned out, she broke up with him before they quite made it down the aisle, but that didn't alter his view of marriage or keep him from marrying Cindy Barstow half a year later.

Pete curled his hand into a fist and pressed it against the phone-booth wall. Cindy. The biggest mistake of his life, a classic case of marriage on the rebound. At twenty-one, though, he'd believed he was in love again.

Cindy was cute, sweet and affectionate, and she fell for Pete very hard, very fast. By their second date they were making love and she was saying, "I love you," which was exactly what his shattered ego had needed then. Three months after that they were married.

Cindy had another endearing trait that had bolstered his self-image, a soft feminine helplessness that made him feel strong, protective and needed. Like a rescuing knight.

But it didn't take long for her dependence on him to wear thin and for him to see how draining it was. He began to resent her. He wanted a partner, a helpmate, someone who could occasionally nurture him when he was down—not a little girl.

He soon discovered other things about her that were equally annoying. There were her constant small "tests" to prove he loved her—calls in the middle of the day, for instance, to ask him to leave work to pick up something at the market for her, usually when he was most involved in an important project. She also made unreasonable demands, like having him account for all his time. And then there was the way she said "I love you," with that plaintive little question mark at the end, her way of asking him to reassure her he loved her, too. Constantly. On the phone, during dinner, in the middle of the night.

Only months into their marriage, he knew he'd made a mistake. Cindy was desperate for love, starving for it, and that scared the hell out of him. Although she claimed to love him, all he saw was her fierce need to *be* loved, a need that soon became a bottomless pit. No matter what he did to reassure her, her emotional needs remained unsated and insatiable.

How they'd lasted two years he'd never know, but finally there came a day he couldn't take it anymore. The ante in Cindy's games had risen to the point where, if he didn't walk out, he felt sure that dark bottomless pit of her insecurity would swallow him up. In the end it almost did, but that was a time in his life he didn't like to dwell on.

The only solace he derived from looking back on his marriage with Cindy lay in the fact that they'd never had a child. He'd wanted one, but not with her. Lord, not her. He couldn't imagine a child growing up with that woman.

After that, Pete was pretty well soured on the idea of marriage. Oh, he'd had relationships with other women, some serious, most too casual even to remember. But marriage? No, never again.

Aside from being incurably gun-shy, he simply liked his freedom too much. Single, he could come and go as he pleased, see whom he wanted—or not. He could smoke smelly cigars, eat chili for breakfast, or drop a bundle on a bike that was forty years old. No one would be at home waiting to chew off his head.

So, why was he suddenly feeling twinges of envy for his brother? And why hadn't he felt those twinges while Sue Ellen was still married? He didn't want to marry anyone, even her. She might have been his first love, maybe even his best love, but, no, not even her. She'd hurt him too much when she broke up with him to marry that guy she'd met in college, and he still blamed her for the consequences, his marriage to Cindy.

Cindy. Sue Ellen. They were a mess from his past he'd just as soon forget. And that was exactly what he was going to do. Pete pushed away from the phone, opened the bi-fold door and stepped outside. He had nine days until the wedding, nine glorious, freewheeling days before he had to deal with Sue Ellen again and his interfering relatives. In the meantime—he smiled—it was time to get back on the road.

ALL THE WAY OUT OF TOWN Mary Elizabeth cried. Tears obscured her vision so badly that, turning a corner, she drove over the curb, nearly hitting a mailbox, and a block after that she ran a red light. By the time she reached the highway, the floor around her was littered with tissues, and the fluffy orange cat lying on the seat beside her was eyeing her with aloof disdain. But she couldn't stop.

She was leaving behind everything she knew—her family, her friends, her job and hometown—and was going to a place that was totally unfamiliar. The climate, the architecture, the landscape, everything in Florida would be different.

But then, everything in Maine felt different now, too. Learning she wasn't who she'd always thought she was had changed things. Charles wasn't her father anymore. Susan and Charlie were only half sister, half brother. Aunt Julia wasn't even her aunt. And her mother? Mary Elizabeth reached for another tissue from the box on the dash.

As had happened innumerable times that week, the moment when Charles had informed her of her true parentage replayed itself in her mind. Again she felt her initial shock, the confusion and numbing incredulity that had prevented his words from really registering for several minutes. It was sort of like watching the demolition of a high-rise building, she thought. Hearing the boom of the explosives, seeing the jolt through the structure—and then that strange moment when the building simply hangs in place, mortally wounded but still appearing sound, right before dropping story by story into a thundering cloud of devastation. That was how she felt every time she recalled the destruction of her world.

She wiped her eyes, but they filled again almost immediately. Oh, this had to stop. She couldn't afford to dwell on her illegitimacy anymore or wallow in self-pity. Facing a solitary drive down the entire Eastern seaboard, she needed to be alert, defensive and tough, even though in all her life she'd never been any of those things. Growing up affluent in a quiet New England town, she'd never had to be.

But after several minutes of focusing on her trip, her sadness had been replaced by fear, fear of the journey, fear of the unknown. No, that wouldn't do, either.

"How hard can it be, huh, Monet?" she asked the fat feline riding beside her. "People make this trip all the time—college kids on spring break, retired folks." She blotted her eyes one last time and pocketed the tissue. "I have Triple A insurance, my route clearly mapped out, even the best campgrounds to stay in each night. I've got food, shelter, credit cards, everything I need. And," she said with added emphasis, "it's only three days."

Morning sunshine warmed her left shoulder as she drove down the highway heading south. She relaxed into the warmth, flexing her stiff neck to one side and then the other. "Actually," she said, addressing the cat again, "the drive isn't hard at all. I-95 all the way until we reach Daytona. Just one long road. Amazing, isn't it? Then at Daytona we'll cut across Florida to a highway that runs down the gulf side of the state straight to Sarasota. The gentleman I talked to at Triple A told me that only New York and Washington might give us trouble, but if we avoid those cities during commuter hours, we'll be okay. And once we reach Florida everything's going to be more than okay. It'll be great. I've got a job interview lined up already. My best friend'll be there. The weather'll be forever warm...."

The cat gave her a look that said he'd had enough bothersome conversation. He settled his chin on his paws, closed his yellow eyes and went to sleep.

Mary Elizabeth shrugged and turned on the radio, trying to find a classical station. When she had, she settled back.

But a few minutes later her mind had wandered again, away from the music to the countless school concerts

Charles had sat through when she was a girl. He'd attended her plays and art exhibits, as well. But he'd usually grumbled beforehand, looked impatient during and been irritable after. At times she'd thought she was merely being overly sensitive, but now she knew better. Now a lot of Charles's behavior made sense. So did his words. *You've always been a burden, Mary Elizabeth.* A burden. More than she'd ever suspected, apparently.

It must have been terribly difficult raising a child who was the taunting proof of his wife's infidelity, a child he clearly didn't want and had hoped Eliza would give up for adoption. And how maddening it must have been when that child, given every advantage, had continually failed to live up to the Drummond name.

Or maybe she had, she thought, but in his pain and resentment Charles had simply refused to acknowledge it.

Mary Elizabeth's fingers tightened around the wheel. She wished she'd seen things in that light when she was younger. Instead, she'd spent her youth trying to win his approval and love, trying, always trying, but growing increasingly certain that in some mysterious way she was inferior and deserved to be treated differently from her brother and sister.

Damn! It shouldn't have been that way. Her mother should have told her about her illegitimacy instead of keeping it a secret. It would have explained so much. Besides, it was her very identity her mother had withheld. And what if there was some unpleasant surprise lurking in her gene pool such as heart disease or diabetes? It was only right a person be told such a thing, or at least be given the opportunity to find out. The likelihood of that happening now was slim. Mrs. Pidgin had told her that after her biological father left the area, her mother had never heard from him again. No one knew where he was or if he was even still alive.

Mary Elizabeth came to with a start, realizing she'd done it again. She'd fallen into thinking about Charles and her illegitimacy when her mind ought to be on the road. With a determined effort she put them from her thoughts, reached for the radio and turned up the volume.

She stopped at a roadside rest area south of Boston shortly after noon to feed Monet, who thought he was human and insisted on three meals a day. Although anxiety had destroyed Mary Elizabeth's appetite, she knew that for the baby's sake she ought to eat, as well.

While she was putting together a lobster salad sandwich, she realized her stomach was knotted with a curious new tension. Her hands trembled with a nervousness she couldn't quite define.

She was opening a cupboard to look for her copper tea kettle when the thought abruptly hit her: survival. That's what this nervousness was about—preparing her first solitary meal, in the first home that could truly be called her own. It didn't matter that she'd prepared innumerable meals before. This one cut through time and all common sense to feelings that were obscure and primitive. The need to survive. The fear that she wouldn't, just as Charles had predicted.

Conscious of her every move, she found the kettle, set it on the propane stove and turned the knob. Ridiculously, her heart leapt when a flame appeared.

She considered going out to a picnic table with her food, but an eighteen-wheeler was parked nearby, and while the driver was probably just having his lunch, too, she felt it was wiser to stay inside.

She sat instead at the small kitchen table and cranked open the window to catch the fresh September breeze. Gazing outside at her unfamiliar surroundings, her stomach suddenly clenched again. She was alone now, truly disconnected from everything she knew, and she *felt* alone, *felt* disconnected.

But there was simply no way she could have stayed in Deerfield. Feeling alone and disconnected wasn't nearly as bad as having to deal with Charles. Or with Roger, she thought. In a town as small as Deerfield, Roger would have found out about her pregnancy sooner or later.

Mary Elizabeth picked up her sandwich and took a small, tasteless bite. Charles was right; Roger *was* a decent person, and although he and Mary Elizabeth didn't love each other, he'd want to marry her. He'd think it was the right thing to do.

It wasn't. She'd never been more certain about anything in her life. It wasn't her own happiness she was considering, although she'd always assumed she'd marry a man she was in love with. It was the child's welfare that concerned her. Roger would feel trapped in a situation he hadn't planned and didn't need or want.

Of course she wouldn't have to marry him, despite her father's considerable influence on both her and Roger. But even single, Roger was sure to resent the child. Maybe not at first. At first he might ask for visitation rights, maybe even insist on paying child support, but eventually he would feel he'd been dealt an unfair hand, especially when he met a woman he wanted to marry. He'd resent having to explain this embarrassment from the past, this bastard. He'd resent having to justify the drain on his time and his wallet. The child would become an issue between them. His wife might even be jealous and ask him to stop seeing the child altogether.

No, Mary Elizabeth didn't want any baby she brought

into the world to grow up like that, resented and unwanted by its father—the way she'd been raised.

She regretted not being able to tell Roger she was pregnant. Fathers had their rights, and what she was doing to him was morally wrong and probably legally wrong, as well. But whatever guilt she felt was dwarfed by her conviction she was doing the right thing for the baby. And in the end, would it really matter whether Roger knew or not? She planned to give the baby up for adoption, anyway.

Taking a sip of tea, she let her gaze wander the motor home, crammed full of her possessions. She'd brought along most of the necessities to start a new life, but she'd also brought some frills. The Steuben goblets she'd inherited from her grandmother, her Crabtree & Evelyn clothing sachets, nearly twenty years of needlework, even her Salem rocker. She knew personal, homey touches had little to do with survival, but she needed them, anyway. Her soul needed them.

Mary Elizabeth smiled softly, her sense of well-being returning. She might be alone now, detached from home and everyone she knew, but ultimately she'd be okay. She had this RV to comfort her and shelter her from all the wide-open unknowns beyond.

And she had a tiny life growing inside her, she thought, placing her hand on her stomach. As always, that realization intensified her resolve. She *would* reach Florida, she *would* make a new life for herself. And she *would* provide a happy future for the baby. There would be no more talk of abortion, no more pressure to marry a man she didn't love, no more fear that that man would begrudge and mistreat his own child. The legacy of resentment stopped here.

She finished her lunch, washed her dishes and, with fresh determination and optimism, got back on the road.

Mary Elizabeth's spirits remained buoyed through most

of the afternoon, down the Massachusetts interstate, into Rhode Island and on through Connecticut. She played the radio, listened to a book on tape, and when she got tired of that, simply drifted along with her thoughts.

She pulled into another rest area just before New Rochelle. Traffic was bumper-to-bumper on the opposite side of the highway, commuters leaving New York for their homes in the suburbs. And while this side of the highway was relatively free-flowing, she knew she'd hit similarly clogged arteries once she reached the city and the lanes outbound south.

Instead, she parked the RV and passed the hectic rush hour over a leisurely dinner of quiche, salad and crisp bottled water with a twist of lemon. For dessert she had tea and a slice of Mrs. Pidgin's spice cake.

Feeling replete, she took to the road again at dusk. With any luck she'd reach the recommended campground in New Jersey around seven-thirty. She smiled, struck by a childlike sense of anticipation.

Everything was going well. The tires were humming, *she* was humming, the cat had even awakened to keep her company again.

And then she reached the Bronx.

There, highway signs and exit ramps became so confusing that before she knew it she'd gotten off I-95 and entered a labyrinth of streets that seemed to have no way out. It was, by far, the most frightening terrain she'd ever seen, except on "NYPD Blue." She drove in circles, went down blind alleys and sped past loitering, leather-clad gangs. Occasionally she thought of her St. Christopher riding solemnly along on the dash, but mostly her prayers just went up to anybody who'd listen. She wanted to find her way out, but more than that, she was terrified of breaking down. All along the dark, potholed streets, cars lay stripped of everything but their shells. She didn't want to think about what had happened to their owners.

Eventually, and for no reason she could discern, she did find the highway again. But by then she was so weak from having adrenaline rushing through her system, she didn't even care that she was heading in the wrong direction, back toward Connecticut. And when, a few miles later, she realized she wasn't even on I-95, that didn't matter, either. She was on a major highway, she was going somewhere, and that somewhere wasn't New York City.

She took the first exit she came to that displayed the symbol for lodging. It was nearly nine o'clock.

She braked at the end of the exit ramp, peering first to her right, then to her left, wondering which direction to take on the dark two-lane road. Wondering, too, why there weren't any signs. The billboard on the highway had promised a luxury motel three miles east off the exit, but which way was east? She was so tired she didn't know up from down anymore.

She slumped over the wheel, dropping her forehead to her knuckles. She didn't need this. For the last half hour, the only thing keeping her going was the thought of bringing this cumbersome vehicle to a stop and crawling into bed.

Ah, well, she sighed, sitting up. It was only three miles. If she chose the wrong direction, how long could it take to turn around and backtrack? She flexed her shoulders, did a quick eenie-meenie, and went left.

The road was dark and narrow and arched with trees. She passed a cottage set back from the road, a small restaurant and several acres of corn field. After that there was nothing but woods.

She glanced at her odometer several times, and when she was satisfied she'd covered more than the requisite distance without finding the motel—or any other signs of civilization, for that matter—she decided to turn around.

Almost too tired to see anymore, she swung the camper across the road, her headlights cutting a white tunnel into the trees. She shifted and carefully backed up, red brake lights casting an eerie glow over the roadside brush at the rear.

Given the length of her vehicle and the narrowness of the road, however, Mary Elizabeth was forced to go through the maneuver again, cutting across and backing up. Still, the turn wasn't complete, and she wished she'd waited until she'd come upon a driveway or crossroad.

This time would do it, though, she was certain. Forward. Back. Back a bit more…

Without any warning, the rear end of the motor home dropped with a thud. Mary Elizabeth's teeth banged together, while somewhere in the nether regions boxes tumbled. "Oh, God!" she whispered as the engine stalled.

With fingers that quivered, she turned the ignition key and pressed her foot to the gas pedal. But even as she was doing so she knew she was wasting her time. The back tires spun futilely, kicking up dirt and pebbles that hit nearby tree trunks like buckshot. The RV didn't budge. Panic flooded her as she gripped the wheel. Her blood pounded. What was she to do now?

After turning off the engine, she found a flashlight and slipped outside to investigate. Just as she'd suspected, she'd backed the RV right into a roadside ditch. She clutched the top of her head as if it might blow off. How could she be so stupid?

Okay, don't panic. This isn't a problem, she assured herself. *You've got AAA, and they come to the rescue anywhere, any time. Right? Right. All you have to do is find a phone.*

She peered up the road one way and down the other. All black. Just cricket chirps and bullfrog noises mixed with the thick, woodsy smell of humus. This was definitely not her idea of New York. Or was she back in Connecticut? Well, it wasn't her idea of Connecticut, either.

She climbed into the motor home again, brushed her hair, put on lipstick, found her purse, stepped outside, locked the door and, with a shuddery sigh, pocketed the keys.

The solution was easy, she told herself. She'd simply walk back the way she'd come and phone for a tow truck from the restaurant she'd passed just off the exit.

But when she stared down the dark empty road and remembered she'd be on it for more than three miles, her heart grew faint. She reminded herself that every journey, no matter how daunting, begins with a single step. She pulled in a breath and set off.

When she finally reached the restaurant, her legs were ready to give out. But what was worse, now that she'd gotten a good look, she realized it wasn't the sort of establishment she'd ever walked into before. It wasn't the sort she ever wanted to walk into, either.

It was low and dark and seedy-looking. The gravel lot surrounding it teemed with pickup trucks and motorcycles glinting lurid neon color from the beer signs flashing in its windows. Over the door a string of multicolored Christmas lights outlined a peeling sign left over from happier or more hopeful days. Starlight Lounge it read. The *I* was dotted with a star.

Mary Elizabeth looked across the road to the lone cottage huddled beneath a dense grove of pines, pines that made an almost human sighing, and her mind filled with visions straight out of a Stephen King novel.

She glanced from the cottage to the restaurant and back to the cottage again, feeling truly caught between the proverbial rock and a hard place. She decided on the restaurant. At least it was a public building.

As soon as she opened the door she was hit with a wall of country music and cigarette smoke. The next moment she realized she'd made a serious mistake.

CHAPTER TWO

PETE GOT A BAD FEELING the moment she opened the door.

He was sitting along the far leg of the U-shaped bar, near the back exit where he could keep an eye on his bike and still watch the room. He was trying to mind his own business, catch a little of the American League play-off, finish his beer and ribs, and be on his way. He still needed to check into that motel he'd seen up the road. His body ached and his eyelids felt like sandpaper despite the protective glasses he'd worn while riding.

Still, it had been a good day. No, make that a great day. He'd traveled some of the prettiest country he'd ever seen, the weather warm and dry and sweet. But even better was the riding itself, the sense of freedom that came from the open road, a motorcycle, and no agenda to meet. Time seemed to peel away from his thirty-six years as he'd ranged the wooded hills out of New Hampshire and down the Berkshires of western Massachusetts. By early evening, when he'd reached Connecticut, he'd felt eighteen again. Had the urge to buy a pack of Lucky Strikes and try out a few lines from *Rebel Without a Cause*.

Stifling a grin, Pete picked up his thick glass beer mug and took a cool sip.

Over the rim of the mug, his glance returned to the young woman at the door, poised on the threshold, surveying the clientele. His good humor dissolved. Damn! What was she doing here? He lowered the mug and gave serious thought to slipping out the back door.

It wasn't such a bad place, really. A working-class bar, unapologetically masculine. The patrons seemed to be mostly regulars, guys from the nearby town, here to kick back with a cold brew, watch the game on the big-screen TV and gripe about their jobs to somebody other than "the wife." Pete felt comfortable enough here; at least he didn't feel threatened. And the ribs were good, just as the guy at the gas station up the road had said.

But Pete wasn't about to stick around, either. He'd picked up a sense of the place early on and knew that, with just a touch of the wrong ingredient, it could become trouble.

He was pretty sure the wrong ingredient was standing at the door now.

She didn't belong here. She was as polished as the chrome on a classic old Bentley. With her smooth-as-water natural blond hair and her peaches-and-cream complexion glowing only with health, she might as well have dropped in from Venus. The few other women in the joint looked thoroughly shellacked and frizzled.

Pete doubted any of them would've bought the outfit she was wearing, either. The neatly buttoned, maize-colored jacket and matching knee-skimming shorts, worn with tights and loafers, made her look like a model posing for a back-to-college spread in one of those wholesome fashion magazines his sisters used to read when they were teenagers.

His gaze returned to the young woman's hair, those soft gleaming waves that fell from a side part to just below her collarbone. It was a timeless look, as in style now as it had been in the forties or would be again in the next century.

He focused on her face, a collection of refined features

arranged with perfect balance in a perfectly oval setting. She had a small, straight nose and delicately sculpted cheekbones. Her neck was long and thoroughbred, and her eyebrows arched with just the right amount of hauteur. He couldn't rightly judge her mouth—at the moment her lips were pressed too tight—but he thought it would be appropriately aristocratic. Yes, he decided, hers was unquestionably a face born of well-tended genes.

Pete watched her with more fascination than he usually allowed her type. She was on the prowl for something. A walk on the wild side? That was usually the case when a princess like her walked into a dive like this.

But Pete didn't think so. Even from clear across the smoke-filled room, he could see how scared she was. When her large, worried eyes fixed on the phone on the back wall over behind his right shoulder, he put two and two together and came up with car trouble. Probably out of gas, or maybe a flat tire.

Damn! Where was her God-given common sense? There was a service station just a mile up the road. Better yet, why hadn't she ever learned to change her own tires the way his sisters had?

His gaze swept over her fragile features and regal posture. But of course she wasn't the type to change tires. Probably never pumped her own gas, either.

Or, he thought on an unexpected wave of sympathy, maybe she didn't have any older brothers to teach her how. For a moment a picture flashed through his mind of his own sisters caught in a similar situation.

Pete shook his head fractionally. No, she was just a princess. Didn't pump gas. Didn't change tires. Thought she could sashay into any ol' place and not suffer the consequences. No one would dare give her trouble.

From under his lowered lashes, Pete scanned the room and winced. Someone was thinking of daring.

He'd noticed the guy earlier, a muscle-bound, muscle-shirted big-mouth with a taste for Scotch, sitting on the other side of the bar. Pete swore under his breath, glanced over his shoulder at the exit again and began to wipe his hands.

MARY ELIZABETH SERIOUSLY considered retreat, just backing out the door and fleeing up the road to her RV.

But that would mean walking three miles in the dark again, this time with a stitch in her side. And worse, now there was the added risk she might be followed. A few of the men were giving her some decidedly unsettling looks.

In addition, retreat would solve nothing. Even if she did arrive at her motor home safely, it would still be stuck in a ditch. Besides, on the far side of the dimly lit room, beyond the pool table and drifting veils of smoke, hung the solution to her problem—a public telephone. All she needed was the courage to get there.

She pulled in a long breath, gripped the strap of her shoulder bag, and with eyes trained on the floor, made her way through the nearly all-male clientele. It seemed a gauntlet, but eventually she reached her destination.

With her back to the room, she set her purse on the ledge under the phone and took out her wallet. While conversations rose to their natural volume again, she flipped through her credit cards and various forms of identification, searching for the AAA phone number she knew was in there.

It eluded her. A fine tremor of fear shivered over her skin. She started her search again, aware of a sweat breaking out on her neck. Driver's license, social security card, Visa, American Express...

Suddenly, the room dimmed to the degree where she

couldn't see the contents of her wallet at all. She turned and, with a jolt, realized it wasn't the room that had dimmed, but only her particular corner of it. An immense pair of shoulders was blocking the light.

"Hi, how ya doin'?" For someone so big, the man who'd spoken had a remarkably high voice.

Mary Elizabeth could barely catch her breath, so acute was her alarm. "I'm fine, thank you. How are you?" Her eyes flicked upward to a square red face made even blockier by a flat-topped buzz cut. There seemed to be no demarcation between his head and shoulders except a pale border where the hair had recently been trimmed.

"I never seen you in here before." The man inched closer, causing her to back up.

He wasn't really bad-looking. He didn't wear a leather vest or have sinister tattoos like those bikers playing pool, yet she still found him threatening. Something in his depthless, slitty eyes...and he smelled of hard liquor.

"Excuse me, I just need to make a phone call." She attempted to turn and resume searching her wallet.

"And I just come over to help," he said. "This isn't the sort of place a pretty little lady like yourself ought to be wandering into alone."

Mary Elizabeth eyed him guardedly, trying to decide if his offer of help was sincere, wondering if she had perhaps misjudged him. "I...uh...it's car trouble." *Finally,* she found the card. "RV trouble, actually. Nothing mechanical. I just need a tow."

He leaned his beefy shoulder against the wall, hemming her in. The odor of liquor and smoke, combined with too-sweet after-shave, nearly made her gag. "Well, how about that." He chuckled. "You're lookin' at the answer to your prayers, darlin'. I just happen to have a tow rig on the back of my truck."

She stood in horrified numbness as he lifted one hand and ran his moist fingertips down her cheek. "Excuse me," she said, shaking him off and stepping aside. In the process, however, the AAA card slipped from her fingers and fluttered to the floor between them. Swallowing, she bent to retrieve it, but just as she was reaching, his big sneakered foot landed squarely on top.

Heart hammering, she looked up the towering length of him.

With a dry chuckle, he removed his foot, but not until he'd made it clear he was playing a game of cat and mouse, a game he obviously enjoyed and wasn't about to give up.

She retrieved the card and glanced around the room. A few men were watching them, but they didn't seem inclined to interfere. The rest were oblivious, playing pool or pinball or watching a baseball game on TV. Mary Elizabeth glanced toward the bar for help, but as luck would have it, the bartender was female.

"How about a drink?" her unwanted companion asked, wrapping his sausagelike fingers around her upper arm. "Let me buy you a drink, huh? I'm in the mood for another myself."

"Thanks, but I'm not thirsty. All I want is to be left alone so I can call for a tow, then I'll be on my way. So if you'll excuse me…"

"Hell, we can have you towed in no time. I told you that already. Come on, relax." He gave her arm a little shake. "Take a load off."

Mary Elizabeth tried to stay calm, at least on the surface, but inside she was growing frantic. No way was she going to get in a truck with this gorilla and drive off down a dark, isolated road.

"Excuse me. I…I have to go to the ladies' room."

Her friend tilted his thick, squared-off head. "Whatsa matter? Am I bad company?"

She wanted to say yes but had been raised to be impeccably polite. "Excuse me." Surprisingly, he let her go.

Once she was inside the tiny washroom, she knew why he'd been so agreeable. The window was five feet up the wall and so narrow she doubted even her leg would fit through. Mary Elizabeth sighed aloud and would've leaned her weary self against the stall except that it was probably crawling with germs that science hadn't heard of yet.

What am I going to do? she implored her reflection as she patted a wet paper towel to her flushed cheeks. Inside her open purse, set on the rim of the sink, lay the plastic gun Mrs. Pidgin had given her. Mary Elizabeth smiled wanly. Perhaps she could fill the gun with water and squirt the brute to death.

Ah, well, Mrs. P.'s intentions had been good.

Her newfound friend was waiting outside the washroom door, patient as a puppy. "Missed you." He grinned. "Hope you like rum and coke." He held up a glass.

"No, thanks." Trying to ignore him, she headed for the bar. Another female was sure to sympathize. "Excuse me," she called, leaning over an unoccupied stool.

"Wait a sec," the bartender, busy at the cash register, answered distractedly.

"You know," came the high, now nightmarish voice close at Mary Elizabeth's side, "if I didn't have such a sweet, forgiving nature, I'd be mighty ticked off by now. Here I offer to give you a free tow, something worth fifty, sixty bucks..."

The bartender finally headed in Mary Elizabeth's direction.

"Please, could you do me a favor?" Mary Elizabeth's

voice wobbled noticeably now, but at least she'd been able to fend off tears.

The young woman, who looked to be about her own age, glanced up from the tap where she was filling three glass mugs.

"Would you be so kind as to call Triple A for me? All I need is a tow. Here's the number...."

The bartender's left eyebrow arched. "And there's a pay phone, right there." She pointed with her chin.

"I know, but..." Mary Elizabeth rolled her eyes toward the man still crowding her, his breath on her neck.

The young woman huffed. "Sonny, leave 'er alone, huh? You're being a jerk." Then she walked away, delivering the three beers to the far end of the bar. It was apparent *she* didn't consider him a threat. Also apparent was the fact that she'd be of no help.

Mary Elizabeth slipped onto the stool, planted her elbows on the bar and dropped her head into her hands.

"So, what's your name?" Her friend, who was evidently named Sonny, placed the rum and coke under her nose.

Too weary even to look up, she said, "Will you please leave me alone? It's been a very long day." Now tears did flood her vision. "Damn," she spat, embarrassed by her weakness. On a spurt of anger she spun off the stool. This was a public place, and that, a public phone. No one had the right to stop her from going about her business.

"Hey, where you runnin' off to now?" Sonny gripped her arm and gave it a yank. "Here I'm tryin' to be nice... Whatsa matter? Don't you like me?"

Something must've happened behind her because she noticed Sonny's slitty eyes shift and refocus. Suddenly he went still, while a calm, deep voice with just a trace of a slow southern drawl said, "Why don't you give it a rest?"

Mary Elizabeth turned in surprise. A tall, dark-haired

man was lounging back in his bar stool, his eyes fixed on the TV screen. He seemed relaxed, but looking at him, she got a sense of tightly coiled alertness.

For the first time since she'd wandered in here, she drew a clear and easy breath. She wasn't sure why; he certainly didn't look like anybody a woman ought to be breathing easily over.

Sonny released her arm and stepped aside. His eyes narrowed even further. "What did you say?"

"Leave her alone. Let her make her call." The stranger calmly took a sip of his beer and continued to watch the game.

Sonny shifted his considerable weight, one foot to the other. "And who's gonna make me?"

Slowly, the man at the bar set down his mug and carefully got to his feet.

Mary Elizabeth couldn't take her eyes off him. He was over six feet tall and powerfully built. Tough as the road he'd traveled in on, too, she'd bet. He had wind-tossed black hair, steely blue eyes, weathered skin and a jaw that was unrelenting. Dust burnished his black boots, and the edges of his pale denim jacket were frayed. Beneath the jacket, tucked into low-slung, well-worn jeans, he wore a plain black T-shirt.

But the thing about this man that mesmerized her so wasn't his clothing or eyes or build. She didn't know *what* it was, but it wasn't physical…although his physical aspect was certainly impressive, too.

Mary Elizabeth bit her lower lip while her eyes traveled over him, up, down, up and down again. In all her life she'd never met anyone quite like him. He was like a new, unexplored land, and though her stomach jumped with something akin to fright when she gazed at him, she didn't want to miss a single mile.

"Look, I don't want any trouble," he said with easy composure, raising his hands like a gunslinger showing he was unarmed.

Sonny snickered.

"But if you start it, I'll guarantee I won't run away."

"Oh, yeah?" Sonny replied with all the cleverness of a block of cement.

Mary Elizabeth's skin crawled with deepening dread. She'd never witnessed a fight before, but this situation seemed to have all the signs of one brewing.

"Go make your phone call, miss."

With a start, she realized the tall stranger was talking to her. The bright animal darkness of his eyes made her breath catch. She nodded.

But Sonny responded, "I already told her that isn't necessary."

The blue-eyed man impaled Sonny with an immobilizing stare. Then, still holding him in his sights, he took Mary Elizabeth by the arm. "Come on."

Relief flooded her as he began to escort her to the phone.

No sooner had he turned his back, however, than Sonny gave him a hard shove, sending him stumbling forward.

With a plummeting heart, Mary Elizabeth realized that the fight had not been averted, but rather it had just begun.

The stranger who'd come to her aid rebounded quickly and shoved Sonny in return. "Back off," he warned, blue eyes blazing.

"Go to hell," Sonny replied.

And then fists did fly. Mary Elizabeth let out a faint "Yi," the only sound she was capable of, as the two men crashed into bar stools and people retreated.

"I don't believe this!" she whispered, retreating with them.

A table went over, glasses sliding and smashing to the

floor. The room resounded with the smack of fists, with grunts and fabric ripping, and like in a movie, it was all set to music—"Welcome to Earth, Third Rock from the Sun"—thumping from the jukebox.

At least they seemed evenly matched, Mary Elizabeth thought, watching them go at it—though she did sense a quickness in the taller man that Sonny lacked.

What Sonny had was a mean streak. She watched in horrified silence as he grabbed a beer bottle off the bar, smashed it against the brass rail and lunged at her tall dark stranger.

"Get out of here," he called to her just before the jagged bottle came down on the side of his forehead. Immediately blood beaded along the gash.

Rather than rattle him, the cut seemed to deepen his anger and resolve. He picked up a chair and slammed it against Sonny's arm, dislodging the broken bottle from his grip. Then he pushed Sonny against the bar where he kept him pinned until Sonny looked ready to give up.

Mary Elizabeth had no idea where the third guy came from, but suddenly there he was, gripping the dark stranger's shoulder, swinging him around and landing a blow to his midsection that made her nauseated.

Logic told her she should use the diversion to slip away. Nobody was interested in her anymore. Yet she couldn't leave. It was clear that the man who'd come to her aid was as much a stranger in this bar as she was, while Sonny was a local, and if she abandoned him, he'd probably get pulverized by Sonny's friends.

She shouldn't care, she told herself. She didn't know this man, she'd never see him again, and if he was in a bar like this he was probably accustomed to fighting, anyway. Besides, she had a responsibility to the tiny life inside her. That especially had her concerned.

But if she slunk away now, what sort of person would that make her? How would she ever face herself in a mirror?

Without another second's thought, she dug into her purse for the plastic gun. Tossing her bag onto a nearby table, she gripped the gun in two hands and flexed her knees. "All right, everybody freeze!" she called out.

Nobody heard. The debacle continued.

"Hey!" she hollered, affronted. This time a few onlookers turned. She heard someone say, "She's got a gun," and was pleased that the person sounded at least somewhat alarmed.

Within seconds the word passed. Attention turned on her like a tide. Those nearby backed away. A few people slipped out the door.

"Stop fighting," she shouted. "Stop!" To her utter amazement, they did. The three men turned and looked at her, then each of them swore, different epithets, but all at the same time.

"Now...get against the wall there," she ordered as she searched her memory for anything else she could borrow from the police movies she'd seen.

The three men moved, amazing her once again. A hush had fallen over the place. Even the jukebox had obediently shut down.

"Good." She straightened, feeling a heady sense of power. "Now, you..." She waved the gun at the bartender. "I want you to call the police, and this time don't tell me there's a pay phone."

In the dead silence, Mary Elizabeth became aware of sirens wailing in the distance. Confused, she glanced at the young woman behind the bar who made a face that said, *What do you think I am, an idiot?*

In no time flat, blue-and-red lights were throbbing

against the windows, dueling with the neon. The doors banged open and six uniformed officers hurried in, straight to the heart of the fray.

"Thank God you got here so fast," Mary Elizabeth said, but the officers coming toward her didn't return her smile. In fact, every one of them had drawn his weapon.

"Drop the gun," one of them ordered.

She looked at each of the six faces, at each of the six guns pointed her way. "What…?" All at once, she realized what was happening. "Oh. You think…"

But before she could explain the gun was only a toy, three of the policemen had cocked their pistols. She dropped the gun.

A policewoman immediately lunged forward, grasped Mary Elizabeth's right wrist and twisted her arm up behind her back. Another officer, a serious young man with a dedicated, boyish face, carefully picked up the fallen gun.

After that, events swam together in a dreamlike sequence: across the room, the bartender talking excitedly, pointing this way and that; the odious Sonny saying, "But…but he…but…"; and the tall dark stranger scowling at *her*, Mary Elizabeth, where a moment ago he'd been duking it out on her behalf.

"Sonny, Sonny," a craggy-faced sergeant scolded, shaking his head. "It isn't even Saturday night."

Sonny returned a sheepish grin.

"Okay, let's go," the sergeant said. It was then that Mary Elizabeth noticed the handcuffs glinting on the three men's wrists. *No, that's a mistake,* she wanted to cry out. *The tall one is a good guy.* But just then she heard the officer who'd picked up her gun reading her her rights. At the same time something cold and metallic encircled her own wrists.

Mary Elizabeth's face drained of color. "You're hand-cuffing *me?*"

"Yes, ma'am."

"But there's obviously been a misunderstanding."

"We'll straighten it out at the station. Do you have a purse?"

"Uh, yes." Mary Elizabeth indicated a nearby table.

The officer picked up her bag and said, "Come with me, please."

Mary Elizabeth was led through the gawking crowd, close on the heels of her tall, dark stranger. "I don't believe this," she muttered, her eyes hot with humiliation.

"Why the hell not?" he snarled over his shoulder. "Acting as stupid as you just did, you must land in messes like this all the time." His hard lips curled as he muttered something that sounded to her like "Liverpool." She frowned in confusion until she reasoned he'd said "Little fool."

"Sorry," she said.

"You should be."

Outside, she was led to a cruiser, while the three men were taken to a rescue van where medics waited to patch up their injuries.

She was just slipping into the back seat of the cruiser when it occurred to her that she hadn't gotten her hero's name. She peered up at the serious young officer, and with a giggle that rose from hysteria, asked, "Who *was* that masked man?"

He frowned, staring at her oddly, then shut the door.

She sat back and surveyed her surroundings with combined interest and dread. "Oh, Lord, I'm riding in a cage!" she moaned. The next moment, the full significance of what was happening to her hit home, and two hot tears trickled down her cheeks.

After that, events really blurred. She was taken to the

station and booked, only vaguely aware that the three men involved in the fight had been brought in, as well. Her possessions got handed over; she was escorted down a corridor to a cell; handcuffs came off, toilet facilities were pointed out, and then, with a sound that cut right through her, the iron-barred door clanged shut.

And so ended Mary Elizabeth Drummond's first day of independence.

CHAPTER THREE

THE FIRST THING on Pete's mind when he opened his eyes the next morning was his bike. Where the hell was it, and if it had even one scratch, how did the fool who'd scratched it want to die?

The second thing he thought about was Mary Elizabeth Drummond, that preppy little pain in the butt who was trying to wreck his vacation—and doing a pretty good job of it, too. He'd never met anyone so fly-brained in his life, and why he'd stuck his neck out for her was still a mystery.

Pete eased onto his back and scowled at the water-stained ceiling of his cell, recalling the previous night. If she just hadn't walked into that bar, none of this would've happened. He was familiar with places like that, knew the type of guy who frequented them. For the most part, just your ordinary, law-abiding Joe. But add a woman to the equation—an unattached woman, he amended, thinking of the few who'd been there with their husbands or boyfriends—and your ordinary Joe suddenly transmuted into King Kong. She should have known that, too—although, to be fair, he doubted she'd spent much time in bars.

Pete's mouth tightened in a rueful grimace. Of all the gin joints in all the towns in all the world...

Last night after being brought in, they'd sat at adjacent desks while being booked. That's when he'd first heard her name. Mary Elizabeth Drummond. Even in his thoughts he put a spin of mockery on it. He wasn't sure why, except that the name struck him as sort of stuffy and tedious. It had no…give.

Sitting where he was, he'd been able to hear the reluctance in her voice when the officer asked her name, a reluctance that had deepened when she was asked her address, birth date and social security number. Pete got the feeling she didn't want the police to know who she was. For a while, in fact, she'd actually *refused* to give her address. Said she was in transit, moving from one state to another, and at present didn't really have an address. Pete had noted her amazement and dismay when all her vital statistics came up on the computer screen, anyway, just on the cue of her social security number.

What really roused Pete's curiosity, though, was the anxiety he'd detected when she'd been asked if there was anyone she wanted to call. No, there was no one, she'd said, an answer that had compelled him to turn and take a new, harder look at her. A princess like that, you'd think she'd be on the phone right away, a dozen people she wanted to complain to.

Another thing about her that didn't jibe was her voice. It was husky and deep-throated, a Scotch-and-soda voice that belonged more to a torch singer in a smoky piano bar than to someone wearing Bass Weeguns loafers.

Pete winced reflexively when he remembered the turnaround in her attitude after she was asked to explain what had happened at the Starlight Lounge. Suddenly she was a fountain of information. A damn Niagara Falls of information. And she was angry.

Well, maybe *indignant* was a more appropriate word. She didn't seem capable of really ripping loose. He'd noticed that about her last night, first with Sonny and then at the station. Terminally polite, that was her problem.

But Pete knew she'd been angry inside. Her cheeks had

been a feverish pink, her sentences rushed and tumbled, and her slender frame never really stopped shaking. She reminded him of a bottle of carbonated soda, shaken to a froth, but all sealed up.

She was convinced her arrest was a mistake, even after the officer patiently explained the charge against her for the third time. She seemed to think that if she kept yapping, eventually he'd see the error in his logic.

She kept repeating that the gun was only a toy. Couldn't quite grasp the concept that wielding even a toy in a public place was a serious, arrestable offense if that toy was perceived as real and dangerous by those it was pointed at.

Pete and the other two men were booked and on their way to their cells, and she was still sitting there yapping.

Pete swung his feet off the lumpy cot. *Get the broad out of your head,* he told himself. *You've got problems enough of your own.* He rubbed his eyes. "Augh," he said aloud, grimacing under a sudden pain. "Mean left hook you've got there, man," he grumbled to one of two snoring hulks in the cell across the aisle.

Pete watched with deepening disgust. He didn't like bullies. Never had. And if Sonny was anything, it was a bully. *That* was why he'd stuck his neck out for Mary Elizabeth Drummond.

Relieved that he'd finally found an acceptable rationale for his behavior, Pete got up stiffly and studied his face in the mirror over the small white sink. "Great," he said flatly. The area around his right eye had turned brownish purple overnight and his upper lip was puffed.

Ordinarily he wouldn't have cared. It wasn't the first fight he'd been in, or the worst, but he had his brother's wedding coming up in a week. He'd hoped to look at least halfway decent.

Peeling away the tape that held a gauze pad in place,

Pete examined the two-inch gash that Sonny had carved into the side of his forehead. It could've been worse, he thought. He'd seen the swing coming in enough time to pull back and just be grazed.

That was seconds before Sonny's buddy had jumped into the fight. Could've been a lot worse, Pete thought, the lines of his face falling into a study of pensive concentration as he remembered—Mary Elizabeth Drummond pulling that gun from her purse. Fly-brained she might be, but she also had courage. He'd seen the gun shaking in her hands from twelve feet away, yet she'd stood her ground and gone out on a limb…for him?

Pete shook his head to knock away the nonsense and reached for the faucet. He splashed cold water on his face and, straightening, let it trickle down his neck. He couldn't start developing a soft spot for Ms. Drummond now. Because of her he'd been arrested. Because of her he'd spent the night on a cot that felt like a cobblestone road. Because of her he would be wasting a whole morning in court, when what he'd planned was to be riding his new bike.

He heard footsteps in the hall. Pete dried his face on a thin, scratchy towel. A young officer, new with the morning shift, banged on the bars of Sonny's cell, then unlocked Pete's cell and brought in breakfast.

"'Morning. Sleep okay?"

Pete nodded. He might be mad as hell, but the local constabulary would be the last to know it.

The young man set the tray down on the end of the cot. "Half an hour till we go over to the courthouse."

"I'll be ready." Pete reached for his coffee.

The officer paused. "We brought your bike in."

"What?"

"Your motorcycle. Last night you asked if we could re-move it from the parking lot of the Starlight Lounge. I thought you'd like to know that we did and it's safe over at Bernie's Garage. That's on Third Street. You can pick it up after your court appearance."

"Thanks. I appreciate it. How much for moving it?"

"Thirty dollars."

Pete nodded agreeably. "I don't suppose you could tell me what the going rate is for a bar fight in this town?" He smiled—amiably he hoped.

"About a hundred, if you get any judge other than Collins. With Collins, oh, anywhere between one-fifty and three."

Careful to show no reaction, Pete took a sip of coffee. It was hot and surprisingly good, but didn't do much to lessen his irritation.

"How's the girl?" He wasn't sure why he asked, except that she was the source of that irritation.

The policeman grimaced. "Not too happy. Friend of yours?"

Pete cocked an eyebrow.

The officer laughed. "Didn't think so. She asked for tea this morning. Earl Gray, to be exact. With honey and lemon. That was after she insisted someone go feed her cat."

Pete shook his head, lips pressed tight to show he commiserated with the young man.

"Were you able to tow her RV?"

"Yep. It's at Bernie's, too."

"Is it going to be laid up long?" Somehow, the thought of her spending any significant time in this town, with Sonny on the loose, made Pete uneasy.

"Naw. Nothing wrong with it. She just got it stuck in a ditch."

Pete sipped his coffee, keeping his eyes down and his

thoughts to himself. They weren't kind. They weren't too politically correct, either.

"Well, you go ahead and finish eating. I'll be back in half an hour."

The young officer was closing the door when Pete said, "So, did you get it for her? The Earl Gray, I mean?"

The officer's mouth twitched. "What do you think?"

"I think... I'm glad I won't be seeing her after today."

The lock slid shut to the sound of the officer's laughter. Then he said, "Hey, Sonny, rise and shine. Billy, get up, let's go."

THE DISTRICT COURTHOUSE was a three-minute cruiser ride from the police station. Mary Elizabeth was sitting with her police escort in the second row of folding chairs, chewing on her lower lip and wondering how her cat was, when the stranger from the night before walked in. Her whole body seemed to rise a little when he did.

She'd been waiting for him to make an appearance. The previous night, lying sleepless in her cell, she'd thought a lot about what he'd done for her, coming to her defense the way he had. It was enough to make the most hardened cynic have faith in mankind again. Yet she hadn't even had a chance to thank him.

She was reluctant to admit it, but there was another reason she'd been keeping an eye out for his arrival. She just wanted to get another look at him. Even last night, under the most stressful conditions, his looks had been distracting enough for her to take notice.

He walked with his police attendant down the aisle that divided the seats. When he got to Mary Elizabeth's row, he paused, his steely blue eyes meeting hers as if perhaps he'd been curious about her, too, this person he'd risked life and limb for. He didn't look any happier now than he had last night.

She knew she looked awful. She was frightened and embarrassed, and had been that way all night. Now her eyes were bleary and her skin was dull. Her clothes had seen better times, too. Instinctively, she ran her shackled hands along her linen walking shorts in a futile attempt to iron out the wrinkles.

But if she looked bad, the dark-haired stranger looked even worse. Noticing his bruises, her expression crumpled. *I'm sorry,* she wanted to say, and hoped her eyes conveyed the message.

If they did, her apology fell on stone. He merely scowled and turned his head.

Another time, another place, perhaps she wouldn't have minded. But here, today, it would've been nice to have a friend. She felt rather out of her element. Never having been arrested before, she didn't know what she was doing.

She'd thought of hiring a lawyer but had been told it wasn't necessary; her case was too small. Which was just as well since she couldn't afford a lawyer, anyway. Still, she felt vulnerable without defense, helpless without someone to negotiate this unfamiliar system with her.

What if she was found guilty? She'd have a criminal record then. What would that do to her future? To her chances of getting a job? Decent housing? And what if Charles found out? He'd never let her live it down.

With hands that shook visibly, she pressed at the wrinkled linen again as if doing so would iron away those problems. When her hands reached her knees, she surreptitiously tugged up her saggy tights. Just as surreptitiously, she glanced at the tall, loose-limbed stranger, slouched in his chair across the aisle.

He looked so calm, so capable and impregnable to injustice. She'd bet *he* would never allow anyone to pin a guilty verdict on him if he was innocent. Maybe she should take her cue from him. Maybe the time had come for her to accept that she was truly on her own and no one was going to watch out for her but herself.

Pulling in a deep breath, she squared her shoulders, lifted her chin and waited for her case to be called.

"Who's the judge today?" Pete asked the policeman sitting beside him.

"Gertrude Collins."

"Collins," Pete repeated. He sank lower in his seat, giving Mary Elizabeth a dark sidelong look. Nothing had gone right since running into that woman.

She was called first. Pete watched her walk up to the bench, her spine straight as a poker, her mouth tight with righteous indignation. Her charges were read and then the judge asked how she pleaded.

Lifting her chin, but not so high that her invisible crown slipped off her head, she said, "Not guilty." Pete exhaled a long breath through his teeth.

He watched the judge confer with her and the police prosecutor—explaining the options, he guessed. Cases as small as theirs were usually taken care of immediately and on the spot. Court dockets were too overloaded to make a production out of every case that came through. Besides, she was obviously guilty—they all were—and six policemen and a bar full of witnesses could testify to that fact.

But after a long deliberation, she still insisted she wanted to fight the charges. Pete heard the officer beside him sigh. He saw the judge sigh. Three people in front of him looked at their watches.

"Could I have the other defendants in this case?" The judge motioned for Mary Elizabeth to stay.

Pete was escorted up to the front of the courtroom, with

Sonny and Billy close behind. Sonny and Billy were greatly subdued this morning. They stood before the judge as docile as lambs, like Pete, knowing that cooperation was the name of the game here, the key to getting out quickly.

Their charges were read: property damage, public intoxication, and assault and battery with dangerous weapons— the weapons being the broken bottle Sonny had wielded and the chair used by Pete. After spending a few minutes plea bargaining with the police prosecutor, who in turn conferred with the judge, they were each found guilty of simple assault and fined one hundred and fifty dollars. They paid their fines, along with the towing charges for their vehicles, and were told they were free to go.

The judge then looked at Mary Elizabeth, her expression seeming to say, *Got the picture?*

Mary Elizabeth swallowed.

Sonny and his buddy took off as soon as their fines were paid. Pete was pocketing his wallet and thinking of doing the same when Mary Elizabeth turned her eyes on him. He'd noticed they were an unusual shade of warm coffee-brown, and right now they were very large and very lost.

He tried to look away. He didn't like her kind, he told himself. He'd dated a few princesses in his day and found them dull and patronizing. The dull part he could excuse...

Still, there was a bruised look in those eyes that appeared too real, a vulnerability he never would've associated with her.

He caught himself up short, just as he was sliding into sympathy. Aw, no. He wasn't going to fall for that trap again. That's the way things had started with Cindy. He gave his shoulders a flexing roll and set off for the door.

But halfway there he paused. Behind him, Mary Elizabeth was asking the judge to clarify the trial process she'd have to face if she contested the charges. Pete didn't really care what happened, but he was curious enough to want to listen in. He made his way to the side of the courtroom and stood against the wall.

Mary Elizabeth spoke quietly. He couldn't hear everything she said, but he got the sense of it. Capitulation.

The judge sighed in relief. She found Mary Elizabeth not guilty, but fined her two-hundred-and-fifty dollars.

It was a reasonable sum, but Pete could see—could almost feel—Mary Elizabeth's indignation picking up a new head of steam. Why was her fine higher than the men's? she wanted to know. Pete squinched his eyes shut. The men, she said as her handcuffs came off, had smacked each other black and blue while she had done nothing except stop the fight, which you'd think she'd be commended for instead of punished. Furthermore, why was she being fined at all if she was innocent?

Before he could think, Pete cleared his throat, loudly. She glanced over and he shook his head, hoping she understood.

She was breathing hard, conflicting emotions warring in her eyes. Something in their depths made him think that maybe her reaction to her fine wasn't really indignation at all, but fear. Fear of what, he didn't know.

Finally he saw her give in—a slow exhalation of breath, a slumping of her shoulders.

"Sorry, Your Honor," she mumbled, and reached into her bag for her wallet.

Pete stood away from the wall and once again turned to leave. He didn't like what just happened, that small communication between him and her.

He was halfway to the door again when something caught in his peripheral vision: Mary Elizabeth searching through her purse. Dread crawled over him.

"It's not here," she said, no longer speaking in that

Scotch-and-soda voice that so intrigued him. She was practically squeaking now. "I...I can't find my wallet." She searched again, taking several items out. Her face had gone crimson.

"Are you sure it was in your bag?" the judge inquired.

"Positive. I had it last night at the bar." She kept rummaging through the purse, swallowing, turning redder. Finally she looked up, her eyes slightly wild. "I think it was stolen."

"Stolen?" the judge repeated.

Mary Elizabeth nodded. "At the Starlight. After I pulled out the water pistol, I threw my purse onto a table. I don't even remember doing it. I just remember that's where I found it when I left. While it was lying there, somebody must've helped himself to the contents."

"I see." The judge dragged a hand down her face. "Officer Wilson," she called, addressing the policewoman who'd been part of the arresting team at the Starlight, "as soon as Ms. Drummond's business with the court is concluded, take the information regarding her wallet."

The policewoman gave a short nod.

Mary Elizabeth looked up at the judge, dazed. "Your Honor? How am I supposed to pay my fine?"

"Did your wallet contain *all* your money?"

Coffee-brown eyes shimmered with tears. She nodded. "Seven hundred and twenty dollars."

The judge cast her a stern look. "It isn't wise to carry so much money on your person, Ms. Drummond, especially when you're traveling. Better to divide it and put it away in several locations."

Mary Elizabeth lowered her eyes and said nothing, all her uppity self-righteousness gone. Pete was beginning to think it hadn't been very real to begin with.

"Well, I suggest you call your bank and have the money wired to you."

"I'm afraid I can't do that, Your Honor. I closed all my accounts before I set out on this trip."

Standing a few feet away, Pete scowled. Closed all her accounts? And she had only seven hundred bucks? Mary Elizabeth was becoming more of a puzzle every minute.

Then it hit. *That* was why she'd reacted to her fine. She'd been worried about the amount of money she'd have to hand over.

The judge said, "Then I suggest you contact a relative or a friend."

Again, Mary Elizabeth shook her head. "I...I can't do that, either."

The judge was growing impatient. "Unless you want to work out an alternative, I think you had better, young lady."

"May I ask what the alternative is?" Mary Elizabeth inquired, squeezing and twisting the strap of her purse.

"Fifteen days in the county jail."

Mary Elizabeth's eyes went a few degrees wilder.

Pete clasped the nape of his neck. *Don't do it, Mitchell. Get yourself the hell out of here,* he thought, even as he stepped forward and said, "Your Honor, I'll loan Ms. Drummond the money. That way you can get this train moving again." He could've sworn the formidable woman on the bench mouthed the words "Thank you." He didn't say "You're welcome." He was angry at her for assuming Mary Elizabeth had money readily available, an assumption based on the style of her hair and the quality of her clothes.

Mary Elizabeth turned in surprise. Her gaze traveled over him in quick assessment, taking in his black eye, two-day-old beard, faded jacket and jeans whose knee had finally popped a tear.

"That's very generous of you, but I couldn't possibly accept your money."

Instantly he rued his generosity, not knowing whether to laugh at her mistaken assumptions about him or shove her condescension down her throat.

"Fifteen days," he reminded her, half hoping she'd go for the time.

"But…are you sure you can spare it?" she asked.

"For you? Anything." He winked, but there was no mistaking his sarcasm.

She looked confused. "I'll repay you. Just as soon as I reach where I'm going."

"Of course you will. I didn't say it was a gift."

The judge asked, "Are you willing to pay her tow charge as well?"

"Yes. How much?"

"Sixty-five dollars."

Mary Elizabeth's face dropped. "I don't believe this," she muttered, but only loud enough for Pete to hear. He nudged her with his elbow, using restraint to just nudge and not ram. Her muttering ceased.

Pete handed over the cash, making a mental note to stop at the first ATM he came to.

"That's it? I'm free to go?" Mary Elizabeth asked, a conflicted mixture of incredulity and relief.

"Yes. Next case," the judge said quickly.

Mary Elizabeth couldn't shake the feeling she was caught in a nightmare. She felt almost sick from exhaustion and fear, and knew, as she walked away from the bench, her steps were weavy. All she wanted to do was crawl under a rock somewhere and sleep. Instead, Officer Wilson was waiting for her, pad and pen poised.

"The wallet's beige, cowhide, monogrammed in gold with my initials," Mary Elizabeth said.

"Credit cards?"

"Yes. Three." She fought off a tightening in her throat. "And a gasoline card, and four department store cards." Her sense of being caught in a dream world deepened. What was she to do now? No money, no plastic...

"Where would you like us to send the wallet, if it turns up?"

"Oh." Mary Elizabeth passed an unsteady hand over her brow. "My friend's in Sarasota. Yes, definitely my friend's." If it ever went back to Charles, she'd die of humiliation. She could almost hear him saying it now, "I told you you'd never make it on your own."

Unexpectedly, thoughts of home rushed over her, and with them came remembrance of her mother's affair, her shock at learning she was illegitimate, her distress over her pregnancy...so many problems that had somehow gotten relegated to a back burner since last evening.

Having procured all the necessary information, the officer pocketed her pen, wished Mary Elizabeth well, and walked off, leaving her standing alone with the weight of her remembered troubles. Feeling vague and quite disoriented, she turned to go. "Oh," she said in surprise. Peter Mitchell, whose name she'd learned just this hour, was still in the courtroom, standing right behind her.

He had the clearest blue eyes she'd ever seen. The fact that one of them was bruised didn't detract from their impact one bit. Right now those eyes were narrowed under a lowered brow, studying her. She guessed she looked pretty bewildered.

"Yes?" she asked uncertainly.

"Do you want to take my address?"

She blinked, uncomprehending.

"So you'll know where to send the money I lent you."

"Oh, yes, of course." She opened her purse and withdrew a pen and a small notebook. He took them from her and began to write. He had nice hands, she thought distractedly. Strong, broad hands that were cut and callused yet imbued with a certain masculine grace.

He wrote his address on the top sheet of paper, along with the amount she owed him. Then he flipped to the next sheet and wrote out an IOU, to which Mary Elizabeth added her signature and Chloe's address.

"That should do it," Pete said, pocketing the IOU.

"Yes." She glanced down at the address he'd written in a surprisingly neat but firm hand and felt a kick of adrenaline. "You live in Tampa?"

But he had already turned and was heading for the exit. She hurried to catch up. Her head had cleared remarkably. Moreover, her spirits were lifting, probably because it had just begun to sink in that she'd been found not guilty. She would have no criminal record, no impediments standing in the way of establishing herself in a new location.

"This is really a coincidence. I'm going to Florida myself."

Peter opened the courtroom door and made his way through the crowded corridor, his eyes fixed on the exit ahead.

"I'm going to Sarasota," she persisted, following. "That's on the Gulf Coast too, not very far from Tampa, right?"

"No," he said, hurrying on. "It's miles away. Many, many miles."

Mary Elizabeth would've contested his claim, but just then she spotted the policeman with the sincere, youthful face who'd arrested her the previous night. He was standing by the main door, just ending a conversation with someone who looked like a lawyer.

"Excuse me," she said. "Do you know if there's a phone at the garage where my RV was taken?"

"Yes, ma'am, there is."

"Great. Thanks." She'd call the credit card companies from there to notify them that her cards had been stolen. She continued out the door, Peter Mitchell a few brisk paces ahead of her. She'd thought perhaps they'd walk to the garage together or maybe take a cab, but apparently he wanted to go his own way, alone. She drooped with mild disappointment.

"Can I give you a lift?" the policeman asked, jogging down the courthouse steps after them. "I'm on my way to the garage myself. Got to take my vehicle in for a tune-up."

Mary Elizabeth looked toward Peter Mitchell, already chugging along the sidewalk, and her smile returned. "That would be great."

Pete didn't intend to stop. His instincts told him it was time to break away, go find a diner or a bookstore until Mary Elizabeth Drummond was out of town and safely gone from his life. He had no desire to get to know her better, especially if she was going to be living in Sarasota!

"Peter?" she called, and when he didn't respond, she said, "Mr. Mitchell." Damn. She spoke his name in that deep, dusky voice that had the ability to rise and fall and float around a man's imagination like a dancer's silk veil. He glanced over his shoulder.

"Come on." She beckoned him toward the open door of the squad car with a bright, wide-eyed smile. You'd think she'd just copped a ride on a twelve-horse coach. The earnest young officer was looking at him, too, waiting. Pete rolled his eyes heavenward, wondering who had it in for him now.

Bernie's Garage, a five-stall cinderblock building, sat on

a quarter acre of asphalt enclosed by an eight-foot-high chain-link fence. Several impounded vehicles, as well as a few police cars under repair, were parked to one side of the garage. Civilian vehicles occupied the rest of the lot.

Pete spotted his bike as soon as they drove through the gate. His heart kicked over, lovesick. It seemed okay, but he wouldn't breathe easy until he'd had a closer look.

The officer twisted his wiry torso to glance at his passengers through the safety grate. "I hope you have a safe trip from here on."

"I'll certainly try," Mary Elizabeth said, "although it won't be easy."

Pete wished the guy would open the damn door and let him out.

"That wallet contained everything I needed to get by. My money, my credit cards…"

Dread crawled over Pete's skin again. That had been happening a lot lately.

"…My health insurance card…"

He cleared his throat, as he had in court, but she didn't look at him.

"…Important phone numbers…"

Pete nudged her loafer with his boot, and when she finally glanced his way he gave her the blackest warning look he could muster.

"Everything," she said, frowning in vexation at him. "It even contained my driver's license."

Mary Elizabeth watched Pete close his eyes and slap a hand to his brow. The next moment she understood what he had been trying to head off.

Her gaze shot to the police officer, who looked pretty disheartened himself. He looked away, pulled at his nose a few times, looked back.

She winced and slipped low in her seat. The officer had

to have known that her license had been stolen along with her wallet. Would he have let her drive off if she hadn't mentioned it? She felt the irrational urge to apologize for complicating his life.

"Do you have four forms of identification? That's what you'll need to apply for a new license."

Mary Elizabeth thought hard. She'd brought along a birth certificate. And her RV registration was in the glove compartment. But that was all she could come up with. Anything else usable as ID had been stolen.

She supposed she could have her social security card reprocessed and mailed to her here.

Here? She didn't exactly have an address. A tremor of panic ran through her. *Think, Drummond. Concentrate.*

She could rent a post office box, then. She could have her new credit cards mailed here, as well. But the process would take days. Maybe a week or more.

"It might take a while," she replied, her voice unsteady.

The officer flattened his lips. "I'm really sorry about this, but I can't let you drive without a license."

"I understand." She understood, all right. She'd bungled things again. At the rate she was going, she'd never make it to Florida.

The officer stepped out of the squad car and opened the back door, almost being knocked over as Pete shot past. "Well, maybe it's a good thing you've got a camper, ma'am."

"Yes." She gulped, wondering if she'd have to stay here in this fenced-in lot until she got all her paperwork together.

She slid out of the cruiser. Peter Mitchell was crouched alongside a motorcycle, his pale denim jacket pulled taut across his wide back. She should have guessed he'd be riding a motorcycle, though that one looked sort of strange. Although it gleamed in the sunlight as if it were new, it was an older model than the ones she was used to seeing. Much older.

Hmm.

She'd overheard him report that he was self-employed. Was that his way of saying he was *un*employed? Was Peter Mitchell on the road looking for work? And how much of a sacrifice had he made paying her fine? Had she thanked him? She couldn't even remember.

"The phone is inside the garage," the policeman reminded her.

"I'll be along in a minute. I have to check on my cat first."

He nodded and walked off.

Mary Elizabeth did want to check on Monet, but first she turned her attention to Peter Mitchell. He was straddling his rumbling bike, ready to leave. She crossed the lot at a run. "Peter," she called, waving her arms in case he didn't hear.

The bike took a little lurch before stopping. "What's the matter?" he asked, looking at her from behind dark glasses.

"I haven't had a chance to thank you for everything you've done."

He lifted one shoulder in a scant shrug and revved the engine.

"I mean it," she said, placing a staying hand on his upper arm. Even through a layer of heavy denim, she felt the vibrancy of his muscled flesh. Her palm warmed with an unsettling tingle. "Not many people would've done what you did last night," she said, removing her hand. "And then paying my fine today... I want you to know I really, *really* appreciate it. I can't imagine how I could ever repay you."

"Three-hundred-and-fifteen dollars will do," he said. He had a Clint Eastwood kind of voice, she thought, momentarily bemused. Soft as a prayer. Dark as sin. "And as far as last night goes," he added, "consider us even, all debts squared away."

She tilted her head. "How do you figure that?"

"You came to my rescue, too, by pulling that gun. You stopped the fight and kept me from getting the tar knocked out of me. It was a stupid stunt—it got you arrested—but it worked, and as I see it, repaid me in full for whatever I did for you." He shifted his balance and looked toward the open gate.

Mary Elizabeth knew there was nothing left to say. She ought to step aside and let him go. She shouldn't want to hold him back. She knew nothing about this man. And yet...

She reached for his arm again. "Wait."

"What now?" His mouth was so serious it was almost grim. She noticed the upper lip was cracked and slightly swollen. A nice mouth, though, firm but warm-looking, and beautifully shaped.

"What is it?" he repeated.

Her pulse raced. Was she out of her mind? She'd met the man in a *bar,* for heaven's sake. An unquestionably seedy bar, at that. He was no stranger to fighting, no stranger to being jailed. He was tough and huge and dangerous-looking, and he scared her half to death. And yet...

"I don't suppose you'd care to open the ledger again."

He took off his dark glasses and squinted at her. The hard blue energy in his eyes seemed to compress. "What do you mean?"

"Well, I was thinking... " She wondered if he could hear her heart thumping. "It's another crazy idea, but..."

"Spit it out, Mary Elizabeth." He drawled her name with almost singsong mockery.

"Would you consider driving me and my RV out of

town? We could say that you've offered to drive me all the way to Florida, but once we're safely away from here…''

"Mary Elizabeth!" he said, clutching his chest in feigned shock. "That's illegal."

"Yeah, well…" she tried not to grin. "It's the company I've been keeping lately."

His beautifully shaped mouth twitched, and twitched again, before he brought it under proper control.

"To repay you, I could fix you some lunch. How's that?"

He looked off into the distance, seemingly considering the offer. But then he said, "Sorry, it wouldn't work. For one thing, what would I do with my bike? For another, well, I just prefer traveling alone."

Mary Elizabeth rubbed her arms, nodding, lips pressed tight. "It was just a thought."

"Yeah." He slipped on his sunglasses again, looked to the road, looked back. She thought she felt his gaze traveling over her, but wasn't sure. Then, with a nod and a hot blast of exhaust against her shins, he sped away.

She continued to stand there, clutching her elbows and listening to the sound of his bike growing fainter. When it finally faded altogether, the lot seemed unnaturally quiet. She could hear the tiniest metallic clank of a tool being placed or picked up from the cement floor in the garage. In all her life, she thought she'd never heard such a lonely sound.

She didn't have time to dwell on the phenomenon, however, because just then she spotted Sonny and his friend plodding along the sidewalk, heading for the entrance to this very lot. Within a matter of seconds she was inside her RV with every door and window locked.

She was relieved to see that Monet was all right and that someone had refilled his food and water bowls, but after the briefest of pats on the head, she dashed to the bathroom where Sonny couldn't possibly see her if he happened to look through a window.

She knew her behavior was bizarre. What could he possibly do to her here, with a policeman just yards away? Why would he want to do anything?

Nevertheless, she remained flat against the closed bathroom door, her breathing shallow, her heart galloping away. She heard Sonny's distinctively high voice, heard the young officer talking to him, then, after what seemed an eternity, a car engine starting up.

Only when it faded in the distance did she allow herself to relax. When she did, though, she realized she felt wretched. Far too much had happened within the past couple of days. It was finally backing up on her. But for once in her life she was in exactly the right place at the right time. She simply sank to her knees and let herself be sick.

When she finally felt better, she washed her face and lowered her shaky self to the toilet lid. Leaning forward, she dangled the wet washcloth between her knees and stared at the brown linoleum. Her ribs ached.

Maybe Mrs. Pidgin was right; this wasn't such a good idea. She couldn't even make the three-day journey, which she'd thought would be the easiest part of leaving home. How, then, would she start a new life, make new friends, find a job, a place to live? And how in heaven's name would she do all that *and* have a baby?

Maybe she ought to go back. Maybe there was no other way than to tell Roger about her pregnancy and marry him. So what if they didn't love each other? So what if they'd already broken up before she discovered she was pregnant? As Charles had said, it was the right thing to do.

The only question was, right for whom?

She closed her eyes, longing for the sweet oblivion of

sleep. Unfortunately, there were things that demanded her attention—calling the credit card companies, for instance.

She hauled herself to her feet, brushed her teeth, combed her hair and unlocked the bathroom door, preoccupied with thoughts of finding her financial records. She was surprised to find the interior of the RV had darkened. Evidently, the sky had lowered while she'd been closeted in the windowless bathroom.

But she wasn't nearly as surprised by the darkness as by the fact that a light had been turned on in the kitchen. On a rising tide of curiosity and inexplicable hope, she hurried forward.

She was right. A light *had* been turned on, over the table, casting a warm cozy glow over her mother's Battenburg lace.

It also cast its warmth on a man who, after all, had not gone away. When he heard her come forward, he put down the book he was reading, and with one booted foot pushed out the chair opposite him.

It was then she noticed the cup of tea waiting for her. Earl Gray, to be exact. With honey and lemon.

CHAPTER FOUR

I OUGHT TO HAVE MY HEAD examined, Pete thought, putting down his book.

He'd gone five blocks, successfully ignoring his conscience, but then he'd noticed Sonny and his sidekick walking along the street in the direction of the garage. They'd be crazy to start trouble with Mary Elizabeth today, he'd thought; the consequences would be a lot more serious than a simple fine. On the other hand, they just might be vindictive enough not to care. By the time he'd reached the highway Pete had been racked with concern and guilt. So he'd returned, driven all the way back to Bernie's, only to find no trace of Sonny—but Mary Elizabeth in need of assistance anyway.

Mary Elizabeth seated herself opposite him. She looked pale, tired and humiliated, probably at having somebody hear her throw up. "What are you doing here?" she asked weakly. "How did you get in?"

"First things first. Would you like something to eat with that. Toast? Crackers?"

Her smile was faint. "Crackers would be nice."

Pete slid out of the bench and opened the cupboard where he'd found the tea. He returned with the entire box, and then realized maybe he ought to bring her a plate.

"That's fine," she said, reading his thoughts.

He set the box in front of her, slid into the bench and

said, "Now, to answer your question, I came in through the door. How did you think?"

Her eyes widened. "But it was locked."

"No, it wasn't."

Mary Elizabeth dropped her head to one hand and groaned, "Oh, God. I thought I'd locked it. I thought…"

"Eat," he said. "Get something in your stomach."

She pulled a cracker from the box with two fingers, the others crooked daintily, and nibbled off a small bite. Pete watched as she took a sip of tea, turned the cracker and took another tiny bite. It looked like this might take a while. He settled more comfortably into the banquette and gazed around the RV.

As a general principle, he held motor homes in abject contempt. With their microwave ovens and color TVs, they made an utter mockery of camping. But when he'd entered Mary Elizabeth's cluttered motor home, his purist sensibilities had gone into something like sugar-shock.

He was used to traveling light. Even on trips that lasted several weeks, he managed to fit all the necessities of survival into a few well-planned saddlebags.

Trying to be charitable, he reminded himself that Mary Elizabeth wasn't on a camping trip. If what she'd told the police was true, she was moving. Having lots of cartons stacked around was only to be expected.

Cartons he could overlook. He could overlook the rocking chair that obstructed the living space, as well. What he couldn't quite get over, though, was the fancy lace on this table. And the stained-glass dingle-dangles hanging in the windows. And that vanilla-and-cinnamon smell he associated with expensive gift shops. There was a wreath of dry weeds on the door, a huge snoring cat overhanging the edge of the bunk above the cab, and framed embroidery everywhere. He'd never seen a motor home quite like it.

Then again, he'd never met a traveler quite like Mary Elizabeth, either, a woman who'd chosen to set out on a sixteen-hundred-mile journey dressed in an outfit that he'd bet cost hundreds of dollars and could only be dry-cleaned.

"How are you feeling?" he asked her.

"Better." She finished off another cracker. "I really hate being sick. I'm usually not. Usually I have the constitution of a workhorse."

"Do you have the flu?"

"No." She looked aside and said no again, quietly. "A lot's happened to me lately. That's all."

He studied her sidecast eyes and closed expression. The words "Tell me about it" were almost on his lips, when he caught them back. Dammit, he didn't like women with secrets, especially secrets that hinted at problems he didn't want to deal with. He preferred the straightforward kind, women who were undemanding, easy to please, easy to take pleasure from in return. Mary Elizabeth Drummond was none of the above, and he had no desire to get to know her better.

She drained her teacup. Her color was coming back, all peaches and cream. "You answered only one of my questions," she reminded him. "You still haven't told me why you're here."

Pete didn't let himself rethink what he was about to do. Without preamble he said, "I changed my mind."

She closed her eyes and sat very still. "About what?"

"If you'll add the use of your shower to the lunch you offered earlier, I'll accept your deal."

Pent-up anxiety escaped on an explosive breath. "Thank you," she said, opening those big coffee-brown eyes and letting their warmth pour over him.

"Hey, don't get too grateful on me now. It's only until we're safely away from this town."

She nodded vigorously. "Of course. I understand. But what about your motorcycle?" She took another cracker out of the box and popped it into her mouth whole.

"I think I can work something out."

"Really?" Her delicate oval face brightened. Her whole *body* brightened, making him think it might be nice to just sit there and watch her for two or three hours.

"Hold on." Pete raised his hands, trying to stem her too-ready optimism—and maybe his reaction to it, as well. The last thing he wanted was to start liking this woman or finding her attractive. "I might work something out *if* you're willing to add a few bucks to what you already owe me."

Her smooth brow puckered. "What for?"

"I'll have to buy one of those trailers out there, if Bernie will sell one, that is."

"Oh. Oh, well, sure," she agreed, smiling again. "There's already a hitch at the rear of the motor home. The former owners used to tow a small car."

"Yes. I noticed." Pete had known towing his bike wouldn't be a problem even when he'd used it earlier as an excuse.

"Well, let's go ask." She popped out of her seat, combing her fingers through her hair.

"The policeman who gave us a ride is still here," Pete said, following. "You'd better tell him about this setup before he thinks you've skipped town and there's an APB out on you."

Her smile widened, showing off a set of remarkably white and even teeth. "Wouldn't that be something!" Then she opened the door and practically skipped down the RV's two metal steps.

Oh, great, Pete thought miserably. She was the bouncy kind, chirping cheerily just minutes after being sick. He hated bouncy, chirpy people.

The policeman, whose name was Riley, was standing just inside the garage. Pete knew he'd been watching the RV ever since he'd gone into it. "What's up?" he inquired.

"Mr. Mitchell has offered to drive me to Florida."

The officer gave Pete a tight once-over. "That right?"

Pete nodded. "It doesn't make sense, her being stuck here, trying to get her old license renewed. By the time it comes through, she could already be in Sarasota with her new license in her pocket. And since we're both traveling in that direction, anyway..."

The officer looked at Mary Elizabeth. "Are you sure that arrangement's okay with you?"

She nodded spiritedly. "It was my idea to begin with."

"I thought you were on vacation, Mitchell?"

"I was, but those court expenses this morning kind of put a crimp in my plans. A free ride home looks pretty good right about now."

"Well, you watch your p's and q's," Riley warned. "Remember, we have everybody's address, we know where you're going, and I plan to add this latest development to your file."

Just then a mechanic in a gray jumpsuit shambled over. "Car's all set, Pat."

"Thanks, Bernie." The officer turned back to Mary Elizabeth. "Well, good luck to you, ma'am." He touched the visor of his cap and actually cracked a smile before getting into his vehicle and driving away.

As soon as he was gone, Mary Elizabeth shouldered her way around Pete and strode into the garage. "So, you're Bernie?"

"Yuh. Bernie Kearns." The mechanic wiped his hands on a grease-blackened rag.

"You're just the man I want to see, then."

Forty minutes later Mary Elizabeth had convinced the

garage owner to sell them a small wooden trailer, Pete had hooked it to the RV and secured his bike, and she had phoned all the department stores and credit card companies she had needed to contact.

"I feel so much better," she said, leaving the garage at Pete's side. "Whoever stole my wallet went on a shopping spree. They've charged close to two thousand dollars in my name so far, but I'm not going to be held accountable for those charges."

"And are they sending you new cards?"

"Uh-huh. They're being mailed to my friend's in Florida. So, how's your motorcycle?"

Pete led her to the trailer at the rear of the motor home. The Triumph's wheels were locked within deep wooden blocks, its body secured with enough chain and cord to hold down a mad Brahma bull.

"Are you sure it's secure enough?" she asked.

Pete frowned at his handiwork, genuinely concerned for several long seconds before realizing she was joking. He didn't laugh. He'd grown increasingly disgruntled as he'd worked. It was a jury-rigged job and it hadn't been easy. Thoughts of how much vacation time he'd already lost because of Mary Elizabeth had begun to eat away at him, too. On top of that he was starving.

Emitting a low grumble, he grabbed up his duffel bag and said, "Let's get this show on the road."

Inside, Pete tried to get into a better frame of mind, but when he took the front seat, his mood only darkened. He'd driven all sorts of vehicles in his time, from megaton backhoes to powerful sports cars, but never in his life had he expected to one day be sitting at the wheel of a motor home, with a lace potpourri ball swinging from the radio knob and a wind chime of ceramic geese jangling above his left ear.

"Is anything wrong?" Mary Elizabeth's bourbon-over-ice voice drew him out of his thoughts.

"Uh—no. Got a road map?"

She reached for a neatly folded map on the dashboard. Pete took it from her and opened it out over the steering wheel. Interstate 95, from Maine to Florida, had been highlighted with an orange marker.

"Okay. This is where we are," he said, moving the map between them and pointing. She leaned in. Pete picked up her scent, something fresh and floral—orange blossoms?

"Are you sure?"

"Uh-hmm. Northwest of the Tappan Zee Bridge." He smiled fractionally. "Why? Where'd you think you were?"

"Not there." Her lips stretched in a comic grimace. "I thought I was on my way back to Connecticut. Instead, I must've gotten on the Bronx River Parkway or maybe Route 87 and headed north."

"How did that happen?"

Her cheeks warmed to a soft pink. "I sort of got turned around in the Bronx." Quickly she added, "So, Peter, how do I get back to I-95?"

Pete studied the map and all its possibilities. "This way." But instead of drawing his finger due south, backtracking to the Bronx, he inscribed a loop that crossed the Hudson via the Tappan Zee Bridge and came down along the western bank of the river, in New Jersey.

"Isn't that kind of indirect?"

He noticed she had a distracting way of wrinkling her nose when she questioned him.

"Only a little. We're not far from the bridge now. Besides, that route is a little more pleasant. I'll leave you off... let's see, somewhere in here, around Ridgefield. I don't think you'll have much trouble from there."

"That's very kind of you, taking me all that way."

Pete folded the map into a bulging package that began to swell as soon as it hit the dash. "That's me, all right," he mumbled in self-disgust. "Old Mr. Kind."

The orange cat roused itself from sleep and leapt down from the bunk, landing with a thud. He lumbered forward, sat at Mary Elizabeth's feet and looked up at her with an exhausted expression. Apparently, the vault into her lap was too much to expect so soon after his leap from the bunk.

"Come on, Monet." Mary Elizabeth patted her lap.

Pete's left eyebrow curled. *Monet?*

Mary Elizabeth sighed and finally heaved the lazy bundle off the floor. "I hope you don't mind if I sit for a minute. I haven't forgotten that lunch I promised you. I just feel so exhausted all of a sudden."

Pete's stomach was so empty it hurt. "No rush," he said. He turned the ignition. "All right, we're out of here."

The motor home eased its way through Bernie's lot, out the gate and down the street. Mary Elizabeth sank more comfortably into the contoured seat, experiencing the first release from tension she'd felt in days.

She looked out the side window. Commercial buildings flickered by, lamp poles, car lots, trees. She wanted to ask Peter about himself but didn't want to irk him any more than she already had. Obviously, he wasn't happy about this arrangement, but then she couldn't blame him. It was a tremendous imposition.

"By the way—" He spoke so unexpectedly she jumped. "It's Pete, not Peter. Nobody ever calls me Peter."

"Oh." She gave his hard profile a considering study. "How sad."

Frowning, he leaned away from her. She thought she heard his breath hissing like a slow tire leak.

On the outskirts of town, they passed a series of small

strip malls, a vague familiarity making her think she'd come this way in the squad car last night. She saw a gas station, a two-story motel, a green highway sign—and sat up abruptly. She knew this place. This was where her adventure had begun.

Her head swiveled. Behind her the motel was just disappearing around a bend, the very motel she'd come off the highway seeking last night. She swiveled forward, and with sickening clarity the Starlight Lounge came into view. Across the road, under the sighing pines that shielded the cottage she'd been so afraid of, two young children were playing with a spaniel.

She sank back, pressed by the weight of irony. If only she'd started eeny-meenying on the opposite side of the road. If only she'd decided to try the house instead of the lounge.

But then she wouldn't have met Peter Mitchell, she thought unexpectedly, and somehow, on some level she didn't quite comprehend, he seemed worth the trouble.

They took the on ramp to the highway. Mary Elizabeth adjusted the cat to a more comfortable position and watched the trees sail by under a rain-threatening sky. A languorous warmth flowed through her, calming her overwrought nerves, quieting her mind. Not even the oldies station Peter had tuned in to disturbed her lassitude. She turned her body, tucked up her left leg and watched him through her lowered lashes. Even in such a large vehicle he seemed sizable. Though it was unfamiliar to him, he looked competent and in control.

He'd taken off his jacket, revealing a T-shirt-clad body that was solid and well-muscled. But his build wasn't grotesquely bulky like Sonny's. There was fluidity of line to his body, a naturalness to his strength.

Her languorous gaze lifted to his profile. She studied the

hard, down-curving set of his mouth, the cynical squint lines carved into his sun-hammered skin. The heavy shadow along his unshaven jaw, coupled with the black eye and cut lip, gave him a sinister cast. But Mary Elizabeth doubted there was a sinister bone in his entire body. He might be rough and raucous, like the song "Great Balls of Fire" that was playing on the radio. But sinister? No. Anyone who'd come to the aid of a stranger to the extent he'd come to hers had to be honorable right to the core.

From the expressions that flashed across his face, she also sensed he was a considerably intelligent man, which made her wonder why he rode an ancient motorcycle, dressed in ratty denim and habituated country bars. And why, above all, hadn't he risen higher in life?

Perhaps she *should* be concerned about this driving arrangement. Peter Mitchell was a package of contradictions, a package that, when all was said and done, she really didn't know. She just thought she did because they'd been through so much together since last evening. For all she actually knew, she might be riding merrily along with another Jeffrey Dahmer.

She opened her heavy eyes a fluttery crack and took in his profile again. No, he wasn't a Jeffrey Dahmer. He was a good man, an honorable man, tall and quiet, like an old-time cowboy. Peter Mitchell, she thought groggily as sleep overtook her, king of chivalry and rock 'n' roll...

THE MOTOR HOME ROCKED gently over an unevenness in the road. Pete glanced at Mary Elizabeth's slumped form, turned at an angle to face him. The motion of the vehicle must have lulled her to sleep. She looked as zonked as the cat in her arms.

He was surprised. He'd expected her to bend his ear, ask him nosy questions, chirp all the way to Ridgefield. She mustn't have slept too well last night in her jail cell. Pete smiled faintly. Served her right, the little brat.

She was a pretty little brat, though; you couldn't deny her that. The waves in her hair had drooped somewhat overnight, but it still looked nice, better in fact, falling like silk across her face. He liked the color, too, the soft striations of honey and ash.

And then there was that peaches-and-cream complexion. He glanced again as if to confirm his memory of it. Flawless, still.

His glance cut to her mouth. In repose, it looked softer than it usually did. Wider and fuller, too. Awake, she was usually so tense, her lips all but disappeared.

She did have a great smile, though. Great teeth. *Rich* teeth. Probably fluoridated, polished, braced and capped since the first one poked through.

On impulse, Pete flipped down the visor and bared his own teeth in the attached mirror. They weren't as white as hers—he drank too much coffee—but they were strong and straight and all his own, which was saying a lot for someone who hadn't been taken to a dentist...ever. He'd had to take himself, when he was sixteen and becoming self-conscious about such things.

He heard Mary Elizabeth sigh and quickly flipped up the visor, his face warming. What the hell was he doing?

He slanted a look her way, but she continued to sleep. Her left arm had slipped off the cat and come to rest on her leg, her hand hanging limply over the bent knee. Pete gazed at her hand, a hand with long graceful fingers and nails modestly filed and buffed.

It was also a hand with a pale band of skin on its ring finger. He scowled, sensing trouble. She'd told the police she was single, but that telltale ring mark indicated otherwise. What was Mary Elizabeth trying to hide? Was she

on the run from something? From some*one?* For a second
Pete felt the urge to check his sideview mirror, expecting
to find an irate husband trailing in the motor home's wake.

But, no, Mary Elizabeth didn't strike him as anyone's
wife. It could've simply been a piece of meaningless jewelry, he told himself.

Then why the evasive answers when she was being
booked? Why the anxiety?

And why, he wondered irritably, was he wasting his time
puzzling over an up-town girl who'd gotten his face busted,
his police record lengthened, and his wallet drained of three
hundred and sixty bucks? He was never going to see her
after today.

He drove two miles before he caved in and looked at her
again. She was still wearing her jacket, all three buttons
fastened, but the lapels had folded open, exposing the silky
shell she wore underneath. Because of the way she was
sitting, it pulled across her front, revealing a figure that was
slim, graceful and feminine.

Too feminine.

And there she was, trusting him so blindly and completely that she'd fallen asleep. In a motor home, no less.
With a bed in back where visibility from passing motorists
would be virtually nonexistent. How vulnerable could a
woman get? *Ah, Ms. Drummond, you have a lot to learn.*
The question was, why did he feel it was up to him to do
the teaching?

"Mary Elizabeth," he called softly. "Hey. Wake up."
She continued to sleep. "I want to talk to you." *No, I don't.
But, you see, I have these two sisters.* "Yo, princess." He
finally poked her arm.

Mary Elizabeth woke with a start. "Wha'za matter?"
She turned her head, confused. "Oh. Peter." She exhaled
a sigh as she reoriented herself.

"It's Pete," he reminded her. "Sorry to wake you, but we've got to talk." Slowing the RV, he eased it into a roadside rest area.

"We do? About what?"

He parked the vehicle under trees that were dripping with gathered mist. "The facts of life."

She cast him a wry look. "The facts of life?"

"Yes. On the road. The first rule of which is, you've got to be careful. Very, very careful. And I'm afraid you've flunked that one big time."

"By going into the Starlight? I already know that."

"Yeah, that was pretty dumb. But what I'm referring to now is the way you invited me onboard here. You shouldn't have done that. I could've been anybody for all you knew. A maniac, an escaped convict..."

Mary Elizabeth chafed under his criticism. "What's your point, Peter?"

"Pete," he corrected her. "My point is, disaster can happen anytime, anyplace, just like that." He snapped his fingers. "And you were courting disaster—robbery, rape, murder."

"I was not. I trusted you. I wouldn't have invited someone onboard I didn't trust."

"But that's my point. These days you can't tell who's trustworthy and who's not. Appearances are deceiving, and the world is full of creeps waiting to take advantage of the unwary."

"And that's *my* point," she insisted. He apparently thought she had fluff for brains. "I was not vulnerable. I didn't invite just anybody." A tiny part of her also knew he was right, but she didn't want to admit to herself she'd been so careless.

"Yeah? So, what do you know about me?"

She met his challenge with one of her own. "Well, are you or are you not a trustworthy man?"

He studied her a long, silent while. Finally he sniffed and looked away. "You were just lucky it was me."

"I wasn't lucky. I *knew*. And I didn't judge you by appearances only. In fact, not by appearances at all."

His gaze slid back to her. A raised eyebrow seemed to ask the question he refused to voice.

She said, "If you can't judge a person by his actions, how *can* you judge him?"

His penetrating blue eyes, fringed with indecently thick lashes, swept over her with deepening interest. "Yeah, well, just don't do it again. The next guy might not be so 'trustworthy,' and I won't be around to pull your bacon out of the fire."

Although she rarely even raised her voice, she suddenly wanted to hit him. Just haul back and wham that arrogant male superiority complex down his throat. Instead, she removed the cat from her lap and undid her seat belt.

"Where are you going?"

"To make you lunch." The sooner their obligations to each other were paid, the better. Why had she thought she liked this person?

"Well—" he looked out the wet windshield to the quiet rest area "—this is as good a place as any to take a shower. How about I do that first?"

"It makes no difference to me."

When Pete stepped out of the steamy bathroom ten minutes later, he found the table had been set with a platinum-rimmed white plate, a linen napkin and a cut-glass tumbler. Upon the plate lay a sandwich and a pickle. A *thin* sandwich and a pickle. A thin sandwich *with the crusts cut off*, and a pickle. His empty stomach growled.

Mary Elizabeth was sitting in the passenger seat up front,

with her feet resting on the driver's seat. Bathed in the watery green light that poured through the wide front windows, she seemed to be sitting in a strange underwater cave. She didn't bother to look up from the book she was reading when he said, "Aren't you going to eat, too?"

She shook her head, eyes still fixed on the page. "The tea and crackers will hold me for a while." Apparently she was still miffed about his advice concerning her trust in strangers. Fine, let her sulk, he told himself. He didn't want to talk to her, either.

Yet something about her kept Pete rooted to the spot and staring at her. Was it her complete and utter disdain of him? Or was it something else? The aloneness he felt surrounding her? The tragic beauty he read in her delicate features bathed in that strange, green, other-worldly light? *Who are you?* he wanted to ask. *What are you running from? Where are you going?*

She finally looked up and just for a heartbeat he thought he saw an unguarded reaction, the slightest widening of those coffee-brown eyes. But then shutters came down and she said, "Is there something else?" The orange cat in her lap lifted his head and cast him the same disdainful look.

"Do you mind if I get something to drink?"

"Of course not." She flicked back her hair, a minimal gesture that nonetheless conveyed a wealth of pride. Then she went back to her reading, as chilling as any ice princess he'd ever met.

CHAPTER FIVE

MARY ELIZABETH WAS burning up. In spite of his bruises and days-old beard, she had already concluded that Peter Mitchell was an uncommonly handsome man. But when she'd looked up just now, the realization had hit on a purely visceral level. With his thick, still-damp hair combed back from his face, and the rugged planes of that face freshly shaven, he was truly a sight to behold.

He'd changed into a fresh pair of jeans—these were not torn—and an ordinary navy polo shirt that was respectable enough to have come straight from her brother's closet. Unfortunately, she'd never seen anyone looking quite so virile in an ordinary knit shirt before.

In that unguarded moment, she'd found herself responding to him in a frankly feminine way, her body rising to an elemental physical pull. It was bizarre. Showering and shaving hadn't changed his appearance that much, but the changes were sufficient to make her uncomfortably aware of him in a physical way.

She was appalled. What was she doing feeling sexual stirrings for this man? She was pregnant, for heaven's sake. That part of her life had shut down, at least for the foreseeable future. In addition, she didn't think she even liked him anymore.

She heard Pete take a seat at the table. Cautiously she looked up. He was staring at the sandwich she'd prepared, a curious expression on his face. She couldn't imagine what was wrong now.

The next moment he picked up one of the triangular halves, popped the entire thing in his mouth, chewed three times and swallowed. She was so amazed she didn't even try to pretend she wasn't gaping when he met her eyes.

She watched him pick up the other half of the sandwich, demolish it with the same quick ease, and then polish off a ten-ounce glass of milk. He left the pickle.

"Thanks for lunch," he said flatly.

Heat slid up her cheeks. What a dope she was to have thought a man as large as Pete would be satisfied by a meal so insubstantial.

Almost instantly her embarrassment was replaced by anger. At least she'd tried. He didn't have to be so sarcastic.

He went to the sink with his dishes. "Should I wash these?"

Her eyebrows arched. "Should I?"

"What?" He turned from the sink, frowning.

"Are you trying to tell me you're the sort of man who wouldn't be caught dead in a kitchen?"

He placed the glass in the sink with extreme care. "No," he said calmly, but irritation grated just under the surface. "What I'm trying to ask is, are you restricting your water usage?"

Mary Elizabeth swiveled the bucket seat forward, and when she was sure he couldn't see her, winced. "No, there's enough water. I have an extra-large tank." Behind her she heard mutters of exasperation.

Before long they were on the road again, crossing the long Tappan Zee Bridge. On the approaching side of the Hudson rose the steep, picturesque banks known as the Palisades. In the distance to the south shimmered the concrete spires of Manhattan, barely visible today in the mist shrouding the area.

Halfway across the river Pete turned on the wipers. He also sneezed and, pulling a clean handkerchief from his jeans pocket, sneezed again.

"Bless you," Mary Elizabeth responded out of habit. "Catching a cold?"

Turning off the wipers, he grumbled, "No such luck."

"What do you mean, no such luck? You *like* catching colds?"

"Better than I like being allergic to cats." He gave Monet, lounging across her lap, an evil scowl.

"Oh." She folded the cat closer. "Well, you'll only be bothered a little while longer."

"Amen to that." He hung his left wrist over the steering wheel, slouched a little and sneezed.

Mary Elizabeth decided she didn't like the way he drove. He appeared careless, inattentive...and she didn't like the way he looked at her cat.

What she didn't mind so much, though, was his scent. Was it his soap? His after-shave or shampoo? *Something* smelled awfully good. Warm. Outdoorsy. A cross between sandalwood and pine. Nothing like the sweet fruity fragrance that Roger used to ooze.

At the unexpected intrusion of Roger on her thoughts Mary Elizabeth felt a weight press down on her. Guilt again? She turned her head and watched the low gray clouds skulking across the sky. She felt like one of those clouds, slinking away from responsibility, and emitted a sigh.

"What's the matter?" Pete asked.

"Nothing."

After a minute or so, he said, "If it's all the same with you, I'm going to turn off at the first town we come to."

"How come?"

"I have some shopping to do."

"Peter, I'm rather in a hurry. Couldn't you wait until after we've parted company?"

"It's Pete," he bit out, "and, no, I can't wait."

Mary Elizabeth's lips parted on a mute protest.

"What's your hurry?" he inquired.

"Not that it's any business of yours, but I have a job interview waiting for me in Sarasota."

Pete gave her a reassessing once-over. "Important position?"

"Important in the sense that I need it."

His gaze returned to the line of traffic ahead, moving across the long bridge. He turned the wipers on and off again.

"What sort of job is it?"

"It's a temporary clerical position in a dentist's office, just until I can find something in my field."

"Which is?"

She was reluctant to go on. In her continued silence he asked, "What's the matter? Are you in a line of work you can't talk about?"

"Of course not. It's just that I get the feeling you consider my talk of a job trivial. I work, Peter. I always have. Nothing's ever been handed to me."

He cast her a doubtful glance. "So what do you do?"

"Well, for the past five years I've served as curator of a small local-history museum in my home town."

Pete cocked his head, his dark eyebrows lifting. "Really?"

His surprise annoyed her. She derived an unholy amount of satisfaction when he sneezed again, three times in a row, and his eyes began to water.

"Yes, really."

"How'd you get a job like that?" he asked as they left the bridge behind.

"I slept with the entire board of directors."

He choked on a laugh. She rather liked what laughter did to his hard-bitten face.

"I do have a degree in art history, you know," she said.

"Oh? From where?" he asked in nasally interest.

"Smith."

"Figures."

She turned offended eyes on him. "What's wrong with Smith?"

"Other than it's one of the Seven Sisters? Nothing."

"I suppose the college you went to is better."

He turned a probing frown on her, making her realize her remark had been unkind, meant to underscore the fact he didn't have a degree.

"I didn't exactly go to college, Mary Elizabeth. I got most of my training in the army. I finished off my degree nights at a university extension near my home."

Her head swiveled. "You have a degree?"

"Jeez, what a snob!"

"I am not."

"Ha!"

She ignored his derision. "What's it in?"

"Electrical engineering."

Her eyes widened. "Is that what you do for a living?"

"Yes. And no." He paused to blow his nose. "I run my own construction company. I build houses."

Her perception of him fractured, flew apart and reassembled like the colorful chips of a kaleidoscope design.

"Are you really on vacation, then?"

"Yeah. What did you think?"

She knew her color was heightening. She shrugged.

"I saw an ad in a magazine for that bike we're towing,"

he explained. "A guy up in New Hampshire was selling it, so I said to myself, 'Mitchell, take some time off and go check it out.'"

Her confusion deepened. "Is that motorcycle something special?"

"It's a '53 Triumph."

"What does that mean?"

"To me it means Marlon Brando in *The Wild One,* James Dean in *Rebel Without a Cause....*" His left eyebrow arched.

She shook her head. "Never saw them."

"Steve McQueen in *The Great Escape*?"

Again she made a helpless gesture. But suddenly she perked. "Ever see Miss Piggy on *The Muppet Show*?"

"Miss Piggy?" Disbelief opened his expression.

"Yes. She did a motorcycle number once to the song 'I Get Around.'"

Pete pulled on his lower lip. "Uh, gee, no. I missed that one."

"She was great."

"Right up there with Brando, was she?"

"Absolutely." Mary Elizabeth found herself grinning and unable to stop. She noticed he was smiling, too. They rode on in companionable ease for several minutes.

"So, what does being curator of a local museum entail?"

"Well, when I took over, our collection was in pretty sad shape—a few Revolutionary War uniforms, a room dedicated to the logging industry." She raised her index finger and gave it a few sardonic twirls. To her utter delight, Pete smiled again.

"So the first thing I did was study local history. Can you wait a sec?"

She got up, took two steps into the kitchen and returned with a large bowl of M&Ms. "Want some?"

He shook his head, horrified. She'd been sick only a short time ago and had nothing solid in her but crackers.

She deliberated over the bowl and then chose a brown. "I read everything I could get my hands on—books, diaries, old maps, photographs...." With her index finger she stirred the contents of the bowl, found another brown, and popped it into her mouth. "Then I scoured the region—auctions, antiques shops, old estates—looking for artifacts."

Pete watched her picking through the candy, moving it around, popping another brown.

"I also pleaded for bequests through regional newspapers and magazines. And soon stuff was pouring in."

"Mary Elizabeth, what are you doing?"

She raised her head to find him frowning at her. "Pardon?"

"You eat M&Ms by color group?"

She looked from his incredulous face to her bowl and up again. She suspected her smile was rather sheepish.

Pete slapped a hand to his forehead. "What am I doing with this woman?" he muttered.

She popped another brown and placed the offending bowl on the floor.

"Why did you leave your job?" Pete braked carefully and directed the motor home into the parking lot of a shopping mall. The mist was so heavy he hadn't bothered to turn off the wipers for several miles. "You obviously enjoyed it."

Mary Elizabeth tried to keep thoughts of her argument with Charles from telegraphing. "I did, but I'd exhausted it. There wasn't much left for me to do."

"Sounds like you enjoyed the process of pulling the museum together more than the final product."

She thought awhile, then slowly nodded. "I guess I did."

"I can understand that. Not much different from building a house. I love seeing the structure taking shape, but I sure as hell don't want to stick around after the sod is down and the owners have moved in."

She smiled softly, liking the comparison he'd drawn, enjoying the connection they shared.

"I don't imagine there's much money in local museum work, though," he probed.

"No. But it was never an issue—" she grimaced "—until today. I lived at home and didn't have the expenses that most people have. Even though I paid my father for room and board, I was still able to save money."

"Seven hundred dollars?" he asked doubtfully.

She shook her head. "That's just what I've put aside since I bought this RV."

Of course, Pete thought. The RV. That's why she didn't have much money. She'd recently made a huge purchase.

But something else she'd said was now puzzling him. "You still lived at home?" Inadvertently his eyes flicked over her.

"Yes." She gazed at her tightly interlaced hands. "Moving out isn't a high priority with my...um, father. He has fairly old-fashioned standards, and the only satisfactory reason for a daughter to move out is marriage."

"Ah, I see." Satisfied that he had a clearer bead on her, he uncoiled himself from his seat. "I'll be back in a few minutes. Don't go 'way."

By the time Pete emerged from the mall, the mist had turned to unabashed rain. He jogged across the slick parking lot with his purchases tucked into his jacket. His stride was strong and sure. Mary Elizabeth had no trouble picturing him walking a scaffold or balancing on a roof peak.

He bounded up the two metal steps, closed the door and shook his head, wet hair sticking to his forehead. His presence immediately filled the RV. "Getting nasty out there," he muttered right before sneezing.

He went to the sink, drew a glass of water, opened a box of allergy medication and swallowed two tablets.

Mary Elizabeth suppressed a grin. She didn't know why she found his allergy so amusing. The man was obviously in agony. But he was so big, so strong and arrogant, that she couldn't help feeling tickled by the thought of him being done in by a fat, lazy cat.

"Come here."

She huffed. The man certainly loved to give orders.

She got up and stepped closer, but not too close. Dampened by the rain, his scent seemed to have intensified in a disturbingly alluring way.

He slipped his wallet out of his back pocket and thumbed out several twenty dollar bills. "Here." He pushed the bills at her, and when she only stared at them, uncomprehending, he dropped them on the counter. "You won't get far without gas money."

The extent of his generosity brought a tightness to her throat. "I can't let you do this. You've already done too much."

"How do you expect to get this boat to Sarasota then? Wishful thinking?"

She swallowed. "No, I thought I'd find a pawn shop. I have lots of things I can sell—earrings, a pearl necklace that was my moth—"

Pete clamped a swift hand over her mouth and muttered a choice expletive. "Don't tell me what you've got that's valuable, lady!"

"But…" Her lips moved against his warm, rough palm.

"No 'buts,' Mary Elizabeth. Dammit, you've got to be more careful. I mean it." He removed his hand slowly, his eyes traveling over her features and finally coming to rest at her still-parted lips. For a moment they were both quiet, a current of awareness buzzing between them, stirring their blood.

Shaken, Mary Elizabeth stepped back. No, not *between* them, she thought. She was the only one experiencing these inappropriate feelings, she was sure. Why would a man like Peter Mitchell be interested in a woman like her? She was clearly not his type.

But then, he wasn't her type, either. So what was she doing?

She made herself relax, telling herself she'd done nothing to get upset over. He hadn't picked up on what she'd been feeling, and even if he had, they'd be parting soon, never to see each other again.

Turning to the counter, Pete opened a waxed-paper bag. "No offense to the lunch you made me," he said, unwrapping a thick meatball grinder and taking a healthy bite.

Remembering the sandwich she'd made him, her cheeks warmed. "No offense taken," she returned with difficulty.

Pete popped open a can of cola. "Come on. I can eat while I'm driving."

The windshield wipers beat a steady thwock-thwock as they traveled along the Palisades Parkway heading south. To the left, below the cliffs, the Hudson rolled on, slow and gray. Ahead, across the river, the towers of Manhattan grew sharper.

Mary Elizabeth turned down the volume on the radio, interrupting the Flamingos in mid doo-op. "Is that thunder I hear?"

Pete opened his window and listened. "Oh, hell." He reached for the radio and raised the volume. She was about to object—she'd heard just about all the oldies she could take for one day—but then realized he was searching for a local weather report.

"...At times heavy," a female voice chirped liltingly, "with a late afternoon thunderstorm in the Hudson Valley and scattered squalls inland as far south as Trenton. But cheer up, folks. Skies will be clearing by morning and the weekend looks great."

Pete punched a radio button and the Flamingos returned. Mary Elizabeth rolled her eyes. "What's your fascination with this music?"

He thought awhile. "I have absolutely no idea, Mary Elizabeth."

She shook her head, accepted Monet into her lap again and gazed out the rain-streaked windshield. In her peripheral vision she could see that Peter had finished his sandwich but not his drink. He'd wedged the can between his thighs. Without realizing it, she soon became mesmerized by the way his strong hands curled around the aluminum can and lifted it to his lips, by the way he tipped back his head, took a long thirsty pull, then wedged the container between his thighs again.

"Don't hesitate to tell me if you see anything you like," he drawled.

Her gaze shot upward to a pair of laughing blue eyes. Her cheeks flushed, yet she was able to say, "I will. When I see it."

Pete coughed on a sharp laugh.

Mary Elizabeth sat back, smiling. She rather liked this banter they engaged in. It was something new for her. Her father would've thought it common. Roger would've taken offense.

They rode on for another mile. "Tragedy" was playing now, and Mary Elizabeth was paying closer attention to the lyrics than she cared to admit, when she became aware of something rustling. Turning, she noticed Peter unwrapping the cellophane from a thin cigar. He clamped it between his strong even teeth, deftly struck a match one-handedly and lit the end, puffing clouds of foul-smelling smoke into the close air. Her throat closed up in reflexive self-defense.

He held the cigar under a crooked index finger as he steered around a cloverleaf and blew a thin stream of foulness in the general direction of the slightly opened window to his left. Most of the smoke hit the glass and swirled right back in.

Mary Elizabeth cleared her throat. "Do you mind?"

He clamped the cigar between his teeth and shot her a wide, waggish grin. "We're almost there, princess. A few more miles. If I can put up with that fat fur ball, I'm sure you can put up with the aroma of a fine cigarillo."

"Payback. Is that what this is?"

His grin broadened. He chewed on the cigar, closed his gorgeous lips around it and drew in a mouthful of smoke which he released in playful little puffs.

A short time later Peter moved the RV into the breakdown lane and let it slow to a lazy roll before stopping under an overpass.

Mary Elizabeth sat up. "Anything wrong?"

"We're here. There's your ramp onto I-95. I told you it wasn't far."

"Oh." Even to herself she sounded surprised and disappointed.

Attractive lines crinkled outward from the corners of his eyes. "Miss me already?"

She tried to think of a comeback, but her lightheartedness had fled. She merely stared at the highway. Rain fell so hard it was smoking off the asphalt. Vehicles, all with their lights on, had slowed to a crawl.

"Do you think I'll have any trouble from here on—you know, with the police?"

"Hard to say. I'd advise you to keep to the speed limit,

don't drive too late at night and, well, just be careful. The rest is up to dumb luck.''

Mary Elizabeth nodded. "What about you? Are you going to be all right in this rain?''

He puffed thoughtfully for a minute. "Are you really in such a hurry to get where you're going?''

Her blood began to rush. "Well, um, yes.''

"Doesn't your schedule allow for sitting out the occasional monsoon?''

She ran the tip of her tongue over lips that were suddenly paper-dry. "Is that what you'd like to do? Sit here until the storm has passed?''

He squinted ahead. "Rain riding's not my all-time favorite way to spend an afternoon. I'll do it if it's necessary but…''

"No, I wouldn't want you to get wet or anything.''

"Wet?'' He laughed. "Hell, that's the least of it.''

"Oh?''

"Not much traction on wet pavement.'' He puffed on his cigar, letting her imagination paint a running list of horrors. "And then there's always the chance of being hit by lightning,'' he added.

"That happens?''

"Well, sure, Mary Elizabeth.'' He swiveled to face her, filling her eyes with his casually charismatic presence. "Tell you what we could do.'' He glanced at his watch. "Check-in time at most motels is three o'clock, and it's past that now.''

Mary Elizabeth felt an uncomfortable heat crawling up her neck.

"My God, Mary Elizabeth.'' He chuckled. "You are so easy to get a rise out of. I didn't even *mean* that as a tease.''

She struggled to look innocent and baffled.

"All I was suggesting was you drop me off at a motel

somewhere and then be on your way. This rain's not going to let up until morning, so I might as well find a hole to crawl into for the night.''

''I could do that,'' she said in a falsely light voice, not looking at him. ''Where's the nearest motel?''

''I'd guess off the next exit.'' He turned the ignition key, put the RV in gear and carefully eased into traffic.

Just as he'd predicted, they found a motel a few miles ahead. Pete parked in front of the office. ''Let me get a room and detach my bike, then you can be going.''

Mary Elizabeth didn't move. She felt weighted down by the realization that this was it; the time to separate had come. Until now she hadn't fully acknowledged how secure she felt traveling with him.

''Are you sure this is what you want to do?'' she asked. ''What I mean is, if you'd like, you can ride with me the entire way.''

''I can, can I?'' His smile was wry, making it clear he knew exactly who'd be doing whom the favor.

''I'd pay you, of course,'' she added. ''I might have to do it in installments, but I would.''

''Thanks, but it isn't a matter of money. I have a week of vacation time ahead of me and you've got to get to Florida pronto. Right?''

She smiled diffidently.

''Well then, this is where we say adios.''

After registering, Pete drove the RV around to the rear wing of the motel where his room was located. Although he worked quickly to unchain his bike, the rain soaked through his clothes in no time. Mary Elizabeth watched from the open doorway of the RV in stunned disbelief as he hauled the dripping bike right into his first-floor, disabled-access room.

He loped back to the RV to get his duffel bag. ''You

know how to get back to the highway?'' His hair was wet, a puddle forming on the floor at his feet.

For a long bemused moment, Mary Elizabeth stood transfixed. The rain, penetrating his clothes and washing over his skin, intensified his physical presence until she almost couldn't breathe. With an effort, she nodded. ''I know the way.''

He fit the strap of his bag over his shoulder. ''Well, you take care of yourself, Mary Elizabeth,'' he said, his tone soft and dark. ''And stay out of bars.''

She fought the urge to touch him, just one brief touch to that hard, vibrant cheek before he left. ''You, too, Peter.'' She noticed he didn't correct her this time.

He swung out of the RV, went a few steps and turned again. She was still standing in the open door, watching him.

''You know, driving an RV in this weather isn't too much fun, either.'' He blinked futilely at the rain, which continued to pour down, gathering and spilling off his lashes. ''If you'd rather cool your heels till it lets up, you could park outside my room. I put your license plate number on my registration form.''

''Thanks. That was kind of you. I'll consider it.'' Why was he still standing there talking? she wondered. Why didn't he have the good sense to get in out of the rain?

''Well then, I guess I'll be seeing you around, princess.'' He turned and this time sprinted all the way to his room.

Mary Elizabeth continued to stand in the doorway, staring through the sheets of rain. She felt mysteriously let down.

A close clap of thunder brought her to her senses. She closed the door and decided maybe she *would* stay a while. She got behind the wheel and drove the motor home to the far end of the parking lot near the woods where it wouldn't

be in anyone's way. There, she sat, staring at the rain washing down the windshield, wondering if the gods were trying
to tell her something—like maybe this trip wasn't meant to
be?

She was just tired, that was her problem. Tired, it was
easy to start thinking hopeless thoughts. What she should
do was take a hot shower and grab a bite to eat. That would
wake her up and make her feel more cheerful. With renewed conviction she got to her feet.

The rain continued into the evening, drumming on the
metal roof of the motor home, creating what should have
been a lulling white noise. Unfortunately, the thunder and
lightning continued as well, keeping Mary Elizabeth on
edge in spite of her exhaustion.

It was too early to sleep, anyway, she reasoned, watching
TV and sipping yet another cup of after-dinner tea.

Inadvertently, her mind wandered to Peter. She wondered
what he was doing, if he'd gone to a restaurant, if he'd
eaten at all. Maybe she should've invited him over.

But they'd already said their goodbyes. What was the
point of inviting him back? In fact, why would she *want*
to?

To emphasize her point, she slipped out of the banquette,
found a can of room deodorizer, and went through the RV
spraying away the faint, lingering odor of his cigar.

The sweet cloying scent of jasmine caught in the dampness of the closed-up camper and almost made her gag. She
hurried to open windows and flapped her arms.

When the air was breathable again, she decided to call
it a night. Although her body was still going, her brain had
evidently shut down. Besides, if she got to sleep now, she
could be on the road before dawn.

She retired to the bedroom, got into pajamas and crawled
into bed. There, she lay against her propped pillows, knees

bent, and listened to the storm. Light from the parking lot streamed palely into the room through the narrow slats of the window blinds, casting bars of light and shadow over familiar objects that in this setting looked new and strange.

Spying her Walkman amid the jumbled contents of a carton on the adjacent bed, she reached across the light-slatted darkness. Resettling herself, she untangled the cord, fit the earphones over her head and adjusted the switch to "radio." Lord only knew where her cassette tapes were.

The radio came on at a station playing jazz, something dense and screechy. She moved to another station where a full-throated country-rocker was singing about wanting "a real man."

From her position, Mary Elizabeth had a clear view out the window alongside her bed to the room where Peter was staying. The drapes were drawn but his light was still on.

She really was exhausted, tired right to the bone. Then again, wasn't she always now that she was pregnant? But this was nice, being propped in this soft nest of pillows, earphones drowning out the rain and too-frequent thunder. And although she was reluctant to admit it, it was comforting to watch the light from Peter's room and know he was there.

She found a different station. "Oh, brother," she complained when the deep, plaintive crooning of Elvis Presley filled her ears. She'd probably stumbled onto the station Peter had tormented her with all afternoon.

Although this song wasn't half bad.

All right, admit it, Drummond. You really like the song. She closed her eyes, opened them drowsily to take one more look at the motel, and closed them again, while Elvis's anguished voice pleaded for just one night with her, a voice she occasionally mistook for Peter's as she glided off to sleep.

INSIDE HIS ROOM, Pete bent over his king-size bed, folding his freshly laundered clothes. Luckily, he'd landed in a motel with a washer and dryer. In the background the TV flickered and droned. By the door stood his drip-dried bike. On the dresser lay an empty pizza box and two beer cans, also empty.

He'd thought of inviting Mary Elizabeth over. For all his claims to being a loner, he wouldn't have minded company tonight. But then, she'd probably turn up her nose at pepperoni pizza or eat it with a knife and fork. So in the end he'd eaten alone, watching ''Wheel of Fortune'' while his laundry spun in a dryer down the hall.

He packed his folded, still-warm clothes into his bag and buckled the flap. Maybe he'd read to pass the time. Or maybe he'd see if there was something more interesting on the tube. Propping himself on the bed, remote control in hand, he surfed his way through the channels. When he stumbled upon an X-rated movie, he reared back, his head bonging the hollow wall in surprise. What if he'd been a kid innocently looking for a cartoon show? he thought with the proper amount of indignation.

But in spite of that indignation, he lingered awhile.

Growing uncomfortably warm, he snapped the set off. No, he didn't need to watch that sort of stuff, either. He turned on the radio instead, and the room filled with the sounds of Bonnie Raitt singing ''Real Man.'' Her husky voice reminded him of Mary Elizabeth.

He eased off the bed and meandered toward the window, turning off lights before drawing aside the drape. It was still raining.

And she was still parked out there by the trees.

He wiped a hand over his mouth where a smile wanted to form. He hadn't been sure she'd stay.

Pete watched the rain, the lightning bursts in the distance, and thought of the frequent electrical storms that rode in off the Gulf at home. He wondered if Mary Elizabeth knew what sort of weather she was moving to.

Abruptly, he became annoyed. Why did every thought turn inevitably to Mary Elizabeth Drummond? He tried to put his special spin of mockery on her name, but strangely he couldn't find it anymore. It was gone.

And *that* was why he hadn't invited her over for pizza, he finally admitted—not because she'd turn up her nose, but because he'd stopped seeing her as someone he could easily slot and label.

That, and the spark of attraction he'd been fighting all day. There, he admitted it, and it only hurt a little.

It was crazy; he didn't know when he'd stopped wanting to run from her and when he'd started enjoying her company. He only knew it had happened, and if he asked her over, he'd be begging for trouble. Their night might not end with the last slice of pizza.

He couldn't risk that. She was moving to Florida, to a town that was less than a two-hour drive from his place, and he had to ask himself if he really wanted to start something here. She had a gift for landing herself in trouble and then getting him to help her out of it. Now she wanted him to drive the entire distance, and if he invited her over, he just might end up agreeing. It would only be one more favor, but one that would ruin his vacation. And, dammit, he had needs, too.

With a conscious effort he banished Mary Elizabeth from his mind and thought instead of his brother getting married....

And of Sue Ellen getting divorced. It was hard not to. He and Sue Ellen had shared something good at one time. They'd been one of those high school couples who seem like an institution, dating forever, always together. Pete and

Sue Ellen. You could hardly say one name without saying the other.

She'd wanted to get married right after graduation, but he'd convinced her that was out of the question. For one thing, she was already enrolled in college, and her parents damn well expected her to go. For another, what would they live on? The few extra dollars he made painting houses with his father? The paycheck he brought home from his part-time job at the gas station? Sue Ellen said money didn't matter, but that was only because she didn't know what it was like to go without it.

Pete did. Although his family never went hungry or lacked a roof over their heads, he knew the quality of their lives could've been better. A lot better.

Not that his parents didn't try. They worked as hard as they could, both of them, but the small backwater town where they lived didn't offer much opportunity for employment. His mother went from one menial job to another, the only type available to a woman who wasn't a secretary, a nurse or a teacher. In addition, his father suffered chronic back pain from a construction accident, and that limited the types of jobs he could take on.

Pete didn't want to repeat his parents' life, and although he sorely wanted to marry Sue Ellen, he knew that in the end they'd be far better off if she went to college and he got the training he needed to build a solid career.

Going into the army was one of those ideas that had been with him so long he didn't even question it by the time he was eighteen. An older cousin had gone in and done well, and Pete never forgot it. It was the most efficient way of earning and saving a decent wage, that cousin had said, since life in the military provided everything a person would normally spend money on. Equally important was the lure of getting some valuable training on the side, free.

Pete wasn't concerned merely about his own future with Sue Ellen. He was worried about his brother and sisters, too. What sort of livelihood would they eke out if he didn't do something? As the oldest and the one who'd always had to watch out for everyone else, Pete felt their future was riding on his coattails.

He wanted to go into business for himself, and he wanted that business to be prosperous enough to employ them all, the entire Mitchell clan, if need be.

When Pete's mother died unexpectedly a month after his graduation, leaving his increasingly disabled father with three children still in school, the pressure on Pete to provide intensified.

So he'd entered the army, sure that his and Sue Ellen's love would endure. Of course it would endure. They were meant to be together, weren't they?

But two years into his hitch, while Pete was slogging his way through the jungles of Central America, Sue Ellen decided she'd waited long enough and married some northern boy she'd met at college.

Pete's slow exhalation fogged the rain-rippled window. Now she was divorced. Calling him three times a week. Driving down to his office in Tampa. Prompting his sisters to rhapsodize about a reunion at Brad's wedding. Causing him to wonder if maybe they weren't on to something…

He breathed out a sardonic laugh. What the hell was he thinking? There was nothing between him and Sue Ellen anymore. Less than nothing. He suspected she was coming around only because his business was doing so well these days. But even if there were something, he had no intention of ever getting married again.

He sighed. It was the rain. That was what was causing these sentimental thoughts. Just the rain. It brought out the romantic in him every time.

Pete stood back from the window and reached for the remote control. He wanted to change the radio station, find something to divert his attention. He only hoped that in the dark he didn't accidentally click on the TV and tune in the orgy again. It had been too damn long.

Ah! *That* was it! he thought, smiling in relief. *That* was why he'd found himself being drawn to Mary Elizabeth Drummond today.

His smile thinned. How long *had* it been since he'd slept with a woman? A year? Eighteen months? It wasn't just that he was being more careful these days; relationships simply didn't seem worth the hassle.

I'm getting old, he thought, his shoulders slumping. Here he was, pushing thirty-seven, the only Mitchell offspring not married or about to be, and thinking of relationships as hassles. *What's even worse, I'm sleeping in a damn motel instead of a tent the way I used to, and I'm liking it!*

The radio suddenly came in clear, The King begging some woman for just one night with her, that's all he was praying for, the need conveyed by his voice almost painfully desperate. Pete knew the feeling.

He gazed out the window. The motor home across the lot was glazed with rain. All the lights were out, which meant Mary Elizabeth was probably getting some sleep. That was good. She'd looked awfully tired when he'd left her.

He groaned and looked aside, vexed by his continuing preoccupation with her. She'd probably exhausted herself with all that reaching for the radio dial today and turning down the volume on his oldies station.

Actually, he'd heard enough oldies himself for one day. He tuned in a classical station instead. "Opera night," he muttered with automatic derision.

But something in the music caught his attention, something in the expressive soprano voice that cut through pre-conceived notions of what was listenable and what was not. The sound was lush, full of passion and longing, and although Pete didn't understand a word that was sung, he still felt a tightness in his chest. Outside, the rain continued to pour down, and he thought, *Here finally is music made for a night such as this.*

I'm really getting old, he thought defensively. But the aria continued to flow through him, anyway, carrying him off. And he continued to stand in the darkness of his room, gazing out the window, thinking about romance and fate, youth and heartache and Sue Ellen Carlisle....

...But picturing Mary Elizabeth's delicate face on the rain.

CHAPTER SIX

MARY ELIZABETH WOKE shortly after 5:00 a.m. For several seconds she didn't know where she was. Startled, she gazed around the small bedroom, still dark at that predawn hour. Somewhere nearby a whispery voice was asking, "Who's sor-ry now?" Groping over the coverlet, her hand fell upon the source of the whispering, the headphones to her Walkman, and in a flash of remembrance, she knew where she was, and why.

Cool, fresh air was drifting through the open window over her bed. She propped up on an elbow and gazed across the parking lot toward the motel. The rain had stopped, but the world was still soaked and dripping. She sank back into the pillows.

It was then that she became aware of the discomfort in her lower body, a discomfort that felt like indigestion, menstrual cramps and nausea all rolled into one. Was that the reason she'd awakened so early? she wondered, running a light hand over her stomach.

Warily, she sat up, lowering her feet to the floor and clutching the edge of the thin mattress in two tense fists. In the process of sitting up, the tightness in her abdomen seemed to have risen right to her diaphragm, pressing the air out of her lungs and causing perspiration to bead on her upper lip. She took a slow breath, but it brought no relief.

A cup of ginger tea, she thought. That's what she needed. There was nothing like ginger tea to soothe an ailing stomach. Carefully, she got to her feet and shuffled to the kitchen.

But twenty minutes later, as she sat doubled over at the table with a half-drained cup under her nose, Mary Elizabeth felt worse than ever. The tea she'd swallowed seemed to be sitting right on top of that hard ball of cramps, just under her rib cage, with no place to go. Groaning in agony, she curled up in the corner of the banquette that Peter seemed to favor and hugged her arms.

Peter. How she wished he was here.

She lifted aside the lace window curtain and stared across the parking lot to his room. He'd be leaving today, going his own way while she went hers. She didn't know why that thought bothered her so much. She hadn't planned on having him drop into her life, so what difference did it now make if they parted company?

The difference, replied an impatient voice inside her head, was that she'd experienced the sense of security that came from being in the company of a strong, seasoned traveler. She felt there was no calamity Peter couldn't handle, and, quite frankly, after the events of the past two days, she was beginning to feel rather like Chicken Little. If the sky wasn't falling at this precise moment, just wait. Open your umbrella while you were at it, too.

Mary Elizabeth huddled into her bathrobe, feeling increasingly wretched. What was happening to her? she wondered in deepening anxiety, flinching under another cramp.

Suddenly her eyes snapped wide open. Was this the start of a miscarriage? Her strength drained out of her.

The clock on the cooking stove read only 5:35. Outside, the sky was still dark. "Oh, God," she moaned, pressing a hand to her slightly rounded belly. She was alone, sitting in the parking lot of a strange motel somewhere in New

Jersey, without money, without identification, without family—and she was having a miscarriage.

She levered herself to her feet, and on legs that trembled, shuffled back to bed.

PETE DIDN'T KNOW WHY he couldn't sleep. It was only 6:30 and he didn't have to be out of the room till eleven. Yet for the past hour he'd been wide awake, staring at the ceiling, thinking about where he'd go today, what he'd see and do. Occasionally his mind wandered to Mary Elizabeth, to whether she'd get to Florida without being stopped by the police, if her RV would make it without giving her trouble, whether she'd run into any more creeps like Sonny.

All right, so maybe his mind wandered to her a lot. It was understandable, considering all they'd been through together.

Pete finally gave up the idea of sleep. He hauled himself out of his rumpled bed, took a shower and dressed.

Seven o'clock, and the RV was still there, all the curtains drawn.

She'd been tired last night, he conceded, but if she planned to cover any decent amount of road today, she really ought to get moving.

Against his better judgment, Pete crossed the puddled parking lot and tapped at her door. There was no answer. He tapped again, louder, and waited. Tapped again on the rear window.

Finally he heard movement within, saw a curtain lift, and then the door opened.

"Hey, there," he began. "I hope I didn't wake you, but I thought…" His words slowed as her appearance registered—the uncharacteristically hunched posture, the sunken eyes, the tension around her mouth. He bounded up the steps and pulled the door closed behind him. "What's wrong?" he asked, gripping her arms.

She made a valiant effort to straighten her spine. "I'm just feeling a bit indisposed this morning." She smiled wanly. Her face was pale.

"Have you taken anything for it, for whatever's bothering you?"

She nodded. "Some tea, a few antacid tablets…"

"Any relief?"

"Not much." Again she attempted to smile, to appear in control of the situation. "Peter?" Her voice was small and tentative.

Pete found himself stroking her arms, kneading them, feeling them quivering under his fingers. "What is it, princess?" he said in almost a whisper.

"Could I prevail upon you for just one more favor before we say goodbye?"

Pete lifted a hand to her head, cradling it, petting. She was obviously scared to death. "Go ahead, I'm listening."

"Could you drive me to the nearest hospital?"

He worked at keeping his expression set. "Is it that bad? Are you sure a walk-in clinic…?"

She was already shaking her head. "Those places aren't always equipped for…" She paused, her eyes going a little wild.

"For what?" Pete leaned closer.

She swallowed, avoiding his gaze. "Well, you know, they're just not as good as hospitals."

"Can you tell me what's wrong?" He tried to keep his voice calm even though adrenaline was dumping into his system like water from a busted hydrant.

"I…I'm not sure."

"Well, is it a sharp pain or a dull pressure?"

"Both."

"Is it around your appendix?"

She shrugged. She was being vague and evasive. He knew it, but he didn't think it wise to press. Time was passing and apparently she didn't *want* to tell him.

How many secrets do you have, Mary Elizabeth? Pete wondered, frowning down at the top of her mussed blond head.

"Okay. Let me go lock up my room and talk to whoever's at the front desk. I'll ask where the nearest hospital is. Do you feel you can get into some street clothes?"

She nodded. Her eyes were closed, her body rigid.

"What?" Pete asked, tensing. "What's happening?"

She smiled fragilely. "Go. I'm fine. The sooner we get this over with, the sooner you can be on your way."

The hospital emergency room was small but busy. Mary Elizabeth was relieved Pete had come with her. While she continued to battle cramps, he made short order of explaining her missing health insurance card. He was calm and articulate and unexpectedly charming, while still conveying unbending assertiveness. The admissions clerk *would* find Mary Elizabeth in the mammoth computerized system, and she *would* be cleared for coverage.

Although Mary Elizabeth was deeply grateful for Pete's help in tackling the financial bureaucracy, she prayed he wouldn't be around when she had to explain what was wrong with her. No one knew she was pregnant except Charles and Mrs. Pidgin, not even Chloe. For one thing, she'd promised Charles not to tell anyone else. For another, she was simply too embarrassed. She certainly didn't want Peter Mitchell to know.

Unfortunately, her current luck held true and Pete never left her side. While one clerk was handling her admission, another was asking how she felt, if she was in pain, *what was wrong with her.*

"I'm not sure," she said. "I'm having abdominal pain."

"Is it localized, one side or the other?"

"It's hard to say. Will I be able to see a doctor soon?" Unwittingly she pressed a hand to her stomach as another spasm assailed her.

The woman shuffled together forms, fastened them on a clipboard and scooted around her desk. "Charlene," she called to a passing nurse, "take these people down to room three." She then jammed the clipboard into Pete's midsection. "Here, you can finish filling these out while you're waiting for the doctor."

Pete nodded brusquely, took Mary Elizabeth's arm and followed the nurse named Charlene.

Mary Elizabeth balked. "You can wait here. I'll be fine alone. Really I will."

Pete continued to propel her down the corridor. "I've come this far...." he said, leading her into room three.

The nurse handed Mary Elizabeth a blue hospital gown and closed the curtain around the bed. Left alone inside the enclosure, Mary Elizabeth worked herself out of her clothes.

"Are you decent?" Peter's quiet voice, just beyond the curtain, sent her scurrying for the nearest chair, grabbing at the back of the gown as she went.

"Uh-huh."

He stepped inside, gave her a sweeping glance and winked. In spite of her discomfort, she smiled.

"Do you feel up to filling this out?"

"Sure." She took the clipboard from him.

She was almost done with the forms when the doctor came in. He was a tall, thin, stoop-shouldered man with gray hair and a kind face.

"Good morning." He smiled. "What seems to be the problem?"

Mary Elizabeth glanced at Peter, standing at the foot of the bed. "Would you mind?" She tilted her head toward the door.

He hesitated. "Are you sure?"

"Yes."

With lingering reluctance, he drew aside the curtain and ducked out.

"Was that your husband?"

"No, just a friend."

The doctor skimmed her chart, puzzlement etched on his brow.

"I'm moving to Florida. He's keeping me company, helping with the driving," she temporized.

She knew exactly when the doctor reached the line that asked if she was pregnant. The furrows on his forehead deepened.

"Is he the father of the baby you're carrying?" When he looked up she was relieved to see his smile was still kind.

"No. We're just, as I said, friends." She was grateful he didn't pursue the issue.

Instead, he asked her to lie on the bed and proceeded to examine her, while she told him about the nature of her discomfort and her fear that she was having a miscarriage. His movements quickened noticeably.

Standing outside the room, Pete tried to rouse a few pangs of guilt for keeping his heel in the door, but he failed. He was too curious about the mysteries in Mary Elizabeth's eyes and more than a little worried about the pain he read in her body language.

Suddenly he felt he'd been hit with a brick. She was pregnant? Mary Elizabeth Drummond? Impossible. Not the Mary Elizabeth he knew.

He was still grappling with that revelation when the rest

of her words took hold. Pete pushed a hand through his hair and clutched his pounding skull. She was having a miscarriage? Right now? In there?

His pulse skyrocketed. He didn't want to know about this. Enough was enough, goddammit. He was on vacation!

He eased the door closed, looked toward the exit and began to walk away.

"CONSTIPATION?" Mary Elizabeth repeated, sitting up. Her face was red-hot, her eyes incredulous.

"That's my guess." The doctor lowered himself into a vinyl chair.

"You mean, I'm not having a miscarriage?"

"I see no indication of that."

Mary Elizabeth's eyes welled up so fast she didn't have time to check her reaction. "Thank you," she whispered to a deity she couldn't remember praying to.

"Constipation is a common malady during pregnancy," the doctor said. His clinical detachment helped her rein in her billowing emotions. "Surely your physician has told you."

"I haven't seen a physician yet," she explained. "I didn't want to start up with one, knowing I'd be moving."

"Ah, well, let me be the first to tell you, then. Constipation can be a devil of a problem when you're pregnant. In your case I'd guess it's been complicated by the stress of moving. Stress can foul up the plumbing of the healthiest person." He fingered his stethoscope. "Have you found yourself unusually troubled lately? This move, this pregnancy…are they worrying you?"

"Oh, sure," she said, trying to sound intelligently realistic, yet upbeat. If only he knew what else she'd been through lately!

"And you say you haven't had any morning sickness?"

"That's right, but I have been nauseous the past couple of days. Is it possible I'm just starting to have morning sickness now?"

"I doubt it. Not at three months. My guess is your nausea, like your constipation, is tied in with stress. Does that make sense to you?"

"It certainly does."

The doctor chuckled. "Don't look so glum. Constipation can be dealt with easily enough. Morning sickness can't. You're one of the lucky ones."

Mary Elizabeth rubbed her aching stomach and tried to feel lucky. "So, what now?"

"Time to call roto-rooter."

She rolled her eyes.

"Don't worry, it's a very gentle process, quite safe for the baby. There's a mild sedative I could prescribe for you, as well, to ease your anxiety, but quite frankly I'd prefer not to. I'd prefer you try to alleviate your anxiety by more natural means."

Mary Elizabeth nodded. "I can do that. I took a yoga class once, in college."

"Good. Now, until you engage a physician, I recommend a diet high in fiber. Eat lots of fruit and vegetables...." The attending nurse handed him a folder stuffed with pamphlets on pregnancy.

"Think you know everything, don't you, Charlene."

"I do," she parried dryly.

"Ah, nurses. Was a time they knew their place." The good-natured doctor got to his feet, chuckling. "Unfortunately, I have to leave you in this know-it-all's hands and go see another patient. But I'll be back before you're released."

"Thank you, Doctor. Oh, and could you not say anything about this to my friend?"

The doctor frowned at her but agreed, anyway.

Forty minutes later, Mary Elizabeth was feeling infinitely better and ready to leave. The nurse stood at the examining room door while she gathered up her belongings.

"Good luck to you now."

"Thanks. I'll need it."

"What are you hoping for?" The nurse opened the door. "A boy or a girl?"

Mary Elizabeth blanched when she noticed Pete waiting for her out in the hall. Had he heard?

"Yes, one or the other," she said distractedly. The nurse laughed.

Pete slouched against the wall, arms folded high on his chest, Bad Attitude written all over his sullen face. Their eyes met, and in that instant she realized he knew she was pregnant. Moreover, he'd known for a while. Had the doctor told him?

He pushed away from the wall. "How're you doing?"

She pressed her lips together, chagrined. "Okay."

He turned to the nurse. "Is she really?"

"She's tired but otherwise fine."

His eyes darted from one woman to the other. He wore the look of a man who thought something was being put over on him.

"Take care now," the nurse called, walking away.

Pete stared after her, grim and dissatisfied.

"Come on, Peter." Mary Elizabeth poked his chest with the folder of pamphlets and started for the exit.

They weren't even through the entry when he gripped her arm and unloaded the question. "What happened in there?"

Heat slid up her neck. "Not much."

His face grew dark and forbidding. "Did you... miscarry?"

Mary Elizabeth stared at the left pocket of his blue chambray shirt. "No."

His grip tightened. "Are you sure?"

"Of course I'm sure. Now I'd like to ask you something, mister. How did you...?"

"I listened in at the door."

"You've got a nerve. I asked you to leave."

"Why? Why are you hiding your pregnancy?"

"I'm not hiding it. It's simply none of your business." She gathered her indignation around her like a protective cloak, stepped around him and rammed open the glass door. Outside, the clear September sun had dried the pavement and soaked up all but the largest puddles.

Pete overtook her in a few easy strides. "So, what was wrong with you?"

Walking by his side, eyes fixed on her motor home parked in the lot reserved for emergency room patients, Mary Elizabeth felt embarrassment spill over her again. "I had cramps."

"Cramps. What kind of cramps?" he inquired impatiently. "Are they going to come back? Are they the sort associated with miscarriage? Were you spotting? Did you pass any clots?"

Mary Elizabeth stopped in her tracks. "Do you have children, Peter?" He didn't wear a ring, but that didn't mean he wasn't married, or divorced, or a father. She was shaken by the fact that even after everything they'd been through she still knew so little about him.

"No. Five nieces and nephews."

"Ah." Nieces. Nephews. She was dismayed by how easily her equanimity returned.

"My youngest sister had trouble with both her pregnancies."

She resumed walking. His *sister* had had trouble, and *he*

had taken such an interest that he knew things about female physiology that even she didn't?

He must have seen her puzzlement because he explained, "Lindy's husband hasn't been the most responsible of guys. There have been times during their marriage when she's...well—" he looked aside "—come to stay with me."

"During her pregnancies?"

"Yeah. I even went to a few Lamaze classes with her, so do you want to try telling me again what was wrong with you?"

Mary Elizabeth bit her lower lip. "It...it was nothing like that, nothing to do with miscarrying."

They'd reached the RV. Pete unlocked the door and held it open for her. "So, why did you have me rush you to the hospital?"

Tired of being badgered, she spun to face him. "I've never been pregnant before. How was I supposed to know I wasn't aborting? It felt pretty bad."

"*What* did?" He tossed the keys onto the dashboard, the clatter startling the cat, who was sleeping a few inches away.

"All right." She tossed up her hands and, feeling trapped, began to pace. "You want to know? Okay, I'll tell you. Here it is."

Pete folded his arms and leaned against the kitchen counter. "Anytime, Mary Elizabeth."

"Oh, God, this is so undignified."

"Have you ever been strangled?" he asked impatiently.

She glared at him. "I was constipated. There, are you happy?"

As soon as she'd said it, she wished she hadn't. She hurried down the hall and closed herself in the bedroom.

In the mirror behind the door, her face glowed redder than a valentine.

The door flew open. "Constipated?" Pete loomed over her, hands on his hips, disbelief written all over his handsome face.

"Get *out* of here. Did I ask you in here?" She pushed at his unmoving chest. "Get out."

"You had me rush you to the hospital," he went on, ignoring her outrage, "you left me out in the hall, worried half to death for more than an hour, and now all you can say is you were constipated?"

Mary Elizabeth wrapped her arms around her head and emitted a moan. She wanted to die. Just slip under the covers of her unmade bed and die.

Pete began to chuckle. She wanted to smack him.

"It isn't funny, Peter," she mumbled, still hiding like an ostrich.

"Yes, it is," he said, his amusement building

She dropped her arms and glowered. "You have the sense of humor of a ten-year-old."

He cleared his throat and made an attempt to compose himself. "I'm just relieved you're all right. That's partially why I'm laughing."

Her glower softened. "And the other part of you is laughing because it finds me ridiculous."

To her utter amazement, the laughter left his eyes completely. "No. Occasionally I find the things you do funny, but not ridiculous. Never that." His long fingers closed around her shoulders and drew her to him. She stiffened instinctively when their bodies met.

But in spite of the vague impropriety she felt being held in this man's arms, Mary Elizabeth began to relax. Being held with such tender care felt wonderful. So did hearing his strong, reassuring heartbeat under her ear. She sighed, shuddering as she sank further into his comforting warmth and strength.

He moved his hand under her hair and slowly stroked her neck. She closed her eyes, drifting on the delightful, tingly sensations his touch set off.

They both felt the change in their embrace at the same time. His fingers were moving up her neck into her hair when the shift occurred, away from mere friendly consolation toward an unsettling sensual awareness—awareness of the warmth of his breath on her cheek, the lush press of her breasts against his chest, the bracketing fit of his hip bones just above hers, and a flash-fire surge of arousal that was undeniably reciprocal.

I must be imagining things, he thought, his body freezing into position.

And holding her breath, she said to herself, *I must be dreaming.*

But it is happening, he admitted miserably.

He is feeling it, too, she thought, embarrassed.

Maybe if we feign ignorance, it'll just go away, they both decided.

Pete loosened his hold and she immediately stepped back. Neither of them met the other's eyes.

"Sit down, Mary Elizabeth." He guided her to her rumpled bed, then pushed aside a carton on the bed opposite and sat. "Tell me what happened. What did the doctor say?"

Mary Elizabeth looked past him, out the window to the small brick hospital. She continued to feel self-conscious, but she gave Pete a full and honest account of her examination, anyway. He deserved one.

"I'm sorry I got you involved in a false alarm," she murmured when she was done. "Poor Peter, you could've been miles away by now."

"Don't apologize. When you're pregnant it's always better to err on the side of caution."

"I suppose you're right."

"Sure I'm right. Now, will you smile, dammit? Everything turned out fine."

She smiled, but only to please him. Inwardly she'd felt a vague sense of dissatisfaction building all morning, a sadness, a something that weighed on her like guilt. But of course, it *was* guilt. Wasn't it always?

The touch of Pete's hand on her knee startled her. "What's the matter now?" His eyes were too intent.

She forced another smile. "Nothing," she said while a small voice inside her heart nagged, *Why did you wait so long, Mary Elizabeth? Why did you go back to bed instead of calling for help immediately?*

Pete's eyes narrowed, boring into her.

"Honestly, I'm fine."

He dropped his hand. "If you say so."

She nodded and then yawned. In mid-yawn she laughed. "Sorry. Sleepiness is apparently another joy of being pregnant."

Pete smiled with gentle sympathy. "I know. I once saw my sister Pam conk out right at the supper table. Don't worry. Second trimester you'll feel more energetic." He got to his feet. "Look, I've got to get back to the motel to check out. Why don't you just curl up there and catch yourself a nap."

She nodded, already dropping to her side. Pete lifted her feet, pried off her loafers and drew the blanket up to her chin.

"Wake me when you're ready to part company," she said drowsily. "I don't want to be left sleeping in a parking lot."

"No one will bother you."

"I know. I'd just feel, I don't know, creepy."

He stroked her hair. "Okay. Don't worry. Get some sleep now."

Mary Elizabeth drew the blanket up over her ear, imagining that by doing so she'd capture forever the warmth of his touch. By the time the engine started she was soundly asleep.

Pete looked in on Mary Elizabeth after returning his room key. She was still asleep, her honey-and-ash-colored hair fanned out across the pillow like a length of silk, her lips slightly parted, her thick lashes fluttering with a dream.

He sat on the other bed and watched her. He was ready to leave. He'd examined his bike, strapped on his pack and reviewed his road map. It was clearly time to resume his vacation. Time was passing. He'd wasted Thursday night in jail, Friday morning in court, Friday afternoon driving this boat through the rain, and here it was already halfway through Saturday...

So why didn't he just wake her up like she'd asked, say goodbye and leave?

He rose off the bed, and then sat right back down again.

Good Lord! Mary Elizabeth was pregnant. The thought still had the power to knock the wind out of him. Pregnancy usually did. The mere idea of a whole new person being created, cell by cell, within a woman's body never failed to put him in a state of awe. But Mary Elizabeth's being pregnant set off feelings that went beyond that, feelings that were complex and unsettling.

He glanced again at her ringless left hand lying gracefully on the pillow. It wasn't so much the fact that she was pregnant and unmarried, although, in his opinion, that wasn't exactly the best way to bring a new person into the world. It was rather that being pregnant and unmarried *and Mary Elizabeth* just didn't go together. She struck him as a woman for whom there was a proper time and place for everything—and this wasn't it.

His image of her would never be the same. Apparently she wasn't the "princess" he'd dubbed her, but a woman struggling with more problems than he had imagined, and doing so with more dignity than he'd given her credit for, as well.

Pete's mind teemed with questions. Who was the father? Why did they split? Did he leave her? She, him? Had he been abusive? Was he out searching for her, gaining ground even as Pete sat here musing? Was that why she was so tense and eager to reach her friend in Florida?

Pete closed his eyes and pinched the bridge of his nose. He was jumping to wild conclusions. He had to chill out.

He got up and, bracing a hand on the dresser under the rear window, gazed at his bike parked outside his motel room, whispering to him of sun and wind and the open road. Today he planned to ride through rural New Jersey, go someplace he'd never been. He needed to let the white lines soothe his brain, wipe out the emotional garbage that had accumulated with work and family responsibilities. He especially needed to let the vibrations of the engine shake loose those feelings of confinement he got when people tried to set him up, tie him down and marry him off. After a week of white-line tomorrows, he'd be okay. He'd return to Tampa reassured of his autonomy, stronger in himself, and ready to handle whatever came his way.

He stepped back from the window and gazed down at Mary Elizabeth, a sunbeam pouring a diagonal ray of gold across her curved cheek.

He hadn't liked the idea of her traveling alone even before he knew she was pregnant. Now he hated it. His sisters would probably get on his case about his attitude. Mary Elizabeth was pregnant, they'd say, not incapacitated. But he couldn't help feeling extra-protective toward her now. Lots of unforeseen problems could arise—today's problem, for instance.

Pete frowned. The doctor had told her that stress was making her ill, the stress of moving. Pete didn't doubt it, especially when you threw in getting stuck on a dark country road, running into a creep like Sonny, being arrested, having her wallet stolen and spending a night in jail.

And being pregnant, besides! Suddenly Pete felt like a jackass for giving her such a dressing down when they first met. Granted, he was being hauled off to jail because of her at the time, but he still felt bad now.

He lowered himself to the bed again and watched her sleep. He could alleviate that stress. He could drive her all the way to her friend's.

But then he'd be cutting his vacation short. Cutting it short? Hell, he'd be ending it. Getting her to Sarasota as soon as possible didn't include the sort of casual touring he meant to do.

And what about afterward, when she was settled? They'd know each other then, be able to call and visit. But did he really want her in his life? Did he want to know a pregnant woman who was apparently alone in the world except for one old college friend? A woman who was moving to a place she'd never been?

But mostly he worried about the physical pull he felt toward her. If he traveled with her, that pull would have to be denied, no question about it. And just how hard would that be? Would it plague him throughout the drive, turn their time together into a marathon test of willpower?

"What am I going to do with you, Mary Elizabeth?" he whispered on a troubled sigh. "What am I going to do?"

MARY ELIZABETH WOKE slowly to the familiar hum and rock of her motor home. Drifting in the muzzy land halfway between sleep and full wakefulness, she was aware nonetheless that something wasn't quite right.

Pushing back her hair, she squinted at her watch. Twelve forty-two. She sat up abruptly. They should have reached Peter's motel hours ago.

She slipped out of bed and peered out the high rear window. His motorcycle was once again secured to the trailer, rattling like Marley's ghost under its shroud of cord and chain. With a sudden leap in her pulse, she lifted her gaze. Gone was the dense urban sprawl of the New York City area. In its place were hills, wooded hills, and a twisty two-lane road!

"Peter Mitchell, where the devil are we?" She scooped a sleeping Monet out of the passenger seat and set him down in the kitchen. He stood there for a moment, bug-eyed, disoriented, then simply collapsed where he'd landed and went back to sleep.

Pete gave Mary Elizabeth a grin so confident it bordered on arrogance. His teeth gleamed around a cigar. This one, fortunately, was unlit.

"Well, hello there, Mary Elizabeth. Feeling better?"

She plopped into the passenger seat. "Where's the motel? Where's I-95? Why are you still driving?"

"You *sound* better. Look like hell though, if you don't mind my saying."

Mary Elizabeth combed her fingers through her hair. "I suppose you look like a prince when you first roll out of bed."

Not bothering to remove the cigar, he tipped back his head and laughed. He had a wonderful laugh, she admitted through her agitation. Rich, expressive and contagious.

"These here are the hills of northwestern New Jersey, Mary Elizabeth."

"Northwestern New Jersey," she repeated in a flat, dazed tone. "You mean, you've taken me even farther off course than I was before?"

"Well, not by much."

"Did it ever occur to you that I might not want to be in the hills of northwestern New Jersey?"

"Oh, it occurred to me, all right, but I figured you wouldn't mind once you thought about it. You're obviously in need of a little R and R before moving on."

Mary Elizabeth covered her face with her hands and moaned, "I'm on a schedule."

Just then the RV slowed and made a wide turn. Curious, she peeked through her fingers. Pete was nosing the vehicle through a stone gate into a campground.

She dropped her hands. A campground, she thought in a continuing daze. In northwest New Jersey. On Saturday afternoon. When she'd figured to be somewhere in Georgia by now, her trip almost over.

Mary Elizabeth kept her mutters to a minimum, however, while Pete registered them at a rustic cabin and received a site number and a map of the grounds.

By the time he set the RV in motion again, she felt considerably more sanguine. After the clamorous, exhaust-filled air of the New York region, this was really sort of nice, this refreshing scent of pine, the soft swish of a breeze through the trees. Maybe it wouldn't hurt to stop for just a few hours.

Their site was nestled under a canopy of trees on a rise overlooking a lake. A picnic table and a fire pit came with the space, as well as electric, sewer and water hookups. Mary Elizabeth sat at the picnic table—Pete's orders— watching him move around the campsite, engaging hoses and lines with an efficiency that amazed her.

He scrambled up the ladder at the rear of the RV, lithely

stepped along the roof, and squatted to do something mysterious to the air-conditioning unit.

She sighed. These were the responsibilities that had scared her into not venturing far from home on her few weekend outings. She fully intended to read all the instruction manuals that came with the camper—she'd have to if she was going to make it her home—but so far she knew only the basics about the mechanical systems.

Swinging off the ladder, Pete gave her a cavalier grin. "There, all set. Feel like taking a walk?"

She glanced toward the lake, a lake almost as blue and deep as his eyes. Shrugging, she got to her feet and fell into step by his side. All around them families were enjoying a last warm weekend of summer, tossing Frisbees, paddling canoes, cooking over campfires. Mary Elizabeth felt distinctly out of place.

Walking at the water's edge, she finally asked him the question that had been troubling her since she'd awakened. "So, what are we doing here, Peter?"

"I already told you. I thought you needed—"

"To rest? I could've done that back in the parking lot of the motel. You know, the one just a mile off I-95?" she said pointedly.

His arm bumped hers companionably. "But could you go fishing for your supper back at that motel?"

"I don't need to go fishing. I have enough food to get me through a Valley Forge winter."

"Not the way *I* eat. Besides I don't like quiche, and I noticed you have so *much* of it."

Mary Elizabeth opened her mouth, words of protest ready to spill, when all at once his remark took on strange new meaning. Her footsteps slowed, then stopped completely.

"What did you say?" she asked softly.

Pete picked up a flat stone and skimmed it across the surface of the lake. "I've decided to take you up on your suggestion," he replied, giving her a casual over-the-shoulder glance.

She held her breath. "Which one?"

"I'll go the distance with you...."

Her breath escaped on a burst of relief.

"Wait. Hold it. You haven't heard my half of the deal yet. Before we do anything, we have to get a few ground rules straight, the most important being, I'm not making the trip in three days. You have to understand that. I have almost a week's vacation left and I intend to take every minute of it."

Her momentary elation tumbled. "I can't do that. I told my friend I'd be at her place by tonight."

"Sweetheart, I don't think you're going to make it."

She battled a grin. "I know that, but I thought I'd at least make it by Monday."

Pete shook his head. "With me driving, a week. Take it or leave it."

Mary Elizabeth chewed on her bottom lip.

"Another thing," he went on, "I get to stop the bus any time the spirit moves me and go off side-tripping on my bike."

Her lip-chewing picked up fervor. "Anything else?"

"I get to sleep inside. It'll save me a bundle on motel fees."

Mary Elizabeth tried not to react. After all, the idea of having him drive had originally been hers, so of course he must have assumed she'd thought through all the details. *This* detail had gotten by her.

"Oh, one more thing," he added. "After you're settled in Sarasota, I don't expect us to keep in touch."

A tight ache filled her chest. He didn't *expect?* Wasn't it rather he didn't *want?*

They resumed walking. Eventually he said, "You're awfully quiet, Mary Elizabeth. What are you thinking?"

"I'm thinking there's no free lunch. If you're ready to do me this favor, how do you expect me to repay you?"

He began to smile. "Funny you should ask."

CHAPTER SEVEN

"YOU WANT ME TO *what?*"

"Go to my brother's wedding with me next Saturday. Pretend to be my date."

After a taut span of silence, Mary Elizabeth laughed. "I don't think so, Peter."

Pete skipped another stone, the movement from shoulder to wrist fluid and compact. "Why not?"

"Why not?" She planted her spread-fingered hands on her hips and gaped at him. "I'm pregnant!"

"What does that have to do with the price of bananas? You hardly show." His glance swept the green chino jacket she was wearing today which, as usual, was buttoned. "Wear something loose like that and nobody'll notice."

"That's not the point. It's…I don't know. It just feels wrong. Besides, we hardly know each other."

He shrugged nonchalantly. "A week can solve that."

She chewed on her lip, considering the proposition. It was crazy.

It was also tempting…and because it was she replied, "No, thanks," and resumed walking.

"Ah, well." Pete pulled the RV keys from his jeans pocket and dangled them in front of her. "Have it your way, princess."

Her steps slowed. "But why would you want me to pretend I'm your…your date? It doesn't make sense."

"Yes, it does. I have a solid, rational explanation. But

before we start swapping war stories, let's go up to the clubhouse and see if we can rent us a boat and some fishing gear.'' Without waiting to hear what she thought of the idea, he started off, calling over his shoulder, ''And we *will* swap, story for story. That's another stipulation. I'm not going anywhere with you until I find out about that little bombshell you're carrying and the guy who's responsible.''

Mary Elizabeth caught up beside him. ''I don't see how that's any of your business.''

''It will be, if I happen to wake up some night looking up the barrel of a twelve-gauge shotgun.''

Mary Elizabeth rolled her eyes. ''That happen to you often, Peter?''

He chuckled, a down-and-dirty sound that brought on a smile she had trouble suppressing.

''I'll tell you right now,'' she assured him, ''nobody's following me.'' At least she hoped not. She hoped Mrs. Pidgin was able to keep her destination a secret

''I still want to hear about it.''

Mary Elizabeth walked along, puzzled by her reaction to his proposal, by her reluctance to accept it. After all, having him drive had originally been her idea, hadn't it? And it would be to her advantage if she agreed.

Was she balking because, if she complied with his agenda, she'd be arriving at Chloe's a week late? That certainly was a serious consideration. But, oddly, she wasn't nearly as bothered by that as by the idea of spending a week with Peter Mitchell in an eighteen-foot motor home. And that, she knew, was because of the fascination she'd felt for him from the moment she'd laid eyes on him, a fascination that had quickly turned into something more.

She gave him a sidelong glance, taking in the chiseled perfection of his rugged profile. She really didn't know why she was worried. Acting on an attraction was no longer an option open to her. She was pregnant. Her social life had temporarily shut down. Remembering that, surely she could keep these stirrings under control.

Likewise, she shouldn't be concerned about Peter, either. Why would he want to get involved with a woman who was pregnant, a woman carrying another man's child? If anything, her condition should drive him away. She ought to feel safe traveling with him. Her pregnancy acted as a shield.

"When did you say this wedding's supposed to take place?" They'd reached the clubhouse. She paused on the dirt path.

"Next Saturday. I'm Brad's best man, so you'll have to sit with the family during the ceremony, but afterward, at the reception, I'll be all yours."

"Oh, joy."

"So, is that a yes?"

"No! Let me think about it. I still want to hear your reasons."

"Fine. But first, the gear."

"Peter," she called, following him up the porch steps. "I've never fished before."

Opening the wooden screen door, he turned. "You're kidding."

"No."

"You grew up in Maine, and you never fished?"

"No!"

He shook his head. "You've got more to learn than I thought, Mary Elizabeth."

"SO," PETE SAID, WATCHING a dragonfly scissor across the surface of the lake, "are you ready?" The dinghy was designed with two benches. He sat on one, Mary Elizabeth on the other, their poles reaching out over the water in opposite directions.

"For what?" she asked.

"For shoes and ships and sealing wax..."

"Oh."

"Want me to go first?" he offered.

"No, no. I don't mind." She pulled in a breath that lifted her shoulders almost to her ears, then expelled it in a shuddery gust. "Okay, here it is. About a year ago I started seeing this guy named Roger. My...um...father set us up."

"A blind date?"

"Not exactly. Roger works at...with my father, so I already knew him. My...father simply persuaded me to attend a company dinner as Roger's date. We had a good time, he asked me out again, and things progressed from there."

Pete noted the hesitation in her voice, the awkward pauses and leaps over detail, but he didn't interrupt. She'd relaxed significantly in the short time they'd been rocking on the lake. He didn't want to tamper with a good thing.

"Unfortunately," she continued, "there was never any real spark between us. I liked Roger well enough, but I wasn't crazy about him, you know?" Her nose wrinkled with familiar predictability as she reached the end of her sentence.

"Yet everyone seemed to think we were an ideal couple. My...father, especially. He was always talking about our future together, always hyping Roger's virtues, always telling me how lucky I was to be dating him."

Pete's eyes narrowed. Just for a second there, he thought Mary Elizabeth sounded bitter.

"So," she said on a sigh, "we became engaged."

Pete's scowl deepened.

"I know." Two spots of color emerged on her cheeks. "It was a terribly passive thing to do. I'm not proud of it."

Pete returned his gaze to his side of the lake. "I'm not criticizing. God knows I've done plenty of things simply because momentum carried me along."

"Momentum. That's a good way of explaining it." She paused, then abruptly sat up. "Oh!" She swung her leg over the bench to face the water directly. "Peter, something just tugged on my line."

Pete put down his pole and carefully moved from his bench to hers. "I think you're right." He sat behind her, with his thighs bracketing her hips and his hands reaching around to cover hers. Then together, they began to reel in whatever she'd lured.

Positioned as he was, Pete caught the orange blossom fragrance of her hair, felt the supple warmth of her back against his chest, and his body coiled with a purely sexual reaction.

He reminded himself that Mary Elizabeth was not someone he wanted to think about in those terms. He also reminded himself of the multitude of reasons—not least of which was her pregnancy. With a determined effort, he concentrated on the rod and reel, and put his easy responsiveness to this unlikely woman out of his mind.

"It *is* a fish!" She laughed when a silvery walleye splashed through the surface.

"Not a bad size, either. Ah, beginner's luck." Pete deftly unhooked the fish and lowered it into a bucket.

"This is so neat!" she exclaimed, admiring her catch.

Baiting her hook again, Pete glimpsed the sparkle in her soft brown eyes and tried not to feel too pleased that she was having a good time.

' "Continue," he said gruffly. "You and Roger became engaged...."

"Yes. That was last May." She took her pole from him and cast the line clumsily but with obvious delight. "About that time, I also began to give our relationship serious thought—you know, the fact that it was so lukewarm?" Pete watched her nose wrinkle and wondered why he'd ever thought of the quirk as anything but adorable.

She continued, "I came to the conclusion that maybe it was my fault. Maybe I hadn't given our relationship all I could. Before that time, Roger and I hadn't, you know, been intimate?"

Pete was glad her embarrassed gaze was fixed on the water and not his face. Dating all that time, and not intimate?

"But with marriage on the horizon, thoughts of making love occupied my mind more and more. Maybe that would change things between us, I thought. That would add the spark that was missing. And so..." She shrugged and fell broodingly silent.

Finally Pete asked, "Did it work?"

She shook her head. "I don't know why I ever thought it would. I was never really attracted to Roger in that way," she said dismally. "Actually, I'd always found kissing him rather distasteful." She paused. "All right, to be totally honest, it usually felt like I was kissing a plate of wet pasta."

Pete couldn't help laughing and was glad to see Mary Elizabeth smiling, too. He got the feeling this was the first time she'd looked at her relationship with Roger in anything but a tragic light.

"The ironic thing about it was, Roger felt the same way I did. I just didn't know it."

Pete wondered what kind of blood ran in Roger's veins, not to be attracted to this long-legged, blond-haired beauty with a voice that could liquify stone.

"But finally," she continued, "the night my father suggested we start making arrangements for a Christmas wedding, we both came clean and confessed we were unhappy. We broke off our engagement that very night. That was seven weeks ago. Right now I'm about eleven weeks along."

Pete calculated quickly. "You didn't know you were pregnant when you broke up?"

"No. It was too soon for me to miss my...um...monthly cycle. Besides, we'd taken precautions."

Pete turned his gaze on her, one eyebrow raised.

"Condoms are usually reliable," she explained, "but occasionally you hear about an accident happening. I guess it was just my dumb luck to have one of those accidents happen to me."

A flock of geese in V-formation honked their way across the blue sky heading south. Watching them, Pete said, "Does Roger know?"

Mary Elizabeth sighed, frowning. "No."

Pete let his breath hiss through his teeth. This didn't sound like it was going anywhere good. "Do you intend to tell him?"

She gulped. "No."

Pete hesitated, wondering if he really wanted to poke his nose any further into Mary Elizabeth's life, which only got messier the better he knew her.

Curiosity won out over prudence.

"Don't you think he has a right to know?" he asked.

Her mouth hardened, but her voice was surprisingly thin and uncertain when she said, "What about my right to be married to someone I love?"

"Who said anything about marriage?"

She sighed. "Roger is a decent guy. We might not love

each other, but he'd want to marry me. He'd think it was the right thing to do.''

"But you wouldn't have to agree."

"Yes, I would. I come from a small town, Peter. Everyone would know I was the one who'd denied the child a proper home."

"Jeez, Mary Elizabeth! Coming from a small town may be tough, but it doesn't mean you have to roll over and play dead."

"How would you know?"

"I didn't always live in Tampa."

"Oh." She hunched forward, her momentary boldness deflated. "It isn't just that. Good Lord, I'd like to think I have more backbone than that."

He had suspected she was dancing around the issue, avoiding the heart of it. "What is it, then?"

She gnawed on her bottom lip. "I didn't tell Roger because I just don't want him to know."

"Why? If he's such a decent guy..."

"The child, that's why. I don't want to raise a child who's unwanted and resented by its own father."

Pete sat quietly for a while, unsure what to make of the rancor he'd picked up in her voice. He was also puzzled by the erratic leaps and zigzags in her logic.

Eventually he said, "Have you ever considered the possibility that Roger would love the child?"

She shook her head, sending blond hair swirling. "No. Whether we got married or not, Roger would begrudge the child, I'm sure of it. Maybe not outwardly. Outwardly he might claim to want visitation rights and even insist on paying child support because that's the proper thing to do. But inside I know he'd feel trapped in a situation that embarrassed him and burdened him financially and socially."

Pete was intrigued by the strength of conviction in her

voice, by the depth of sadness in her eyes. Was there something about this Roger she wasn't letting on?

She held the forgotten fishing pole at a heedless angle and said, "I don't want that, Peter. I don't want any baby I've brought into the world growing up like that, resented and unwanted. There's got to be a better way."

"Like running off to Florida?" he said with more sympathy than she apparently heard.

She lifted her chin as if challenged. "Yes."

He studied her tensed face, the delicate blue veins throbbing at her temple. "I don't know, kid," he drawled. "In my experience, honesty has usually proved to be the best policy. Keeps things simple, you know?"

She kept her eyes trained on the water, her jaw set with conviction. "It's what's best for the baby."

"But leaving home, quitting a job you liked—that's really a drastic step."

He waited through an interminable silence. During the entire time, her eyes stayed fixed on the water, long lashes hooding whatever was in their depths. Pete had a hunch it was more secrets.

"Your family must be upset by your decision to leave home." Her mouth hardened and he sensed he'd hit a raw nerve.

"Yes," she replied, but her expression told him no. "But I'm leaving for their benefit, too."

"I don't follow...."

"Well, my father is sort of a public figure." She paused. "I guess it doesn't matter, my telling you. He's president of a bank. It's a local bank, but still quite prestigious. He's also head of the chamber of commerce and a deacon in our church. His reputation would be seriously tarnished if I remained in the area—you know, pregnant and unmarried?"

Pete scrubbed at the back of his head. Her *father's* reputation would be tarnished because *she* was pregnant? What kind of crazy logic was that? Come to think of it, what kind of *father* was that? Where was the familial support she needed at this difficult time in her life? Where was the love?

"What about your mother?"

"Died when I was twelve."

Pete's heart contracted. "I'm sorry." He really was. He already had a bad feeling about this father of hers and didn't like the idea of her being left in his care. "Do you have any brothers or sisters?"

"One brother, one sister, but they don't know I'm pregnant. Susan is married and busy with her own life. Charlie's in London." Layers of loneliness darkened her eyes, yet she smiled, briefly, hollowly. She was a paradox, and becoming more of one the more he knew about her.

Pete thought of his own family, how involved they were in one another's lives. Although they often exasperated one another, he couldn't imagine any of them not sharing news as important as a pregnancy.

"What are you going to do when you go back home to visit? Do you plan to leave the baby in Florida, pretend it doesn't exist?"

She began peeling away at some tape wrapped around the grip of her pole. "Lately," she said, concentrating on the tape, "I've been thinking that the best thing I can do for everyone concerned, especially the baby, is give it up for adoption. I mean, what sort of life can *I* offer a child, living in an RV, pawning him off on day-care while I go to work."

To someone who liked his women uncomplicated, Pete thought, Mary Elizabeth Drummond could easily become a nightmare.

"You plan to live in your RV when you get to Florida?"

"Yes."

"I'd wondered why someone like you was traveling in something like that. Is that why you bought it?"

"No. I got it a year ago." She gazed across the lake to the far shore. "I've always wanted to travel," she said simply, but in her eyes he saw emotions that complicated her response, emotions that echoed in his own chest in a way that made him feel they had a lot more in common than they knew.

"And giving up the baby...is that what you really want to do?"

She coughed nervously. "Yes. A husband and wife looking to adopt would give it a much better home than I could. Sometimes those couples have been through excruciating medical problems. They'd cherish my baby."

Pete's glance shot to her face. Her eyes were glassy, her expression set in an effort not to cry.

Just then, however, his line began to whir. He gripped the pole and braced himself, grateful for the diversion. He didn't think he wanted to pursue the reasons for those tears. No, he *knew* he didn't.

BY THE TIME HIS CATCH was flapping around in the bucket with its hapless mate, Mary Elizabeth felt she'd regained an admirable grip on her composure. She hadn't intended to divulge quite so much about her personal life, but Peter had been surprisingly easy to talk to, probably because he was a stranger, she reasoned—although he didn't feel like a stranger anymore. He felt like a friend.

"Okay," she said, "you know my story, now let's hear yours. What's the reason behind your asking me to attend your brother's wedding?"

She watched him settle on the bench facing hers and cast

his line. When the baited hook had sunk, he said, "All right. Here's the way it is. Someone I'd rather avoid is going to be at the wedding, a woman named Sue Ellen Carlisle." The rippling circles around his line widened outward. "She and I used to be an item in high school, but you know how life is. After graduation she went her way, I went mine."

Mary Elizabeth tried to read his expression, but it had gone blank. She hadn't a clue how *life was* with him, and evidently he didn't plan to tell her.

"Now Sue Ellen is divorced, and I've got a hunch people at the wedding are going to be trying to get us together again."

"People?"

"Hmm. My brother. My two sisters. Friends who knew us back in high school."

"Why would they want to do that?"

"Basically, because some folks don't know how to mind their own business."

She sidestepped his cynicism. "Were you and Sue Ellen really serious? Like, king and queen of the prom or something?"

The corner of his mouth lifted lazily. "I wasn't exactly king-of-the-prom material back in high school, Mary Elizabeth." His smile faded. "But, yeah, we were serious."

She wasn't sure she was glad she'd asked. She'd finally picked up a reaction, a thread of sadness in his voice, a hint of remembered heartache that, illogical as it was, made her jealous. Apparently, breaking up hadn't been his idea, and this Sue Ellen was a person capable of hurting the inviolable Peter Mitchell.

Mary Elizabeth murmured, "And now she's divorced."

"Yep. Fifteen years later she's divorced, and people are saying dumb things like, 'Hey, Pete, why don't you ask her out?'" He shook his head in disgust. "Especially my sisters. They're married, so they think the whole world should be. They're always trying to fix me up with somebody. I think it's really just a case of misery-loves-company."

The slap of the water softly lapping the boat filled the ensuing silence. Mary Elizabeth wanted to probe deeper. Each new thing she learned about him only made her hunger to learn more. But she wasn't sure she should.

"What do you have against marriage?" she asked hesitantly.

"Nothing, as long as it doesn't involve me." He gazed out over the sun-shot water, again avoiding her question with flippancy, firming her suspicion there was more to his past than he was letting on.

"You don't intend to ever get married?"

"Nope. Not cut out for marital bliss."

"But how do you know unless you try it?"

His jaw hardened. "I don't have to eat mud to know it's not for me, either. Hell, Mary Elizabeth, lots of men are confirmed bachelors. Why are you having such a difficult time with the concept?"

He'd become prickly enough for her to back off the issue and not say what was on her mind, that she thought he'd carved out a terribly lonely existence for himself.

"Have you seen this Sue Ellen recently? Do you know how she'd react if people actually started matchmaking at the wedding?"

Pete clicked his tongue. "That's part of the problem. I've got a strong notion Sue Ellen wouldn't mind us getting back together herself."

"And you don't want to?"

"You got that right. She's half the reason I decided it was time to leave Tampa for a while, go on vacation."

"The other half being...?"

"That Triumph turning up for sale."

"Ah, now I get it. You want me to be your *date!*"

"Yes. I'll protect you on the road if you'll protect me at the wedding."

She smiled. That was an odd way of looking at the arrangement. "But surely you know other women. Why me?"

"To be perfectly honest, I haven't been seeing anyone special lately. Oh, I've dated, but my family and friends know who and how casual it's been. Now, if I show up with you, a complete stranger, I could say anything about you and nobody'd be the wiser. I could say we're practically engaged, or thinking of moving in together...."

"But won't your family want to know why you'd never mentioned me before?"

"Not really. I don't tell them all my business. But just to be safe I'll say I had a hunch our relationship was special but I didn't want to let them in on it before I was sure."

"But what happens after the wedding, when I'm suddenly not around anymore?"

Pete thought a moment. "Suppose we go with the truth, say you're moving to Sarasota. That way I can pretend we're still seeing each other, but Sarasota's enough of a distance that they wouldn't bother checking. Then, after a couple of months, I'll merely say we broke up."

Mary Elizabeth scowled at the half inch of water at the bottom of the boat sloshing around her shoes. "I don't know, Peter. There are still so many holes in your story. What if someone at the wedding asks me something about you that I should know?"

"We have a week to learn the details of each other's lives."

"But shouldn't we have a past, you and I—how we met, places we've been together?"

"Of course. We'll work on it. We'll come up with something believable."

"And all I have to do at the wedding is…what?"

"Dance with me, sit and talk with me, go along with the pretense that we're crazy about each other—and keep Sue Ellen and my pushy relatives off my back."

Mary Elizabeth closed her eyes and made a sound that was half groan, half laugh. "Oh, Peter, I'm still not sure we can pull it off. Look at us. We're not exactly a made-to-order match."

They sat quietly in the gently rocking boat, faces serious, eyes exploring each other, searching for the reminders that they came from vastly different worlds. Those reminders were becoming increasingly difficult to find.

Finally Pete grinned carelessly and drawled, "You've got a lot of promise, Mary Elizabeth. I can fix you up, make you look almost as good as somebody I might take out."

"Oh? Why do I have to be the one with *promise?* What about you?"

"I'm perfect. Who'd want to change me?"

"Your arrogance, Mr. Mitchell, is second only to your impertinence."

Grinning, he ran his knuckles over his jutting chin. "I knew you'd like me once you got to know me better."

She moved to hit him, but he caught her wrist and laughed. "So, what's it gonna be, sweetheart? Two for the road, or adios, amigo?"

Clasped in his strong grip, with her arm pressed against his muscle-ridged chest, Mary Elizabeth experienced that pull of physical attraction that had plagued her much too often lately. She was sure he was feeling it, too. Everything inside her lifted with the sensation—and then fell.

"It's three for the road, Peter," she reminded him quietly. "Three."

She watched her point hit home. He swallowed, loosened his grip and moved away from her.

Mary Elizabeth glanced toward her camper tucked under the trees. She could be in Florida by Monday night if she left tomorrow morning and drove two ten-hour days.

But she'd be driving without a license. If she got caught, her license might be taken away from her for years. And given her streak of luck lately...

Just twenty hours on the road, she thought.

But what if she fell sick again? What if the RV broke down?

A mere two days.

"When did you say we'd be getting to Tampa?" she asked.

"Friday. And it won't be Tampa. It'll be Elmira, the small town where I grew up, about forty miles away. Brad's fiancée still lives there. So do most of the two families."

"I see. But I wouldn't be free to continue on to my friend's until when, Saturday night?"

"Better make that Sunday morning."

Hmm. Monday night. Sunday morning. Almost a whole week.

But did it really make a difference?

Of course it did, her conscience nagged. What about her job interview? She was supposed to be interviewed on Tuesday.

"I'll have to call my friend and see if my interview can be rescheduled."

"So, is that an answer?"

She shut her eyes and moaned, wondering what she was getting into. "I suppose it is."

PRODDING THE GLOWING coals in the fire pit late that afternoon, Pete thought about Mary Elizabeth's answer and felt a pang of guilt. She was up at the clubhouse now, phoning her friend to ask if the job interview could be put off. But what if it couldn't? What if she lost the position just because he insisted on taking his time getting to Florida?

He shook his head. Why was he feeling guilty? Taking his time was his right. It was a God-given prerogative of being on vacation. Besides, he hadn't forced her to agree to his terms. She could've said no. But she hadn't, and in his experience he'd found that people usually did what they really wanted, even when they claimed it wasn't. And he suspected that what Mary Elizabeth really wanted was to slow down and maybe lose herself on the road for a while. If she didn't, she should. She was wired pretty tight.

He wished he could rationalize his not telling her about his marriage as easily as he rationalized his guilt. But the plain truth was he just hated talking about Cindy and that part of his life. Would he be forced to before he and Mary Elizabeth got to Elmira? Maybe nobody would bring the subject up. If they were polite they wouldn't, but when had his family ever been polite?

He turned the potatoes, poked the coals again and sat back on his heels, his mind wandering to his afternoon on the lake with Mary Elizabeth. The corner of his mouth lifted. She'd looked so damn pretty sitting there in that boat, her silky blond hair gleaming with sunlight, her eyes dancing when she'd reeled in that skinny walleye.

Catching himself in mid-reverie, Pete swore under his breath. He had to stop thinking of her as a woman. Nothing could happen between them. It was a matter of principle with him that he didn't get involved with a woman if he knew he wasn't going to see her again, and he wasn't going to see Mary Elizabeth again after next Sunday.

Considering she was pregnant, a one-week-stand became

even more taboo. A guy didn't start up with a woman who was pregnant unless he was ready to get serious and share his life with her and her baby. It just wasn't right, morally, psychologically, any way you looked at it.

Pete placed four ears of corn on the hot grate and scowled. All right, so he was aware Mary Elizabeth was planning to give up her baby. But so what? If he got involved with her, he'd still have to see her through the pregnancy, and the birth, and the emotional adjustment period afterward. What kind of heel would he be if he didn't? Those were pretty traumatic life events she was facing, and she was facing them alone. But that was a helluva lot for a woman to ask a guy to commit to after knowing her only a few days. It was certainly more than he was ready to commit to.

He'd just have to cool his engines while they were together. He'd be friendly enough—no sense in being miserable for a week—but Mary Elizabeth would know he meant nothing by it. He'd make sure she did.

Pete stood up, wiped his sooty hands on a bandanna and gazed toward the clubhouse through the trees. Mary Elizabeth was coming along the path, returning to the campsite, her pale hair swinging with each long stride she took. Without any warning his body betrayed him, responding to the merest sight of her with an involuntary flush of heat and need.

He jammed the bandanna into his back pocket and scowled at the fire. Something told him cooling his engines was going to be one of the hardest jobs he'd ever tackled.

CHAPTER EIGHT

MARY ELIZABETH'S CALL to Chloe wasn't the most honest of communications. She needed to tell her friend about her new travel plans, but not wanting to alarm her, she didn't mention Peter. She merely said she had decided to slow down, maybe visit Pennsylvania Dutch country or the Carolina coast, places she really had always wanted to see. Chloe seemed confused, but Mary Elizabeth didn't know how else to explain this strange new turn of events.

The job interview was another sticky matter. Chloe's husband had arranged the interview, and while it was only for a temporary position as a receptionist in a dentist's office, that dentist was a friend of his and the interview, a personal favor.

"I'm not sure it can be put off," Chloe said. "Dr. Taylor has already postponed hiring somebody because we asked him to wait for you."

"I'm sorry, Chloe."

"Oh, it's all right. I'll see what can be arranged."

Before hanging up, Mary Elizabeth remembered her wallet. She told Chloe not to be alarmed if it arrived in the mail. Skipping details, she merely said she'd lost it and had given Chloe's address to the police. She also asked Chloe to watch the mail for her new credit cards. Chloe was full of questions, but Mary Elizabeth dodged them by saying her supper was on the fire and needed tending.

And, in fact, it was. By the time she got back to the

campsite, Peter had the fish cleaned, seasoned and wrapped in foil, and ready to place over the coals in the fire pit, alongside the three potatoes that were already baking there and the four ears of corn he'd bartered from the family camping next to them. In exchange, he'd given them three of her lovely little quiches. Looked mighty pleased with himself for doing so, too.

She sat at the picnic table, watching him. "You're very good at this," she commented.

He looked up from the fire, the angles and planes of his face emphasized by the warm glow. One corner of his mouth lifted. "Good at lots of things."

Although she didn't doubt it, she said, "You need a healthy dose of humility."

"Me?" He pretended to look offended.

"Yes, you." In the silence that followed, she questioned again the wisdom of agreeing to travel with this man for an entire week. How totally different from her original travel plan on leaving home. She tried to figure out how she'd reached this place in her life, but the chain of events eluded her. If her call to Chloe had accomplished anything, it was to underscore how truly bizarre her course had become. She wasn't a bizarre person. Things like this didn't normally happen to her.

She watched Peter move around the fire, the muscles of his thighs rippling and bunching as he reached for things, knelt, got up. It was because of him, she thought, feeling a quiver of indefinable fear shoot through her. She'd chosen this path because she'd wanted to remain with him.

The fear expanded and rose to her throat. Oh, Lord, what had she done? The answer came back to her in the stirring of her senses as she continued to watch him, this tall, forceful man who intrigued her more than any mystery.

Okay, this isn't a problem, she assured herself on a shaky

sigh. All she had to do was remember her circumstances. She was pregnant. She needed a job, medical care, a semipermanent place to park her RV. And those were only the physical problems. What about the emotional ones she was carrying—her myriad insecurities, the shock she still felt over her parentage? She had so many issues to deal with, no man in his right mind would *want* to touch her—if he knew about those issues. Pete didn't, not fully.

Okay, so she'd just have to be careful, make sure she didn't send out any signals that might give him the wrong idea. That might be difficult. There were times she caught herself just staring at the man. But she could do it if she set her mind to it. She knew she could. She'd always had good self-control.

She watched him peel away the foil from the fish, careful not to tear it—and she refused to think of those large rough hands being so capable.

"Have you done a lot of camping?" she asked with forced nonchalance.

He nodded. "Ever since I was a boy. Of course, back then I thought of it as running away from home."

She was relieved; here was something safe they could talk about. "You used to run away?"

"All the time." He chuckled. "Got my backside warmed every time I did, too."

"Why'd you run away?"

He came to sit beside her at the table, bringing along the long steel tongs he'd been using to turn the vegetables. "Is this our first session of getting to know each other?" He cast her a grin that was both playful and seductive. She didn't think he meant it to be; that was just the way he was.

She looked at the fire. "I suppose it could be."

He leaned forward, swinging the tongs between his knees. "I was a punk, that's why I ran away."

"Well, I assumed that. But why else?"

"I wanted to see the world." He laughed, a tight, self-conscious sound that told her he was uneasy with talking about his past.

"Where'd that ambition come from?"

His grin changed subtly at the edges, then gradually faded. "I was the oldest of four, both my parents worked, and I had the responsibility of taking care of the kids while they were gone. I had to get the girls' breakfast, walk them to school, entertain them afterward, pick up Brad from the baby-sitter's, start supper—" He broke off abruptly. "Let's just say I wasn't too happy about the situation, so occasionally I took off, just me and my Schwinn and the horizon."

Mary Elizabeth barely breathed. She hadn't expected him to open up to her like that.

"Somebody would always find me, though—a neighbor, the police." He shook his head, smiling faintly. "By the time I was twelve I had quite a reputation around town. That crazy Mitchell boy, people used to say. Gonna put his mama in the ground."

"This was all before you were *twelve?* Taking care of your siblings? The running away?"

"Well, sure, Mary Elizabeth. Kids grow up fast in small cracker towns. When I turned thirteen my sister Pam took my place, 'cause I was old enough to go to work with my daddy paintin' houses."

She noticed he'd slipped into a more pronounced southern drawl, a deliberate attempt at levity that nonetheless conveyed a heavy measure of derision.

"When was this, during summer vacations?"

"Yep, summer vacations, winter vacations, afternoons

after school, too. If we were lucky enough to get a job, it didn't matter what time of year it was. We just worked.''

How different from her own youth, she thought. She realized she must've been frowning because he said, ''That's okay. I never wanted to be on the debate team, anyway.''

Her frown deepened. Maybe he'd never wanted to be on the debate team, but given his size and strength and athletic grace, surely he must have wanted to go out for sports.

''It must've been awful,'' she commiserated.

''Awful?'' He ran his knuckles along his jaw, thinking back. ''No, not really. Sure, it was hard, but it taught me a lot about responsibility and survival. And there was no question that my parents loved us. I may have sometimes been angry as a kid, but I hold no grudges now. They did the best they could. My mother certainly didn't want to be away from us so much. She would've much preferred being a stay-at-home mom. I would've preferred it, too. I hated seeing her so tired, but there was simply no other way my parents could've made ends meet.''

''Do your parents still work?''

Pete swallowed, then gave his head a brisk shake. ''They're gone. My mother died young, only forty-one. My father passed away eight months ago.''

''Oh, I'm sorry,'' Mary Elizabeth murmured. She wished she hadn't asked. Pete's voice had fallen into a monotone that betrayed a lingering sorrow. ''Um, how did you learn to fight so well?'' she asked to change the subject.

''The usual way. Got into lots of brawls.'' The tongs, she noticed, were swinging at a more agitated pace.

''Why was that?''

He exhaled a derisive laugh. ''For a while, I had a chip on my shoulder the size of Ohio.''

''From feeling trapped in a family situation you didn't like?''

"I guess. I was sick of just scraping by, angry at people who labeled us. And I didn't much like that tiny backwater town I was stuck in." He paused thoughtfully. "Hell, I don't know why I fought. I was just a punk, I guess." He reached forward and prodded the potatoes. "These are done," he said, getting up. She sensed him pulling away from her.

She tried to pull him back. "So, Peter, when did you get your first motorcycle?"

He wiped his hands on a red bandanna and grinned. "I was fifteen, too young to ride it, but that didn't matter. It was junkyard salvage. Needed major repair before I could put it on the road, anyway."

"And when you got it working, did you try to leave town on it the way you used to on your bicycle?"

His grin faded. "No, I started dating Sue Ellen then."

That knife twist of irrational jealousy returned to puncture Mary Elizabeth's sense of detachment. Her levity was forced when she said, "I see. Kicked the wheels out from under you, did she?"

"For a while," he admitted. "But I'd always planned on going into the army after high school, and I did. Come on, let's eat."

With a bit of nudging, Peter continued to talk about himself during the meal. Mary Elizabeth was especially curious about his stint in the military. At first he tried to pass it off simply as a way of escaping the small town of Elmira and the burden of watching over his siblings, who then had ranged in age from fifteen to eight. And while she didn't doubt those reasons were true, she felt they weren't the entire truth.

Sure enough, as he continued to talk, a far broader picture came into view. Peter had been consumed with the idea of starting his own business, a business substantial enough to employ his entire family and bring them financial independence and security. In short, he'd seen the military as the first and most vital step toward that end.

Apparently, he'd seen right. Brad now worked as his foreman. Pam did the books. Her husband and Lindy's were general laborers, and Lindy was studying carpentry. And that didn't take into account the smattering of second-rung relatives who were also on Pete's payroll.

"I'm not sure the military was the right decision," he said thoughtfully. "Maybe I would've been better off staying at home, working part-time, going to school nights. But back then, I didn't have much guidance in those matters. It seemed like a good idea."

"And you got to see the world."

He grimaced. "Yeah. The jungles of Central America." He paused, glancing at her plate. "Eat your corn, Mary Elizabeth. Lots of fibre in corn."

She made a face at him but followed his directive anyway.

"What made you decide to settle in Tampa?"

"Oh, it's a big city, lots of opportunity for a guy with ambition. If I'd stayed in Elmira, I'd be just one more guy with a pickup truck calling himself a contractor and scratching for work."

"But what about your family? They didn't move, did they?"

"Brad did, but the girls stayed. It's a long commute, but that doesn't seem to bother my relatives."

There was just enough derision in his tone for her to say, "I thought you liked your relatives."

"I do, most of the time," he admitted. "And most of the time I enjoy working with them. It's just that sometimes…" His voice thinned.

"Sometimes, what?"

"Nothing," he said, and concentrated on eating.

"Sometimes you feel you've never left home? That you're still twelve years old and forced to baby-sit everybody?"

He moved the food around on his plate, a slow grin forming those creases around his mouth and eyes that she was quickly coming to love. "You're a lot smarter than you look, Mary Elizabeth."

Her grin matched his. "And you, Mr. Mitchell, are a lot more complicated than you like to let on."

"Complicated? Uh-uh." He bit into his corn with his strong, even teeth.

"Yes, you are."

He shook his head. "What you see is what you get, a simple man with simple tastes. Beer, sports and rock 'n' roll—that's what makes me tick."

"A regular Renaissance man, by golly."

"I like my work, too. Add that to the list."

"And motorcycles," she teased dryly.

"Goes without saying. So, how are we doing? Think you know me yet?"

"I'm getting there."

"Jeez Louise! How much more do you want to know?"

Everything, her heart replied. She noticed him look at her strangely, and her breath seized up on her. Had she just telegraphed that thought?

Quickly, she drank the last of her milk, got to her feet and, mumbling something about just wanting to be prepared for the wedding, began clearing her place.

After she went inside, Pete sat at the table, smoking a cigarillo in the golden light of the lowering sun. Why had he told her so much about himself, all those stories about his childhood? His private life was usually off limits to outsiders. How had she gotten through his defenses? One minute she was asking him a simple question about camping, and the next he was telling her how he *felt,* explaining *reasons* for things, explaining...himself. Why?

He took a puff on his cigar, determined to shake off those bothersome questions. A guy could go crazy thinking too hard. He and Mary Elizabeth had just been talking, that's all, and he wasn't going to read anything more into it. Besides, they had a bigger problem. The sun was almost on the horizon, and night was coming on. It was nearly bedtime.

No, this isn't a problem, he assured himself. Mary Elizabeth might be an attractive woman, but he certainly didn't want to get involved with her. He knew that. He knew all the reasons, too. All he had to do was keep reminding himself of them and they'd get through this week with no trouble.

Feeling more at ease, he snuffed out his cigarillo and headed for the RV.

Mary Elizabeth was filling the dishpan when he came in. He placed his plate and cutlery on the counter and, without a word, wandered off to the bedroom. Puzzled, she perked her ears, trying to hear what he was doing.

"Where do you want me to put these boxes?" he called casually.

"What boxes?"

"The ones on my bed."

"*Your* bed? Your bed's out here."

Pete returned, his gaze combing the kitchen. When he saw she was motioning toward the bunk, his eyebrows almost disappeared under his hair. "You don't really expect me to sleep up there?"

"Why not?" She lowered their plates into the sudsy water.

"I'll show you why not." He climbed the short ladder,

crawled onto the thin mattress and, lying down, rolled carefully onto his side.

Mary Elizabeth studied his cramped body in its boxlike quarters and abruptly burst out laughing. "You look like you're in a coffin."

"And we all know how comfy those things are. How about I move the stuff from the bedroom to here?"

She sobered. "No, don't bother. I'll sleep up there."

"You shouldn't be climbing ladders in your condition."

"I'm only three months along, Peter. I think I can manage."

"Yeah, well, what if you fall out?"

"I won't f—" In mid-sentence, Mary Elizabeth froze. Pete's shoulder dropped forward, the weight of his upper body carrying the rest of him along, over the side of the bunk. "Peter!"

All in one lithe move, he tumbled, rotated and landed soundly on his feet. "You're not sleeping up there," he declared flatly.

Puddles had formed where the soap dripped off her motionless hands. "Peter Mitchell," she swore, eyes narrowed, "you're going to be the death of me yet." She reached for a paper towel and made a hasty pass at the wet floor.

"Better me than a tumble from a bunk. Now, if you want those boxes someplace else, tell me now. Otherwise..." He started to walk off.

Mary Elizabeth dried her hands and followed him into the bedroom. Her heart was racing. "But we can't sleep in the same room."

"Why not? Do you snore?"

She shot him an impatient look. "I read late."

"Great. So do I."

She gazed at the paper towel she was absentmindedly wringing. "You know that's not the problem."

Looking amused and thoroughly self-possessed, he said, "I'd suggest we hang a rope between the beds and throw a blanket over it—you know, like in *It Happened One Night*? But this is the 1990s, sweetheart, not the 1930s."

"I don't care." She folded her arms.

"Question. Have you ever slept with a man?"

"What, are you deaf? I told you about me and Roger."

"You're not listening. I didn't ask if you'd had sex, I asked if you'd slept with a man."

She didn't know where to settle her uneasy gaze. Hesitantly she replied, "No."

"That college you went to...that was an all-female college, right?"

Again, her nod was slow in coming.

"You never took baths with your brother when you were a kid?"

"Don't be ridiculous."

"You never..."

"Stop." She cut the air with a wide motion of her hands. "Whether I bathed with my brother or didn't bathe with him has nothing to do with you and me now, sleeping in the same room."

"Sure it does. You're obviously uncomfortable around the opposite sex. I, on the other hand, couldn't care less."

Mary Elizabeth gave him a slightly startled once-over. She was amused to see the tips of his ears turn pink.

"That didn't come out quite right. What I mean is..." He paused and she got the idea he was searching his mind. "You and I have an agreement, sort of like a business contract, and I never mix business with sex. The complications just aren't worth it." He paused again as if reviewing what he'd said.

Apparently finding something lacking in his argument, he went on. "Secondly, I'm just not interested. That's not a reflection on you, Mary Elizabeth. God knows you're a desirable woman." He could've been saying *You're a tall woman* or *You have a nose and two eyes* for all the fervor he invested in his words. "But with this traveling arrangement lasting only a week, I'd feel like a heel getting involved with you. I'd feel I was using you, and, well, I just don't do that sort of thing." He paused a moment, looking at her, but not really meeting her eyes. "Have I made myself clear? Do you know where we stand?"

Yes, to both questions, she thought, surprised by his forthrightness. Paradoxically, she felt both relieved and let down. She lowered herself to the edge of her bed and looked across the way, testing the view, trying to imagine Peter stretched out there. Despite his avowals of disinterest, ribbons of discomfiting heat fluttered through her.

"We'll respect each other's privacy when we're dressing?"

His lips twitched. "Undressing, too."

"Well... I suppose we could give it a try."

"Atta girl." Pete hoisted an instrument case off the cluttered bed. "After the first night, you'll be looking at me like one of your old sorority sisters, you'll see."

Somehow Mary Elizabeth doubted that.

"Be careful with that thing."

"What is it?"

"My violin."

"Do you play?"

"Sort of."

"Will you promise not to while we're traveling together?"

"What do I get out of that?"

"I won't light up my cigars in your presence."

"Oh, yay," she replied vapidly—right before being hit with a pillow.

Mary Elizabeth got ready for bed first. By the time Pete was done using the bathroom she was under the covers with Monet curled up at her feet and her tiny book light glowing over a page of a hardcover novel. Spotting the cat, Pete groaned and returned to the bathroom to take his allergy medicine.

When he returned, she tried not to look up, tried not to feel his presence filling the small room. She failed. Pete had the body of a man who does physical labor for a living—strong and lean and solid. Just a glance at his thick, tanned forearms did more for her than all of Roger's lovemaking combined. When he peeled off his shirt, the sight of all that hair and chest muscle was almost her undoing.

"You might want to turn," he suggested matter-of-factly, unbuckling his belt.

"Oh." She rotated onto her side, eyes to the wall, her mind filled with images that refused to go away, no matter what grim thoughts she forced on herself. She waited until she heard his mattress sigh to ease onto her back again.

They read for several minutes without speaking.

"It isn't a question of modesty or prudishness," she said clear out of the blue.

"Really?" Uncannily, he knew exactly what she was talking about. "Is that why you're wearing pajamas *and* a robe to bed?"

"Oh. I...I was cold." Okay, so maybe she was a tad prudish, too. "It's the intimacy of this arrangement. I'm not used to intimacy. Growing up, I didn't even share a room with my sister."

Pete laid his book on his dark chest and stacked his hands under his head. "I understand."

She looked over. "Do you? What I'm referring to has

more to do with talking and sharing what's in one's heart than with anything physical." *You know, like what we've been doing today.*

He caught her in his bright, knowing gaze and repeated more softly, "I understand. Intimacy is pretty scary business. It opens the door to our deepest vulnerabilities. Nobody likes to be seen as vulnerable."

She couldn't picture Peter feeling vulnerable about anything, not anything physical, anyway. Unlike her, he lay comfortably exposed, covers to his waist, pale underarms subjected to the scrutiny of anyone who wanted to look.

But emotional intimacy might be a different story. He'd let her into his life today, but only with trepidation and, at times, resistance. It had been a limited tour, too, whole rooms of his past closed off to her inspection. Oddly, she didn't mind that now. Knowing he wasn't invulnerable made him more human. Approachable.

She smiled and went back to her reading. He did the same. But within minutes, her mind had wandered again. "It's been quite a day, hasn't it." She spoke softly, almost to herself.

"I'll say. It's not every day that starts off with a run to the emergency room." He turned a page of his Tony Hillerman mystery. Outside, crickets sang a subdued September song. The breeze swished through the pines. Television sounds drifted from nearby campers.

She swallowed. "Peter?"

In the next bed, Pete felt a quickening of his pulse. Something in the way she said his name made him wary. It was a prelude to something he didn't think he wanted to explore.

"Mmm," he replied lazily.

"Can I tell you something?"

Keep it light, Mitchell. "You will, anyway, with or without my permission," he tossed off, "so shoot."

And she did. "I hate being pregnant."

Oh, man. This was going to be worse than he thought. He lay unmoving. He didn't want to even look over.

"I just hate it. It's complicated my life something awful." Her voice didn't wobble, but he didn't like the way it had thinned.

"The plain truth is I'm embarrassed by my condition. I'm disappointed and I'm angry." Pete listened to her swallow. "I keep asking myself why. Why did this have to happen to me?"

He looked over then, and the anguish he saw in her face tore at him. "Well, for cryin' out loud, Mary Elizabeth, that's perfectly understandable."

"Is it?" she said with bitter doubt, and then fell silent. She seemed hesitant to go any further.

Pete knew he could use that hesitancy as leverage to vault himself out of this little tête-à-tête. He *should* use it...but he noticed a tear caught at the outer corner of her eye, hanging there, quivering.

"What is it, sweetheart?" he asked softly. "You can tell me. There isn't much I haven't heard already. I have very colorful friends."

She smiled faintly, but continued to stare up at the ceiling. "Life would be so much easier if I weren't pregnant. I could return to Maine, continue working at my job, remain a part of my family. And I'm afraid that's the reason I didn't go into the hospital right away when I thought I was having a miscarriage."

Pete braced himself up on one elbow. "What's this?"

"This morning, I woke around five, but instead of calling for help and going straight to the hospital, I went back to bed."

"Are you trying to tell me you *wanted* to lose the baby?"

Her lips trembled. "Yes. Maybe."

"But you could've terminated the pregnancy yourself, back home. Nobody would've even had to know—Roger, your father, anybody." Objectively, Pete marveled at himself. He sounded so calm, so wise, even while his heart was thumping in his chest like a car about to blow a rod.

"No, I couldn't have. That's the point I'm trying to make," she said, finally turning her head. The tear at the corner of her eye spilled into her hair.

"Why not?"

"I'm basically a coward. Abortion would've involved a conscious choice on my part, a decision I couldn't make. But a miscarriage is a different story. A miscarriage would remove the decision from my hands."

He thought of lying back, turning off his light, burying himself deep under the covers and forgetting any of this conversation had happened. Instead, he swung his bare feet to the floor, making sure to keep the sheet across his lap. "Would it make you feel any better if I told you you probably did the right thing, going back to bed? My sister Lindy had false labor during both her pregnancies, and her doctor's advice was to lie down. If the contractions didn't go away after a rest, *then* she should call him. But invariably they went away."

"Interesting…but, no, I don't feel better."

"How about the fact that when we're feeling sick, our first instinct is to crawl into bed?"

She rocked her head on the pillow.

"You couldn't have been positive it was a miscarriage. You probably had lots of other ideas swimming around in your head, clouding your judgment."

"Nope. Doesn't wash."

Pete got so frustrated he threw off the covers and moved to her bed. He didn't even care about his lack of clothing. At least he had his shorts on, and even if he hadn't, this was too important an issue for modesty to interfere.

Gripping her arms, he hauled her to a sitting position. "Will you give yourself a break, goddammit? You're so hard on yourself." His fingers pressed into her soft flesh. "I hate to disillusion you, Mary Elizabeth, but you're only human, and humans sometimes feel the way you do. If you got a kick out of being pregnant in your situation, then I'd really think you were nuts. But being disappointed and angry?" He shook his head. "Welcome to the human race, princess."

He watched relief enter her eyes, felt it wash through her body. For a moment he thought she was going to cry. It came out a laugh instead.

"That's better." He loosened his grip. "Now, about that cockeyed idea about subconsciously wanting to miscarry, I don't buy that. First of all, I was there, remember? I saw you leaving the examining room. I talked to you after. I talked to you after. You were happy not to've lost the baby. Your feelings came out in ways you probably weren't even aware of. Sighs of relief. Smiles as you spoke."

The tension was melting visibly from her face, loosening her shoulders, steadying her breathing.

"And secondly," Pete continued, "you made your decision regarding the life of this baby a long time ago, back in Maine. You did," he insisted when he saw doubt momentarily darken her expression. "Remember that the next time you start feeling depressed or angry at yourself, will you? And while you're at it, give yourself a pat on the back. It took courage to do what you did. This going to Florida isn't just a running away. You deliberately chose to give up your home, your job and your family for this baby, and in my book, kid, a person can't get any more heroic.''

Mary Elizabeth wanted to cry again. She also wanted to dance. She ended up just sitting there, enjoying how light Peter had made her feel. They were close enough for her to see the starburst of violet rays surrounding the dark pupils of his blue eyes. Such beautiful eyes, she thought. Such a beautiful man.

''How'd you get to be so nice?'' Her smile trembled.

''Jeez, Mary Elizabeth—'' he released her and pushed away ''—I'm a lot of things, but nice isn't one of them.''

''Stupendous, then.''

Pete got to his feet. ''That's more like it.''

He noticed her eyes had lowered and spots of color had emerged on her cheeks. He looked down at his shorts, then quickly got back into bed and turned off his light.

Arranging the covers, he saw her reach for her book. ''Get some sleep,'' he said gruffly. ''Sleep's important when you're pregnant.''

''I know.'' But she continued to lie there, staring at the book. He noticed her eyes weren't moving.

He finally reached across the distance that separated them, moved her book to the floor and turned off the tiny light. Darkness wrapped over them.

Unfortunately that's all the darkness did. Pete lay back, still hearing the soft rasp of her breathing, still catching the fragrance of her hair, knowing she was lying there as aware of him as he was of her.

He wished sleep would come. Wished he could drive out that last lingering image of her before he'd snapped off the light. Bathed in the intimate glow cast by the small bulb, she'd looked warm, mysterious and absolutely beautiful. He especially wished he could ignore how close he felt to her at this moment. That was something else you had to worry about with intimacy. He wished he had remembered.

He released a long breath through his teeth. Maybe this sleeping arrangement wasn't such a good idea after all. He hoped he knew what he was doing.

CHAPTER NINE

MORNING CAME as a surprise. Mary Elizabeth lay in the pearl gray light, listening to Peter's steady breathing, and realized the intimacy of falling asleep with a man couldn't begin to compare with the intimacy of waking up with him.

He lay facing her, his eyes closed, one arm draped atop the covers, his shoulder and part of his chest exposed. He looked younger in sleep, another surprise.

He stirred fractionally. The silence of the hour magnified the rustle of the bed linens out of all proportion. He made a sound in his throat, his eyelids twitched, and before Mary Elizabeth could turn away, he was looking at her.

She froze, breath suspended, body throbbing with self-consciousness at pulse points she hadn't even known existed before. She wondered how she looked, what he saw. Were there sleep lines on her cheeks? Sand in the corners of her eyes?

She felt his focus sharpen, his awareness of her deepening. Should she say good morning? For a confused moment she felt they already had. Should she get up and go to the bathroom? Ask if he needed to use the facilities first? And if he did, should she pretend indifference to his parading in his B.V.D.s? How did people *do* this?

He said nothing, did nothing. Just closed his sleepy eyes, opened them, and lay there watching her, a riveting connectedness riding on their gaze.

God, this wasn't good. What was she doing, sleeping

bed-to-bed with a man she'd met only three days ago? They'd become much too familiar in too short a time.

But that didn't mean they couldn't back up. If they kept the mood between them light, surely they could reclaim some of their emotional distance—couldn't they?

Peter rolled away from her, a gesture of blatant indifference that made her feel foolish for thinking he shared her sharpened sensitivity. She had to relax. If she kept taking everything so seriously, she'd never survive the week.

She watched his back, measured the rise and fall of his breathing, and when she thought he was asleep, she eased out of bed, collected her clothing and tiptoed to the bathroom....

...Leaving Pete behind, staring at the wall and trying to calm his speeding heart. What a way to wake up, to open your eyes and have Mary Elizabeth filling your vision. What scared him, though, was that he hadn't been surprised or even disoriented. It had felt quite natural to find her there, looking all soft and warm just an arm's length away. For one wild moment he wondered if he had been dreaming about her. She'd seemed such a natural extension of his thoughts.

All at once Pete felt claustrophobic. He turned onto his back and wiped his wrist over his clammy brow. His heart was palpitating. Such a small room...there wasn't enough air to breathe in here. He had to get outside. He had to have more space.

He threw off the covers, got out of bed, yanked on some clothes and reached for his helmet.

He didn't come back from his ride for an hour. He felt a lot better when he did. The sky today was a deep china blue, and the air sparkled with the crisp clarity of approaching autumn, a weather condition he just didn't get down in Tampa. It cleared his mind and let him see he still had control of his life; he still had his freedom. He shouldn't let sexual urges or even dreams trick him into thinking he didn't.

The only detail that marred his ride was his concern about not leaving a note. Mary Elizabeth was going to be worried. She'd think he had cut out. His oversight bothered him so much that he returned sooner than he'd planned.

Vaulting off his bike, he bounded into the RV...and found she was still in the bathroom!

"Oh, hi!" she said with a blithe smile when she eventually stepped out. "I thought you'd still be asleep."

Pete slapped a hand to his forehead. The woman was going to drive him nuts.

She'd obviously been fussing with herself the entire time he'd been gone. Fresh, deep waves were back in her hair, every strand in place, and although he couldn't see any makeup, that didn't mean she wasn't wearing any. She'd probably just applied it with expert care. Today she was wearing brown corduroy pants, a beige tweed jacket with brown elbow patches, and a blouse with a flouncy tie, held down with a brooch in the shape of a horseshoe.

It was probably that brooch that made him say, "Where are you off to, a polo match?"

For a moment she looked confused, and then quietly embarrassed. Pete wanted to kick himself. He'd only meant to tease her, but apparently he'd caught her blindside.

Looking down at her outfit she murmured something almost incoherent about choosing it because the day was chilly. Then she made a quick cup of tea and some toast and took her breakfast into the bedroom.

Just as well, Pete thought, alone with his guilt in the kitchen. This was exactly what he wanted, a mutual respect for each other's right to space and privacy, and he hadn't even needed to bring up the issue with her. She'd agreed tacitly. He ought to be pleased. And he was. He was so damn pleased he'd be doing cartwheels soon if he didn't contain himself.

Restlessly, Pete walked outside. The sky didn't look quite so blue anymore. A few minutes later he walked back in. She was still in the bedroom. "Hi," he ventured, standing in the doorway. "What are you doing?" Yep, he sure was pleased they understood their need for space.

Mary Elizabeth didn't turn from the closet. She didn't want Peter to see the tears she knew were still clinging to her eyelashes. Damn, she'd thought she looked nice—until he made that sarcastic comment about her being dressed for a polo match.

Which only went to prove what a fool she was. She hadn't spent all that time in the bathroom, primping in front of a mirror, just to look nice. She'd done it to please him, a man who obviously couldn't be pleased. Not by her, anyway. She was clearly not his type. He found everything about her laughable.

And why not? She was laughable. Who in their right mind still curled their hair on rollers? Who wore tweed jackets with elbow patches?

The daughter of Charles Drummond, that's who. But she wasn't Charles Drummond's daughter anymore. She only owned the woman's wardrobe. And shared her habits. Walked like her and talked like her. Mary Elizabeth suddenly disliked everything about the daughter of Charles Drummond.

"Um...I'm looking for something to wear to your brother's wedding," she replied, surreptitiously wiping her eyes.

"Ah. Good idea. What've you got?"

"Oh, I don't know. I've just started looking." She still hadn't turned around. She hoped he got her message.

He did. "Well, I'll leave you to your task." Peter stood away from the door frame, but before leaving he added, "I'm sorry I made that comment before. I was only trying to crack a joke. I guess I haven't quite figured out yet when that's okay and when it's not."

She turned from the closet then, but he was already gone. A few minutes later the RV started up and they were on the road again.

For the next thirty miles, Mary Elizabeth plowed through her wardrobe, trying on clothes. She had several outfits she could wear to a wedding, several that she *had* worn, but none of them pleased her. Time and again she looked in the mirror and thought, *Would Peter Mitchell really be involved with that person?* The best she could say about her was she looked nice. Inoffensive. Ladylike. She lived up to the expected standard of propriety set by Charles Drummond.

Mary Elizabeth had another problem she hadn't counted on. Nothing fit right anymore. For the past couple of weeks she'd worn jackets or baggy sweaters that hid the fact that the skirt or pants beneath were unzipped and held in place with a loose belt. She couldn't do this with her wedding finery. The roomiest dresses either revealed her small pot belly or refused to zip.

She finally abandoned her search and went to sit up front. "I can't go to your brother's wedding," she announced glumly, slumping in her seat.

"Why not?" Pete moved an unlit cigar from one corner of his scowl to the other.

"None of my clothes fit right anymore."

He glanced over, down at her waist, up again. One eyebrow cocked.

"You don't believe me? Here, look." She lifted her tweed jacket to reveal the undone zipper of her trousers.

Both Pete's eyebrows shot up. He swallowed, and a strange look came into his eyes, something between terror and awe.

Mary Elizabeth tensed. "You don't think this means I'm having twins, do you?"

Pete removed his cigar. "No. You're slim. Light-boned. You were bound to show early."

Just when she was enjoying a moment of relief, embarrassment overtook her. What was she doing, showing this man her pregnant stomach? Such an intimate thing to do. No wonder he'd looked ready to swallow his tongue. She sank in her seat, convinced she could do absolutely nothing right.

"Tell you what," he said. "Tomorrow, we'll swing into Baltimore and get you something new to wear. How does that sound?"

It sounded wonderful, until she remembered she had no money. She shrugged and mumbled something gloomy about making do with what she had.

"Aren't you in a mood!" Pete chuckled. "Don't worry. It's only your hormones. During pregnancy, they don't know if they're coming or going."

She didn't find the insight amusing.

He brought the RV to an abrupt stop, swung out of his seat, went into the kitchen, then returned with her bowl of M&Ms, which he planted in her lap. "*That's* what's wrong. You haven't had your daily dose of sugar yet."

She glanced at him out of the corner of her eye, feeling a faint smile tugging at her lips. He started up the RV again and eased onto the quiet country road. For the next couple of miles the only sound between them was the ticking tumble of candy being stirred and picked over.

Pete was fiddling with the radio, trying to find another

oldies station, when she said clear out of the blue, "What about my hair?"

"Huh?" His head swiveled.

"My hair. Do you think I should change it for the wedding?"

He glanced at her, frowning. "It looks okay to me."

"High praise, indeed," she said, still in a snappish mood.

Pete huffed. "Look, Mary Elizabeth, that remark I made yesterday about changing you into somebody I'd be more likely to date…I was only kidding."

"No, you weren't."

"Now you're telling me what I was thinking?"

"Yes."

He slouched away from her, grumbling. "All right, you want a small suggestion?"

"Yes. That's why I asked."

"Now, remember, I think you have beautiful hair. I love the color and the way it shines. But maybe…" He hesitated. "Maybe you could find a more casual style. Something, I don't know, swingier, looser, less Laura Petrie."

Mary Elizabeth gasped audibly.

Pete suddenly looked as if he'd been hit with a two-by-four. "Oh, hell! Did I just say what I think I said? I'm sorry, Mary Elizabeth. I'm really… Honest, I didn't mean it."

"Laura Petrie? The sixties? Is that what you think of my hair?" Without thinking, she beaned him with an M&M. It felt so good, she beaned him with another. After firing off at least a dozen shots, she sat back with a contented sigh and said, "You're right. I fuss way too much with my appearance. Actually, I'm obsessive. A more casual look is exactly what I want, too. I only wanted your stamp of approval."

Looking at Monet sprawled on the warm dash, Pete muttered, "We're riding with a bona fide crazy lady, did you know that?"

They rolled on another mile.

"What about my makeup?"

"It's fine. Perfect," Pete said quickly. "I'll tell you one thing I *would* like to change."

She sat up straighter. "What?"

"Your name."

"My name? You don't like my name?"

"Well, it is sort of long, don't you think? By the time I finish saying it, I've usually forgotten what I wanted to say in the first place. I also find it—" he paused "—sort of starchy."

She refused to be hurt. After all, she wanted to change, didn't she? "What do you want to call me?"

He shrugged. "Doesn't anybody call you by a nickname? Beth? Liz? Marybeth?"

"No. I've always been Mary Elizabeth."

"Hmm. Let's see, then. Besides those options, there's Liza, Lizzy, Betty…"

"I don't mind Beth."

"I don't, either. It suits you."

She looked at him warily. "So, you're going to call me Beth from now on?"

"Let's try it for a day, see how it fits."

She grimaced. "This is weird, but okay." After a while she said, "So, where are we going today, Peter?"

"Pennsylvania."

"Really?" She perked. "Where in Pennsylvania?"

"Wherever the road takes us."

"Penn Dutch country?" she asked, exaggeratedly batting her eyelashes.

He laughed and in a teasing Maine accent said, "Sorry. You cahn't get theah from heah."

"Why not?"

"I'm morally opposed to tourist traps."

"Well, I'm not."

"Too bad. Who's driving?"

"Whose RV is it?"

He growled.

"What a grump," she muttered happily as the motor home crossed the state line. Between them swung the lace potpourri ball, tied to the radio where Jerry Lee Lewis belted out "Let the Good Times Roll."

"You should call your brother and let him know I'll be coming to the wedding. They'll need to set another place at dinner."

"I know. I will."

They'd covered another mile when Pete asked, "Hey, Beth? Do you dance?"

"Sure. Pretty well, too. I had two years of ballroom lessons."

"Yeah, well, I'm not exactly a fox-trot kind of guy. Do you dance fast?"

"A little."

He pulled the RV off the road again, this time into the lot of a feed and grain store. "A little isn't good enough if you're going to be my woman." He gave her a teasing smirk.

"Huh?"

He unfastened his seat belt and got to his feet. "We should practice, Beth. People will be watching us at the wedding."

With a sigh of exasperation, she got up, but, in truth, she wasn't as annoyed as she pretended. The idea of picking up a few new moves from this man was rather exciting, in fact. She followed him into the kitchen area, where she drew the blinds before they began.

For a long while, Pete ignored the music that was playing on the radio and simply walked her through his moves. They worked on steps they bungled, repeating them until they eventually flowed with instinctive ease.

They'd been practicing for fifteen minutes when the song "Splish Splash" came on. Pete grinned and said, "You're ready."

But apparently she was not. With the addition of music, her movements became too bouncy and loose. "Tighten up," he admonished, gripping her hand more securely, afraid that in her exuberance she might fly off and bash into the cabinets.

"What do you mean?" Undeterred, she beamed her incandescent smile at him.

"Don't be so perky, Beth. A little movement goes a long way."

"All right. I'll try." And she did. Still…

"Your arms," he said, waggling them up and down in easy ripples. "They're looser than spaghetti. Control them, Beth. Pull in."

"Okay," she chirped, bobbing like a bright balloon on the end of a string.

The problem, he realized, resided in her attitude. Didn't it always? It simply wasn't in her nature to be cool. Not that he was exactly an expert on what "cool" entailed, but he thought it had a lot to do with containment. Contained, her moves would become sinuous and seductive.

Pete's mood darkened when he realized he was thinking about Sue Ellen Carlisle, a woman who certainly understood her feminine powers and how to use them. No doubt about it, Sue Ellen had always been one helluva dance partner.

"This is so neat!" Mary Elizabeth ducked under his arm, twirled, and came up bobbing on the other side.

To his complete surprise, Pete found himself laughing, a rich satisfying laugh that came from a part of him he thought he'd lost. Maybe Mary Elizabeth wasn't cool, but there was a lot to be said for enthusiasm.

And for a willingness to learn.

And courage in the face of adversity.

And eyes the color of warm coffee.

The song ended. He caught her to his side, laughing and spinning. Under the span of his hand, her ribs rose and fell. He felt the heat of her exertion, caught her scent intensified, and before he could think, he'd dipped his head and pressed a kiss to her cheek. He wasn't sure why, except the urge just suddenly overwhelmed him.

She stood very still, eyes wide and fixed on the floor, a pulse racing at the base of her throat. *Oh, hell, what did I just do?* he thought. But before he could think of a way out of his dilemma, she broke away, beaming a smile that said she chose to ignore that dilemma.

"Thanks for the dance lesson, Peter. It was great fun." She was already heading back to her seat.

Pete breathed a lot easier.

They had covered a couple of miles when Mary Elizabeth, still thinking about the wedding, remarked, "What about our history? You know, how we met and all that?"

"Got any ideas?"

"A few."

"Good. So do I. But first, could you get me a cup of coffee?"

As the RV rolled along, they shared ideas and built a magical relationship out of thin air. They decided they'd met the previous winter while she was on a month-long vacation in Clearwater. *With a girlfriend,* Mary Elizabeth insisted. Vacationing alone smacked too much of man-hunting.

Before long they were bantering with enough friendly sarcasm to chase away any awkwardness still lingering between them because of that kiss.

"Now, let's suppose we met at a supermarket," she went on. "We were both shopping and you asked me..."

"Stop. Where'd you get the idea *anybody* meets in a supermarket—some silly woman's magazine?"

"Well, where do *you* want us to meet? A *bar?*"

"A bar's more believable. Besides, where *did* we meet, Mary Elizabeth?"

She fought back a grin. "All right, we met in a bar. A *nice* bar."

"A very nice bar." Pete's blue eyes laughed at her. "You were there to listen to the music, a jazz combo."

"My girlfriend, too. I don't hang out in bars alone."

Pete rolled his eyes. "God, you're such a Mary Elizabeth."

An M&M binged off the window to his left. He caught it in mid-ricochet and popped it into his mouth.

"Were you there for the music, too?" she asked.

"No. I stopped by to meet a client and lingered after he left." He spoke with conviction, as if the incident had actually occurred. "You'd noticed me earlier, and now that I was alone you asked the bartender to send over a drink."

Seconds stretched out, long and silent, and then she blurted, "In your dreams, Mitchell."

"You don't like that idea?"

"'Don't like' is too mild a term. I'd never buy a man a drink."

"That's too bad. It's a great way to break the ice."

"Not in my book." She drummed her long fingers on her thigh. Gradually her finger drumming slowed and she glanced at him in quick, speculative forays. "Has any woman ever bought *you* a drink?"

Sipping his coffee, he waggled his eyebrows at her over the rim of the mug.

"Figures," she muttered.

They rode on, continuing to add to their story long after it was necessary. Mary Elizabeth knew they were supplying details they would never use. The yellow roses he'd sent her on Valentine's day, for example, because she liked yellow roses best. A bed-and-breakfast at Bar Harbor, where they'd stayed in April when he flew up to see her. But it was hard not to get carried away. This project of creating a past was so much fun. Anything was possible and *everything* was possible—although she tried not to think as far as "everything."

They were well into Pennsylvania when a billboard advertising a flea market appeared on the side of the road. Five miles ahead, it said.

"Pay dirt," Pete exclaimed. "I had a feeling this route would lead to something interesting."

"A flea market?"

"A giant flea market," he corrected her.

Just beyond that billboard there stood another, advertising a comprehensive tour of Amish country. Mary Elizabeth eyed the turnoff with sad longing as it zipped by.

The flea market surpassed even Pete's expectations. It filled an entire barn, two floors. It being Sunday, the place was crowded with eager rummagers.

Pete loved flea markets. Didn't know why, except he always found the most extraordinary things when he visited one. This visit fell true to form.

"Serendipity-do-da!" he exclaimed, slapping his hands together when he spotted the tin roller coaster.

Mary Elizabeth, walking close by his side, laughed at his expression, which was precisely his point in using it. He loved hearing her laugh. The musicality of it fascinated him.

He approached the toy with feigned nonchalance, not wanting to appear too eager. "Does it work?"

The vendor seated behind the junk-heaped table nodded. Pete searched and found the built-in key, then wound the mechanism.

"Careful," the vendor warned. Pete nodded, and stepped back. The little car took off, zipping up and down and around the track.

"Oh, that's delightful, Peter," Mary Elizabeth whispered, leaning in.

He thought so, too, although at the moment his attention was more taken with the warm curves pressing against his arm. He'd been doing well today, he thought—except for that kiss and the little episode when she'd lifted her jacket. He'd realized then that knowing she was pregnant and *seeing* she was pregnant were two different things.

His mind had suddenly galloped out of control. Forward to how she'd look at six months, eight months, nine. Backward to a faceless man named Roger, whom Pete had suddenly disliked immensely. Forward again to the feel of a little person swimming around in there, pressing a foot or an elbow against his palm—*his* palm. He didn't admit it to himself often, but he missed having children of his own.

Other than those two episodes, he'd done well today ignoring Mary Elizabeth's feminine side. She'd just been a person who happened to be traveling with him, a sidekick he enjoyed the hell out of teasing. But walking through this flea market, he began to notice things, like how close she stayed by his side, how his senses stirred when she brushed against him. He was unaccountably fascinated by her height, too. Five-eight, maybe? He didn't see her in feet and inches, though, but rather in how well she'd fit him if they were standing together...kissing.

He also noticed the glances she drew from other men, even some who were there with their wives or girlfriends. Despite Pete's teasing about her hair and clothes, she was one class act. She just didn't seem to know it. She had a real wide gap where her ego should have been.

That didn't bode well. Ultimately, lack of self-esteem had been Cindy's problem, too. He remembered only too well the black hole it had created in their lives, a hole that nothing he did or said could fill. *You're beautiful, Cindy,* he'd tell her, and she'd want to know how beautiful. Would he pick her if he had a choice between her and Farrah Fawcett? He'd say of course he'd pick her, and she'd want him to say it again and again. Tell me, Pete. Hold me, Pete. Don't go in to work today, Pete. Love me, instead. Love me more. Prove you love. Love me or else—

"Pete?" Mary Elizabeth's voice jolted him out of his dark thoughts. "Can I buy it for you?" she asked quietly.

"The roller coaster? I don't think so."

"But it's only seventy-five cents."

Pete dragged a hand over his twitching mouth. "That's dollars, Mary Elizabeth, not cents."

She swallowed. "Oh."

Her chagrin was just what he needed to banish Cindy from his thoughts. "It's probably forty years old, maybe fifty, and in excellent condition." Turning to the vendor, he said, "I'll give you fifty bucks."

The man shook his bald head, jowls waggling. Pete shrugged and began to walk away.

"I can't take anything less than seventy."

Pete slowed, turned and offered sixty. Again the vendor shook his head.

They finally settled on sixty-five, and Pete walked away a happy man.

He and Mary Elizabeth stayed at the flea market almost three hours. The time flew for him. Mary Elizabeth claimed to be having a good time, too, although he wasn't sure. Not until they reached a booth with an unusually large collection of fine china. She lingered so long, picking up this dish and that bowl, that she finally told Pete to go on; she'd catch up later. It was then he knew she'd caught the junking bug.

When she did find him, she was lugging a cardboard carton in two straining arms. "I'm sorry, I spent some of the money you loaned me, but I have a thing for china," she explained with a shy smile. "I don't know why I continually add to my collection—I certainly don't need the stuff—but I can't seem to stop. Whenever I do settle, my house will have to have an entire pantry just to hold dishes."

Pete took the heavy carton from her in exchange for his roller coaster. "Stop apologizing. I understand. I'm addicted to this collecting stuff myself."

She stared at him, quietly, her soft brown eyes fixed on his. The next moment those eyes filled with a luminosity he didn't recognize as tears until she swung away from him, blinking.

They walked on through the crowded barn, walking just to move. Finally Pete said, "What was that all about?"

She sniffed, then laughed, which seemed to be a familiar emotional pattern with her. "I like your company, Peter. I've never enjoyed a man's company so much."

Even as he felt an absurd flush of pleasure, he knew he ought to refute her. "But half the time we're fighting."

"I know. Isn't it wonderful?" She walked off, zeroing

in on a Royal Doulton soup tureen, leaving Pete more baffled by her than ever.

"Would you care to explain that remark?" he asked later, as they tried to fit their purchases into a motor home that didn't need any more clutter. Besides the roller coaster, Pete had bought a yellow plastic radio from the 1950s that didn't work and a lava lamp that did. Besides the box of china, Mary Elizabeth had found three wine goblets that matched a set she already owned.

"I came from a polite family," she replied, closing the storage cupboard in the hall. "We didn't argue, no matter how angry we got."

Pete plugged his lava lamp into the toaster outlet. It would take a while to activate. "Were you and your family angry often?" He turned and found her standing stiff and red-faced.

"I didn't really mean *angry* angry, just, you know...."

"Angry," he supplied. He hooked his hands on his hips and gazed at her. She looked ashamed just for having admitted she sometimes felt anger. "Nothing wrong with ripping loose once in a while. What's stupid is *not* venting your anger, letting it eat away at you." He watched her nod and fidget and compress her lips. She was twitchier than a spider on a hot plate.

"Who were you angry at?"

She shook off his question. "I didn't mean to complain. I had a wonderful home, a wonderful family."

"But?" Pete wondered why he was probing. For days he'd been telling himself he didn't want to know her any better than he already did. So, why was he inviting her to mess up his peace of mind?

Surprisingly, it was Mary Elizabeth who backed off. "Let's just drop it, okay? I honestly don't know where I was going with that thought, anyway."

Somehow he doubted that, but he didn't argue. "Fine," he agreed, moving to the driver's seat.

When they were both buckled in, he opened the wrinkled map and laid it across her knees.

"Okay, Beth, find us the quickest route to Pennsylvania Dutch country."

Her head jerked upward, her eyes alight. "Are you serious?"

"Would I joke about something like that?" he said, turning the ignition. "You did say you wanted to go there, didn't you?"

She didn't answer, just hunched forward and began an avid study of the map. But as the RV left the flea market grounds, Pete thought he heard her mutter something—something that sounded suspiciously like "Serendipity-do-da!"

THAT NIGHT, AFTER THEY'D settled into a campground, Pete took his bike off the trailer and went for another ride, this one purely for enjoyment.

He was on a quiet country road when he spotted a pay phone beaming its lonely white light into the dark Lancaster County night. Suddenly he remembered he ought to call home and tell somebody he was bringing a guest to the wedding.

He called his sister Pam. She could contact the bride and make the seating adjustment as well as anybody.

Calling Pam was a mistake. Sue Ellen was there.

"Since when are you two friends?" he asked, sulking into the receiver.

As usual, Pam ignored him. "Want to talk to her?"

"No!" He straightened out of his slouch.

"Too bad. Here she is."

He was still cursing when Sue Ellen came on the line.

"Peter? Hello. What a surprise." Her voice brought to mind long mink-colored hair, soft pink lips, and betrayal.

"Uh...yeah."

"I heard you got the bike you wanted."

"You did, huh?" Pete wondered if monosyllabism was his usual mode of speaking, or if it only came on when he was talking to women he had loved and planned to marry.

"Any chance of me getting a ride when you get back? I don't think I've been on a motorcycle since, God, I don't know..."

Yes, you do.

"We'll see." His answer was noncommittal, his tone reserved.

Yet she replied, "Great. Thanks. So, where are you?"

"Sue Ellen, I haven't got a whole lot of change to feed this phone. Could you put my sister back on?"

"Sure enough. I'll see you at the wedding."

He remained silent and eventually she handed over the phone.

"Don't do this to me, Pam."

"I don't know what you're talking about."

"Sure you don't. The reason I'm calling is, I'm bringing a date to Brad's wedding, someone really special." Pete went on, telling her briefly about Mary Elizabeth, sketching in some of the background they'd made up earlier in the day. He thought he did a convincing job, too, until Pam laughed.

"You expect me to believe that? She's probably just somebody you picked up on the road."

Pete felt the blood drain from his face.

"Just give Jill a call for me, okay? Tell her to reserve another place at the family table. I gotta go." He slammed down the phone.

All around him the cool night pulsed with cricket sounds.

A quarter moon hung like a silver charm at the end of the empty road, washing it with the palest of pale light. Objectively he knew it was a beautiful night, but he no longer cared whether he was a part of it or not. He got on his bike and rode back to Mary Elizabeth.

She was lying in bed reading, Monet curled up by her side. "Hi." She smiled when he strolled in. The smell of minty toothpaste hovered in the air. Tonight, he noticed, she wasn't wearing her robe, only pajamas—seersucker creations he associated with dry old spinsters.

And he still wanted her, God help him, seersucker pajamas and all.

He used the bathroom, and by the time he came out she'd turned off her light, which made undressing easier on both of them.

"Do you want to read?" she asked softly after he'd slipped between the sheets. "It won't bother me if you turn on your light."

"Nah. It's been a long day." He relaxed into the cool bed, feeling the ghosts of vibrations still haunting his muscles.

"It's been a good day, too." There was a smile in her voice. "We did so much!"

Pete imagined the smile reaching her eyes. "Yes, we did."

"Actually, this has been one of the best days of my life." She sighed. "Isn't life strange! Yesterday was one of the worst—the hospital part of it, anyway."

Pete wasn't sure he wanted to be someone with whom she experienced superlatives. But the truth was, today had been pretty high on his list of good days, too.

Actually, it was right at the top.

CHAPTER TEN

THEY REACHED BALTIMORE by 9:00 a.m.

Mary Elizabeth had tried to argue she didn't need a new dress for the wedding, but Pete insisted she did. He knew she probably *could* make do with what she had, but she'd seemed so down on herself, so depressed over her appearance, he thought buying something new might give her a brighter outlook. He suggested she visit a beauty salon, too, although he hoped she didn't do anything drastic with her hair. He sort of liked it the way it was.

He told her he'd spend the morning grocery shopping since they were running low on some basics. After that he'd visit the baseball museum or simply walk around and enjoy the architecture of the new harbor complex.

They left the motor home in a parking garage, picked up bus schedules and diagrams of the subway system, agreed to meet for lunch in front of the aquarium, and went their separate ways.

Peter had given her money, but Mary Elizabeth hoped she wouldn't have to use it. Coming into the city, she'd spotted a shop that bought gold and gemstones, and decided to make that her first stop.

She left the shop more pleased than she'd expected to be, having sold a pair of diamond earrings she'd never liked, as well as three gold chains, a class ring and several earrings whose mates she'd lost.

After the tranquillity of rural Pennsylvania, Mary Elizabeth found the bustle of Baltimore a pleasant contrast. Just walking through the downtown area energized her.

With little trouble, she located a quality salon that welcomed walk-in customers, went in and explained what she wanted. She had several pictures marked off in a fashion magazine but the stylist seemed more interested in studying the shape of Mary Elizabeth's face and fingering the texture of her hair.

The outcome of the woman's scrutiny was a trim that kept Mary Elizabeth's hair at shoulder length but added the wispiest of bangs and a few long layers curving toward her cheeks and jaw. Mary Elizabeth loved the look. It was straighter, fuller, more contemporary and, she thought, quite sensual. She immediately wondered what Peter would think.

On a whim she asked the stylist if she knew of any stores that specialized in skin analysis and customized makeup. She did, and after paying for her haircut, Mary Elizabeth walked up the block, had her skin and coloring analyzed, and subjected herself to yet another stranger's diagnosis.

The result was amazing. Gazing at herself in the mirror, Mary Elizabeth wondered why she hadn't done something like this sooner. She didn't look made up, which had been her fear coming into this shop. She just looked better, more vibrant, her mouth and eyes defined, her cheekbones polished.

From the cosmetics shop she went to The Gallery to shop for a dress for the wedding. She found just what she needed in one of the larger department stores that was running a half-price sale on its summer stock, a pale champagne two-piece ensemble whose full chiffon skirt was gathered in a comfortable elasticized waist and topped by a hip-length tapestry jacket. Very chic. Also very concealing.

Standing before the dressing-room mirror, gazing at her

radiant reflection, she thought, *Yes, here finally is a woman Peter Mitchell would consider taking out.*

With time to spare before meeting him, she wandered the store, drifting inexorably into the maternity department. She dreaded it, imagining the racks full of huge flowered dresses with Peter Pan collars and big perky bows.

Mary Elizabeth was pleasantly surprised. She bought a pair of slim black leggings whose stomach panel would expand as she did. However, she passed over the matching jersey. She could make do with roomy shirts and long sweaters for quite a while yet.

She was almost out of the mall when she saw a sign for a sweater sale. Actually, she didn't have that many long sweaters. Two that were wearable, maybe? She went in.

Twelve minutes later she came out, not only having purchased a sweater—a cream-colored angora with a soft shawl collar—but wearing that sweater, too, along with her new leggings. *Won't Peter be surprised,* she thought, hurrying down the sidewalk. The next moment it hit her; she'd been thinking about Peter all morning. Every one of her choices had been made with an eye on his reaction.

Her steps slowed. She was doing it again—dressing to please him, believing it would make a difference. A difference in what?

She walked on, trying not to acknowledge the fact that she had been thinking of them as having a relationship. After all, they would be living less than two hours apart in Florida. It was certainly feasible that they could see each other beyond this week. But of course, Peter would have to want to see her, wouldn't he? And that was the crux of the matter, the point in her thinking where she always came out feeling like the fool.

She was pregnant. Why would Peter want to see her beyond this road trip? For that matter, how could *she* even consider it? Hadn't Charles made a valid point when he'd said a pregnant woman who dated ran the risk of appearing indiscriminate?

Her spirits were sinking fast, threatening to ruin what had been a wonderful day only moments ago. She took a purposeful look at her reflection in a store window, examined her swingy hair, her stylish new clothes—even her vibrant coloring was visible in the glass—and her cheerfulness returned. Even if her makeover generated no change between her and Peter, and it wouldn't, she'd done something nice for herself. That was enough.

Pete spotted Mary Elizabeth coming almost two blocks away. Funny thing was, he didn't recognize her at first. He only knew that one foxy lady was sashaying up the street in his direction.

When she waved, his gaze jerked upward to her face, away from those rounded hips swaying under that soft white knit stuff. In that moment of recognition he knew he was in deep trouble. He'd been trying to deny his attraction to her these last few days, but his libido apparently had its own agenda. The attraction had grown in leaps and bounds, waking him in the dead of night, dropping her into his thoughts at unexpected times throughout the day. He knew something had to give, soon. Trouble was, he also knew it would be a sweet, very sweet, surrender. That was why he'd begun to think that maybe the consequences of giving in wouldn't be as bad as he'd thought.

"Well, what do you think?" She put down her shopping bags and turned a slow circle for his perusal. A couple of lawyer types, passing on their way to lunch, applauded.

Her already glowing cheeks warmed to a higher tint. To Pete's utter delight, she paid them no attention but kept her gaze fixed on him.

"Oh, mercy!" For the life of him, Pete couldn't think

of anything else to say. He guessed she understood, though. Catching her glossy coral-pink lips in her teeth, she smiled, pleased that he liked what he saw.

As his gaze roamed over her, however, he realized her beauty wasn't due directly to any of the physical changes she'd wrought. Those changes were too minor. Rather, her beauty was emanating from a source within.

Well, I'll be damned! Pete thought. She'd needed to feel better about herself, and although the changes were only physical, they'd worked. Maybe his sisters were right; shopping really was good for the soul.

He lifted his hand and fingered her newly styled hair. He liked it. She looked half pixie, half seductress. He caught her warm floral scent, became captivated by the curve of her graceful neck, imagined his lips pressed there right under her jaw—and for a moment forgot they were standing on a busy city thoroughfare.

He was going to kiss her. Kissing her would open a Pandora's box of woes, but the urge tearing through him was too overwhelming to curb. He was going to do it, right here, right now, and caution be damned.

She looked up quite suddenly as if sensing his thoughts. The moment froze and became measureless, an infinite expanse of mutual awareness and shared anticipation, echoing all the other moments of attraction they'd experienced over the last few days and denied.

And then she blinked and looked away, effectively breaking the spell. Pete cursed her common sense. But of course, she was right.

"Oh, here's your money," she said, reaching into her purse. "I didn't use it. I had my own."

"What did you do, hold up a convenience store?"

She cast him an impatient look. "I sold some of my jewelry at a pawn shop."

"Aw, hell, Beth!" He hoped she hadn't sold any heirlooms. Hoped she hadn't been ripped off.

"It's okay. I wanted to. It felt good doing this—" she flipped her hair "—on my own. So," she went on quickly, "where would you like to eat?"

"I got a recommendation from a cashier at the supermarket. A place that specializes in seafood. Come on, it's just a couple of blocks away."

In a city that made specializing in seafood a matter of pride, the restaurant they chose was truly superb. They ordered crab cakes, spicy steamed blue crabs and roasted oysters, served with rice pilaf and warm crusty bread.

While they ate they memorized the vital statistics of their lives: birth dates, height, weight, the names of their parents and siblings, a few family anecdotes, peculiarities of their hometowns, and whatever else they could think of that a couple who were in love ought to know.

They walked back to the parking garage testing each other. Mary Elizabeth fumbled only once, on the name of his best friend in elementary school. Pete, she realized, had a remarkable memory, which by now didn't come as much of a surprise.

She climbed up the steps of the RV feeling mildly euphoric, a mood she attributed to the delicious, leisurely meal they'd just enjoyed. When she stepped into the kitchen, her euphoria soared.

The first thing she noticed was the plush bear sitting on the counter, surrounded by pastel baby outfits still on their hangers. From there her gaze flew to the table, then the passenger seat up front. Gifts were everywhere, and not all of them looked to be for the baby.

She felt weak-kneed. She reached blindly for Peter, and when she found his arm, she closed her fingers around it.

"Peter!" That's all she got out before her voice deserted her.

Pete cleared his throat gruffly. "After picking up the groceries, I had some time to kill."

She walked unsteadily toward the table where she found a set of soft bath towels, a squeaky yellow duck, a basket of baby toiletries and four dozen cloth diapers. She stared, happy, sad, mostly confused. "But...I'm not keeping the baby."

"That's okay." Pete stepped closer. "I just thought you might like to pass some things on to the new mom, let her know this is no ordinary kid she's dealing with. This one comes fully equipped and ready to rumble, compliments of her first—and best—mom."

Mary Elizabeth was choking on tears and affection for this man. She had to move away from him before she did something embarrassing. "What's all this?" Draped over the passenger seat were a pair of denim jeans—maternity jeans—and a large white T-shirt with bold blue letters that read Baby under Construction.

"Considering my occupation, I couldn't resist," Pete murmured, smiling almost shyly.

Mary Elizabeth fingered a second outfit, yellow cotton tights with a blue T-shirt that read Baby on Board, the words printed within a yellow square. On the seat she found two pairs of maternity shorts, two more tops and a book titled *What to Expect When You're Expecting*. She could contain her tears no longer.

"My sisters swear by that book," Pete said with casual disregard.

Before turning, Mary Elizabeth swiped at her eyes. She moved to the counter and picked up one of the baby outfits, a mint-green sleeper. So tiny. So soft. She held it up and for an instant actually imagined a baby filling it out. The image was so vivid she could almost feel the warmth and weight of it. Her eyes threatened to spill over again. Quickly she put the outfit down.

"Thank you, Peter. This is—" she spread her hands "—just overwhelming."

"Aw, hell, this is nothing compared to what—" He broke off abruptly, hitched his right shoulder and glanced aside, looking embarrassed again.

Compared to what? she wondered. What a baby would ultimately need? What he would like to buy?

She said, "I bet you didn't get to the baseball museum."

"If you've seen one, you've seen them all. Here, let me pick up this stuff so we can get rolling." He stepped toward the front seat.

"No, that's okay," she said, reaching at the same time. "I can do it." Their hands landed on the T-shirt simultaneously, their arms crossed one over the other.

In a college psychology class, she'd once seen a documentary about the aura that surrounds the human body. It included actual footage of auras, captured on a particular sort of film capable of photographing those strange energy waves. Mary Elizabeth remembered being especially fascinated by two people in the experiment who happened to be attracted to each other. Standing about a foot apart, their auras literally flared and elongated as if reaching out toward each other, trying to meet.

At this moment, with her right hand and his left resting on the shirt, she imagined a virtual bonfire of flares rising from the skin where their forearms crossed and touched.

Instantly, awareness was there, resonating between them more forcefully than ever. One minute they'd been just friends, the next a man and a woman alone, drawn to each other, minds and bodies rife with all the possibilities that existed between them.

Mary Elizabeth lifted her gaze to his face. She loved everything about it. Every angle and crease and curve seemed perfect. Even the imperfections seemed perfect.

Desire blindsided her and before she could disguise it, it was burning in her eyes, pulsing from her skin.

The moment will pass, she told herself, just as it had earlier when they'd met for lunch. All she had to do was move, resume talking. But the strange thing was, she didn't want to. She was tired of fighting it.

And so was Peter, it seemed. She watched his mouth soften, become serious and sensual. Watched his eyes darken and felt a shiver of anticipation while his head lowered, slowly, giving her ample time to pull away. She didn't. If anything, she swayed forward to shorten the agonizing wait. And then his lips met hers in a kiss that brushed and moved apart and brushed again, acquainting her with little more than the heat of his breath. It left her disappointed, leaning in, wanting more.

Pete's eyes glittered down at her, apparently pleased with her reaction. The next moment he angled his head and joined his mouth to hers again. This time there was nothing hesitant about the move. His arms slid across her back and gathered her close, while his lips continued to move on hers, smooth, warm, supple, and so very, very arousing.

Mary Elizabeth returned his kiss with a fervor that would have embarrassed her if she'd had time to think about it. But at the moment all she was capable of thinking was *Yes! Finally, yes!*

She felt Peter's body tauten against hers and happily let the kiss deepen and intensify. As it did, her body came awake…and she awakened to her body.

Suddenly she was aware that her breasts were crushed against Peter's chest—her swollen, tender breasts. Her *pregnant* breasts. Her pregnant belly arced against his jeans.

Pete felt a change in her and lifted his head. "What's the matter?" He watched a frown slide into her eyes where an instant ago there had been desire. Trembling, she pulled away.

He was rather shaken himself. He should have expected an unusually strong reaction. He'd wanted her for days. But he hadn't been ready for *that*.

"Peter, this can't happen," she said shakily.

"I know," he agreed, disgusted with his lack of control. "Come Sunday, we'll never see each other again."

She folded her arms and gazed at the floor. "It isn't just that."

Pete tried not to ask. He lasted about two heartbeats. "What is it, then?"

"I'm pregnant." Her voice scratched with anguish.

"I know you're pregnant. Believe me, I know." He thought about little else these days. "But that doesn't mean you aren't still desirable." He slouched against the counter and crossed his legs, trying to diminish the visual proof of exactly how desirable she was.

She groaned and shook her head again. "I'm sorry. I should never have let that happen. I feel so embarrassed."

Should I ask? he wondered. Oh, hell, in for a dime…

"I'm not sure I understand where that's coming from, that embarrassment."

"Isn't it obvious?"

"Would I be asking if it were?"

She thought awhile, her mouth working. "It's just wrong, that's all."

"What is? Kissing?"

"Yes!"

"It felt pretty right to me."

She started to pace, arms clutched tight under her breasts. "But don't you find it cheap?"

Pete's mouth dropped open. Cheap was the last thing on his mind. Before he could tell her, though, she added, "Most men would, no matter how broad-minded they say they are."

"Whoa. I'm not following this. Come over here and sit."

They slid into the banquette, taking different sides of the ell. "All right, now let's try that again. Most men would find *what* cheap?"

She sat huddled, arms still crossed, her hands gripping her elbows. The proud glow she'd acquired as a result of her makeover was gone, confirming his suspicion that what needed mending resided at a far deeper level. "Well," she said, "to begin with, nice girls don't get pregnant outside marriage."

Pete emitted a choked laugh.

"Okay, they do," she amended, "but they usually marry the guy who got them pregnant, fast. A woman who chooses not to go that route is still the exception. She has to, well, really watch what she does."

"Why? Because she's chosen an unconventional path?"

She lifted one shoulder halfheartedly.

"So people won't talk?"

Two shoulders lifted. "Sure. And because guys might get the wrong idea and think she's..."

"Cheap?"

"Well, yes." She kneaded her upper arms, nervously twisting the soft white sweater. "That's definitely a risk she runs. Her pregnancy is obvious proof she's recently been with another man."

Pete frowned incredulously. "Do you think, because you let me kiss you, I now consider you easy or immoral? Do you think I see your pregnancy as the result of indiscriminate behavior? Is that it?''

She swallowed again. ''I guess.''

''You know something, kid.'' He leaned far over the table, his eyes fixed hard on hers. ''You're nuts.''

She backed away. He leaned even closer. ''It's the intimacy of this arrangement, the close quarters,'' he explained. ''It was bound to happen. We're only human.''

''You think what we did was right?''

''No, I believe it was wrong, too, and I'll try not to let it happen again—but for different reasons. As I've said before, I don't have one-night stands.''

Her face took on a hard, belligerent look that stymied him. ''We'll only be a two-hour drive from each other.'' She let the logical conclusion tumble through the ensuing silence. She was daring him to admit he just didn't want to continue seeing her.

There was no use in trying to refute her. Although lately he'd been toying with the idea of seeing her through her pregnancy, he still believed he lacked the fortitude. ''I like my freedom, Mary Elizabeth. I don't enjoy serious, long-term relationships. They take too much time and energy. In your condition, you deserve better than that.''

He saw her ice up right before his eyes. ''In other words, what I 'deserve' is a guy who's willing to take on used goods and a brat who's somebody else's. Well, let me be the first to inform you, that animal doesn't exist.''

''Lady, you *are* crazy.''

''Am I? Tell me, what do *you* think my worth is on the dating scene these days?''

Pete suddenly surged with anger. ''You have as much worth as you give yourself, Mary Elizabeth.''

He saw her eyes fill and felt his heart contract. ''What

happened to calling me Beth?'' As if that was the issue here!

''You can change your hair and your clothes, but I'm afraid you're still a Mary Elizabeth inside.'' He tipped her face so she had to look at him. ''What you need is a serious attitude adjustment, kid.''

She jerked away from his hold. ''Yeah, well...'' she said vaguely, blinking away tears.

''Who was he?'' Pete asked sharply.

''Who was who?''

''The person who did the tune on you.''

''I don't know what you're talking about.''

''Yeah? Well, somebody sure did a bang-up job on your self-esteem. I'm gonna take a wild guess and say...your father?''

The color drained from her face. Still, she managed to say, ''Where did you ever get an idea like that?''

''From you, things you've said. The way he pushed Roger at you. The extremes you went to to make that relationship work. I can't help thinking the entire Roger fiasco was just an attempt to please your father. Then, when you told me he wasn't upset to see you leave home, well, what else could I think except the guy's a royal jackass. Oh, by the way, you also stammer whenever you mention him.''

''I do not.''

''You do.''

She sagged into the seat, sighing. ''All right. I admit my father had a few things to say to me before I left, but...''

''Did those things happen to include words like 'cheap' and 'used goods'?'' Pete was still amazed that she'd used such phrases. ''Is he the one who told you no man would want you because you're pregnant? That's all crap, Mary Elizabeth, and if that's the sort of line he dished up while he was raising you, then you damn well *should* be angry with him. You should be fit to be tied."

A knock at the door brought a curse to his lips. "Who the hell can that be?"

Opening the door, Pete found a young security officer with his knuckles poised, ready to knock again. Pete looked past him, remembering quite suddenly that they were parked in a garage in Baltimore. "Yes?"

"Just checking to see if things are all right here."

"Things are fine."

The young man poked his head in warily. "That right, ma'am?"

Mary Elizabeth had risen from the bench. "Yes. We were just about to set off."

Pete closed the door, grumbling. Damn kid looked about fifteen years old. When he turned, Mary Elizabeth was already in the passenger seat, her cheeks flushed. Maybe, he decided, her attitude adjustment would begin today.

CHAPTER ELEVEN

THEY DROVE OUT of Baltimore in tense silence. The countryside was beautiful. Lots of thoroughbred horse farms, but Mary Elizabeth wasn't interested. All she wanted was... what? For this trip to be over? Was it still only Monday? She closed her eyes, knowing only half of her wanted that. The other half wouldn't mind if her journey with Pete went on forever. She sighed, longing for relief from this tug-of-war between her heart and her brain.

She awoke sometime later, not having realized she'd drifted off to sleep. The motor home had stopped and Pete was unbuckling his seat belt.

"Where are we?"

"A park. Somewhere in western Maryland. It seems a nice quiet place to walk." He uncoiled from his seat. "And talk."

She wasn't sure she liked the sound of that, but she was awfully stiff from riding, so got up, anyway.

They walked at a revitalizing pace, past flower beds and jungle gyms, down one path and another. It was just what she needed. Her blood was flowing again, her head clearing. Eventually, though, their pace slowed to a conversational amble.

"I don't know a hell of a lot, Mary Elizabeth," Pete drawled, squinting ahead, hands tucked in his back pockets, "but I have learned it's easier to live with certain situations if you talk about them to somebody."

She threw him a skeptical glance. "Like you?"

"I'm a great listener. Why I was born with big ears."

Her lips twitched.

He guided her off the path, across a springy lawn to the shade of an ancient beech tree, where he spread his flannel shirt and they sat.

"It's nice here," she admitted softly as Pete fit himself behind her and began massaging her shoulders.

"You're so tight," he said, and then, pressing forward, grumbled against her ear, "you don't need this. Neither does the baby. Why not get rid of it, all this old emotional baggage? You're supposed to be starting a new life, so do it. Throw it overboard."

She sighed. "I wish I could."

"Well?"

"How?" she challenged, shrugging off his hands and turning to face him.

"Tell me about it. Talk to me."

She sat for several minutes, still as the afternoon sun on the grass, legs crossed Indian-style, fingers loosely interlaced under her gently protruded belly. Pete watched her sink into herself, examining her thoughts, weighing her trust in him. *Come on, you can do it,* he assured her silently, willing her to take that first step. He saw her wet her lips, take in a breath, and thought jubilantly, *Yes!*

"The day I told my father I was pregnant, I learned something about myself I didn't know, something that changed my life irrevocably." She paused. He waited. "I learned I'm not his daughter." Her eyes darted to Pete's to measure his reaction. He kept his expression set, although inwardly he was reeling.

"Go on," he urged gently.

She returned her gaze to the safe middle space between

them. "It seems my mother had an affair during their marriage and I was the result."

"Do you know your biological father?"

She shook her head. "He was someone working at the house, adding on a sun room." The corners of her mouth turned downward. "A guy just passing through, hired for the season by a local contractor."

"Was your mother in love with him?"

"Mrs. Pidgin, our housekeeper, claims she was, but I have my doubts. She stayed with my...with Charles, didn't she?" Bitterness slid into her voice. "She even went on to have another child with him."

"Well, dissolving an established marriage isn't always an easy matter."

The bitterness spread to her eyes.

Pete frowned. "Are you angry at your mother?"

He watched her emotions gather and rise until finally she couldn't contain them any longer. "Yes! She had no right to do that to me."

"Do what to you?"

She focused on him with startled eyes. "I...ah...have me, I guess." Her brow creased. "Get pregnant by someone just passing through and then let her husband know about it."

Pete watched her swallow convulsively, waiting till she seemed more composed to say, "You think it would've been better for her not to tell him?"

"For me it would have been." Her features appeared chipped from ice. Pete imagined a wealth of heartache behind her statement, behind all that ice. Charles had probably put her through hell, playing her for a scapegoat.

"The other day," he said carefully, "when you were telling me about Roger and your reasons for not wanting him to know about your pregnancy, you mentioned several times you feared he'd resent the baby, think of it as a burden and an embarrassment."

She plucked a blade of grass and pulled it apart again and again.

"Does that fear have anything to do with the way your father raised you?"

She tossed the shredded grass. "Charles had his reasons."

"That's not what I asked. Did he resent you, make you feel unwanted?"

"My mother betrayed him. She had an affair. Every time he looked at me he must have been reminded of that infidelity."

"And that's why you're mad at *her?*"

He knew he'd confused her. He'd meant to.

In her continued silence he said, "You remind me of my sister Lindy. Her husband has a drinking problem, but for a long time she refused to admit it. She used to make excuses for him. It was his job, his friends. Most of the time she felt guilty as sin, too, thinking his problem was really her fault, that there was something wrong with her that drove him to drink." Pete knew he had Mary Elizabeth's attention.

"Then one day I convinced her to go to Al-Anon, and she learned drinking was *his* problem and had nothing to do with her. She stopped making excuses and, to make a long story short, eventually got her life together."

Pete could see thoughts moving behind Mary Elizabeth's eyes, memories churning, the pain deepening.

"Okay, maybe Charles did make me feel unwanted," she admitted, blinking rapidly. "How could he not? I *was* unwanted. When we were talking about my options, the day I told him I was pregnant, one of his suggestions was for me to go away, have the baby and give it up for adoption. When I refused, he said I was just like my mother. I guess they had discussed options, too.'' Her voice went faint. ''Ways of getting rid of me.''

''But she refused?''

Mary Elizabeth's eyes swam with tears. ''Yes.''

Pete let her mull over that thought for a moment before he said, ''But you're doing just what he suggested. Going away, giving up the baby.''

''I know, but now it's my decision. I didn't like the way he was dictating something so important.''

''I see.'' Pete mentally chalked one up for Mary Elizabeth. ''How did Charles make you feel resented? Do you remember any specific things he did or said?''

She breathed out a sharp laugh. ''Millions of things.''

''Like?''

She waved a hand at him. ''What's the use in digging up trash like that now?''

''Although talk won't change the past, sometimes it can change the future.''

She shook her head. ''No, I wouldn't feel right talking about it now.''

''Why not?''

''I don't know. It's just…unbecoming.''

''Unbecoming?'' Pete almost laughed. ''Do you see it as whining or something? As slandering Charles's character? Or being a…a bad girl?'' he mocked.

She twisted her lips and scrunched her nose. Pete wanted to take her in his arms right there and smother her with kisses. Instead, he plucked some grass and, like her a moment before, began shredding.

''The past has a hold on you,'' he said, regaining his seriousness. ''*Charles* has a hold, one of the most destructive there is, too. He seems to be dictating what you think about yourself, and most of it is negative. What you've got to do is take that power away from him, kid. It doesn't belong to him.''

"That's why I left home," she mumbled, chin tucked.

Her statement caught him from an unexpected angle. His fingers stilled. ''Of course! I'm just beginning to realize… That was a really big step for you, wasn't it, physically removing yourself from him. It was your way of saying you weren't going to take his guff anymore. You were sick of the guilt and the pain.''

"Yeah, well, I don't see my leaving as anything to be particularly proud of. In fact, I see it as sort of selfish.''

"Well, stop it, dammit," he mock-scolded. "Start thinking of it as right, as strong, as an affirmation of your self-worth.'' He paused. ''Did I just say 'affirmation of self-worth'?'' He gave an exaggerated shudder. ''Next thing you know I'll be listening to New Age music and wearing crystals.''

Her glance could only be called coy. "Or maybe taking your sister to some other group meeting where the phrase 'self-worth' might happen to come up?''

Pete whistled through his teeth. ''You really are smarter than you look.''

Smiling, Mary Elizabeth stretched her right leg and kneaded the calf.

"A cramp?''

She nodded. He got up and helped her to her feet. When they'd resumed walking, he said, ''One thing I've found that helps me when I've been hurt is to stop thinking of myself as a victim. I do that by turning my pain into anger.''

She looked at him askance. ''That doesn't sound very enlightened.''

"What can I say? It works.''

"So, what do you do? Go around punching people?''

"Ah, the damage of first impressions. No, what I usually do is confront the person who's wronged me and let him know exactly how I feel. It gets a weight off my chest and usually leads to our clearing the air."

She was shaking her head. "Oh, I couldn't do that, Peter. Not with Charles."

"I understand. Some people you just can't confront. That's why I own a punching bag."

She laughed, a sound that poured through him like warm brandy.

"I've converted one of the bedrooms in my condo into a gym, and when somebody or something's bugging me and there's no other way I can get rid of my frustration, I pound a punching bag for about an hour. The madder I get, the better I feel afterward. So, as I'm punching, I'm saying things like, 'You sonuvabitch. You *promised* me, you *swore on your mother's grave* that you'd deliver those special shingles by Monday! And I only gave you the order as a *favor*. As a reward for my generosity, I had to face the owner. *I* had to tell him why we won't be finished with his house on time! And he wasn't happy.'" Pete paused. "I really focus on what happened, too, let my memories get as specific as possible so that I can feel the original emotions flowing through me again. And all the while I'm punching away."

"And that helps?"

"Yep. By the time my hour is up, I'm feeling much better."

"Yeah, well, I don't own a punching bag, Peter."

"Maybe you can find a substitute... not me," he added quickly, shielding himself with his raised hands.

When they reached the RV, she said, "You really think it'll help?"

"It's worth a shot."

She nodded. "I'll give it some thought."

Inside, they microwaved a bag of popcorn, got bottles of apple juice from the fridge, and soon were under way again.

"I have one other suggestion I think'll help." Pete tipped back his bottle and swallowed some juice. "Call Roger."

She stiffened. "Uh-uh. I don't even want him to know where I've gone, never mind that I'm pregnant."

Pete glanced at her, puzzled. "But he's bound to find out where you are, working with your father and all."

She sighed heavily. "I told Charles I was going to Chicago."

Pete slumped away from her, staring at the road. After a moment he began to laugh, a dark, wicked rumble. "There's no end to the mess you've created, is there. Do I dare ask why?"

She stuffed her mouth with popcorn, making him wait for the answer. "When I refused to tell Roger, Charles threatened to tell him himself and bring about a marriage. That's how badly he wanted this little unpleasantness taken care of." She patted her waist. "He seemed to be appeased when I said I'd leave the area, but that didn't last long. He's afraid I might return with the baby. I knew he'd started thinking about telling Roger again. I think he still might."

"All the more reason for you to call the guy and tell him yourself. Right now you're running scared. Charles is calling all the shots. Take that power away from him. A phone call'll do it."

She knew he was right. Keeping this news from Roger had been bothering her from the beginning of her pregnancy. Guilt was weighing her down, exhausting her. "I'll consider your advice."

"Good. And if you decide to take it, do yourself a favor. Decide how *you* want to handle the matter before you call.

Don't wait for Roger to tell you what to do. Have a plan of your own.''

"That's it? You're not going to tell me I should keep the baby or give Roger joint custody or—''

"Hell, no. Those are your decisions.''

She moaned, sinking into her seat.

"Nobody ever said growing up was easy, Mary Elizabeth.''

Pete turned on the radio, hung his wrist over the wheel and let The Shirelles and The Platters carry them over the Virginia line and on into the Shenandoah Valley.

It was dusk when they arrived. They hadn't quite made it to the national park, but Pete found an adequate campground, anyway. It was small and privately owned, and on this Monday evening in late September, only sparsely occupied. He parked at a distance from the other campers in a secluded spot by a rushing stream. The site lacked the convenience of hookups but offered a view of the Alleghenies that was beyond price.

Mary Elizabeth had started their supper while still on the road—a porterhouse steak, brown rice and broccoli, provisions Pete had bought that morning in Baltimore. By the time he had the RV settled into its site, the meal was done and laid out on the table. She had hoped they'd be able to eat outside, but night was simply coming on too fast.

Their dinner conversation was quiet and thoughtful, and revolved on the subject of her illegitimacy. Though they'd tried to ignore it, it had been on their minds all afternoon.

"Don't you ever wonder about your father?" Peter asked. "Who he was, what he was like, things like that?"

Reluctantly, she nodded and told him the few crumbs of information Mrs. Pidgin had given her, that his name was John Avery, that he was originally from Minnesota, that he liked to travel and worked as a carpenter mainly, it seemed, to support his love of wandering. "Aside from that…" She fell silent again, moving the food around on her plate, then suddenly tossed down her fork. "I know absolutely nothing about him."

Pete looked at her, surprised by her fit of pique. She was thinking about her mother again. He knew it without even asking. *How* he knew, he wasn't certain, but their wordless communications were increasing, their empathetic instincts deepening.

He asked quietly, "Do you blame your mother for that?"

"Yes." She pushed aside her plate. "She had no right to withhold that information. It was part of my very identity. I feel cheated. I feel betrayed." Pete watched pain crease her smooth face. He reached across the table and took her hand in his. He didn't care if it was the wrong thing to do. It was what felt right at the moment.

"Something tells me you're not so much mad at her as hurt."

Slowly, she gave in and nodded. "You know what really hurts? She kept *her* identity a secret from me, too. I used to think I knew her. All those years, the memories I carried, memories I *treasured*…" Mary Elizabeth's voice thinned as some of those memories crowded her.

Giving her head a small shake, she continued, "But suddenly I learn she wasn't that person at all. It's like…" Her hand had gone lifeless in Pete's. "It's like she's died for me all over again."

Her grief tore at him. She'd been through a lot, more than most people had to endure in twenty-seven years. What made it worse was that she was extremely sensitive.

"Have you ever considered that she believed not telling you was the best thing for you? Whether it was or wasn't is irrelevant. It's what she believed was best."

Mary Elizabeth nodded reluctantly. "It couldn't have been an easy decision."

"You would know."

Her eyes met his and filled. "Mrs. Pidgin says Charles threatened to fight for custody of Susan if my mother left him. She believed he'd win, too. That's why she stayed with him and told my real father it was over between them. After that Charles made her promise she'd never tell anyone about her affair. He's an extremely proud person, very conscious of the family's reputation. Mrs. Pidgin thinks that's why they went on to have a third child, so he could show the world nothing was amiss with the Drummonds." A tear spilled down her cheek. "My mother died seven years later—pneumonia that got so bad her heart failed her. Mrs. Pidgin claims it was her heart all along, a problem that started when my father, my real father, left town."

The silence lengthened, made soothing by the plash of the stream outside their open window.

"Sounds like one pitiful mess," Pete finally commented.

"Yes, it does." Embarrassed, she looked aside. "I'm sorry."

"For what?"

"Being such a drag."

"You apologize too much."

"Yeah, but…"

"Yeah, but," he mocked. "Honestly, I don't mind. Who knows, maybe I'll need your shoulder to cry on some day."

Mary Elizabeth broke into a smile that ignited a small fire in his chest. "That, I would pay to see." She got to her feet and began clearing the table. Unexpectedly she said, "Peter, would you mind leaving me alone for about an hour tonight?"

He studied her through narrowed eyes. He was about to ask why and then it happened again; without exchanging a word, he understood. She had an appointment tonight, with Charles Drummond.

"Not at all. My bike needs a workout, anyway."

They took their dishes to the sink and left them to soak. Pete went to the bedroom for his jacket, gloves and helmet. When he returned, Mary Elizabeth was still standing at the sink, eyes fixed on the darkness outside. She looked inconsolably alone.

He swayed on his feet, physically wavering with the indecision that rocked inside him. Finally he just came up to her from behind and wrapped her in his arms.

She stiffened, as he knew she would. "It's okay. I just want to hold you."

He felt her relax. Her shoulders released, her arms softened, she exhaled a held breath. Fitting himself closer, he laid his cheek against her hair. He was surprised to realize he was nervous for her.

Holding her the way he was, he was something more than nervous, but that didn't surprise him. He was getting used to being in a near-constant state of arousal.

Before Mary Elizabeth found that out, though, he gave her a squeeze of encouragement and said, "Give 'em hell." Then he released her and slipped out the door.

Mary Elizabeth waited until the roar of his bike faded before going in search of her tennis racket. She felt distinctly foolish, but it was the best substitute for a punching bag she was able to come up with.

She found the racket deep within the bunk bed over the cab. To get to it, she had to take down her rocking chair, which Pete had fit in there somehow, and two boxes of books.

In the bedroom she tried lifting the racket over her head. It thumped the ceiling. Slowly she swung it downward toward her mattress. On the way it hit the over-the-bed cupboards and grazed a light fixture. No, this wasn't going to work.

A few minutes later she had solved her problem. Outside, working by the pale light that streamed from the RV's windows, she placed a bed pillow, minus its embroidered case, atop a hip-high rock by the stream. Her sense of foolishness had grown acute, even though no one could see her. The nearest campers were too far away, and the RV shielded her from view, anyway.

She lifted the racket in two hands and brought it down experimentally. It landed on the feather pillow with a satisfying wump.

Exhaling, she adjusted her stance, wiggling her bottom and planting her feet like a ball player at bat. Then she lifted the racket again and thought, *Okay, Charles Drummond, this one's for you.* Wump!

In the ensuing stillness, she looked around self-consciously. Nothing stirred. No eyes peeked out of the woods. No twitters arose.

She raised the racket again and thought, *I lived in your house for twenty-seven years without complaining about the way you treated me, but I guess the time has come. You made me miserable, Charles.* She whacked the pillow. *No matter how I tried to please you, you found fault. And I did try. Pleasing you practically became my life's work. But you always made me feel I'd failed or there was something inherently wrong with me.*

She hit the pillow again and paused to take measure of her feelings. Guilt had joined her self-consciousness. What right did she have to complain, she who'd been given the best of everything? Most of the world had it so much worse.

"Excuses," she said out loud, cutting off that train of thought.

Gripping the racket handle, she focused on her grievances again. *Mrs. Pidgin was right. She said if you hadn't
given me those things, people would've wondered why not,
why you'd singled me out. And we all know the worst fate
in life is to have people talk.* She beat the pillow very hard,
then paused once again. She was beginning to feel genuinely irate. *But you did single me out, didn't you? At home
where no one could witness it.*

An episode sprang to mind so unexpectedly, bringing
with it an upsurge of forgotten pain, that she'd pummeled
the pillow several times before she'd even examined the
memory.

How old had she been? Eight, maybe? Nine? She was
riding her bicycle out on the road in front of their house
when Charles approached from the other direction returning
from work. She remembered pedaling hard to meet him at
the mailbox, so hard her leg muscles burned, then bringing
the bike to a skidding stop using the hand brake and ultimately her feet. She was beaming, happy because she'd
made it; she'd gotten to him in time to say hi and give him
a welcome-home hug.

But, reaching for the mail through the open window of
his Lincoln, he met her with a thin-lipped scowl that was
followed by a lecture on how she mustn't drag her feet
when she was riding her bicycle. Didn't she know she was
wearing out her shoes? And shoes were expensive, he said.
What did she think, money grew on trees? He'd gone on
and on, until even now at twenty-seven, Mary Elizabeth
felt shriveled with embarrassment and guilt. She
felt…unlovable.

Damn you, Charles! She clubbed the pillow. *I didn't deserve all those lectures on the cost of things—books,
clothes, even food. You made me feel like a burden just for*

breathing. Susan and Charlie were downright careless with their things, but you never lectured them.

Her insides were shaking and that frightened her. But before she could decide whether to stop or continue this exercise, another memory assailed her—the Father's Day she'd spent hours in her room making a greeting card for Charles, a card she'd found later that night still lying on the chair where he had opened it earlier in the day. It was creased and flattened as if it had been sat on, while on the mantel Susan's and Charlie's store-bought cards were on proud display.

Tears stung her eyes as she remembered that hand-painted gift into which she'd poured so much love.

Damn you, Charles. Maybe you were hurt, too. I was the product of an affair, proof of a betrayal. But I was only a child. I just wanted your love. You shouldn't have taken your feelings out on me.

She hit the pillow so hard she felt the twang of impact up her arms and right into her chest. But she was beyond stopping now. Memories kept rising, pain seizing her, anger pouring out.

And this is for all the A's I got that you never mentioned and all the C's that you did. Mary Elizabeth began to perspire. Her clothing stuck to her back.

And this is for all the times I heard "Why can't you be more like Susan?"

Feathers were beginning to shoot through the ticking.

And this is for the time I had a crush on Kevin Manchester in eighth grade and you said I looked trashy. This memory elicited a double wump, and then one more, a backhand, for good measure. For she truly felt thirteen again, infatuated with the opposite sex for the first time, and totally insecure about the whole business. She remembered the hours she spent studying fashion magazines, felt again the misery of looking at herself in the mirror, the frustration of rearranging her hair, her clothes, her facial expressions. And then, just when she'd thought she might have done something right, Charles had said, "What's wrong with you these days, Mary Elizabeth? You're looking so trashy."

Well, Charles Drummond, let me finally tell you. You're the one who had the problem, not me. I only wish I'd known it then. What you did to me was sick, sick, sick. With each "sick" she pounded the pillow. Her muscles were quivering, her eyes blazed, and feathers were now flying like snow through the torn ticking. Yet she didn't stop.

As the stars grew big in the sky above, she continued to travel the dark roads of her life, reliving old hurts and some that weren't so old, as well.

And about my job, maybe you did pull a few strings, but I was qualified, too, and I did good work. But you never stopped reminding me you'd pulled those strings. You couldn't let me forget that even as an adult I was beholden to you, a burden you had to provide for.

She seemed a woman possessed. Every memory she brought to light was tied to a dozen more, reaching deep into murky places in the heart she hadn't known existed.

And Roger—oooh, now there's an issue that's long overdue....

There were so many grievances she'd buried, so many unkind words that had accrued until she'd actually believed them herself.

But as was inevitable, she eventually gave the racket a swing that would be her last. *It's over, Charles,* she thought. *You're history.* Then she just stood there, breathing hard, arms weak, staring at the battered pillow and the bent racket, and feeling absolutely empty.

After a while, when no other thoughts came to fill the

void, she gathered up what she could of the pillow, stuffed it in a trash bin and went inside. She drank a full glass of water, noticing that the hand that held the glass was shaking, like her stomach and her legs.

Turning from the sink, she bumped her knee on the rocker she'd taken down earlier from the bunk. It seemed to be waiting there on purpose.

The chair had come from her bedroom back home and was the only piece of furniture she'd felt comfortable removing from Charles's house. Her mother had bought it when Mary Elizabeth was born and had used it to rock her while she was nursing. Mary Elizabeth didn't remember those days, but she did remember being rocked to sleep as a toddler, especially after nightmares. She also recalled sitting in her mother's lap and being read to in that chair, and later being taught to cross-stitch.

Too weary even to sigh, she sank into the padded seat and huddled like a person pulled to safety from a raging sea. She set to rocking and closed her eyes, seeking balm in the rhythmic movement. Instinctively, she crossed her arms over her stomach, as if comforting and protecting the child within.

And that was exactly how Pete found her when he returned—asleep, arms wrapped around herself, a childlike peace reposing on her face.

CHAPTER TWELVE

PETE DIDN'T HAVE TO ASK how she felt the next morning. He found her wading in the cold stream, singing "Oh, Shenandoah" off-key at the top of her lungs. Standing on the bank, he scratched his bare chest and grinned.

She'd been so wiped out the previous night she hadn't even awakened when he'd carried her to bed. Which was no surprise. Their day had started early and had been active right to the end.

Pete thought back on all they'd done, all the ground they'd covered—both physical and otherwise—and felt something close to astonishment. Time had never seemed so elastic, so unbounded or saturable to experiences, not even when he was a boy. Either he was having one helluva vacation or Mary Elizabeth had taken him clear into another dimension.

She noticed him standing on the bank and broke into one of her thousand-watt smiles. His stomach hollowed out with the sensation he imagined he'd get if he were falling off a sixty-story building.

"Good morning," she said, her long honey-and-ash hair gleaming with morning sun. Her eyes met his, and when he should have looked away he didn't. Neither did she. They just stood there, openly taking pleasure in each other, and in that moment Pete felt a sense of inevitability about the course of this day.

"Oh, your eye is looking so much better today. There's just the slightest tinge of yellow."

He nodded, glad she'd noticed, glad she liked what she saw. She was wearing the maternity jeans he'd bought her, rolled to the knees, and the shirt that read Baby under Construction, with a bulky red cardigan slung over it all.

She plucked at the shirt. "I know I don't really need it yet but..." She just shrugged.

But you're feeling pretty damn good this morning about being pregnant, he finished silently.

"Looks nice on you."

She waded to shore and dried her feet on a bath towel. Admiring the curve of her ankle, he noticed the ground nearby was strewn with feathers. Had a duck or bird been mauled here by some woodland animal?

"Where are we going today?" Her warm brandy voice scattered his thoughts of ducks and maulings. Morning sun lit flecks of gold in her brown eyes.

"I thought we'd get on the Skyline Drive and head south. It's the touristy thing to do, but in this case I'll make an exception."

"Oh?" She tilted her head, drawing attention to the sweeping length of her neck, a neck that seemed made for kissing. "Nice driving?"

He clicked his tongue. "Most scenic route there is through these old mountains. It becomes the Blue Ridge Parkway farther south."

"Oh! Are we heading toward the Blue Ridge Mountains?"

"Uh-huh."

Her expression took on a dreamy softness as she said, "There's just so much..." She didn't finish her thought, just lifted her arms to the horizon as if she were embracing all that it encompassed.

Yes, so much, he thought, realizing with some surprise he was enjoying showing her the world. Enjoying? He was having the time of his life.

"Is there anything in particular you'd like to see today? Any place you'd like to go?"

Mary Elizabeth's smooth brow furrowed in thought. Suddenly she brightened. "I remember reading about some wonderful caves in this region. You know, the kind with stalagmites and stalactites?"

"Caves?" Pete nodded. "Sure. Why not?"

Coming around the RV, Mary Elizabeth noticed his Triumph parked by the door where he'd left it the previous night. "Can we also spend part of today riding?" she asked, swinging her leg over the leather seat.

Pete grinned. "You look mighty pretty sitting there, Mary Elizabeth." After trying out other names, he'd decided he liked "Mary Elizabeth" best, after all.

"Well?" she prodded. "If I'm supposed to be a serious girlfriend of yours, won't your family expect me to ride with you?"

"Sorry. In your condition you don't need all that shake-rattle-and-rolling." *Besides, motorcycles are dangerous.* The thought popped into his head from out of nowhere.

No, not nowhere. He couldn't count the number of times he'd skidded on roadside sand or hit a pothole and almost gone over the bars—and he was a careful driver. And what about his friend Mark who'd tangled with a Buick? A minor collision if he'd been in a car, but instead he'd died.

Pete scrubbed his face with two hands. Where were these thoughts coming from? He'd never worried about being hurt before.

"Can I at least sit here awhile?" She clutched the handlegrips and hunched forward, trying to look menacing.

And Pete thought, *If I died now, I'd never see that funny*

face again, never know if she had a boy or a girl. And what if she needed my help...?

Suddenly he began to think that maybe it wouldn't be such a big chore to drive from Tampa to Sarasota every once in a while. Maybe he did have the staying power to see her through her pregnancy. He might even go to Lamaze classes with her, be her birthing partner if she wanted. He'd gone to a few classes with Lindy, so it wasn't as if he didn't know what he was getting into. And after the baby was adopted, she'd need someone to help her adjust, get back in the swing...

Pete emerged from his thoughts with a start. Oh, hell! He couldn't mean what he was thinking. He couldn't really want to complicate his life by getting involved with a woman who had so many needs. Could he?

He noticed Mary Elizabeth looking at him curiously, still waiting for an answer. "Sure you can sit there. Have a ball," he said with more gruffness than her simple question should have elicited. "But it goes back on the trailer right after breakfast."

They were rolling again by nine. Mary Elizabeth felt wonderful. Much of her exhilaration came from having unburdened herself of the grievances she'd harbored while living as Charles Drummond's daughter. Well, some of the grievances. She wasn't naive enough to think that beating up one bed pillow had rid her of a lifetime of anguish. But it certainly had helped.

Just being on the road gladdened her, too. As Pete had predicted, the scenery along the Drive and the Parkway was magnificent—the endlessly rolling peaks, the mysterious, mist-shrouded valleys, the silver-blue sparkle of lakes and streams.

That day they stopped at three scenic lookouts and snapped innumerable pictures of each other with her Pentax. They visited a cavern and were appropriately awed by its soaring walls and immense columns of colorful, glittering stone. They saw a natural bridge purported to be a wonder of the world, and at a roadside stand bought gaudy key chains in the shape of the state of Virginia.

But mostly what Mary Elizabeth saw that day was Peter Mitchell. He filled her eyes, consumed her thoughts, and made everything else a minor distraction.

When he spoke she hung on every soft, dark note. When he walked, she reveled in his manly stride. She loved the way his clothes fit, how the blue of his shirt picked up the blue of his eyes. She loved the habit his hair had of curling over his ears. She even loved the size and shape of his feet. What Mary Elizabeth had trouble admitting, though, was that, quite simply, she loved *him.*

The thought stymied her. How could that be after less than a week? In six days people could discover they were attracted to each other, maybe even blindly infatuated. But love, real love, took time.

So maybe what she was feeling was just attraction?

Well, if that was so, it was the damnedest attraction she'd ever experienced! When in her life had she ever been fascinated by how long a man brushed his teeth? When had she daydreamed about his feet?

It was the intimacy of this arrangement, she told herself, leaping on Peter's excuse from the previous day. She'd never lived in such tight quarters with a man before, and the man in question wasn't just any ordinary man. Peter was very nearly overwhelming.

Improbable as it still seemed to her, she knew sparks were jumping both ways. She felt it in the heat of his eyes as they followed her, in the countless times he touched her for no apparent reason, his hand lingering, fingers stroking.

And of course there was that kiss yesterday, that sweet, drugging kiss that had left her addicted and craving more.

The trouble was, as the day wore on, she became less and less sure what she would do if he kissed her again. The issue wasn't that she still felt "cheap." She'd laid that warped idea to rest last night. The issue was making love, which was where any degree of physical contact between them now would lead. She wanted to. Oh, how she wanted to. But where would that leave her emotionally when they parted on Sunday?

Despite her misgivings, the idea of making love with Peter occupied her mind with increasing frequency. What would it be like? she wondered a dozen times that day. He was so different from Roger. Physically, he was so much larger. His hands were callused, the tendons of his arms hard as oak.

She imagined that what he knew about lovemaking lifted him head and shoulders above Roger, as well. Which led to some fairly warm images cropping up in her mind... which lengthened to steamy scenarios...which had her sweating in her seat more often than she cared to admit.

Would it happen, then? The question hung between them every time they spoke or even just looked at each other.

Lord, what was she thinking? Of course it wouldn't happen. Peter had made it perfectly clear he didn't get involved with anyone he wasn't going to see again. It was a matter of principle with him. He'd also said he wasn't interested in serious relationships, and in her condition she deserved more from a man.

But Peter had said lots of things these past six days and then changed his mind, and in his eyes she thought she saw a change of mind. So, ultimately, would their making love be up to her? Would it depend on whether she was willing to accept an on-the-road affair? Strong enough to let it go in four days? It was a question that rode with her all day, unanswered.

They made it all the way to the North Carolina border that day, compensating for the slow-going scenic route by switching to the interstate for the last two hours of their drive. They found a state park about ten miles from the highway and settled in with a couple of hours of daylight to spare.

They were cooking up their supper—linguini and clam sauce from a can—when Mary Elizabeth suddenly announced, "I've decided I'm going to call Roger."

For some reason Pete's lungs seized up on him. "When?"

"Right after we eat."

The spoon he was stirring the sauce with scraped faster against the pan. "Hey, there's no need to rush."

"Yes, there is." She stirred the pasta and their elbows bumped. "I'm eager to get it over with, to be free of this whole mess."

Pete walked away from the stove to set the table and try not to think of the alternative, that she might not end up free but mired even deeper than she was now.

GOLD FROM THE SETTING SUN gilded the tops of the towering pines that edged the clearing outside the recreation hall. Mary Elizabeth stood inside, phone cord stretched to its maximum, gazing out the window, waiting for Roger to pick up at the other end. Outside, Peter was shooting baskets with two teenage girls and a boy. The girls were flirting.

"Hello?"

The smile dropped from her lips. She swung from the window and stammered, "R-Roger?"

"Who's... Mary Elizabeth?" His voice slid up an octave.

"Yes. Hi." Sweat trickled down her sides. "How are you, Rog?"

He ignored her polite inquiry. "Where are you, for God's sake? People here are pretty worried. Are you all right?"

She wet her dry lips. "Yes, I'm fine. I'm in North Carolina, just over the Virginia border." She laughed nervously. "Why are people worried?"

"North Carolina? My God, Mary Elizabeth! Your father told me..."

"I know. Chicago. Never mind that right now. Why are people worried?"

"Oh. Oh, well, your wallet showed up a couple of days ago. Some woman in upstate New York found it on her front lawn. Your housekeeper almost had a stroke, and your father's ready to notify the FBI. You'd better call home."

Mary Elizabeth clutched her head. "I will. I promise." Poor Mrs. Pidgin. She'd forgotten, the woman had been expecting her to phone when she reached Chloe's, two days ago.

"Listen, Roger, the reason I'm calling...I have something to tell you."

"Oh?" He sounded wary.

"It concerns you and me and the last week we were dating."

"Oh?" he repeated, his wariness intensifying.

"I don't know any painless way to say this, so I'll just come right out and say it. Roger, I'm pregnant."

Silence roared between them for several incredulous seconds.

"Are you sure?"

"Yes. I'm almost three months along."

"Three..." Another span of silence enfolded them. "Is that the reason you've moved?"

"Yes. One of the reasons."

"To North Carolina?" He seemed to want to find something in her location to be astounded at.

"No, I'm on my way to Florida, to my friend Chloe's. I'm just taking my time, going the tourist route, you know?" She heard him swallow, and swallow again. "I'm calling because I thought you might want to know." She massaged her forehead. "About the baby, I mean."

"Oh, uh, yes, of course. Do you need money?" Roger's voice had lowered, although she was pretty sure he was alone in his apartment.

"No," she said. "I'm planning to have the baby and give it up for adoption."

"In Florida?"

"Yes." What was this obsession he had with states? "Do you have a problem with that? Adoption, I mean."

"Uh...no." He exhaled so hard the sound of rushing air hurt her ear. "Actually, that seems like a very wise plan." His voice had loosened noticeably. It struck her as almost comical that for weeks she had feared he'd want to marry her. Apparently, that was the furthest thing from his mind.

He sounded practically magnanimous when he asked, "Would you like me to fly down there for the birth or anything?"

"No. That isn't necessary. I'll have Chloe. But thanks for offering. It's really decent of you." And it was. Why had she been so frightened to call?

"Your father doesn't know about this, does he?"

"Yes, he does."

"But not that I'm..."

"Yes, that too."

"Oh, God. I had lunch with him just this afternoon. He didn't say a word."

"That's Charles Drummond for you. He doesn't exactly

like information of this sort getting around. If you don't say anything, I guarantee he won't, either.''

"Well, that's something, I suppose." Roger was quiet awhile. "If I tell you something in confidence, will you promise to keep it under your hat?''

"Roger, I'm a thousand miles away. Who am I going to tell?''

"Okay. All right. It's just that nobody knows yet except my parents. I'm thinking of running for town council next fall. I don't need to tell you how damaging this news could be if it leaked during an election campaign.''

Mary Elizabeth felt disillusionment creeping over her, like spidery frost over a window. "You needn't worry, Rog. No one will hear it from me.''

"Thanks. I knew you'd understand. Now, are you sure you don't need anything?''

"I'm sure.''

"Well, if you do, let me know. How've you been feeling?''

"Very well, thanks. I—''

He interrupted with a nervous laugh. "God, this is just so weird, you pregnant. It still hasn't fully registered. It's been hitting me in bits and pieces.''

She held her breath, wondering if paternal feelings were coming in bits and pieces, too. "Rog, I've got to ask you something—purely hypothetical, of course. What if I were to keep the baby?'' She heard a small gasp. "It's just a what-if.''

"Okay,'' he responded shakily. "What if?''

"Would you acknowledge it or want to help me raise it?''

"Gee, I don't know.''

"I don't mean to put you on the spot. I know it's a

difficult question, especially when you factor in running for political office.''

He sighed. "I suppose I would. It would be my child. Yes, I guess I'd make room for it."

"But would it be an imposition?"

"Well, sure. You can understand that, can't you? A child would be an imposition on you, too. More so. You'd be its primary parent. Think of the effect it would have on your career. And what about your social life?"

Mary Elizabeth watched a parade of ants scurrying single-file along the baseboard.

"Aw, hell, Mary Elizabeth. It isn't just my running for office. It's…" He hesitated.

"It's what, Rog?"

"Well," he hemmed, "I've met somebody."

"Ah. Say no more."

"I'm sorry for feeling the way I do. It's just…"

"No need to apologize. I understand."

"I hope so. Well, maybe it's a good thing your question was only hypothetical." Tension with an undercurrent of challenge buzzed over the wire.

"Mmm. Good thing." She poised the toe of her shoe over the line of ants, feeling momentarily evil, then drew it back. From the other end of the line came the familiar ring of Roger's door buzzer.

"Sounds like you've got company."

"Yes."

"You'd better go." Irrationally, she felt a pang of regret, for him, for her, for the love they'd never quite achieved.

"Stay in touch, Mary Elizabeth," he said softly. "I mean that."

"Sure. You, too." Mary Elizabeth hung up the receiver and dropped back against the wall. Her emotions were so tangled she didn't know whether to laugh or cry.

Roger's disinclination to acknowledge the baby left her hollow with disappointment. Peter had almost convinced her that her dismal opinion of Roger was incorrect, that it had been unfairly tainted by her relationship with Charles. But Roger had just confirmed her conviction. He *would* consider the baby a burden, and though he hadn't said it, he *would* resent it in time. She knew it as surely as she knew anything.

Oddly, however, Roger's disinterest also put her at ease. Without his interference, she was now free, really free, to go about her life and make her own decisions regarding the baby.

But most of all, Mary Elizabeth felt relieved. She'd done it, made the call, faced the dragon, and in so doing had rid herself of the guilt she'd lived with while Roger had remained in the dark. She'd also beat Charles to the punch and jettisoned her fear of not knowing Roger's reaction. Peter was right; she'd taken the reins of her life into her own hands and become empowered.

How did one man get to be so smart? she wondered, pushing away from the wall and gazing out the window. He was still shooting baskets with the teenagers. A little girl, four or five years old, had joined them, and Peter had lifted her onto his shoulders. Her giggles, as she dunked the ball, brought a smile to Mary Elizabeth's eyes and an unsettling image to her heart—of Peter as a father.

She gave her head a hard shake. What foolishness was that, casting a confirmed bachelor into the role of parent? She swung back to the phone with a stern reminder she had one more call to make.

Pete was waiting for her on the steps outside. "Well?" he asked as they walked the path back to their campsite.

"Roger took the news well. He offered me money and

his company during labor. But bottom line is, he isn't really interested in becoming a father.''

They continued to walk, the silence between them so dense it practically throbbed.

Without warning, Pete stopped, hooked an arm around her neck and pulled her to him, holding her close, holding her tight. His muscles trembled. He didn't say anything, and neither did Mary Elizabeth. She was rather too astounded to speak. She hadn't realized he was so concerned about the outcome.

As they stood on the path, the resinous scent of pine spiced the dusk. The trill of a bird she'd never heard before rode the warm southern air. And Mary Elizabeth thought, *This is a moment I'll remember forever. This piny scent. That bird. And Peter's wordless rejoicing.*

Back at the campsite they built a fire. The sun had just dipped behind the farthest ridge, but an afterglow of peach still warmed the western sky, throwing the distant peaks into hazy relief.

Pete and Mary Elizabeth sat on a blanket, watching the fire, talking quietly about her call to Roger and nibbling on a late dessert of cheese and green grapes.

Pete was grateful she hadn't asked him to explain that incident on the path. He still found the depth of his relief unsettling. It confirmed his suspicion he was beginning to have feelings for Mary Elizabeth. Not just appreciation of her fine looks. Not just physical desire. *Feelings*. He hadn't let that happen since his divorce.

Mary Elizabeth sank her teeth into a grape, and while she was chewing mumbled, ''Oh, I called home, too.'' Pete's head swung around. ''Well, to Mrs. Pidgin's. I wasn't ready to talk to Charles.'' She then explained how her wallet had been sent to the house in Maine. ''I needed to let Mrs. P. know I was all right. She has too fertile an imagination for her own good.'' She smiled, betraying her deep affection for the housekeeper.

''My license and other important ID were still in it, so I asked her to ship it to your sister Pam's first thing tomorrow.''

''Oh, is that why you interrupted the best game of one on one I ever played to ask for her address?''

''Uh-huh. That way I'll be able to drive legally from there to Chloe's after the wedding.''

''Smart thinking.'' Pete noticed her arching and pressing the small of her back. ''Come here. Scoot around front and rest against me. You look uncomfortable.'' Bending one knee, he made a cradle for her between his legs and held out a hand.

She smiled. ''Thanks.'' With a sigh of relief, she settled back, into the rise and fall of his chest, into the warmth of his arms lying crossed over hers.

''Did you also tell your Mrs. Pidgin how you've been traveling?'' Pete rubbed his chin over the silk of her hair.

''No. I hate lying to her, but she'd just worry herself sick, wondering who you were and if I was all right.''

Pete adjusted their fit, tucking her closer, his arms coming to rest right under her breasts. Under her voluminous new T-shirt she was all womanly curves, soft and enticing. It took a moment before he found his voice. ''You did well today, Mary Elizabeth. Got a lot done.''

''I guess. At least I handled the mess I left behind me. Now all I need to tackle is the future.'' She moaned and buried herself deeper in his safe, encircling embrace.

He laughed. ''You'll be all right.''

''Easy for you to say. You've got a job. You've got a condo.''

''There you go again, underestimating yourself.''

"I'm not underestimating myself. I'm simply being a realist."

He chuckled. "Yeah, but your vision of reality is skewed."

She tilted back her head and gazed up into his fire-lit face. "Spoken by a man who buys lava lamps and thinks they're neat."

"Cool, Mary Elizabeth. Cool. *You* think things are neat."

He bent forward, smiling against her cheek, and she thought, *This is reckless. But frankly, I don't care anymore.*

She laid her hand on his knee, and he thought, *This is going to get us into trouble. But when have I ever run from trouble?*

They sat in silence, listening to the crackle and hiss of the fire, feeling their heartbeats accelerating, both gripped by that strange sensation of inevitability that had begun the day.

"Mary Elizabeth?" Peter's voice rumbled, deep and soft, but something about it sounded different, a note that hinted at...vulnerability?

She sat up and turned to face him, laying her hands on his chest. She needed to see what that uncharacteristic note was about. "Yes?"

His brows were low slashes over his eyes. All the lines of his face had gone serious. "The other day when I said I was against marrying..."

Her pulse quickened.

"I want you to know that isn't a decision I made casually simply because I like my freedom."

She could see that whatever he was thinking about was distressing him. She combed her fingers through the hair over his ears and watched his eyes. For a moment she thought he'd changed his mind. He looked past her, his mouth tight.

But then he said, "The reason I intend to stay single is—" he swallowed "—I've been married already."

Mary Elizabeth felt the earth spin. Everything blurred with the speed of it, and then abruptly settled. "Married. Ah." Her composure amazed her.

"I was young and it lasted only a couple of years. But it was a painful-enough experience to turn me off marriage for a lifetime."

Under her hands his chest heaved like a bellows. "What happened?" she inquired. Her face warmed immediately. "I'm sorry. I shouldn't pry."

"It's okay." His face looked craggy in the flickering firelight. He drew a long breath and then proceeded to tell her about Cindy, about her endless insecurities, about everything.

"Toward the end of our marriage, things were really bad." By this point in his narrative, his eyes appeared lost, his face bleak. "She knew I wanted to leave her, so she upped the ante in her games. She said if I left, she'd kill herself."

Mary Elizabeth hadn't expected that. She flinched. "Dear Lord, she...didn't, did she?"

He shook his head. "But that wasn't for lack of trying. They were feeble attempts, though. She wasn't really suicidal. She only meant to scare me." He looked into Mary Elizabeth's eyes and his mouth lifted in a sad, lopsided smile. On that look rode a wealth of things unsaid, a wealth of pain undivulged.

"Her behavior also convinced me to leave the marriage as soon as possible, not just for my own good, but for hers, too. I wasn't familiar with the term 'enabler' back then, but

I must've understood the basic concept and realized that's what I was for her.''

He paused, eyes fixed on the past. ''Thank God we didn't have a baby. I can't imagine how that would've complicated things.''

After a protracted silence, Mary Elizabeth asked, ''What happened to her?''

''Oh, I made sure she moved back with her folks and got psychiatric help.''

A muscle pulled in his cheek, the slightest of reactions that nonetheless caused Mary Elizabeth to wonder what he meant by making sure she got psychiatric help. Had he paid? And for how long?

''The last I heard, she'd moved to Denver and married and divorced twice more.''

Pete stroked Mary Elizabeth's arm, his fingers coming to rest over hers against his chest. ''So, that's the way it is with me.'' He gazed straight into her eyes. ''I just thought you ought to know.''

Under her hand his heart beat hard, an echo of her own. She suddenly knew exactly why he'd shared this part of himself with her. He wanted her to understand, really understand, he was serious about not wanting to ever marry again, so that if she got involved with him she did so with eyes wide open.

So it *was* up to her, just as she'd feared all day. But as she sat there watching this magnificent man, she realized she had already arrived at a decision. She leaned forward, slowly, and pressed a kiss to his firm, dry lips.

Backing away, she momentarily feared she'd misread the situation—he sat so still—until he said, ''You're sure?'' The dark undercurrents of passion in his voice sent heat spilling through her. With her eyes wide open and fixed on his, she nodded.

CHAPTER THIRTEEN

WATCHING THE SOFT CORONA of firelight shining off Mary Elizabeth's pale hair, Pete thought she was just about the most beautiful sight there was. Angelic almost. He might live to regret this some day, a day when he was facing the long drive to Sarasota, or sitting through another boring Lamaze class. And what if he discovered she really didn't interest him, after all?

Unfortunately, he didn't care about any of those what-ifs at present. He only listened to the need coursing through him, thrilling in the knowledge that it coursed through her, as well.

He dipped his head forward and finally took what he'd been dreaming about night and day, sighing his pleasure into her mouth. What a sweet mouth it was, too, warm and soft and eager. He immediately wanted to immerse himself in its mysteries and ravage its secrets.

But he didn't. He was too concerned about rushing her. Although she wasn't a novice to lovemaking, he sensed limitations to her experience that caused him trepidation. The last thing he wanted was to overwhelm her. He needed to move carefully. He wanted this first time to be special.

He was somewhat confused, therefore, when she tipped back onto the blanket, taking him down with her. And he was more than confused as she plowed her fingers through his hair, her nails scraping his scalp, and joined her open mouth to his once more. Pete momentarily lost control. The

night swirled, the stars and the earth and everything between, with Mary Elizabeth at its center.

Fighting for breath, he broke the seal of their kiss and
buried his face in her hair. He needed to catch his bearings.

"We don't have to do this if you don't want." She
sounded a little embarrassed.

"Don't want?" Pete laughed, rolling onto his side and
pulling her against him. "You enjoy seeing men explode,
do you?" He felt her smile against his neck.

He got to his feet, towing her with him. "I think we
ought to go somewhere less public, though."

While she folded the blanket, he doused the campfire.
He felt like a raw kid again, excited and scared, and the
feeling amazed him. In thirty-six years he'd had lots of first
times with women, but this felt like *the* first time.

As soon as the door of the RV closed behind them, he
turned her into his arms and kissed her. Mary Elizabeth
dropped the blanket and kissed him back, fitting herself to
him, winding her arms around his shoulders, holding him
tight. Her lips glided over his, supple and seductive, then
opened, inviting him to deepen their union.

Pete started to burn, a fire that kindled at his center and
quickly spread to the rest of him. Tipping his head to the
side, he fit his mouth to hers more aggressively, tasting her,
circling the inner softness of her lips, delving the deeper
secrets within. She responded with a low wanting sound,
and then her tongue ventured forward to meet his. He let
her explore, and explore she did, her forays becoming more
emboldened with each passing second. Dear Lord, what
was she doing to him? Maybe he was wrong about needing
to move carefully. He was beginning to fear he was the
one who was being swept along too fast.

He tried to slow down, tucking her head under his chin
while he caught his breath. But even the innocent slide of

his hands across her back became for him an erotic act. He spread his hands wide, palms rasping against her cotton shirt, fingers exploring each ridge and hollow from her nape to her firm little bottom.

He soon realized that trying to slow down was impossible. He couldn't remember the last time he'd wanted a woman so badly. He kissed her again, caressing her breasts with one hand while he held her to him with the other. The hunger roaring inside both of them radiated like heat from a furnace.

He left her mouth to trail kisses along her neck. She moved against him, arching, inviting him to continue his journey south. He obliged, kissing her through her clothing, feeling her respond even through layers of fabric.

Looking up, he saw her eyes were passion-glazed, her lips full and flushed with desire. He returned to them, kissing her deeply, deeper, backing her up to the refrigerator and resting against her—although resting was hardly the term for what they were doing.

What *were* they doing, he wondered with the last part of his brain that was still functioning—two grown adults, behaving like oversexed teenagers? She was so responsive though, he couldn't help himself. God, so responsive.

He thrust against her, consumed by a building, driving lust. With a soft desperate cry, she lifted her left foot off the floor and wrapped it around the back of his right knee.

Pete curled his hands under her and lifted her to meet him. She made it easy, practically shimmying up his body, using the refrigerator for leverage. She looked wild and wanton, and Pete wanted nothing more than to be wild and wanton with her.

Against her mouth he growled, "Let's go someplace more comfortable."

But she shook her head, blond hair flying. "No time," she gasped.

He didn't realize how close she was to completion until she emitted a breathless little cry and her body tautened in his arms. He watched, somewhat dazed, as her head fell back and she cried out, her moist heat burning through her clothing and his.

He held her tight, and when she finally finished shuddering, he gently eased her to her feet. Holding her close, Pete stroked her hair and smiled in satisfaction, even though his own body still thrummed with need.

Her head lay heavily on his breastbone while she fought to catch her breath. Her hands rested on his arms, slack-fingered. He could feel her racing heartbeat slowly decelerating.

She remained in that position so long that Pete finally tipped up her chin, thinking she might've gone to sleep. He wanted to see her face at this moment, wanted to look into her eyes.

What he saw was not what he expected. Instead of a soft-mouthed, dreamy-eyed woman floating in the afterglow of orgasm, Mary Elizabeth looked distraught, her eyes luminous with unshed tears. His first thought was that he'd hurt her.

"Are you all right?" He pulled her away from the refrigerator, checking to see if maybe he'd driven her against the door handle. He smoothed his hands down her back, up her arms, touched her cheek, her hair, wanting to find the source of her pain.

She shook her head, never meeting his eyes. "I'm all right."

His second fear was that she was still a victim of Charles's warped influence, that she was feeling she'd done something tawdry.

"I'm all right," she repeated. "Just feeling a little ridiculous."

"Oh, sweetheart." He pulled her to him in relief, folding her close, wanting to laugh but knowing better. "You should never feel ridiculous about what just happened."

Her breath warmed his chest in a long, displeased sigh. "Oh, really. How would you feel if it had happened to you?"

"If you had held out for half a minute more, you might've found out." He smiled gently. "But you're right. I'd feel ridiculous." He released her but continued to hold her by the shoulders. "But with you... It's different with a woman. I feel flattered, Mary Elizabeth. Honest-to-God flattered." He scrunched down a few inches to meet her sullen eyes and let her see he was sincere.

"Yeah, well..." Her gaze slid off to one side. But he could see she was thinking about it. One corner of her mouth tightened, forming a dimple in her cheek. "Some society we live in. A man prematurely climaxes and he's considered a flop. A woman does it and the man's ego gets pumped up."

"It *is* kinda crazy, isn't it." Pete smiled as the comedy in the situation struck him. He watched her emerging from her embarrassment, her face melting into a matching smile.

"Then you're not disappointed?" she asked. "You don't think I'm a failure at this sort of thing?"

"Are you kidding? How can I be disappointed when you've just proved you're absolutely crazy about me?"

Her eyes widened. "Oh! The arrogance of the man!" she gasped, swatting his arm and suppressing a laugh, which bubbled out, anyway.

Pete caught up her wrists. "You are. Admit it."

"In your dreams," she scoffed. They were both laughing now for no apparent reason Pete could discern, and he thought, *This is amazing, this relationship we have, this resilient, always-surprising relationship.*

The thought made what happened next flow as naturally as breathing. He released her wrists, gathered her close, rested his cheek on the crown of her head and rocked her in an embrace of pure affection. Their jovial mood slipped away, and when they gazed at each other a moment later it was as a man and a woman aware of their mutual respect and shared need.

Pete lightly fingered a strand of her hair, then traced the contour of her cheek while she stood before him, immobile, shivering under his sweet exploration. With his thumb he outlined her lips, coming to rest on the lower one full center. His eyes darkened and his soft, sinful voice whispered, "How about we try doing it right this time, Mary Elizabeth?"

She swayed on her feet like a woman under a hypnotist's trance. "I thought you'd never ask."

TO AWAKEN IN THE ARMS of Peter Mitchell defied description. Mary Elizabeth's gaze roamed his face, from the sun-creases around his still-closed eyes to his irregular hairline to the small mole on his right cheek. She thought she could look at that face forever and never get enough.

They lay on their sides on her narrow bed, his arm heavy across her waist, hers tucked against his chest, their legs entwined.

They'd tried to be sensible last night, tried separating after they'd made love, but she hadn't gotten any sleep with him gone from her bed. She'd just lain there in the dark, eyes wide open, restive, thinking about what had happened.

She'd never known making love could be that wonderful. Peter had taken such slow, thorough care with her, lifting her to a height of arousal she'd thought she might die from—and then keeping her there until she was mindless and virtually begging for release. And when it came, oh...

She hadn't realized he was still awake and restive, too, until he whispered her name. She'd answered by throwing aside the covers and making room for him. Then, what had been on their minds became reality for a second time, and a third.

Buttery morning sunshine poured across the room, spilling over Peter's smooth shoulder and into his tousled black hair. Outside, mockingbirds experimented with song. Other campers were stirring. Pots and utensils clinked. Voices carried on the early stillness. And Mary Elizabeth thought, To be able to wake like this every day of one's life would be better than having all the riches on earth.

She was so deeply happy that she began to think she'd made a grave mistake in making love with Peter. Already she didn't know how she was going to say goodbye to him come Sunday. But say goodbye she would. She had no choice. She wanted to think that he shared what she felt, that there was something that drew them and bound them that went beyond mere sensuality. But no words of love had been spoken last night, no mention of a shared future. But then, she hadn't expected any, so she had no reason to complain now. And she wouldn't. Knowing what he'd gone through with Cindy, she wouldn't ever push the issue. She couldn't ask of him what he couldn't give.

She eased onto her back and stared out the window at the brightening sky through the trees. No, making love with Peter hadn't been a mistake. It had been beautiful and special, a memory she would treasure all her life.

As she lay there, with the glow of his loving still lighting her eyes, she realized also that *she* felt beautiful this morning, *she* felt special.

Her hand drifted to her stomach, and she smiled. Her

entire being seemed to be singing with emotion—happiness, optimism, and yes, maternal love for the little person developing inside her. She couldn't deny it any longer. Her love for this baby—her baby—had been growing steadily, day by day. So had her hopes for it and her dreams.

As she lay there watching the golden sunlight slide into the high branches of the trees, the truth quietly slid into her heart: she wanted to keep this baby. She wanted to love it and nurture it and share in its life. Until now she had felt inadequate, unable to provide for a baby. But she wasn't inadequate. She had a great deal to offer as a mother. In fact, she might even become a great mother. Why hadn't she seen it sooner?

She turned her head and let her gaze caress the man beside her. She wanted to wake him and tell him how she felt. She wanted him to know she'd just arrived at a miraculous new decision, to keep her baby. She wanted to run outside and shout the news to the world.

But she didn't wake Peter. He might think her idea was imprudent or consider her fickle. Neither did she run outside. Her decision to keep her baby was no one's business but her own. Besides, the idea was so new she needed to hold it to herself a little longer. So she just closed her eyes, tucked herself into Peter's warmth, and when he woke and asked her why she was smiling, she only kissed his cheek and said it was because of him.

In a sense, that was right.

THEY MADE IT ALL THE WAY to Georgia that day. Pete considered taking a swing into the Smokies. He loved those misty old mountains and wanted to share them with Mary Elizabeth. But visiting the Smokies would take them too far off course, so he continued on a southerly route through the Carolinas.

It wasn't very interesting driving—he could've made it so if he'd had a mind to—but the scenery didn't seem to matter that much anymore. Everything that was important in the world had condensed to the interior of this RV. To Mary Elizabeth.

He had hoped making love with her wouldn't be as good as he'd suspected. But it was. And then some.

You're in deep trouble now, boy, he admitted as they crossed the South Carolina line. But funny thing was, he was laughing when he admitted it.

They made love twice that day. That, ultimately, was what Pete remembered about Wednesday. They'd pretended interest in food or a certain tourist site, but all they'd really wanted was an excuse to stop and surrender to their rekindled needs.

Somewhere along the way—was it during the tour of that restored antebellum mansion they visited?—Pete decided he definitely wanted to continue seeing Mary Elizabeth after they got to Florida. They had something truly special going on between them, something he couldn't possibly say goodbye to on Sunday. As for seeing her through her pregnancy, of course he had the staying power. And of course he'd help her through the birth. He couldn't imagine not helping her. And after the adoption, they would have all the time in the world just to enjoy each other.

That night as he was showering, he decided he should broach the subject soon. Sooner than soon. Immediately. He had noticed her sinking into a pensive mood a few times that day and suspected she was feeling secretly upset about their relationship. How could she not when he'd led her to believe he didn't want to see her after this road trip?

With a towel tucked at his waist, he sat on the edge of her bed where she lay reading. She put down her book and stroked his damp arm.

"Hi." She rolled toward him and pressed a kiss to his knee. "Something on your mind?"

"Mmm." He clasped her hands to stop their roaming. "I've been doing some thinking about us, and I've come to the conclusion that not seeing each other after Sunday doesn't make sense."

She looked up at him with a startled sort of expression on her face. "You want to continue seeing me?" she repeated. "Dating, you mean?"

"Yes."

"Oh."

It wasn't quite the reaction he'd expected. His disappointment must have shown because she sat up and pressed her cheek to his. "Of course. That would be lovely."

Pete wondered why getting closer to this woman felt so much like drifting apart. "Are you sure that's what you want?"

Her eyes filled quite suddenly. "Oh, yes." Her voice broke over the affirmation. But again Pete sensed a contradictory tug within her that he couldn't explain.

"That leaves us with a slight problem, though," he said, lying down alongside her. "It renders the story we made up about ourselves pretty useless."

She turned on her side, looking confused. "How so?"

"Well, if we go ahead with it and tell my family we met last winter while you were on vacation, et cetera, et cetera, what will they think when we continue to see each other and your pregnancy begins to show? I'll tell you what they'll think. Either the baby is mine, or it's someone else's and you were fooling around while you were supposed to be pining away for me up in Maine. Either way I'm mincemeat."

She didn't smile. "Oh, I see. What do you want to do, then?"

"As I've said before, the truth keeps things simple." He lifted himself over her and kissed her long and deep. She didn't respond. She seemed a shell of herself.

He backed away, frowning. "Do you have a better idea?"

Mary Elizabeth stared at his chest, trying to calm her speeding heart. *I've got to tell him,* she thought. *My wanting to keep the baby will make a difference.* She bit her lip, her mind racing ahead to the consequences. *But not yet. Oh, please, not yet. Let me enjoy him one more day.*

"No," she said softly. "Your idea is fine." The last few syllables were lost as her lips met his.

THEY WOKE TO A GRAY drizzle on Thursday that seemed to reflect the mood that had descended on the RV. For much of that day Mary Elizabeth sat at the kitchen table alternately reading or embroidering while Peter drove. Occasionally, Peter tossed a remark over his shoulder, and sometimes those remarks lengthened to entire conversations.

But mostly she just rode along in silence, staring out the window at field upon field of red Georgia mud, wondering why she hadn't told him yet. The baby would make a difference. Why did she have this persistent fear of consequences?

Because consequences hurt, she answered herself, and this one would be a humdinger. He was going to renege on his offer to keep seeing her.

For a while she let herself entertain the possibility he'd be happy with her decision, that he'd say it made no difference to him. At one point she even ventured so far as to imagining him confessing he'd love to be the baby's father. It was a beautiful daydream, the three of them living as a family. But reality brought her down with a thump. If

Roger, the baby's very own father, didn't want it, did she think a stranger would?

She lowered her head as Charles's words crept into her fantasy: "What man wants to take on another man's child?" She didn't want to be influenced by Charles anymore. His bitterness had warped his outlook. But she knew there was a grain of truth to what he'd said. Babies were a heavy responsibility. They were expensive and taxed one's time and patience and stamina. Did she really think Peter would enjoy taking on all that responsibility? He seemed to already have enough on his plate with his family and his construction company. And what about that remark he made when he was telling her about Cindy? *Thank God we didn't have a baby.*

Her thoughts jumped. Would he resent her baby? If he continued to see her, would he be annoyed by its crying? Begrudge how it cut into their time together?

Her thoughts took another leap. TV news was rife with stories of men being abusive to their girlfriends' children—beatings, molestation, murder. Nearly every night, she tuned in to another terrible incident.

Of course, those stories represented the extreme, and she couldn't imagine Peter being physically abusive. But Charles hadn't been physically abusive, either. Distrust began to build inside her, alongside a deepening protectiveness.

Was it a choice then between the baby and Peter?

And what about any other man who might come into her life in the future? She couldn't imagine other men, didn't want other men, but she forced herself to consider the possibility, anyway. What sort of relationship would they have with her child? Would it always be a choice? The thought of raising a child alone was intimidating, but it didn't disturb her nearly as much as the thought of raising that child in partnership with someone else, someone who'd be emotionally abusive.

They crossed the Florida line late in the afternoon, and as if obeying a cue from a benevolent god, the sun came out, slanting under the canopy of quickly dissipating clouds and momentarily chasing Mary Elizabeth's brooding thoughts. She moved up to the passenger seat and leaned forward on the dash, gazing in wonder at palm trees and Spanish moss and pastel stucco houses. Florida! She'd finally made it!

They stopped at a restaurant to celebrate their arrival, and over a dinner of sweet coconut shrimp talked about the upcoming day. The thought of meeting Peter's family put Mary Elizabeth on such a sharp edge she almost suggested they call off their bargain. But Peter had gotten her here; she'd be a welsher to cut out before repaying him.

That night they made camp in Osceola National Park. The air was hot and still and heavy with humidity. As if on cue, but from a different and decidedly malevolent god, the air-conditioning system broke down. Pete and Mary Elizabeth opened every window as far as it would go, and would've left the doors opened, too, except for the army of mosquitoes outside.

Flopping into bed wearing only his shorts, Pete grunted. "Welcome to Florida, sweetheart."

He looked across the way. She was wearing a burgundy nightgown—short, satiny, spaghetti-strapped. He hadn't thought she owned such a thing. Oh, hell! It was too hot to make love.

It was too hot not to.

He swung out of bed and went to her. But as soon as their kisses reached the melting stage, she sat up, shaking her head.

"I can't do this anymore, Peter."

He'd known something was brewing all day. "Why? What's the matter? Have I done something wrong?"

"No. It's me. I just…I feel uncomfortable being with you."

His eyes narrowed and burned into her, stripping her defenses.

"What I mean is, I've decided maybe…no, *definitely,* I'm thinking about keeping the baby." She didn't breathe. Just watched Peter's face, watched his eyes.

What she saw tore at her. He looked as if he'd been sucker-punched. Well, what had she expected? she chided herself. Him to be happy?

But then it hit her. Yes, she *had* been expecting that, or perhaps *hoping* was a better word. She'd hoped he'd be different from Charles and Roger and the other men she imagined were out there waiting to reject her. Peter had so many wonderful facets that had surprised her, she'd hoped he would surprise her again by embracing her decision.

She watched the astonishment leave his eyes as fast as it had appeared, to be replaced with a smile as thin as water on glass. "That's wonderful, Mary Elizabeth."

"Yes, well, I just thought you ought to know."

Peter retreated to his own bed and sat hunched forward with his elbows on his knees. "Okay. Now I know. So what's the problem?"

She sat facing him, frowning in thought. "Don't you see it as a complication to our relationship?"

"I'd be blind not to. But I'm still not sure I understand what you're getting at."

Oh, don't you? As hot and sticky as the night was, Peter seemed to be losing color.

"The problem, I suppose, is I want more." Later she would realize how poorly phrased her answer was, but at the moment she was too taken with her insight to censor her words.

''More? What more?'' A bead of sweat trickled down Pete's left temple.

''Oh, sometimes I fantasize about having the baby, a home...'' She swallowed, and swallowed again. ''And a man who'll love us both forever.''

Peter laughed, a chuckle as thin as his smile had been. ''Hell, Mary Elizabeth, I'm not in the habit of marrying a woman unless I've known her at least a full week.''

She burned with humiliation. ''I said it was a fantasy. I didn't mean I expected you to marry me, for heaven's sake. Just the opposite. All I was trying to say was, now that I'm planning to keep the baby, I feel uncomfortable being intimate with a man knowing the relationship is a dead end.'' Her eyes quickly shifted, but not before they'd dropped the question into the space between them: *And this is a dead end, isn't it?*

When she looked back, Peter's face was an unreadable blank. He reached for his jeans, tugged on one leg, then the other, and rose to fit them over his narrow hips. She noticed he was breathing hard. He pulled on his boots, found a musty shirt, polished his helmet with a sleeve and drifted toward door.

''Where are you going?''

He paused but didn't turn when he said, ''For a ride. It's mighty close in here tonight. I just...need some air.''

CHAPTER FOURTEEN

THE RV PULLED UP to Pam's pink suburban ranch house just after noon on Friday. Since Peter and Brad lived in Tampa and Lindy's household was too chaotic, Pam's house had become, by default, the center of operation for the Mitchell side of the wedding party.

Mary Elizabeth ran her palms down her thighs as she scanned the battalion of cars already parked around it. "Do I look all right?" she asked nervously.

"Sure, you look great," Peter replied without even glancing at her. He wasn't in the best of moods. Not bad, just quiet. Distant. He'd been that way since the previous night when she'd told him about her decision to keep her baby.

She wanted to ask him what they were doing, where they stood, if he still intended to see her after this weekend. But whenever she was about to ask the question, it stuck in her throat. She'd grown uncomfortable with him, put off by the shell he'd closed around himself.

Uncoiling from his seat, he finally gave her a glance. "Stop worrying." He placed his hand on her head and gave it a friendly back-and-forth tug. "They're my family, all jerks, just like me."

She smiled at that, some of the tension melting from her face, but not all. Hardly all. On an instinctive level, she felt he'd abandoned her somewhere down the road, and from here on she was on her own.

"Come on," he urged. "Folks are waiting to meet you."

And they were: Pam and Lindy, Brad, who'd taken the day off work, and three of the five children, the oldest two being in school. There were also two cousins and an aunt in the kitchen helping with preparations for the rehearsal dinner, which Pam would be hosting that evening.

Peter and Mary Elizabeth weren't even in the house yet when conversation erupted. "Hey, look who finally came home," Brad called out the door, while Pam, gaping at the RV, said, "Oh, my God! You *are* traveling in a motor home." Meanwhile, two nephews and a niece were climbing up Peter's legs and hanging on his neck, to the tune of Lindy's ineffective "Behave yourselves. Uncle Petie's not a jungle gym."

Mary Elizabeth found them a most outgoing, likable bunch. They welcomed her into their midst, insisted she have some lunch and accepted her help afterward as if she were an old family friend. Still, she felt a tension buzzing under the surface of their smiles, a curiosity they held in polite reserve. She saw it in the way they looked from her to Peter, and in their shrugged eyebrows when they looked at each other. She got the feeling she wasn't what they'd expected.

By midafternoon they had apparently banked their curiosity long enough. Peter was fitting the extra leaves in the dining-room table when Lindy said, "Pam says you told her you've been seeing Mary Elizabeth since last February. Is that right?"

Mary Elizabeth was carrying in an extra chair from the garage at the time. She tensed, suddenly remembering the flaw in the fiction they'd created. If they continued to see each other, how would they explain her increasingly evident pregnancy? Would Peter go with the truth? Embarrassing as it was, the truth would ultimately make their relationship easier to understand and accept.

Across the room their eyes met. She waited, sensing his reply to Lindy's question would answer the one that had been haunting her since last night: what were they doing, where did they stand?

Peter blinked, cutting off their connection, and said, "Yes, we met while she was on vacation in Clearwater."

She grabbed a polishing rag off the floor and began to clean the chair she'd just carried in, while Peter went on, reeling out the story they'd invented to give their romance dimension—a story that would end with them parting in two days and only pretending to see each other afterward.

Their eyes never really met again that afternoon.

If anyone noticed, they didn't comment. The children came home from school, Pam's and Lindy's husbands returned from work, and the happy tumult expanded. Which was fortunate, Mary Elizabeth decided. It drew attention away from her and Peter and the fact that they hardly ever spoke. It also made it easier for Mary Elizabeth to conceal the heartache that was building inside her.

At five o'clock, with those who would be going to rehearsal arguing whose car they'd take, and the coffee urn refusing to perk, and the children chasing Monet around the kitchen table with doll's clothes, a voice called from the living room, "Hello-o. Anybody home?"

Mary Elizabeth felt a reaction jump through the people around her like an electric current. There was a hush, a sense of the room holding its breath....

And then, from Pam, "In here, Sue Ellen."

Mary Elizabeth swiveled just as a woman balancing a half dozen white florist boxes appeared in the kitchen doorway.

"Hi. Just came by to drop off..." Her words slowed

noticeably when her eyes met Peter's. She smiled. "Hello, Peter. What a surprise."

Peter? Mary Elizabeth glanced from one to the other. Sue Ellen called him Peter?

Sue Ellen tossed back her full head of dark waves. "Here are your flowers for tomorrow. Boutonnieres for the men, corsages for the women. They were delivered to the bride's house by mistake along with the rest of the flowers. Jill was so busy though, I thought I'd run them over here for her."

"Thanks, Sue Ellen." Pam took the boxes to the refrigerator, while everyone else resumed breathing and going about their business.

Sue Ellen was tall, shapely and absolutely gorgeous, Mary Elizabeth decided, but in an approachable sort of way, with big green eyes that looked right at a person and a forthright femininity that existed in perfect harmony with an air of strong independence. She'd been eyeing Mary Elizabeth unashamedly from the moment she'd walked in.

"Since no one else seems inclined to introduce us—" she stepped up to Mary Elizabeth, smiling confidently "—I'm Sue Ellen Carlisle, an old friend of the family. And you're…?"

Through a sudden avalanche of feelings—jealousy foremost among them—Mary Elizabeth somehow found her voice. "Mary Elizabeth Drummond." She shook Sue Ellen's hand, which clasped hers firmly.

"Nice meeting you." Then stepping away, Sue Ellen teased, "I said hello, Peter." She placed two graceful hands on his biceps as if to kiss him. "So far I haven't heard a hello back."

He flicked a glance at Mary Elizabeth—why, she'd never know, because when his eyes returned to Sue Ellen they positively smoldered. "Sue Ellen," he greeted with a lazy half smile.

"So, are you ready to see that baby brother of yours tie the knot?" Her hands still hadn't left his biceps.

"I guess."

Mary Elizabeth left the room then to rescue her cat, who'd taken refuge in the living room. Or maybe she left so she wouldn't have to listen to Sue Ellen asking Peter to save her a dance tomorrow, and Peter replying he'd save her two. *And that's the last time I think of him as Peter!* she decided, carrying Monet out to the RV where she fed him and cuddled him until they both felt better.

When she returned to the house, Pete was ready to leave for rehearsal. "Would you like to come along?" he asked her.

When she replied no, she'd stay behind to help with the buffet, he didn't push the issue. Push? He barely gave it a shrug as he walked by her. Sue Ellen left at the same time, chatting up a storm.

"Sorry 'bout Sue Ellen dropping by like that," Pam apologized later when she and Mary Elizabeth had a rare moment alone. She'd asked what Mary Elizabeth planned to wear to the wedding, and Mary Elizabeth had brought her out to the RV to show her.

"Nothing to be sorry about," she replied, draping her new outfit over the kitchen table. "She was just doing the bride a favor by delivering the flowers."

Pam snickered. "If I know Sue Ellen... Oh, never mind. No sense in bad-mouthing somebody I myself wanted to set up with Pete—until I met you." Her eyes, as blue as her brother's, roamed the RV, picking up evidence of him everywhere. "There's something really strong between you two, isn't there?"

Mary Elizabeth's throat ached. "I thought there was, but now..." She shook her head.

"Have patience with him. That's the only advice I can give you. He's had a couple of really bad experiences with marriage and..."

"A couple?" Mary Elizabeth's heart contracted. "He's told me about Cindy. Who else is there?"

"Sue Ellen, of course." Hearing Mary Elizabeth gasp, Pam hastened to add, "Oh, but they never actually made it down the aisle. They were supposed to get married, though. He asked her the night of their senior prom, and naturally she said yes. They were crazy about each other, had been for years. But then he went into the army and she went to college." A frown slid into Pam's expression. "She sent him a Dear John letter while he was stationed in Central America, poor guy. It was a cruel way to break up, him being so far away and all. And then to say she was getting married to somebody else." Pam shook her head. "It close to broke that poor boy's heart."

If Pam's intention was to cheer Mary Elizabeth, she was failing. "I may be way off base, but do you think that's why he married Cindy?"

"Afraid so. He admits it himself, although at the time he didn't realize he was acting on the rebound. He thought he really loved her. That's why he feels so shaky about his judgment in women now, why he's so terrified he'll make another mistake. He already has two strikes against him."

Just then a car pulled up to the curb, its horn beeping playfully. "Company," Pam murmured. They started for the door, but at the steps she paused again. "Until today I thought what my brother needed was to have Sue Ellen back in his life. But I was wrong. You're what he needs. Only thing is, he might not admit it for a while. Hang in. He's a great guy. He'll be worth the trouble."

Mary Elizabeth tried to keep Pam's encouraging words in mind, but matters only got worse that evening. Sue Ellen had apparently followed the wedding party to the church and finagled an invitation to the gathering afterward. She reentered the house draped on Pete's arm and remained there through most of the evening. Although he didn't forget Mary Elizabeth altogether and occasionally wandered over to ask if she was all right, he seemed happier to be sitting with Sue Ellen, talking and laughing over old times.

And why shouldn't he? Mary Elizabeth admitted, watching them from across the living room. Sue Ellen was a beautiful woman—confident, feminine and highly entertaining. Pete had planned to marry her once. Why wouldn't he be sitting with Sue Ellen, looking as crazy about her as he'd been at eighteen? What did Mary Elizabeth have to offer in comparison? She'd overheard them talking about taking a spin on his new bike. Because she was pregnant, Mary Elizabeth couldn't even ride it out of the driveway. *Why did he bring me here?* she asked herself time and again. *What was this past week all about?*

As hurt as she was, Mary Elizabeth still managed to hang on to her pride. She drew on her vast store of social skills, and mingled and chatted as if nothing was wrong.

By dessert, however, she'd had enough. Not only was she hurt, she was quietly seething. Pete had one hell of a nerve to treat her so poorly.

She hated slipping out without saying goodbye to anyone, but she thought it was best. She didn't want to upset the celebratory mood of the occasion. She'd be sure to write to Pam and extend her thanks and apologies as soon as possible.

She was struggling with the hitch at the back of her RV, trying to detach the trailer that still carried Pete's precious

Triumph, when a familiar voice cut through the evening shadows. "What are you doing, princess?"

"What does it look like I'm doing?" she snapped. She hadn't thought he'd noticed her leave. She'd hoped to get away without a confrontation.

"Step aside," he said, nudging her away. With a few effortless moves, Pete had the contrivance free. "Now, let me ask you again, what are you doing?"

Red-faced with pent-up anger, Mary Elizabeth stomped past him without answering, flung open the door of the RV and stomped inside. She returned momentarily and pitched his duffel bag onto his toes. "You needed protection, huh? Wanted me to keep her away, huh?"

In she went again, to appear at the door a moment later with a bundle of laundry. Pete ducked, but her aim was good. The bundle came apart on his head and spilled over him like a cracked egg.

Tossing aside a pair of black B.V.D.s, he bounded up the steps, slamming the door so hard the RV rocked. Mary Elizabeth wasn't intimidated. She met him chin first.

"What kind of game were you playing?" she demanded. "Lying to me about her, not telling me you really wanted to get back with her and only brought me along to...to what? Make her jealous?"

Pete frowned in deepening puzzlement. "I didn't lie to you. I don't want to get back with her."

Mary Elizabeth folded her arms tight. "You think I don't know you two had planned to get married once? Your sister Pam is a very talkative person, Pete. So you want to try telling me again what you needed protection from?"

"Goddammit, Mary Elizabeth!" He planted two fists on his hips. He was breathing heavily but looked more frustrated than angry. "Wise up."

She gasped when his meaning came clear. "Me? You

needed protection from me? Well, thank you very much."
With that she marched to the bedroom and returned bearing
his tin roller coaster. "You could've just told me to get
lost, y'know. You didn't have to embarrass me in front of
everybody in order to get rid of me."

Pete lunged forward and snatched the roller coaster from
her before she tossed that, too. He went outside and carefully set it on the lawn.

He came back in recharged. "How long have we known
each other, Mary Elizabeth? Seven days?" He followed her
into the bedroom. "And yet you went ahead without the
slightest compunction and put me on the spot last night.
Well, I'd say you've got some damn nerve."

She thrust his helmet into his midsection. "On the spot?
What spot?" The lava lamp came next, dropping into the
bowl of the helmet with a clatter.

Pete's face darkened. "You know what I'm talking
about."

She paced the room, searching for the rest of his belongings, shaking her head continuously. "You don't listen,
do you. I said I didn't expect you to marry me. That's why
I suggested we end our relationship."

"Sure. Right after saying you wanted more—the baby,
a home, a husband, the whole enchilada."

"I said that was a fantasy."

"Yeah, right." His eyes blazed. "You realize what you
were doing, don't you?"

"Oh, please, enlighten me."

"You were upping the ante in our relationship. Just
like…"

"Cindy? Oh!" She gasped in outrage. "Is that what you
think?"

"It's what I know. Just when I was getting used to the
idea of seeing you through your pregnancy, bingo, you drop

a whole new scene on me. It's been that way from the beginning. There was always just one more little favor I could do. Well, I'm sorry, princess. You've pushed me one time too many."

Mary Elizabeth felt she'd been struck physically. "You big, dumb jerk!" She threw his can of foot powder at him. "I'm leaving. Going. Right now." She spun away, clutching her arms. "Pam gave me my wallet. I have my license...."

"What about the wedding?"

She lowered her head and shook it, suddenly fighting a lump in her throat. "Congratulate your brother for me. Under different circumstances I'd love to attend his wedding. I like him. I like all your family, but, no—" she gazed at her bed where they'd made love so often and so well "—I won't subject myself to any more humiliation."

"Leaving isn't necessary."

She spun around. "You just don't get it, do you. You think I'm playing a game, trying to trick you into marrying me. Well, I've got news for you. I wouldn't marry you if you begged me. Sorry to disillusion you, but this baby is far more important to me than you are."

Pete stared hard at her, frowning. "What the hell is *that* supposed to mean?"

She pushed past him and entered the bathroom to pack up his shaving kit. "It means," she said crisply, "I don't want any man, even you, interfering with my child."

When his toiletries were stuffed in the bag she turned. Pete was shaking his head. "Still letting Charles color your world, aren't you."

"No, I'm just calling it the way it is. If the baby's natural father has no interest in it, how do you think a stranger will feel?"

"You still don't think there are any decent men out there?"

She looked straight at him, feeling mean. "I haven't found one yet."

He flinched ever so slightly, but then rallied with, "You're living in the past, kid. Letting Charles call the shots."

"You have a nerve, accusing me of being stuck in the past, you, a man who can't get over a marriage he walked out of fifteen years ago."

"Thirteen."

"Oh, that makes a big difference! Here." She stuffed his shaving kit in the bowl of his helmet. "I think that's everything. Now, get out of my house."

His eyes glittered coldly. "Gladly." But he continued to stand there, filling the passageway. He pulled a cigarillo from his shirt pocket and one-handedly lit the tip. "You know how to get to the highway from here?"

She crossed her arms. "I can read a map."

He took a long, disrespectful pull before answering, "Fine."

"I'll send a check for everything I owe you within two weeks."

Pete puffed a cloud of foulness into the air. "I'll count on it."

She turned her head. "Well, have a good life, Pete."

"You, too." He walked into the kitchen, his helmet caught under one casually draped arm. "Wherever the road takes you."

When she turned her head again, the door was just clicking shut.

Mary Elizabeth slumped against the wall in abject mortification. *Have a good life?* What did she think she was doing, auditioning for a soap opera?

Outside, Pete gathered his laundry with a grimace. *Wherever the road takes you?* Judas Priest! Why not just quote her the last scene from *Casablanca*?

Mary Elizabeth tiptoed to the front seat, where she watched Pete from the corner of her eye. When he'd stuffed his clothes in his bag, he tossed it toward his bike and headed for the house. *Good riddance,* she thought.

Hearing the engine of the RV turn over, Pete hitched his shoulders and thought, *At last.* He felt like a man who'd escaped a physical danger, a convict on death row receiving a reprieve at the eleventh hour. No more potpourri balls swinging from the radio knob. No more cat hair making him sneeze.

But as the RV chugged down the street he turned to gaze after it. "And no more Mary Elizabeth looking all soft and warm in the morning when I open my eyes," he whispered into the empty night.

MARY ELIZABETH'S FIRST month in Florida was a time of rapid adjustment and change. She arrived at her old roommate's door not only distraught over her debacle with Pete but also uncertain of her welcome. They'd roomed together for only two years, and that had been long ago. After an hour with Chloe, though, Mary Elizabeth wondered where her uncertainty had come from.

They talked long into the night, rediscovering a cherished friendship, and Mary Elizabeth finally understood why her first instinct, when she'd decided to leave home, had been to call here.

She was met with one disappointing bit of news, however. The job at the dentist's office had already been filled. But on the up side, her new credit cards had arrived and she was able to draw a cash advance to tide her over. She made sure to draw enough to also write out a check for Pete.

She remained with Chloe for a week. They shopped and went to the beach, drove around to acquaint her with the area, and talked until their jaws were sore. It was wonderful, but by the end of the week Mary Elizabeth insisted she move to a campground. It was time she started getting her life together.

The first step she took was to file a résumé with a temp agency. Living on credit made her nervous. Her next move was to buy a cellular phone so the temp agency could contact her. While she was waiting to hear from them, she scoured the help-wanted ads in various local newspapers.

Though she'd started with a bang, by the end of her second week in Florida Mary Elizabeth was feeling pretty low. The temp agency hadn't called, not even once, and she hadn't found anything in the want ads she felt qualified to do. She had never been a waitress, couldn't type sixty words a minute, knew nothing about selling cars, and she was beginning to think Charles was right—she'd never survive on her own.

One of the few joys in Mary Elizabeth's life those days was the weather. Having lived in cold, rugged Maine all her life, she thought she'd never get enough of the heat and sun.

Another joy was phoning Mrs. Pidgin, which she did often. She was astounded to hear that after thirty-two years of service, the woman had quit her job with Charles. Her husband was already retired, she said, and she wanted to enjoy his free time with him.

"I only stayed on because of you, anyway," she explained to a speechless Mary Elizabeth. "Your mother asked me to before she died, to watch over you. She knew

Susan and your brother would be all right with Charles, but you she worried about.''

"Oh, Mrs. P., I had no idea." Mary Elizabeth's heart overflowed with love and gratitude. If it hadn't been for this woman, her life would've been bleak, indeed. "How can I ever repay you?"

"Just be happy, love, and don't look back."

Mary Elizabeth tried to follow that advice. She submitted her résumé to a job placement service. She found an obstetrician and went for a physical exam. She visited with Chloe and went to the beach. But abiding happiness eluded her—even when, at the end of her third week, a promising job opportunity came through.

The placement agency had found an opening on the staff of a small museum in St. Petersburg, a position that seemed custom-made for Mary Elizabeth. The salary wasn't anything to write home about, her placement officer explained, but on the other hand, the personnel director was agreeable to paid maternity leave.

Mary Elizabeth went for an interview and spent the next three days on tenterhooks. When her acceptance came through, she danced around the RV with Monet, crying and laughing in relief.

But throughout her days, beneath her determination and busyness and momentary upswings, there remained a dark undercurrent of sadness, a barely heard but always present murmur that things were not right in her world.

"It's because of Pete," she finally admitted one night a week after she'd been working. She was lying in bed reading when she glanced toward the empty bed alongside hers and admitted, "I miss him. More than I can bear."

Cleaning the RV, she'd found a stray sock of his, a red bandanna, the can of foot powder that had ricocheted off his chest when she threw it at him, and a pair of dark glasses. Vaguely planning to mail the forgotten items to him, she'd placed them on his bed and there they'd stayed. Artifacts, she thought. Her own private Pete Mitchell museum. A memorial to the deepest happiness she'd ever known.

Reaching, she plucked the bandanna off the bed and buried her nose in its soft folds. It still smelled faintly of Pete. She closed her eyes, used the bandanna to wipe the tears that squeezed through her lashes, and then held it clutched in a fist at her mouth.

Four weeks away from him had given her ample time to rethink their parting argument, and each time she did she felt worse. Pete had had a valid case.

She hadn't meant to cast him in the role of husband and father, but subconsciously that was exactly what she'd done. She'd been so fixated on the baby and on the sort of relationship it would have with any man she became involved with, that she'd leapt miles ahead of where she and Pete were and started speculating whether he would resent her baby or not. She'd had no right to do that. It *had* been only a week since they'd met. No wonder he'd reacted negatively. Any man would've run.

She should have been satisfied with his suggestion they continue to see each other. Satisfied? She should have been jumping for joy. That was quite a step for him after just a week, offering to stand by her through her pregnancy, even go to Lamaze classes with her. A step that might have led to more, eventually.

But did she give their just-seeded relationship time to take root? Time to grow at its own natural pace? No, she'd poisoned it right at the outset by leaping ahead, rushing him, scaring him half to death.

And what *about* that obsession she had regarding her baby, her fear that any man she became involved with would resent it? That might be true in some cases, but Pete? Pete was an incredibly giving person. His family depended on him in innumerable ways, but he didn't resent them. He *loved* them. And he loved children. She'd seen with her own eyes how he interacted with his nieces and nephews. So what was her problem? Why wasn't she able to trust that he'd be just as wonderful and unresentful with her and her baby? *Was* she still living in the past? Was Charles still somewhere inside her telling her she was an unlovable burden?

"Damn!" She shot straight out of bed. She wasn't unlovable. She wasn't ugly or stupid or helpless. She had lots of fine qualities and more strength than she'd ever dreamed possible. In the five weeks since leaving home, she'd had to face and overcome so many obstacles, she felt downright proud of herself.

As she stood there between the two beds counting her virtues, it suddenly struck her. She was free of Charles. She'd freed herself.

Unfortunately, her relationship with Pete had perished in the struggle to reach this point.

Or had it? Was there any possibility it could be salvaged? Hope began a light, rapid cadence in her heart. Of course, she had to keep in mind Pete's aversion to marriage. She shouldn't start thinking he might get over that aversion someday. His radar would pick up her expectations and he'd bolt again.

That was presuming he'd even talk to her.

A sudden fear snaked around her newly risen hopes. What if he was back with Sue Ellen? The woman was lovely and spirited and...

Mary Elizabeth stopped abruptly, realizing what she was doing. She was comparing herself, selling herself short. She refused to do that anymore. Pete might very well be back with Sue Ellen, but that didn't diminish her own unique qualities.

She walked into the kitchen and made herself a cup of chamomile tea. While she was sipping it, she decided to call Pete from work the next day to see if they could meet somewhere to talk. He might say no, or their meeting might lead nowhere, or if he agreed to resume a friendship, that friendship might end next month. There were no guarantees when it came to matters of the heart. But she'd never know unless she gave it a shot. If nothing else, she would apologize for causing their friendship to end so badly. He'd done a lot for her on the road. He deserved at least that much in return.

She finished her tea, went back to bed and was asleep almost before her head touched the pillow.

PETE WALKED OUT of the beachside restaurant in Clearwater with the middle-aged couple whose three-quarter-million-dollar house he was building. They had fiddled with the blueprints again and figured a meal and a couple of drinks would smooth his ruffled feathers. He took them up on their offer. These days, eating with people, even pains in the butt, was far better than eating alone.

After the couple drove off, he mounted his Triumph and set off down the busy coastal road. The sun was just a small orange crescent on the horizon, but its radiance still managed to flood the Gulf and the sky above with blushing color.

Inadvertently he wondered if Mary Elizabeth was watching the sun go down. Wondered what she thought of it, if she liked her new home, if she was all right.

He gave his head a quick snap. Damn! He didn't know why he continued to worry about her. He was sure she'd landed on her feet. She had more lives than a cat. Besides, he had his own life to look after, his own obligations. The fact that he and Mary Elizabeth had met at all was simply a quirk of fate. An accident. A meaningless detour in the course of their lives. Now it was time to move on.

And he did, for about half a mile. Then he let himself admit he was throwing up a smoke screen to avoid what was really bothering him, those feelings he had for Mary Elizabeth. They hadn't gone away. If anything, they'd grown, and he didn't know what he was going to do about them anymore. They were interfering with everything—his sleep, his appetite, his work.

He'd thought of calling her at her friend's, dozens of times. Thought he might at least apologize for his jackass behavior at his sister's. He'd even gotten as far as dialing the number a few times, but he'd always lost heart before anyone answered. And the longer he didn't speak to her, the worse it got. By now she was probably mad enough to spit through the phone.

Maybe he should go see her in person. Or maybe take an extended trip somewhere, like Australia...

Or maybe he would simply drop into that little bar he'd just passed. Jimmy's Shack, it was called. It looked like his kind of joint. He made a U-turn and pulled into the lot.

The place was dimly lit and sparsely filled. The whizzing and binging of an intergalactic war, played out on a pinball machine, intertwined with a twangy song thumping from the jukebox. Pete's mouth twitched when he recognized Ricky Skaggs' "Highway 40 Blues."

Out of habit he chose a bar stool close to the back exit. Two men looked at him with subdued curiosity. He nodded a benign hello and they turned back to the game show they were watching on the TV behind the bar.

Pete ordered a beer, put a quarter in the jukebox and sat back to enjoy the ambience of Jimmy's as "Since I Met

You, Baby'' began to play. This was exactly how he liked spending his life. Alone, freewheeling, discovering charming pockets of America like this here Jimmy's Shack.

Only problem was, he wasn't having such a good time anymore. He hadn't for a while. After Brad's wedding he'd taken a few days off by himself down in the Keys. He'd needed to put some distance between himself and Sue Ellen. After the stupid stunt he'd pulled at Pam's, she'd expected all sorts of things from him. She'd even invited him to stay at her place that night, and he'd had to tell her point blank he wasn't interested—which didn't exactly make Brad's wedding an easy day to get through.

So he'd gone off to the Keys. But he hadn't had fun even there and had returned early. He'd never done that before. He felt restless, discontented. Uncharmed. Pete scowled and wondered why. What had changed?

He lifted his beer glass and took a long swallow. Simultaneously, he met his reflection in the mirror behind the bar. He tilted his head to better catch the light. It picked up the crow's feet at his eyes, a few strands of silver in his hair.

Maybe he was having a midlife crisis. With Brad getting married and all, it was understandable. Brad was the youngest of the bunch, and his marriage just underscored the fact that Pete, the oldest, was still at loose ends. Still coming home to an empty house. Still buying Christmas gifts for other people's kids. Hell, he'd always wanted kids. He'd always seen himself with a wife and a home.

No, that wasn't what was eating him tonight. Those things were certainly true, but they didn't cover the whole picture. He knew damn well what had changed. He'd met Mary Elizabeth, a woman he had feelings for.

Go on, admit it, Mitchell, you fell crazy in love with her. And the reason he'd treated her so badly at Pam's was that, like her, he'd already begun to fantasize, too—about the baby, a home, the three of them together—and it had scared him out of his skin.

He tipped back the glass, drained it dry and set it down. He'd run like a coward, proving he was no better than the imaginary jerks she feared she'd meet up with who would reject her because of the added burden of her baby. Instead of helping her see that not all men were like Charles, he'd confirmed the crippling legacy Charles had imparted. He'd deepened her distrust.

And why? Because he was afraid of being burned again? Mary Elizabeth was nothing like Cindy. Sure, she had needs, but she didn't have that desperate, hungry edge that Cindy had hounded him with. She'd left Charles, she hadn't married Roger, and she'd walked away from *him*, proving she was prouder and more independent than most people he knew.

Pete was staring at the foamy dregs in his glass when another revelation struck him. There was nothing wrong with needs. Everybody had them, one kind or another. They didn't necessarily mean a person was needy.

Neither was there anything wrong with two people depending on each other, in a healthy way. That's what friends and family were for—and what marriage was all about. Trouble was, Cindy's dependence on him hadn't been healthy. He shouldn't have let his experience with her pollute his entire attitude toward marriage.

He swore under his breath. Had he messed up the best opportunity of his life?

He was still staring into his empty glass when the bartender came over and set down a fresh, brimming mug. Pete frowned. He hadn't ordered another beer.

"Compliments of the lady down the end of the bar." The man gave Pete a sly half smile before walking off.

Pete felt none of the pleasure he should have felt. He didn't want to talk to a strange woman in a strange bar, wasn't in the mood to play seduction games. He wasn't even sure he wanted this beer. But the least he could do was acknowledge the woman's generosity.

He leaned forward, resting his forearms on the thickly varnished bar, and scanned the line of faces to his far right. The place was filling fast, he thought idly...right before he found her and his heart exploded through his chest.

CHAPTER FIFTEEN

MARY ELIZABETH WAS a bundle of nerves. She sipped her club soda, kept her eyes on the TV screen and hoped she didn't jitter right off this bar stool.

Finding Pete had not been easy. His home phone was unlisted, so she'd called his office. But he'd been out, working at a remote job site all day. When his secretary asked if Mary Elizabeth wanted her to page him, she'd said no, she'd call back later. And she had, at five, which was the time the secretary had said Pete was most likely to be there. But he wasn't. Luckily, Brad was. In fact, he answered the phone. He seemed quite pleased to hear from her, too.

It was Brad who'd informed her Pete was scheduled to have dinner with a client over in Clearwater. He'd also suggested she try to meet up with him at the restaurant. When she'd asked rather doubtfully if that was a good idea, he'd laughed and declared it a great idea.

On that encouraging, if somewhat mysterious, note she'd changed her outfit, repaired her makeup and hurried up the highway, cursing the fact that the only vehicle at her disposal was still her cumbersome RV.

When she'd arrived at the restaurant nearly two hours later, however, Pete had been nowhere in sight. Dejected, she'd started back, calling herself every kind of fool she could think of.

But a few miles down the road, she'd thought she'd spotted a bike like his parked outside a bar. She'd turned around and investigated...and finally stopped calling herself a fool.

She'd wanted to run straight in, but then reminded herself to show a little restraint. Pete might take one look at her and bolt out the back door, or worse, he might be here with a woman, maybe even Sue Ellen.

Mary Elizabeth had decided to slip in as unobtrusively as possible. When she'd found him, not only was he quite alone, but he appeared so melancholy she had ached for him. He looked tired, too, and he'd lost some weight. Was it possible he'd been as miserable as she? Her heart raced with hope mixed with fear and anxiety.

What that overburdened heart lacked, however, was the courage to look down the bar to observe his reaction to her being here—to her buying him a drink. What if he was angry? What if he was laughing in ridicule? No, she couldn't look. If he wanted to slip out the back door, she would leave the way open for him.

From over her left shoulder, someone asked, "Would you care to dance?"

She swiveled quickly in the direction of the voice, her pulse accelerating, only to find a stranger standing there, a young man with a very bright sunburn. She flicked an uncertain glance down the line of bar stools and her heart plummeted. Pete's was empty. Her instincts had been right.

But suddenly, a voice behind her answered, "Sorry, son. The lady's taken." The voice was soft as a prayer, dark as sin.

The young man backed off immediately.

Pete watched Mary Elizabeth set her glass down with a slow, very shaky hand. He had to use every ounce of willpower he owned to keep from reaching out to her and gathering her into his arms. She took in a long breath, exhaled in ragged shudders, then turned to face him.

"Hello, Pete," she said calmly.

The corner of his mouth lifted. "Mary Elizabeth," he replied with painful restraint.

God, she looked great. Really pulled together. Sexy as hell, too, but in a classy sort of Mary Elizabeth way. She was wearing something he'd never seen before, a jade green, watered-silk pants-and-shirt outfit that was drapey and flowing. It didn't quite conceal her pregnancy, though. One month had made a big difference. The sight of her and her rounded belly filled him with indescribable joy.

He watched her tip back her head so that her hair grazed her shoulder blades. He remembered the silken feel of that hair, not with his mind, but with his body. With the tips of his fingers, the flat of his cheek, his lips. Every part of him that had touched her hair suddenly remembered...as it also remembered her hands, her breasts, her feet, her lips. Without realizing it, Mary Elizabeth had burned herself into his sense memory.

And into his life, because the joy he was feeling wasn't just sensual. Here before him was everything he'd ever wanted—friend, lover, partner.

He set the beer she'd bought him on the bar. "What are you doing here?"

"Oh, I saw your bike, thought I'd stop in, say hello."

Mary Elizabeth watched Pete's eyes narrow to two glittering points of doubt as he said, "With all the roads you and I could've traveled, do you know what the odds are of our meeting up like this?"

"Small," she agreed, fighting off a smile. "Astronomically small. It makes a person wonder, doesn't it?"

"About what?" His eyes had become seductive and heavy-lidded, teasing her, burning into her.

Still, she answered with cool insouciance. "You know,

about things like chance and fate and maybe we were meant to travel together?''

Pete had been thinking along pretty similar lines, but he only grinned and said, ''Or maybe you tracked me down because you're nuttier than a box of Cracker Jack about me.''

He held his breath, waiting for a snappy comeback. Joking would be good. But apparently she wasn't in a joking mood. She merely lifted her long blond lashes and said quite seriously, ''Maybe.''

They stared at each other until the air fairly sizzled between them. Abruptly Pete declared, ''I am *so* sorry, sweetheart,'' just as she was saying, ''I hope you'll forgive me.'' They paused a heartbeat, smiled uncertainly and then fell together into a laughing embrace that made explanations unnecessary.

''Oh, lady, you feel so good,'' Pete whispered against her hair.

''Mmm,'' she agreed, holding him tight, unable to speak for the lump in her throat.

In deference to the other patrons in the bar, they moved apart, but they didn't quite relinquish each other.

''Would you like to dance?'' Pete asked softly.

She glanced toward the small open area where five other couples were swaying to a slow jukebox number. ''I'd love to.''

Reaching the dance floor, Pete took her in his arms and she nestled against him.

''How have you been?'' he murmured. He felt her smile against his neck.

''Miserable,'' she replied, ''but at least I have a job.'' She then proceeded to fill him in on the latest developments in her life.

Pete was pleased for her but not surprised. "I knew you could do it."

"And how have you been?" She drew back to look into his eyes.

"Pretty damn miserable, too, if you want to know the truth." He adjusted their fit and encircled her with both arms. "Mary Elizabeth, I need to apologize for what happened at Pam's."

"You already did that."

"Explain, then."

"I think I already understand. You were right, I *did* put you on the spot. After knowing you only a week, too. That was grossly unfair of me. And for that I can only say I'm sorry."

Pete's weathered face took on an uncharacteristic softness. "It's true, I was worried that it had only been a week. But I learned something this month away from you."

"Oh? What's that?"

"I learned that sometimes a week is enough time to know."

She tilted her head. "Know what?"

He held her a little tighter. "When you've found the person you want to spend the rest of your life with."

Mary Elizabeth stood absolutely still, afraid she hadn't heard right. The music receded, the other dancers ebbed from their awareness, leaving them in a private, spellbound dimension where only they existed.

"The baby, too?" she asked hesitantly.

Pete smiled softly. "Of course, the baby, too. Mary Elizabeth, you've got to understand, part of me might have turned coward when you said you wanted to keep the baby. That was the part of me that had been burned twice. But another part wanted to shout alleluia to the rafters." Pete laughed. "My God, a baby!" he said, awestruck. "A brand-new little person."

Mary Elizabeth ran the knuckles of her index fingers under her eyes and gave a snuffling laugh. "With any luck, it won't be anything like me."

Pete folded her close and began to dance again, swaying, barely scuffing the floor. "No. That's what I'm looking forward to especially, having another person around as wonderful as you."

Her smile abruptly dropped. "What'll we do about Roger? He thinks I'm giving up the baby."

Pete gave her a pointed what-do-you-think look.

"I know, I know. Honesty keeps things simple. But telling him might open a whole new can of worms."

"Don't worry about Roger, we'll handle him together."

The number ended and they walked off the dance floor.

"There is one area where I'll bend my policy on the truth," Pete offered, turning to face her when they reached the bar. "If you'd rather not let on who the father is around my family and friends, I understand. I don't mind pretending the baby's mine."

Mary Elizabeth bit her lip. "Would *you* feel better if they thought it was yours?"

He shrugged. "Makes no difference. I intend to be enough of a father to it to make even us forget I'm not."

"In that case, it makes no difference to me, either. We can tell people to whom it might matter, and let others assume what they like."

"Does that include the baby?"

"Uh-huh. When the child is old enough to understand and handle the news, I intend to tell him, or her. That's the one thing I'm still not at peace with, my mother's not telling me about my real father. Even if I'd never gotten to meet him, it would've been nice to hear about him from her. It would've explained a lot about Charles, too, and maybe I wouldn't have let him affect me as deeply as he did.''

Pete opened the door and stepped aside for her to pass through. The late October night was warm and humid. Sultry. But a fresh breeze was sliding in off the Gulf. The traffic on the strip wasn't as heavy as it would be in winter, but it still ran steady. Lights from high-rise hotels and condominiums blotted out the stars.

Pete strolled with Mary Elizabeth at a snail's pace to the RV. It was parked alongside his bike.

He paused, studying the two vehicles. ''Hmm. Seems we have a problem, sweetheart.''

''Oh?'' Her heart tripped.

He rubbed his chin. ''Well, I guess you'll just have to follow me.''

''Follow you? Where?''

''To my place, of course. You can leave the RV parked there—there's great security—and take my car to work. It'll be a lot easier than trying to maneuver this elephant through the city every day.''

She planted her hands on her hips. ''Whoa. Wait a sec. What are you proposing? That I move in with you? Tonight?''

Even in the tinted light cast by the neon sign flashing Jimmy's Shack—Jimmy's Shack—Jimmy's Shack, she was able to see Pete's color deepen.

''Talk about jumping the gun! Sorry, sweetheart.'' He hitched a shoulder. ''So, what are you going to do? Return to your campground?''

''Yep,'' she answered, imitating him. ''I don't ever want you saying I rushed you into anything.''

''But I don't feel...''

She shook her head. "Besides, a woman deserves at least a few weeks of courtship, don't you think?"

"Courtship?" He looked as if he'd swallowed a bug. "You mean, flowers and candy and going to the movies?"

"Yep." Her smile grew wide and wicked. "I want every bribe and seduction ever devised by the mind of man."

"But we're already...I mean, back there, weren't we discussing...?"

"I don't remember being proposed to, and I definitely don't remember giving you an answer." She shook back her hair, her chin lifted.

Pete thrust his hands in his jeans pockets and scuffed the gravel. "Aw, hell, Mary Elizabeth, are you gonna give me a hard time for the rest of my life?"

She opened the door of the RV and took one step up before looking over her shoulder. "If you're lucky."

She was about to close the door when he bounded in and took her in his arms. "Guess what, princess," he said, laughing a low, dangerous laugh. "I feel lucky." His eyes glittered. "So, what do you say? Will you marry me?"

She shrugged unenthusiastically, trying to pretend her heart wasn't turning cartwheels.

He tried again. "Will you *please* marry me?"

She rocked her head in a considering manner.

Pete held her tighter. "Please. I love you, Mary Elizabeth, and can't live without you. You'd make me the happiest man alive if you'd do me the honor of agreeing to be my wife."

"Well!" Mary Elizabeth didn't need to pretend astonishment. "I...I'll give your offer serious consideration."

Apparently, Pete wasn't satisfied with that answer because the next moment he was kissing her, subjecting her to the most powerful argument of all, his sexual proficiency.

By the time he lifted his head, she was as limp as seaweed.

"Y—" Unable to speak, she merely nodded.

"Is that a yes?"

She nodded again and managed to croak, "I love you, too, Pete."

"Glad to hear it." Pete gathered her close. "Very, very glad," he said as he fit his mouth to hers.

EPILOGUE

MARY ELIZABETH LOOKED down from the second-story window. Mrs. Pidgin was lumbering along the walk that led from the condominium to the parking area, a plastic grocery bag gripped in each hand. The bright June sun beamed down on her newly permed hair and radiated off the roof of the waiting RV.

"What's all that?" Pete inquired, slamming shut the hood where he'd been checking the oil.

"Oh, just a little something extra. You never know."

Upstairs, Mary Elizabeth chuckled. She and Pete were about to set off on a drive that would include a visit to the Grand Canyon and Yosemite National Park. They planned to be gone only three weeks, but Mrs. Pidgin had already packed enough food to last them three months.

She heard Pete say, "Thanks, doll." He always called Mrs. Pidgin doll, and she always blushed.

She and her husband, Alfred, had ventured to Florida on a rare vacation the previous November to spend Thanksgiving with her sister in Gainesville. Mary Elizabeth suspected her real motive was to inspect "this new fella, Pete" Mary Elizabeth had been seeing. Whatever the reason, after a week of sunshine and shuffleboard, she and Alfred had stunned everyone by announcing this was the life for them. They made the move in time for the wedding in December, which they would've attended, anyway, since Mary Elizabeth asked them to serve in place of her parents.

They'd done so beautifully, too, walking her down the chapel aisle, right behind Chloe, her matron of honor, and giving her away in a touching ceremony that was witnessed by nearly one hundred and fifty guests. Among those guests was a contingent from Maine—friends Mary Elizabeth had left behind, a few relatives, and most moving of all, her sister and brother, who were outraged that their father had refused to attend.

Mary Elizabeth had called Charles to tell him she was getting married and to ask if he would walk her down the aisle. But he'd declined. Drummonds, he said, did not walk down church aisles dressed in white when six months pregnant.

Mary Elizabeth hadn't argued. She hadn't been angry, hadn't even been hurt. All she'd felt was pity. "That's too bad," she'd replied in a calm, dispassionate voice. "You're going to miss a great time. We'll send you pictures."

And they had, and apparently Charles had taken a good look at what he'd missed, because a couple of days into February, he'd called to see how she was feeling. He'd called after the baby was born in March, as well, and sent a sizable savings bond as the beginning of a college fund.

"I don't know what to make of this," Mary Elizabeth had said, looking at the bond in a daze.

Pete had replied, "You can make of it whatever you'd like, Mary Elizabeth."

The better she got to know her husband, the more she learned to listen. Often, a casually tossed remark resonated with profundity that only hit her later and stunned her when it did. *You can make of it whatever you'd like.* Wasn't that a prescription for life?

She decided that what she would make of the call and the savings bond was a cordial line of communication. After all, Charles had been an integral part of the first twenty-seven years of her life. She couldn't just pretend he didn't exist.

But she found writing letters easier than phoning, and did so about once a month, sending a photo of the baby each time. It was hardly a warm relationship, but that didn't bother her. It was enough. Besides, she was too busy and too happy these days to let anything bother her.

Below the window, she heard Pete mutter something about coming up to see what was keeping them.

"What's keeping them is little Miss Eliza." Mrs. Pidgin laughed. "You can't rush that child. She already has the appetite of her daddy." The remark poured out with such total spontaneity, Mary Elizabeth wondered if Mrs. Pidgin had actually begun to think of Pete as Eliza's father. He'd like that.

She heard him enter the house, jog up the stairs...then silence. She looked up to find him standing in the bedroom doorway, watching her with that goofy, awed, lovestruck expression she was beginning to think wasn't ever going to go away.

Pete cleared his throat and approached. Mary Elizabeth was sitting in her Salem rocker by the window, the very chair her mother used to rock her in. The baby had just finished nursing. Her plump left cheek was flushed from pressing against Mary Elizabeth's warm skin.

"Hey, Eliza," Pete said softly. He went down on one knee and cupped the baby's downy head in his right hand. "Are you ready to go on your very first vacation?" The baby beamed a gummy smile at him that turned him to mush right before Mary Elizabeth's eyes.

"Oh, are you in trouble. She's got you wrapped right around this." Mary Elizabeth raised and wiggled her little finger.

"You've got that right. Tell Daddy what you want him to buy. A pony? Is that what you want? A Porsche?"

Mary Elizabeth gazed at Pete, murmuring to the baby, and fell in love all over again. He had taken to fatherhood faster and with more enthusiasm than she'd ever dreamed possible...although she should have expected it from the zeal he'd poured into preparing for Eliza's birth.

And that moment when Eliza had slipped into the world—oh, what a look on his face, what a look in those eyes! She could only call it transcendent.

It had been a normal pregnancy, and an equally normal labor, but Mary Elizabeth had been exhausted by the time the baby was born, drifting in and out of consciousness as the doctor placed Eliza on Mary Elizabeth's stomach and Pete cut the cord. She vaguely recollected the baby being there, on her stomach, and fearing she didn't have the strength to hold her and keep her from sliding off. She'd wanted to tell Pete so, warn him, ask him to take charge, but he was less help than she was.

It was a sight to see—a six-foot, three-inch man, broad as a barn, with muscles like oak and a face as hard as granite, this man, slumped in a chair, holding his head in his hands and bawling his heart out. Mary Elizabeth would cherish the image forever.

"She had a great feeding. Should leave us in peace for at least a couple of hours." Mary Elizabeth handed the baby to Pete and fastened her clothing. Eliza was sizable for her three months, yet she looked tiny against Pete's shoulder, and so fair.

Mrs. Pidgin had offered to baby-sit, but Mary Elizabeth couldn't imagine parting with Eliza for three weeks. Traveling with her at this age would probably be as easy as it was ever going to get, too. They would, however, leave

Monet behind in Mrs. P.'s care—with Pete's deepest gratitude.

Mary Elizabeth looped the diaper bag over her shoulder, scanned the room and declared them ready to leave.

Pete had made a few alterations to the interior of the motor home—a queen-size bed in place of the two narrow singles, and a two-person bench where the passenger seat had been. It wasn't quite as comfortable as its bulky, contoured predecessor, but now Eliza could ride with them up front, securely fastened in her car seat.

Pete turned the ignition. Mrs. Pidgin stepped farther back on the sidewalk, pulled a rumpled tissue from the pocket of her housedress and mopped her eyes. Mary Elizabeth smiled and blew her a kiss.

"Okay, I'm ready." Mary Elizabeth slapped her thighs. "More than ready." She loved being a wife and mother, but after months of near-confinement, she was eager to get rolling.

"Wait. There's one thing I've got to do first." Pete leaned across Eliza, who was gurgling happily, and took Mary Elizabeth's face in two hands. The next moment he was kissing her, a kiss that was bold and sensual yet sweetly familiar.

Backing away, he opened his eyes slowly and sighed, "Okay, now I'm ready." He put the vehicle in gear and moved carefully away from the curb, waving goodbye to Mrs. Pidgin.

They'd covered only a few miles when Mary Elizabeth said rather pensively, "You know, if you ever want to do this alone, take one of your bike trips, I mean, I'll understand."

Pete hung his wrist over the steering wheel and thought about it awhile. "No, those days are over."

"Are you sure?"

He nodded. "There's no need. There's nothing to run away from anymore, nothing to go searching for. When I met you last September," he murmured, his eyes soft with love, "I reached my destination."

His image rippled through her tears.

Returning his eyes to the road, Pete said, "This is the only kind of traveling I want to do from now on. The three of us together."

She cleared the sentimentality clogging her throat and smiled. "How about four of us?"

"That sounds good, too." He sobered immediately. "You aren't—?"

"Good heavens, no. I was just speaking hypothetically."

"Oh." He blew out a sigh of relief. "Since we're in a hypothetical mood, how about five for the road?"

She took a long considering moment before replying, "Yeah, I could handle that."

"How about six?"

"Don't push your luck, Mitchell."

He threw back his head and laughed.

Mary Elizabeth settled into her seat with a contented smile and let her gaze fix on the horizon. What a strange journey her life had taken since leaving Maine. How rootless and alone she'd felt then. How blessed she felt now.

She no longer thought of Maine as home. Nor did she really think of Florida in that way, either. Home, she'd learned, was not so much about place as it was about people. Home, as the old adage said, was where the heart was.

She gazed at Eliza, who'd drifted off to sleep, looked over at Pete fiddling with the radio, trying to find an oldies station, and her heart overflowed. It didn't matter where the road took them. They were home.